This is a work of fiction. Names, characters, businesses, places, events, and incidents are either the products of the author's imagination and used in a fictitious manner. Any resemblance to actual persons, living or dead, or actual events is purely coincidental.

Cover Design: Coffin Prints Designs

Formatting : PS. Black

Editor: EJL Editing

Proofreader: Mackenzie @ Nicegirlnaughtyedits

SHATTERED *Ice*

PS. BLACK

Playlist

This story wouldn't have been created without this playlist.

Iris – The Goo Goo Dolls
Paralyzed – NF
I Miss the Days – NF
Twin Flame – MGK
Last November – MGK
How to Save a Life – The Fray
You Found Me – The Fray
Fix You – Coldplay
The Scientist – Coldplay
Chasing Cars – Snow Patrol
I'd Rather Overdose – honestav, Z
She Will Be Loved – Radio Mix
Half a Man – Dean Lewis
How Do I Say Goodbye – Dean Lewis
Bring Me Home – G Flip
Nobody Gets Me – SZA
Lose Control – Teddy Swims
Let Me Hurt (Acoustic) – Emily Rowed
I Found (Acoustic) – Amber Run
More Than Life – Chanin

Wokin On Me – Russ, 6BLACK
Somebody Save Me – Eminem, Jelly Roll
Wires - Athlete

FOREWORD

Shattered Ice includes themes that some readers may find difficult to read. It also contains mature content. For a list of potential triggers, please go to the last page in this book.

"I don't think people truly understand how beautiful the darkness can be if you have the right person there with you."

-Bohdi Stiles

Series

Hawksview University Series is written as an interconnected character series. If you were thinking of reading my *Lost & Found Duet*, I would suggest reading this first. *Shattered Ice* will give all the spoilers for my duet. Although you don't have to, you do get a deeper understanding of Bohdi who is the MMC in *Shattered Ice* You have been warned. :)

Dedication

For those who aren't looking for the light, they just want some-one to sit with them in the dark.

Prologue

Bohdi, Baltimore, MD

February

With the sun beaming brightly, warming our faces, the sound of, "Hi, Jace," reverberates along the shoreline. I witness the tulips we placed in the water being carried away by the ripples of the waves.

The waves take them to Jace.

While glancing to my right, I observe people standing and facing the water, their reactions varying from tears to laughter, clearly immersed in their treasured memories of Jace. As I look at Rylee, I can't help but notice the small smile on her tear-streaked face while she peers back at me. I move my gaze toward my brother, his grasp on her firm, his mouth tight as he watches the tulips fade away. I avoid looking at anyone else, even the flowers and the sun that remind me of my nephew. The sand beneath me has lost its golden hue and now appears ashen, the same as everything else in my life. Instead of joy, the beach now evokes a feeling of emptiness, the longing for a hello from someone I'll never hear from again.

The pain of losing someone is significant, but it becomes unbearable when that person is your best friend and nephew.

With each passing day, the pain twists like a blunt knife, serving as a persistent reminder of its existence and torment. Gradually, I move away from the crowd, dragging my steel-like legs along the shoreline. As I faintly hear my name, I glance behind me to find Rylee gazing at me, sharing the same pain. Six years she was with Jace, six whole years of being loved by him, and six years of being in our family. Losing my nephew and the aftermath of loss has shattered her entirely. I offer a small smile and nod to reassure her, but my focus shifts back to my brother beyond her. His reddened eyes stare at me. Cash knows I need this time to myself. With a subtle nod, he signals to me. And Rylee appears to understand as she turns away and heads back to Cash.

I've been focusing on keeping my family together while disregarding my own pain. The realization that there's no one to share your pain with comes when you return to an empty home at night. It's strange to be consumed by grief. Each day becomes a repetitive blur, devoid of any meaningful experiences, simply a means to get through and start afresh. I come across a secluded area of the beach and decide to take a seat in the sand. Eventually, I run my fingers through the chilling sand. The setting sun casts an orange haze over the shimmering waves.

"One year without you, Jace." The seagulls and waves harmonize with my exhale, creating a peaceful atmosphere.

How is it that my nephew was killed a year ago, and now, I am sitting on a beach, paying tribute by placing a flower in the sea for everyone to remember him? When did life get so fucked?

"I wish you were here, Jace. I would do anything to see that big smile of yours. I miss us shooting the shit. I miss our weekly catchups at the bar after work. I miss it all." My voice cracks. Taking a deep inhale, I close my eyes and tilt my head backward. For days, I struggle to move. I barely eat, barely drink, when Jace plagues my mind all day. I won't let myself return to that state. I need to focus on the future and keep moving forward.

"Jace, do you think I'm making the right decision by changing jobs and moving states?" Despite talking to myself, uttering his name creates the illusion of his presence. If he were here, he'd be the one taking me to the airport. He would be pushing me on to that flight.

Taking my phone out of my pocket, I quickly glance at the screen. I didn't realize I had been sitting here for so long. In three hours, I will leave Baltimore on my flight. I had decided this morning that I wasn't going, feeling both connected to Jace and held back by it at the same time. But as the day went on, the constant reminders of him around me made it impossible to move forward. So, I changed my mind. I needed to get away, to process everything on my own.

"I'm going, Jace. Even though I'm leaving, I still want to remember you. I need to change things up and clear my head. I'll come back to talk to you again. I promise." I ready myself by inhaling deeply before standing. Pivoting on my heels, I retrace my steps toward the parking lot, but I steal a glance at the sea, observing the shimmering ripples under the now rising moonlight.

"Goodbye, Jace."

13
Brayden 'Quake' Anders

Chapter One
Brayden

Lansing, MI

October

The sensation of winning is one of the best feelings. The electrifying surge in your body as the buzzer declares your victory. That, along with the adrenaline high you get when burying yourself in some tight hole of someone I can't even remember the name of. It sends a shiver up my spine and sets every hair on my body to a sharp standing point. I am consumed by primal instincts, driven to thrust relentlessly by his muffled moans. A shiver runs beneath my bare fingertips as I trace my hand up his spine. I push against his upper back, allowing me to arch over him more and push myself even deeper into him.

"Ahh, fuck, fuck," he groans in pleasure, his hands gripping the sheets beneath him, struggling to take me as I increase in intensity and speed. I move my hand, lacing my fingers through his tousled blond hair and gripping tightly. I hear the slight sound of a wince between the cries that leave his lips. When I pull on his hair, his back bends and his face lifts beside mine. While I slide my lips along his neck, his breath quickens, and the sounds grow louder. I softly graze his ear with my lips.

"I promise you, if you keep up with those sounds, I will make you leave here in pain. Now, shut the fuck up and take this dick like the little bitch you are," I hiss as I smack his head down into the bed, muffling his noises. With a firm grip on his hair, I relentlessly thrust into him, pushing from the back of his head. My muscles tighten, and a familiar tingling sensation spreads in my stomach. I apply even more pressure on the guy's head as his hands flail in panic on either side of him. Probably due to the lack of oxygen, but I couldn't care less. I'm only concerned with this sensation I crave, this sensation I relentlessly chase. As I shut my eyes and let my head fall back, my stomach churns and my muscles tighten. I find myself in a state of bliss, floating on dark clouds as I continue to fall without end. With a sigh, I pour myself into the tight hole, letting everything go. With every second of my descent, I experience a release of tension throughout my body.

My ears fill with the sound of loud gasping. "Fuck. Shit."

And just like that, *splat!* The falling stops and I hit the ground. Naturally, he had to ruin the moment by opening his mouth. Reality strikes as the buzzing euphoria in my veins fades away. I swiftly withdraw from him, still catching the sound of his wincing. This isn't my first time with . . . Lance? Lanson? It begins with 'La,' I know that, but I swear I tell him every time to shut the fuck up, and he never does.

"Fuck, Brayden, that was—" he splutters, still lying on his front with his head bent sideways, peering up at me while he uncontrollably heaves. He appears spaced out, as if he doesn't know what year it is.

I don't need to hear what he has to say about what he did or didn't enjoy. The sensation is gone now, and I need him to be too. I grab a towel from my gym bag and walk toward the bathroom, but then I hear the click of my door before it flies open.

"Yo, Qua—" My best friend, who doesn't know how to knock, stops in his tracks. He takes in my naked form and the guy's bare ass laid out on my bed. Lanson desperately tries to stand and cover himself, but his legs give out and he falls to the ground, taking the sheet down with him.

Kal collapses in laughter, dramatically throwing his head back and hitting my door with his fit of hysterics.

"Quake, what did you do to him?" Kal puts his hand out toward him. Lanson is pulling his clothes on as best as he can, still with his ass on the floor. With a wince, he tries to stand up and awkwardly pulls his jeans back on. Maybe I was slightly too rough. I kinda tapped out toward the end.

"Lanson was just leaving." I deadpan, keeping my stare fixed on him with a bored expression. I remain exposed, like the day I was born, but I quickly conceal my now limp and sensitive dick with the towel in my hand.

"Lanson?" His eyebrows raise to his hairline as he stares at me in utter shock and what seems like amazement. Obviously, he's happy, I remembered his name.

"It's Lance." He sighs.

Oh. "That's what I said," I huff. "Time to get going, places to be, people to see," I wince while scratching the back of my head. Lanson blushes and tries to regain his composure. Without making a move, Kal keeps his eyes fixed on Lanson. Both of us remain motionless, fixated on him, urging him to hurry faster. Kal doesn't give a shit. The guy has seen me in worse positions than this. He has had to bathe me while I laid in my own vomit; the guy has more or less saved my life more times than I can count, so this is nothing. Lanson, or was it Lance? I forgot already which one it was, takes his glasses from the side table and puts them on. My jaw tightens as I observe his nerdy self, grabbing his jacket and glancing at Kal and then me. It's the fucking nerdy glasses appearance that does it for me with him. The first time I saw him in the halls, I noticed his wide eyes fixed on me, drinking me in, unaware that I was watching him the entire time. When our eyes finally met, his cheeks turned red, and he quickly snapped his head away, almost as if he might hurt himself with the sudden movement. Later, I realized we shared some classes. The next day, I made a point to keep my stare pinned on him. I could tell I made him nervous, the way he squirmed on his chair, but his eyes always found mine. That one look was what had me dragging him into the bathroom after class and pushing him to his knees. Watching my dick feed into his mouth while he looked up at me through those black-rimmed glasses, with his big innocent brown eyes drowning in fear and desire, had me emptying my load down his throat embarrassingly quickly. I acknowledge him with a nod as his lips tighten and his shoulders slightly slump. Despite knowing this move, I'm confused why he consistently appears disappointed. While nearing Kal, who has shifted to the side, he suddenly comes to a stop, his stare still locked on the ground. Then, his eyes lift gradually to meet mine. He tilts his head slightly, furrowing his brow in confusion. I respond with a questioning stare, raising one eyebrow.

"What's Quake?" he questions, picking up on my nickname on the ice.

Chuckling, Kal responds to him, saying, "Bray is Quake," before I can intervene and tell him not to worry and to leave. Kal leans in close to Lanson's ear and whispers, "Brayden Quake Anders is an earthquake on the ice, shattering any opponent he faces." Lanson draws his head back and turns to face Kal, who observes, "It seems like he's good at shattering people off the ice too." Kal's wide grin is clear as he laughs, playfully smacking Lanson on the ass.

Lanson yelps and hastily makes his way out of my dorm, not bothering to glance back.

"Bye, Lanson!" I call out, and Kal and Lanson both shout in unison, "It's Lance!"

Rolling my eyes, I toss my towel at Kal. He does come out with some weird shit.

"Sorry, sweetness, you're not shattering this heart; my ass doesn't take dick," he teases in a girlie voice as he throws my towel back. "Hurry and clean that snake of yours. We got a party to get to." Sporting a menacing smile, he moves his eyebrows up and down.

"Now you're talking," I grin, spinning on my heels and heading for the shower. It appears that my night isn't coming to an end just yet, and there's a slight chance I'll recapture that feeling of euphoria before it's over.

Chapter Two

Bohdi

Lansing, MI

O*ctober*

I pause to soak in the moment, taking a deep inhale as I observe the classroom. I'm here. My fresh start is finally here. I moved to Lansing in February, but before starting my new job, I had to get myself in the right mindset. From my new desk, I see the empty seats waiting to be filled by students. I hoped for a sign this morning that would make me nervous and confirm that this was the right choice, but there was nothing. No nervousness, no excitement, no eagerness. Just a consistent numbness for the past fourteen months. Rolling my shoulders and craning my neck, I wait for the satisfying crack with each movement. *You've got this. Finally, the fresh start you've been longing for. It's here now. Own it. Live in it.* As I contemplate my inner thoughts, I am interrupted by the sound of distant voices filtering into the classroom, as students hurriedly take their seats and steal glances at me. The majority go up high, but a small number walk in the front row. I rise from my desk and position myself in front of it. Leaning back on my desk, I cross my arms and legs. I don't have to pretend or put on a false display. I am who I am; I'm relaxed and easygoing. Respect me and I'll respect you in return. I aim to create an environment where my students feel free to ask me questions without thinking I'm uptight. I carefully observe every student that enters my classroom. There are approximately thirty, so it's not a large number. I was informed that I might receive additional students as the term progresses, but to be honest, I'm out of practice and thirty is already more than sufficient. I quickly survey the students. Girls occupy the front row while the guys opt for seats in the back of the classroom.

"Good morning, all. Allow me to introduce myself as your new marketing management teacher, Mr. Stiles." I ensure my gaze flickers across as many students as I can. The wide-eyed, grinning faces in the front row slightly distract me, but I ignore it. Denny informed me that the female students would constantly seek my attention when I accepted this job. Being both the hockey coach and relatively young, he had to endure it for some time. I expected this, but I didn't think it would happen so soon.

"Hey, professor," a few girls in the front row say while fluttering their eyelashes. I maintain a tight-lipped smile while nervously rubbing the back of my neck.

"That's another thing. I would appreciate it if you could refrain from calling me professor." I extend my hands in surrender. "I admit, it's the norm, but it makes me feel old and I despise it." I chuckle, as a few students, both male and female, join in laughter.

"What do we call you then?" someone in the front row asks.

"Mr. Stiles or sir will be fine." I clap my hands together, eager to continue the class. "I understand it's a typical icebreaker, but I'd like everyone to briefly share their name. Will I remember? It's unlikely, but I'll give it a shot, anyway." This leads to more laughter from the students. I direct attention toward the girl on the far left at the front as she introduces herself, along with the following individuals. I attempt to remember all the names, but I must confess, they all blend together. I noticed a guy ignoring his turn, too engrossed in his phone, when the last person finished.

"You with the beanie," I say. Several individuals in the front face backward, and the guy briefly lifts his gaze away from his phone, stares directly at me, then returns his attention to his device. *There's always fucking one.*

"Introduce yourself," I simply say. He completely ignores me, and the guy next to him, who I believe goes by Kal, nudges him. Beanie boy casts a sidelong glance at his friend and then shifts his focus toward me.

"Brayden," he murmurs, before diverting his attention back to his phone. I'm not going to call my students out on the first day, but I will be if he continues to act like this going forward. I make a mental note and proceed with the class. I hand out the Syllabus to the front row and tell everyone to come and grab a copy. A few individuals from the back walk forward to collect their paper, but I realize Brayden is not among them. He sits slouched in his chair, staring into space. Another student, who I believe is called Trayton King, walks back to his seat on the other side of Brayden and smacks the syllabus playfully in Brayden's face. It's then I see a small smirk, but only for a moment before he's back to looking straight faced and moody. I can already tell that he's going to cause problems. Unfortunately for him, he will discover that I don't tolerate disrespect, especially from a student.

"Okay, in marketing management, I will provide you with an all-round understanding of marketing, studying key areas including consumer behavior, marketing communications and global markets. You will study all aspects of Market research and gain a practical understanding of how marketing and advertising work in an organizational context." I pause. Happy with how I put that across. I try to maintain eye contact with different students. Some seem keenly interested; some appear as if they're ready to go to sleep. Marketing is known for being tedious to learn, but once you begin experimenting with it, you'll uncover a wealth of intriguing concepts. "To prevent putting you to sleep or overwhelming you, let's start with the basics and gradually explore more. What is the purpose of marketing and why is it necessary?" I continue by elaborating on everything while quickly going through the slides I created during my break. Surprisingly, the class concludes faster than I thought, and shortly after, students begin to leave the classroom.

"Hey, Brayden," I shout. He stops momentarily while walking down the steps, about to leave. Snapping his head up at me, his jaw tightens with a flicker of tension. "Can you hold back a minute?" I state as I close the slide displayed on the screen.

His voice, dripping with sarcasm, floats through the room as he asks, "Why?"

I raise my eyebrows in surprise as I glance up from my laptop and force my words out.

"Because I asked." I try my best to suppress my temper. One aspect of being a teacher is requiring patience, which, unfortunately, I lack. His friend pats him on the back, lowers his head, and leaves the classroom. I move closer to him, but he barely acknowledges my presence. I clear my throat, and his gaze gradually meets mine. My breath hitches and a burning sensation sears through my chest. Holding my stare, he watches as my eyes flicker between his. The eyes transform from crystal blue to thin slits. His eyes are just like- so blue, they are— No. I close my eyes, taking a deep breath and regaining myself.

Fuck. Don't go there.

"Don't really feel like talking, huh?" I assess him, opting to move nearer to him. At that moment, I notice that one of his eyes is surrounded by darkness. A black eye. He drops himself into the chair near the front, casually kicking his leg out to the side. He nonchalantly shrugs his shoulders, seemingly indifferent to this class or me, and there's one thing I won't stand for: disrespect. The moment I'm about to tell him, the classroom door suddenly opens.

"How did my boy's first cla—" I swing my attention to the door; Denny saunters in, clearly thinking I'm on my own, but then sees Brayden.

"Apologies." He raises his hand, but instead of leaving, he approaches me. "Brayden." He nods to him. I notice Brayden's change in expression, and he quickly adjusts his posture, his eyes widening as he tracks Denny standing by my side. He visibly gulps, and instantly, he resembles the ideal appearance of my students. Intriguing. With a scowl and crossed arms, Denny stands next to me, keeping his eyes fixed on Brayden. It's interesting to see how Denny's role as a hockey coach brings out his intimidating side, despite his soft demeanor. It becomes clear that Brayden is a hockey player, and Denny strongly disapproves of his players not paying attention in class.

"Brayden, care to explain why you're here?" Denny snaps. I remain silent and position myself to the side, patiently awaiting Brayden's words. Glancing at the desk, Brayden's hand instinctively goes to his neck. He doesn't make any effort to speak. I give Denny a firm pat on the shoulder with my hand.

"It's good. During class, he raised a question about the syllabus. I was breaking down the explanation of its meaning for him." Moving my attention to Brayden, he appears slightly taken back, but still nods in agreement while turning his attention to Denny. To be honest, I'm not sure why I lied. Something in those eyes of his tells me he could use a break. "Brayden, I hope everything was clear to you. My email is at the bottom of the Syllabus if you have any more questions before the next class." Which I'm pretty sure he crumpled up and chucked in his bag. The sight of his wide blue eyes stirs up a dull ache in my chest once again. I can no longer bear to make eye contact with him. I gesture toward the door, signaling him to leave, and redirect my attention to Denny.

"Don't be late to practice." Denny clicks his finger and points at Brayden.

Without even sparing a second glance, Brayden picks up his bag and exits the classroom after mumbling, "Yes, Coach."

"He's a little shit, that one. Watch him, and if he gives you lip, tell me," Denny quips as soon as the classroom door closes. "He's the one player who could give me gray hair before my time."

I quickly glance at Denny's disheveled hair, with hints of gray, which seem to defy gravity in various directions. Possibly because of his habit of tugging on it while coaching. "Don't say a word," he grits before I say anything.

I burst into laughter, raising my hands simultaneously on either side.

"Wouldn't dream of it."

"How did it go today?"

"Uh—"

"Actually, what are you doing tonight? Fancy a couple of beers?" he interrupts before I have a chance to answer. The thought of going out after work doesn't really excite me, but a bar visit usually results in meeting women. Now, all I can think about is losing myself in someone for the night, which makes me immediately answer Denny.

"Sounds good. Give me a time and location, and I'll be there."

He snaps his fingers at me. "You got it, man. I'll catch up with you later. I've gotta go get ready for practice," he says as he runs out of the classroom.

I collapse onto my chair and lean back, taking off my glasses. Sighing deeply, I soothe my tired eyes, tilting my head. The familiar feeling quickly sinks in as I find myself alone in an empty classroom once more.

Numbness.

13
Brayden 'Quake' Anders

Chapter Three

Brayden

"Yo." Kal slumps himself down next to me, already dressed in his gear. Me? I'm behind, as usual. Trayton follows behind him, ruffling my hair and sitting on the other side of me.

"Quake," Tray mumbles around a mouthful of food. He's the only guy I know that can eat at any time in the day, whether it's before practice or right before a game and never feels ill.

"Sup," I say to both of my closest friends as I lean down and tie my laces up on my skates.

"I bumped into Coach walking toward the classroom. I tried talking to him, hoping you would get out of class before he went in there, but he brushed me off and told me he was in a rush. Sorry, man."

Kal is always attempting to save me. That's his nature. He's the brother I wish I had—he always has my back and does everything he can to stop me from getting in shit when it comes to hockey. He knows how much this means to me, and it's all I have. So why do I keep jeopardizing it? Why do I keep fucking up?

I sit up, rubbing my hands down my face.

"Thanks, man. Don't worry about it. I didn't get in trouble, anyway." I slap him on the back before standing up.

Kal stands up next to me. "What?" His brow furrows in confusion as his eyes skate between mine.

"The new teacher didn't tell on me." I frown at my own words, staring down at the floor. "He lied and said I waited behind to ask him a question about the syllabus." Voicing it aloud causes me more confusion. I thought little about it when I left, my head everywhere except where it should be, but now, why did he even lie for me? Maybe he's new and trying to get on the students' good side. I don't have a good side, so I don't know what he expects from me, but he will be sorely disappointed.

"He seems cool then," Kal says, smacking each knee pad with his stick before stalking off to the rink. Tapping my knee pads is something he has always done before a game, but also practice. Everyone has the thing they do before a game. It's a superstitious thing. It's well known in hockey, but Kal even feels the need to do it before practice. It can't be anyone but me. If I'm not here, Kal instantly thinks he won't be able to play properly. I'm sure it's his way of making sure I always show up, even on the bad days.

"Anders!" Kal bellows as I jump on the ice, skating toward the team standing in the middle of the rink, listening to their captain. Yep, Kal is the captain, and a fucking good one at that. No one deserves this position more than him. He worked his ass for it.

But I know it takes his toll on him, especially being my best friend. He wants to do the best friend duties, but also has an image to uphold. No matter how many times I tell him to stop getting me out of shit, he still does, but sometimes he needs to draw the line in front of our teammates and coach. Take today, for example. I'm late.

"You're putting away all the equipment after practice," he mumbles.

I salute him because I know he hates it. "Yes, Cap."

His jaw tightens, and he sighs loudly. "Shut the fuck up and listen." A small smirk appears as his eyes move from mine and land on the rest of the team.

"We have a tough fucking game on Saturday, and I need you to be on your fucking A-plus game." Kal glances over his shoulder to Coach, who is writing something down on the players benches, and then looks back at us.

"Between us, I heard there are scouts coming from the AHL and not just AHL, but the NHL as well." Kal's eyes immediately lock onto mine as murmurs and gasps surround me, and my eyes seem ready to pop out of my head.

Why didn't he tell me this before? He knows how much this means to me. He knows how much I need this, and this is my only way out of this fucking shit life I have. Kal's eyes slightly wince, and I see the guilt written all over his face. I don't blame him. I know he held it back for a reason, but this means I desperately need to focus now. Hockey is the way out. Hockey is the answer to escaping a life I'm sick of living. It's the answer to stop all this pain.

Kal stands taller and gathers everyone in a huddle on the ice. "Yo, Hawks! Coach has a meeting he needs to get to soon, so you've got me until he's finished. Let's do some drills, but I'm putting a spin on it. I want six stations and get into groups at each station. Station one." Kal points to one corner of the ice rink. "I want lateral hops side to side, Station two, I want you on the blue line, working on your balance. Station three: crunches; Station four: hockey net dips; Station five: shuttle sprints; and Station six: close grip push-ups. When each player has completed the sets, move to the next station. Set yourself a set amount and don't be a pussy. Remember what you're doing this for." Kal pauses, his eyes flicking to each of us. "Who are we?" he shouts.

"Devil Hawks!" we all shout in unison. Each one slaps the other on the back before easily skating to their stations.

Dropping myself into my cubby, I let my head flop back and smack against my locker. Taking a few deep inhales, completely worn from the strength and conditioning sets Kal ran us through today. A fresh surge of excitement courses through my veins at the thought of scouts possibly being here on Saturday. My adrenaline spikes, flooding my body with a new sense of anticipation and hope.

Going pro was never something I thought about as a kid. It wasn't only a matter of ambition; it was something I simply couldn't afford to dream about. But once I began playing, it became the most important thing in my life. I remember skating at the community rink, wishing my life was different, wishing for a normal family. Those thoughts still come back sometimes, but then I think of Kal and Tray, both skating over to me with huge grins on their faces and Tray telling me how my form was off.

I was ready to quit that day, to never return to the rink. But that's when everything changed. The dark cloud that had been hanging over my life began to lift. Kal's dad got a new job in town, and they moved to Michigan. Kal and Tray quickly became my best friends, and the best part? They loved ice hockey, too. Tray met Kal outside the rink that day, and from then on, we practiced together, always discussing how it would be to emulate the players on TV.

Playing professionally has been our dream for years. We've spent countless hours on the ice, pushing each other, dreaming together. And now, for the first time, it appears to be within reach. The dream that once appeared distant is now closer than ever.

"You were killing it out there, Quake," Tray mutters in his cubby next to mine. He stands directly facing me, his flaccid dick hanging in my eye level as I muster up the energy to undo my skates. This is normal in the locker room. We never hide ourselves away. We're guys and all friends. However, Tray does this on purpose. He loves getting his dick out because it's the biggest fucking dick I've ever seen. Any excuse and that weapon is waving around, ready to take you out. Tray is also gay, and he makes sure everyone knows it. He gives no shits what people think of him and to be honest, I admire it. I sigh, sitting up, as he leans against the wall of my cubby. Trayton has the best banter between the three of us. And taunting each other is what we do best.

"I'm not sucking it," I joke. Keeping a straight face, I hold eye contact as I punch his stomach. Tray folds himself in half, sucking in a breath after the one I punched out of him.

"In your dreams," he wheezes while staggering to the showers.

"Bray," I hear quietly as I attempt to remove my skates again. I worked too hard today, and the ache is already setting in. My arms and legs feel as if they are made of jelly. I sigh again, sitting up, and Kal stands there facing me. He rarely calls me Bray, but the way his eyes cast downward, refusing every contact, tells me he's feeling guilty about something. Before he can even continue, I put my hand up.

"You don't need to feel guilty for not telling me about the scouts."

He sits down next to me.

"I wanted to, but I didn't want to get your hopes up. It wasn't definite, and this is them getting a feel for us. It's not them coming and hoping to sign anyone. I wasn't even meant to know. I think Coach was going to keep it to himself, but I overheard a phone call and confronted him."

"It's cool, Kal. Don't worry, I will forgive you 100 percent if you take my skates off for me though. My arms are jelly after that practice session. You weren't taking prisoners today."

"You fucker." Kal laughs as he drops in front of me and takes my skates off. Kal never has to feel guilty. Everything he and his family have done for me has always been in my best interests. Kal's mom is like the mom I wish I had, and his dad kitted me out with the finest hockey gear. I spent many nights and weekends at their house growing up. Even though Kal's dad is one of the most important board members on Hawksview, I always maintained good grades. I didn't want to get a position in this college, because I knew Kal. I wanted to work for it, and I did. I still do.

"I need you all on your top form, especially you, Bray." His eyes soften as he glances up at me. "I need you to control your anger on the ice on Saturday. You need to show them you're a killer on the ice but a killer that sinks pucks, not fists. Got it, champ?" He smacks my thigh as he takes the last skate off.

"Got it, Cap." I salute him.

"Go shower, you stink." He throws his towel at me and spins on his heels, heading for the shower.

Honestly, I could lay my head back right here and go sleep, but I need to hit up the gym and get myself in that sauna and steam room to try to loosen these muscles. Otherwise, I won't be moving, let alone skating on Saturday.

Chapter Four

Bohdi

I forcefully slam my glass on the bar and motion to the bartender to pour me another. Denny told me to get here at eight; I'm thirty minutes early and already on my second drink. Today was good, but despite everything, when the day was over, I still carried the weight of a boulder that seemed impossible to remove. Typically, drinking can provide some relief, but I can't use it as a permanent escape. Today was my first day; I'm celebrating, right?

Seeing that kid set me back a bit. He doesn't resemble Jace or behave the way Jace did, but it's his eyes. They are the exact same color. Similar to mine, but more crystal-clear. It messed with my head. I found myself wanting to know him more: does he enjoy the same things Jace did? My thoughts were all over the place, and I couldn't help but cringe. This is a fresh start for me. I need to let things progress naturally. It's expected that I'll still be thinking about him. He was my nephew, and although there were eleven years between us, he was like my best friend.

I fixate on the beer that was brought to me a couple of minutes ago. A sigh escapes my lips as I run my fingers through my wavy hair, now sticking up in unruly tufts instead of neatly styled. Do

I really want to drink this and let my mind plague more thoughts of Jace? No, I can't stand it because it's torturous and gradually wears me down.

A firm hand grips my shoulder, pulling me back from the dark depths of my thoughts.

"Bohdi, my man."

"Denny," I say as I slide my untouched beer his way. "I got you a beer ready." Denny's face lights up as he grabs the beer.

"Five-star service, you can stay," he playfully teases and takes a big gulp, leaving white froth on his upper lip before wiping it clean.

I gesture to the bartender once more and request a soda.

Denny raises his eyebrow, halting his glass in midair. "Not drinking?" he asks before taking a second big sip, leaving the glass more than half empty. This guy can drink.

"I've had a couple. I got some papers to sort, ready for tomorrow; the hangovers don't leave as quickly as they used to. After turning forty last month, it all went downhill." The lie and excuse roll off my tongue effortlessly. I even believe it myself. However, that's not the reason, is it? It's because I crawl myself into this dark cave where the remains of my shattered soul lie, waiting to feel whole again, but I don't think it ever will.

"I hear you, brother. My back got strained when I was shouting at my players the other day. Make it make sense." He sighs while rolling his eyes.

I burst into laughter when I think of him coaching and shouting, because it's not only his mouth involved. Denny expresses himself a lot with his hands and arms.

"How was the first day? Any kids test you. We have some right dicks in that place," he declares, finishing his drink and signaling the bartender for another. Suppressing a laugh, I shake my head in disbelief. Denny always speaks his mind, but the truth is, those guys are some of his players whom he loves, like his own children.

"Nah, they were good. They're kids. You have to expect them to be dicks sometimes." My mind immediately recalls Jace at eighteen, sneaking around and causing trouble behind his father's back. To this day, there are things I saved him from that his dad has no knowledge of. We always kept it as our little secret. Even though you're not considered a kid at eighteen, boys still behave like children.

"My boys are always dicks, but sometimes I need them to be, makes them play better."

"Do players often end up with many black eyes?" I question, remembering Brayden's black eye in class. Denny halts his glass in midair, lifts an eyebrow at me, and proceeds to fix his stare on me.

"I am a hockey coach, not a ballet coach. Having black eyes is the least of their concerns," he utters before taking another sip of his drink. Nodding, I sip my soda. His face crinkles into a frown as he asks, "Why did you ask that?"

"That kid—Brayden. His black eye was pretty bad."

Denny audibly sighs and nods repeatedly in agreement, acknowledging how severe his black eye was.

"Brayden Anders," he mutters, visibly unsettled by the mere mention of his name. "The only kid to make me want to hug him and scream with rage all at once." He sighs again. While holding the glass, he gestures toward me. "This kid will push every limit of your patience. Don't let him skate rings around you, Boh. If he's slacking in class, kick him up the ass."

My head tilts back, eyebrows arching up to my hairline.

"When have I ever let anyone skate rings around me, Den?"

He brings his hands out in front of him as a surrender.

"Just watch him. Don't get me wrong, I consider him to be my top player, and I have love for him. He's an absolute beast when it comes to playing on the ice. His rage can be both detrimental and advantageous, but when it works in his favor, he becomes unstoppable." He stares absentmindedly ahead, a faint smile forming on his face, as if Brayden's play is unfolding before him, but then the smile fades away slowly. "Something is brewing beneath him, but not in a good way. Even though he's quiet around me, I make sure to watch him because the dean shared a few things with me."

This piques my interest. For what reason? I can't quite figure it out, but there's something intriguing about this kid. I want to know more about him.

"What did the dean say?" I immediately question. Denny moves nearer.

"You can't say anything." Pausing, he drinks the last of his second beer in the last ten minutes.

"His home life is quite bad. His mom is an alcoholic and drug addict, I believe. He's also a twin. I know that from one of the other teachers, but I don't know who or where the twin is." He shrugs before continuing, "I asked Brayden about him, but he said he decided to work and not continue his education."

Denny scans the bar as if he has something else to say but doesn't want anyone to overhear. Leaning in down, he gestures for me to come closer. I lean forward, eager to hear. "I heard from someone that his brother is a drug addict, similar to the mother."

I inhale sharply, and Denny raises his hand in defense.

"Now, it could be hearsay, I don't know, but there's something in Brayden's eyes that indicates he's seen it all. He's too young to have that expression already. I'm concerned. I try to keep an eye on him, but he's incredibly withdrawn." Denny rubs his eyes before saying, "I need to stop drinking now and take a page out of your book, I think. Soda, please." He raises his hand to the bartender.

Dread floods my system. A dysfunctional household, with a drug-addicted mother and brother. It triggers thoughts of the one person I never wanted to remember. My nephew's murderer, my nephew's half fucking brother. The child, victimized and neglected by his drug-addicted mother and her despicable pimps. His life shaped him into the monster who took my best friend from me.

"To clarify, you've never seen the twin?" I'm desperate to understand what's happening here.

"To my knowledge, no teachers have. It's quite a mystery. I assume he's not as smart as Brayden and couldn't secure a scholarship at Hawksview." Denny's frown deepens as he examines the glass before him, as though it holds the answers. I have a thousand questions to ask.

"He's a scholar?" It's bad to think this way, but the smart kids typically stand out. I didn't get that impression from Brayden. Inwardly whistling, Denny tilts his head toward me.

"Not only is he my star player, but he also boasts some of the best grades at the college. Well, *had* the best grades. Something is going on with him. More than it normally is. Lately, he's been slacking a lot more. I'm requesting all teachers to provide me with a monthly report on him and his work next week. I need him to keep it up. Losing this scholarship is not an option, and losing him from my team is not an option either. I refuse to lose him."

My attention drifts as I nod, my eyes focused on my soda. Too many damn questions and not a single answer. What is it about this kid that compels me to dig deep and reveal the truth by peeling away each layer that he hides himself with?

We don't need another James in this society.

We don't need another monster.

"Bohdi, help me, help me!" The echo of a piercing scream fills every corner of my house. It's Jace. He needs me.

I keep screaming, "Jace!" as I open door after door, but his voice fades with each door I open. Since when did my house have so many goddamn doors?

The longer time moves, panic courses through me. "Fuck!" I scream, finding myself opening doors I have already opened.

A sense of dread washes through me as it becomes increasingly difficult to swallow, wondering where Jace is. "Jace, where are you?"

Harder to breathe.

"Here, Bohdi. I'm right here." His voice cracks at the end. He's no longer panicked but sad, as if he doesn't see a way out. But where is he?

"Please hold on, Jace." In desperation, I pull my hair and open every door, crying out for help. He's not here.

"Jace." I spin on the spot, not knowing what to do, but that's when I see it.

Blood. So much blood. It seeps through underneath the front door. Slowly flooding my floor. My heart beats erratically. It's attempting to shatter my chest. I approach the door with hesitation. My shoes sink into the blood that continues to flow from under the door, causing me to wince. Holding my breath, I extend my hand, uncertain of what I will encounter. Opening the door, I am met with the sight of a hooded figure, standing with legs slightly apart, arms and hands hanging down. But I don't see Jace. Only more blood. This time, it drips from his fingers. His gray hoody is no longer gray, but red.

"Where is he?" Rage and panic take over. "Where's my fucking nephew?" I charge toward the hooded figure.

I know who it is. It's him.

"James!" I shout, my voice echoing, as I forcefully grip him and shake him. However, a deranged laughter envelops me as he slowly raises his gaze, causing everything around me to halt.

It's not James.

"No!" My voice trembles, shaking my head from side to side. "No!" I gasp again.

His face twists into a malicious grin. "Jace is gone, Bohdi, and he's not coming back."

"Brayden?"

As I gasp, I soar upward, and my vision gradually clears. My eyes wander around the room while my head sways back and forth.

"It was a dream, it was a dream," I repeat to myself. Adjusting my legs and placing them on the edge of the bed, I feel my slippery, slick skin sticking to the sheet beneath me. Leaning my elbows on my knees, I wipe the sweat off my face with my hands. The moment I open my bedside cabinet, I quickly find what I am searching for. Jace's picture in a black frame. The sight of him makes me sick with grief that I have to hide his picture in my bedside cabinet, but sometimes I need him. I need to see him. I lock eyes with him.

It's going to be okay.

13
Brayden 'Quake' Anders

Chapter Five
Brayden

YUNGBLUD filters through my headphones as I shut my eyes tight and let the lyrics wash away the reality surrounding me. I heard aggressive, loud voices through the thin trailer walls around thirty minutes ago, which warned me to prepare for the sound of shattering glass that would inevitably follow. There's nothing that can disrupt the connection between me and my music. It transports me to a different reality, weaving through the lyrics. I can almost trick myself into believing that I'm not in this messed up place when I close my eyes and listen to music. Leaning toward my old bedside drawer, I open it and search until my hand finds the worn leather binding. I grasp it and pull it out, finding it open to the page I left a message on last week after writing. I turn the UV light on from the pen.

There's no reply.

I skim through the recent pages, reading all the messages I've written to my twin brother, but he never replies. I texted him before I came, letting him know I'd be here, but he's not, which isn't surprising. Sometimes, he'll be here waiting for me. Other times, he'll leave me alone all night in the old bed we used to share, and I won't see him for days. And sometimes, I'll wake up to find him curled up beside me, as he did when we were kids.

I read the last message I wrote.

> *Hey, Bex, I miss you. Hockey is going sick. I can't wait to show you some new tricks I learned. Kal recorded them on his phone. You should come hang soon.*

It's been a week since I last saw him. He stumbled into my old room—his room—at 2 a.m., covered in blood and bruises. He collapsed next to me, reeking of a combination of alcohol and vomit. One week since he whispered he loves me before drifting off to sleep, and one week since he left a message for me before leaving the trailer.

> *I had to go. I'll be back tomorrow for when you finish school.*

Even though I had hockey practice after school, I skipped it. I was so excited to see Bex. I hurried home with a bag of candy, ready to have a casual conversation while enjoying our favorite treats.

He never showed.

I shouldn't be shocked when he's a no-show, but when he does appear, it's as if I've regained my other half. When he's not here, I don't feel fully myself. He's my twin, and I miss him. I reminisce about our old days, but something went astray with Bexley.

Instead of my cozy dorm room bed, I find myself lying in Bexley's bed, which carries the scent of smoke and stale alcohol, a smell I've grown used to. Despite his absence, being here gives me a sense of closeness to him. I haven't been myself lately, as if something's wrong—a constant ache sits in my chest, and I know the only way it will go away is if I see Bexley. I had hoped for a written reply from him. Shutting off the bedside lamp, I grab the invisible ink pen with a built-in UV light. I blindly write on the paper and then press the light button while shining it down on the paper.

I need you, Bex, please come home.

The smell of smoke and alcohol wraps around me until I smile. The warmth I miss every damn day when I lay in my dorm bed warms my bones. My eyes flicker open and close again, my fatigue from today's practice taking all the energy from my body. My eyes flutter and meet a mirroring version of mine. I exhale deeply, my body relaxing and the worries that surround me each day fade away in a heartbeat.

He's here.

He's okay.

"Bray," he whispers, nestling deeper into the pillow and drawing as close to me as possible, our noses nearly touching. Bex takes a few deep breaths, inhaling my scent. I'm his haven, just as much as he is mine.

"Bex," I murmur back, both of us closing our eyes.

I love my twin. He's the reason I fight hard for a future, a good future. I need to help him. I need to get him away from this life he's in because of me. Throughout my childhood, Bexley was my best friend. We were those typical twins that didn't leave each other's side; you wouldn't see one without the other.

He was always the more grown-up of the two; even though I was born ten minutes before him, he always protected me and cared for me. He would comfort me in bed, covering my ears to shield me from Mom's outbursts. Whenever my mother drunkenly stumbled into our room and collapsed on our bed, he would forcefully press my face against his chest. Without any concern, she would lie on us, oblivious to the fact that she was squishing our small bodies at only ten years old. Bexley always shuffled me aside, though, he bared all her weight. Or he would simply get out and lay on the floor next to my side of the bed so Mom could sleep while he lay on the cold, hard floor with only a towel to cover him and keep him warm, which it never did. No matter how hard I tried, he would never allow me to sleep on the floor. He would attempt to make a joke, claiming that I kicked him excessively. That's when we began exchanging written messages. To stop Mom's anger from being woken, we resorted to writing notes and using this invisible pen with a UV light that we got in a magazine. The light displayed a dinosaur when directed at a plain wall or paper—it was the best we could do.

U OK?

Mom snores loudly.

The floor is OK.

Want to go park after skool tomos?

We were inseparable.

Until we weren't.

"Kal mentioned he saw you in town earlier," I whisper, eyes closed, trying to unwind as we lay together. Our demons are at bay now that we're in touching distance. It's as if his demons call to mine.

"Hmm," he murmurs, likely avoiding the topic of what he was doing in town. He never wants to talk about it, and sometimes I'm grateful for that. The less I know, the less I panic, and the better I sleep.

"I've missed you, Bex."

"I've missed you more."

We lie in a tense silence for a while longer, but then Bex shifts, and I open my eyes. The demons begin to stir, rattling the cage of my anxiety, firing it up again. He appears skinnier than when I saw him last week, his clothes hanging off him. His eyes flutter open and stare straight at me. The blue circles shine bright but are rimmed with darkness, sunken in more than usual. His skin is grayer than the skies on a stormy day.

"Are you not sleeping?" I sit up, frowning at him. Bexley visibly sighs, running his fingers through his greasy, overgrown hair.

"I'm fine, Bray." He huffs, sitting up. I know he gets annoyed when I worry about him, but I can't help it. He's on my mind every minute of every day. He turns his head more toward me. Now I can see him fully. His eyes sweep me and then move over my face, his brow furrowing deeper as frown lines appear on his forehead. He reaches his hand out, his fingers gently grazing around my eye.

"What is this?"

Shaking my head, I dip my face down. "It's nothing." I sigh, rolling out of bed and walking toward the window. Bexley stands up next to me, pulling my face toward him.

"This isn't nothing. What happened?"

"Practice."

"You would have said that the first time. Now stop lying to me."

I turn my attention to Bex. His worrying eyes, drawn down, flicking between mine, bore into me. "There was some creep here the other day when I came to see you. He tried getting in here. It got slightly heated."

"What did he look like?"

"Does it matter?"

"Well, yeah, he touched you."

"I don't—" I begin, but Bexley's intense gaze stops me. I drag in a deep inhale, trying to steady my racing heart.

"Bray, please. I need to know," he insists, his voice softer now, filled with concern.

I sigh, sensing the weight of his worry. "He was tall, with a scar across his cheek. He seemed rough, as if he'd been in a few fights."

Bexley's jaw tightens. "Did he hurt you?"

"No, not really. I managed to get him to leave before anything happened."

Bexley pulls me into a tight embrace, his arms trembling slightly. "I'm so sorry, Bray. I should have been here."

"It's not your fault," I whisper, holding him close.

Nodding, his grip on me tightens. "I won't let anything happen to you. I promise."

We stand there for a moment, holding each other, the weight of our fears and promises hanging in the air.

Bexley walks over and lays down on the bed, the mattress creaking slightly under his weight. He reaches over to the nightstand and picks up our shared diary, the worn leather cover familiar under his fingers as he runs his hands over it. Flipping it open, he finds the last page I was on, which he can tell from the dog-eared page. He shines the UV light on the page. His eyes scan the page, taking in the words.

A soft smile tugs at Bexley's lips as he reads my words, his smile broadening more and heart swelling with pride while he learns how well hockey has been going. Just as he's about to turn the page, his phone rings, the sound jarring in the quiet room. He glances at the screen, and his expression darkens.

"I have to take this," he mutters, answering the call. After a brief, tense conversation, he hangs up and glances over at me, regret etched on his face. "I have to go."

"No, please," I plead, reaching out to him as I flop on the bed. "Stay a little longer. I've missed you Bex, so much."

Bexley sighs and runs a hand through his hair. "I don't want to leave, but I have to. It's important."

"Can't it wait? I wanted to tell you about my hockey game, which is coming up this weekend."

Bexley's eyes soften, a small smile forming. "I'm so proud of you, Bray. I wish I could stay and hear all about it."

"Then stay," I whisper, my voice breaking. "Just for a little while longer."

Bexley hesitates before he stands. "I'll be back as soon as I can," he promises, leaning over me and placing a kiss on my forehead. "We'll talk then, I swear."

I nod, trying to hold back the tears as Bexley heads for the door. "Be safe," I call after him, my voice trembling.

Bexley turns back to give me one last, lingering look and says, "I know you need me. But know I will always need you more. I'm sorry, Bray."

His words hang in the air, heavy with emotion. I watch him leave, my heart aching. Every time I watch my brother turn his back on me and leave, I never know if I will see him again. The room is colder, emptier without him. I clutch the diary to my chest, hoping he'll return soon, safe and sound.

Chapter Six

Bohdi

Rubbing my hands over my face, I attempt to erase the tiredness and dark circles, which of course don't work. I frequently have nightmares, but this one felt vivid and involves someone I know. It's even worse because it's my student.

Even though I attempt to gather my composure as students filter in, the lingering sickness persists. It's bad today, worse than usual.

Keeping my eyes fixed on the door, I anxiously wait for each student to pass through. I know who I'm subconsciously waiting for. I only need to see him to know he's not evil. Not like the monster who took my best friend from me. Having a tough home life doesn't mean he's equal to others in that situation.

Five minutes later, the students talk quietly among themselves while waiting for me to begin the class. I get fidgety that Brayden isn't here; I scan the area he was sitting in last, in case I missed him, and I see a few of his friends from before, one being Kal, who he seemed pretty close to. But Kal has an empty seat next to him, which I assume was for Brayden. When I glance back at Kal, he's watching me, and it's then I realize I recognize him from somewhere, but I can't pinpoint where.

Weird.

The sound of the classroom door opening grabs my attention. I think it's Brayden, but it turns out to be someone I haven't seen before. With each stomp of his chunky black boots, the chains on his black jeans create a jingling sound that fills the classroom. He approaches and stands in front of me. A black slipknot sweater engulfs him completely. His green eyes stand out from the black hard edges of the eyeliner that surrounds them. The lip piercing shifts while his lips create a firm, straight line. I clear my throat.

In a barely audible voice, he states, "I'm new." Ah, this is Daxton. I saw something in my emails the other day, explaining someone new would be joining today.

"Daxton Rivers?" I question. He gives me a sharp nod.

"I'm Mr. Stiles," I announce, quickly retrieving a syllabus and forcing a smile, trying to hide the chaos in my mind. "Okay, you only missed one class. Please review the syllabus and remain after the class. I'll bring you up to speed with whatever you need."

He gives me a quick once-over, nods subtly, and finds a seat at the far left, keeping his distance from everyone.

Okay then.

I glance again at the spot where Brayden sat yesterday, but he's not there. Instead, my attention is drawn to Trayton, who is intensely brooding and staring at Daxton. His anger is clear and palpable, and something tells me I need to keep a close eye on whatever's brewing.

As I face the class to begin today's lesson, my mind continues to reel, consumed by thoughts of Brayden's whereabouts. I assign a research task for the class to complete on their laptops and slump down at my desk. As I scan the students, my attention is drawn to Kal, who hastily glances away from me and focuses on his paper as if he hadn't been staring at me moments ago. His tense shoulders give away his discomfort after I caught him staring at me. I squint my eyes staring at his head, which is cast down, concentrating on his work, and decide to get up and take a walk up to speak to him. When I approach, Trayton remains fixated on me without saying a word. Trayton and I exchange nods, his eyes briefly shifting to Kal, and then back to me.

"Kal," I utter, causing Kal's head to tilt up as he directs his attention toward me.

Clearing his throat, he says "Sir," and then resumes working with his head down. There's something about this kid and his inability to make eye contact with me I can't understand.

"Where is Brayden today?" I question whoever wants to give me an answer.

Kal inhales deeply and mutters under his breath, "Not sure."

Trayton's eyes flicker down to the front again at the new kid, and then back to me. I shoot him a skeptical glance, raising my eyebrow. While crouching down, I catch Kal giving me a side-eye and Trayton maintaining his usual blank expression. "Look, I know he's your friend, and I get it, and I don't want to have to tell Denny that Brayden didn't show up today. Are you going to tell me where he is?"

Inhaling deeply, Kal's shoulders sink down as he keeps his focus on the paper, idly toying with the pen in his hand. However, Trayton clenches his fists, and stares down at the newcomer.

"Does Daxton know where he is?" I question, causing heads to turn in our direction. I arch my eyebrow at Trayton.

"Sir, he's probably not feeling well. I'm sure he will be in bright and early Monday morning," Kal says through clenched teeth, clearly irritated at my questioning.

"I'm going to the bathroom," Trayton bites out. I signal my approval with a nod, and he walks past me, his eyes never leaving the new kid. As Trayton reaches the front, their eyes lock, and the tension is palpable. It's clear that something has happened. Is this kid a friend of Brayden's? I'm assuming he was at some point. Fucking students.

"You know I'm going to have to tell Denny," I sigh out to Kal, but Kal shrugs

"You do what's necessary. It's your job after all," he remarks indifferently, and continues working. I exhale in frustration and make my way back to the front, sinking into my chair.

I miss my office job already.

When class comes to an end, I signal Daxton to stay seated so I can go over the syllabus with him. He doesn't appear best pleased by the exaggerated sigh he makes as he slouches down in his chair, but after today I truly couldn't give a fuck. I knew my students were going to test me, but fuck. They're a bunch of nineteen-year-olds and some of them act as if they're fourteen-year-olds. Too much drama for my liking.

"How did you find today?" I try to keep my tone calm as if what happened earlier with Trayton didn't happen. Daxton shrugs, his leg bouncing up and down frantically.

"It was okay," he mumbles, his eyes darting everywhere except toward me. Before I can continue, he interrupts. "I glanced at the syllabus. I got it. If I have questions, I'll let you know." He stands, picking up his bag.

"Wait." I place my hands in my pockets, trying to come across casually, not wanting to put pressure on him to answer me. He glances over his shoulder at me. "What was all that earlier? I won't stand for any kind of bullying in—"

"It's cool, sir. There's no trouble," he interjects with a tight-lipped smile. "See you next week." He turns and heads for the door and all I can do is watch him leave, knowing for a fact there is trouble. I saw the way Trayton stared at him. It was pure hatred, indicating this isn't something minor either.

13
Brayden 'Quake' Anders

Chapter Seven

Brayden

Everyone waits for the coach to enter the locker room. The tension ramps up every minute that goes by. Kal paces the length of the dressing room in front of me. His head cast down and his eyes harsh on the floor as if the bare sight of it disgusts him. He's game-ready, but anyone from a mile away can see the nerves that strum through us, and we aren't even meant to know about the scouts. King flips his lucky coin in his hand, staring into space. The locker room is deadly silent. I get my headphones out of my pocket and get myself into my zone. I can't start a game day without listening to my song. "We Will Rock You" by Queen, blasts through my headphones as I let my head slip back against the locker and I close my eyes. Every time I listen to this song, it takes me back to the good days. Days when Mom was sober, and not drunk, or on drugs. A day we would wake up, and she would have breakfast at the table waiting for us. "We Will Rock You" was Mom's favorite song. The song used to blast through the trailer every day sometimes. On the good days, Mom would play air guitar with Bex and me. When we were fully immersed in the groove, we would stand on the kitchen table and strum the guitars. These were the days when our beautiful mom would gaze at us as if we were her sunshine.

I still don't know what went wrong. We were eight years old with a great life and an even greater mom. Then the next thing I know, we were nine years old, and our mom was no longer our mom; she was a shell of the woman she was before. Life was easier before the change. Not like yesterday morning when I woke up to a message from someone in the trailer park telling me there had been trouble at my mom's trailer again. This is happening way too much. When I arrived, everything was eerily silent. No one was outside, everyone's doors were closed. When I entered the trailer, everything was trashed. Mom was locked in her bedroom and Bex was lying on the bed, covered in cuts and bruises. After cleaning up the trailer and Bex waking up, he told me there was some trouble with the guy he deals with. Karl is a piece of work and doesn't care about anything other than, alcohol, drugs and money. I ended up being there all morning cleaning Bex up, which caused me to miss morning classes. I still haven't had a chance to properly thank Kal and Tray for covering for me in class this yesterday.

Everything in my mind changes, and images of Bexley's sunken cheeks and soulless eyes flash in my mind. I played the song to him and did the air guitar while he lay there, staring at me as if I had lost my mind, his lips tipping up slightly, but he was too drugged up to care or move.

The days I would try to get my brother back, but he was already gone.

Then my eyes spring open as the claps and stomping filter through the headphones from the beat, and the reasons I need this so badly swarm to the front of my mind.

For Bexley. This is all for my twin brother.

The song ends, and I pull my headphones out as Coach walks in, and we all stand up and huddle together. Coach gives us our usual prep talk, and we all slap each other's helmets and head toward the ice. The tension is thick, you could cut it with a knife the minute our skates hit the ice. My eyes glance over at the other team, who seem out for blood. I smile, baring my teeth through the helmet.

Good. Because I'm fucking thirsty.

Something happens to me the minute my skates touch the ice on game days. Something takes over my mind, almost as if a different version of me emerges. People say it's passion, and I guess it is, but the anger that fills me sometimes even shocks me.

I want blood when I'm on the ice.

I want to see people crumble before me.

I want to see them fucking shatter.

"Quake," Kal mutters, grabbing my attention as his stick hits the puck toward me. We warm up together as we always do, and then, before we know it, the game is about to start. Kal skates around me in a circle before tapping both of my knee pads with his stick.

"Remember Quake, sinking pucks, not fists," he says before hitting his helmet against my own. Kal is on the left wing, and King is the right wing. Me, I'm in center, and it's known that our line is the nightmare line. There are no three-line players out there that work better than me, Kal, and Tray together. I stand head-on with the other team's center. Mackey, who plays for Ice Hogs, stares back at me, his eyes brimming with hatred. I may or may not have let him suck my dick at a party one night last year and didn't bother to tell him that his girlfriend had walked in around two minutes prior to me coming down his throat. I still remember the horror on her face watching her boyfriend on his knees deep throating my dick like a fucking pro. Of course, I didn't know it was his girlfriend until he stood and turned around, and she backhanded him around his face. I thought she only wanted to watch and, to be honest, it was hot as fuck. It absolutely made me come quicker. Safe to say, Mackey didn't find it as funny as I did when I was not subtly laughing while tucking my dick back in my jeans.

Apparently, I should have said something.

Who the fuck interrupts a blow job because someone decided they wanted to watch? His lips lift in a small smirk.

"You ain't shattering no one today," he subtly growls, his eyes on the spot between us the whole time.

"Really?" I pause. "Pretty sure your dad shattered right in front of me last night while my dick was—"

The moment the puck makes contact with the ice, I snatch it with my stick. I don't hear what Mackey says as I breeze past him and pass the puck to Kal. I fly up the rink, swerving the opponent's defense as they try bodycheck me. Smoothly sailing past every player, I effortlessly dance around them as if they were under my control. This moment is when I come alive. It's the only time I'm temporarily able to escape from all the negative shit in my life.

I'm me on the ice. Brayden "Quake" Anders.

I quickly shift my focus to the left and spot Kal swiftly advancing. I slide the puck over to him. Getting closer to the goal, his lightning-fast movements become more apparent next to me. I anticipate the opposing defense on Kal and can already predict the outcome. Kal also sees it coming, as the puck swiftly connects with my stick while three players trap Kal.

We're too quick for them.

The goal is in my line, and the goalie's eyes are fixed on the puck. I know for a fact that he doesn't stand a chance, and I know he's aware of it, too. As I swing my stick back, our eyes briefly lock before I make contact. I strike the puck with all my strength, and it reaches the net before the goalie can react. Each leg pad is struck by Kal's sticks before he head-butts me using his helmet. It's a celebration that we share. My team is crowding around me, constantly tapping my shoulders and pulling me around.

"Bray!" I hear someone call out on the ice, and when I turn around, Kal nods toward the crowd. I quickly scan the crowd, following Kal's gesture, and then I spot it.

Me. But a broken version of me.

"Bexley," I whisper into the empty air. Uttering those words amplifies its reality. Bexley gazes at me intently; a smile I haven't seen in a long time appears on his face. Tears spring to my eyes instantly. While I may be uncertain about some things, I am familiar with the feeling of happiness.

He's here.

He saw me score.

He's happy.

My eyes meet Kal's again, and he points at me and winks. No one knew about Bexley until a couple of years back when we were at a party, and he turned up high as a kite and paralytic drunk. I can still hear the gasps echoing in the room as they witnessed what seemed to be me, but wasn't. Word soon got around about Bexley and, as always, the truth came out. I had a twin who was a drug addict. It's safe to say, that year, I had more fights than I ever have had. I couldn't stand the name calling. It didn't last long. Some other gossip came along, which was more interesting. I don't know if all the teachers know about Bex. No one has said anything, except Coach. He out right asked me. Coach doesn't hold back on anything. I told him I have a twin, yes, but I told him what I told everyone else that asked. He's a worker, didn't fancy going to college.

They don't need to know he's a worker, but an illegal one.

I have the excitement of a child wanting to show his father a new trick. My veins ignite with fire as I face Mackey, eagerly awaiting the puck to be released, knowing it will be mine without a doubt. I'm already moving past Mackey with the puck, not hearing anything he has to say. My eyes keep flicking up to Bex, who sits on the edge of his seat, watching my every move. A smile spreads across my face as we move nearer to the goal. The puck is passed between the three of us as we press ahead. I see Tray has an opening, and he doesn't waste it as he shoots the puck toward me. Before my stick meets it, something hard slams into me and my feet slid out from underneath me. I hit the ice hard and wince at the contact. Squeezing my eyes shut, I hiss through my teeth at the sharp pain shooting through my right arm. I open my eyes and Mackey stares down at me grinning with his teeth bared through the gaps in the helmet. He then glances up and I already know where he's staring. He stares right at Bexley. Soon enough everyone is swarming me, players are being shoved, Kal leans down, with his arm outstretched to pull me back up. When I do, me and Mackey come helmet to helmet, allowing them to smack off each other as we both shove each other's shoulders. I inhale staggered breaths as I think back to what Kal said.

"Remember Quake, sinking pucks, not fists." I clench my teeth and drift away from Mackey. I have to remember the scouts and what I'm doing this for. Before I skate away, Mackey's voice interrupts my internal thoughts.

"Your bro is looking angry. Maybe he needs a hit." Everything in my vision goes blurry. I don't see the bright lights anymore. I see gray, surrounded by darkness as I turn on my skates to face Mackey.

"I'm sure I could spare a twenty if he sucks my dick good enough." One minute, he's in front of me, and the next, his helmet is in one hand while the other grips the side of his head and smashes it against the wall of the rink.

The gray and darkness disappear.

Now all I see is red.

All I see is his blood.

Chapter Eight

Bohdi

I can't say that ice hockey has ever been my thing. I'm a massive soccer fan, but Denny persuaded me to come to tonight's game. He said it's good to get an understanding of my students when they're in their element.

His wasn't wrong because this is fucking amazing watching them. They all work incredibly well together. I can also see why they call Brayden Quake. I never knew about this until Denny was telling me on the phone earlier and was getting way too excited about me seeing his star player in action. I hate to say, I was slightly too intrigued. He has an attitude about him, but he comes alive on the ice. He's quiet in class, but on the ice, it's his home. Even though he glows out there, my heart has been in my stomach watching him play, the way he skates circles around the other team. They don't even know what to do with him. They are a puck to him; he simply plays with them how he wants.

I was warned about his temper and was disappointed to see it come to blows on the ice. I don't know what caused it, but one minute, he was in game focus; the next he was fouled, and he got up. I see him skate away, but then in the blink of an eye, it all changed. He grabbed the guy's helmet, yanked it off, and slammed his head into the side of the rink before pouncing on him and pummeling him on the floor. Something set him off, and I can't stand how much I want to know what it was. I don't know why I'm so intrigued by this kid, but it's fucking annoying.

I wait for Denny to come out, and when he does, it appears he's aged.

"Great game," I wince, slapping him on his shoulder.

"Let's not go there. I got to go find his brother. He's on a rampage in there," Denny sighs out, moving past me before I can ask what he means.

"Wait up. What do you mean by his brother? I thought you have never seen him before. And what happened out there? He was playing great from the looks of it." I jog to keep up with Denny, who is moving through people, his eyes moving over the crowd at a quick pace. "Denny," I shout as we get squeezed between people leaving the stadium.

"Boh, do me a favor find a kid who resembles Brayden exactly. When you do, grab him," he repeats before pushing more people aside. I shift to the side and let my eyes scan the crowd, but I don't spot anyone resembling Brayden. I continue moving and keep my eyes on the surrounding people. By the time the crowd begins to thin, I still don't see anyone matching Brayden's description, and I don't see Denny. I assume Denny has gone back to the locker room, so I head back but then bump into someone exiting the public restroom.

"Sorry, man," I mutter as I brush past him.

"No problem," the deep voice replies, but it's not the voice that has me stopping. It's the dark floppy hair that shadows over porcelain white skin. Black-rimmed eyes that hide the bright blue I know those eyes can shine.

"Bray—" I stop myself, realizing one thing already. This is definitely Brayden's brother, and I know what he was up to in the bathroom if his half-lidded eyes and the way he stands there, swaying slightly, staring at me—more as if staring through me—are any indication. He's high. High as a fucking kite. Will he even remember the game? Is this the reason Brayden kicked off on the ice? Did someone say something to him about his brother? Is that why Denny is searching for his brother? Because Brayden needs him.

Not like this, he doesn't.

I grab the boy by the arm and drag him down the hall toward the doors.

"Hey!" He puts up a pathetic protest and barely has the strength to put up even the slightest of a fight. Once, the iron doors slam behind me, and it's only me and him on the quiet sidewalk, from where everyone has disappeared, no doubt to the bar. I push him up again against the wall. His head rolls back, bouncing off the brick. But right now, I don't care. He fucked it for his brother today. Brayden may not think it, but he did. Denny told me there were scouts. His brother would have been fine if he hadn't turned up. He winces, but his eyes blink slowly while gazing up at me, towering over him.

"You're going to listen up now," I grit out, already sensing my temper slip. "You're going to take your mess of a self home and fix up before you see Brayden. When you see him, you make up a piss-poor excuse for why you had to go. He isn't seeing you in this state. You got it?"

His eyes lazily shift between mine before he huffs out a laugh.

"I'll see my brother whenever I want, old man. You ain't stopping me."

My resolve slips slightly as I grip his neck in a tight grip and bring myself nose to nose with him. His scrawny hand scratches at mine, trying to get me to loosen his neck, but I don't; if anything, I squeeze tighter. His eyes go wider. I know I'm projecting my own issues right now, but I need to make him understand what addiction can do to the people that love you.

"You listen here, and you listen fucking good. Your brother could go places. You? You won't. You hear me? All the time you're being you, he won't because he won't leave you. You will drag him into your dark, sad life and remove all the good in him. Is that what you want for your brother? You want him to have the life you have?" I let my eyes dance between him and raise my eyebrows at him for him to answer me. I see it in his eyes, though. The small fight he was trying with me, slips from him right in front of me. His half-lidded eyes turn downcast as he stops tearing at my hand. As if he would be happy for me to take his final breath right here. I loosen my hand and let go of his neck altogether. He takes a few deep gasps and rubs his neck but avoids meeting my gaze. He keeps his eyes on the floor and pulls at the scraggly broken fabric around the wrists of his old sweater.

"Everything." He stops talking and slowly lifts his head, raising his head higher, giving off a false sense of bravery. "Everything I have done in our life was for my brother. I would rather take my last breath right here than Brayden ever have to live a single minute of the life I do." And with that, he shoulders past me and walks away.

"You don't think him seeing you live your life like this isn't chipping away at him day by day. He's living this life with you, whether or not you want that!" I shout.

He stops, his shoulders tensing, but he doesn't turn around; He walks forward again. This time, his head is lower than it ever was.

I pace back through the building and end up back near the rink when I see Denny come from around the corner.

"Did you find him?" he asks, appearing more stressed than ever. I shake my head.

"No."

Denny might think bringing Brayden's brother to him is going to help. But bringing his brother, who is high as a kite, to the locker room in front of his friends will not help. It's going to make Brayden feel even shittier than he already does. He just potentially put a strain on his future, all for what? A brother who can't stay sober for a couple of fucking hours.

"Brayden is in a bad way. And if he doesn't get his fucking head together, he is going to ruin any fucking future he has in hockey," Denny bellows out, throwing a puck at the floor. Turning away from me, he walks back to the locker room, and I automatically follow him, wondering what I'm going to see when I walk through those doors.

As we reach the doors to the locker rooms. Denny stops and turns around.

"Remember, you're not in the classroom here, Boh. Whatever you see or whatever he might say doesn't go against him in the classroom. He can have a nasty mouth."

Den seems worried. I know he is protective of his boys. He makes out they do his head in, but he loves them, and the joke is, he talks about these kids more than he does his own. I nod quickly.

"Of course. I'm here as Bohdi. Not Mr. Stiles today, Den." We both walk in and it's silent. His players sit there, now dressed, staring down at the floor. All their kits packed away.

"Boys," Denny says in a stern voice, as if he hadn't been running the halls moments ago, frantically trying to find the one thing he thinks his player needs. I scan each kid, and when my eyes land on Brayden, still in his hockey gear, my heart breaks a little. His head is cast down, staring at the floor, at his broken stick. Kal sits beside him, staring down at the same spot, while Trayton sits on the other side of Brayden, flipping a coin, staring up at me blankly.

Brayden's head slowly rises, and confusion mars his face the minute he sees me. I can see the devastation on his face, but most of all, I see hurt; he is trying to mask it with anger, but I see it. I see him.

"You good?" I softly whisper, holding his stare. He frowns, as if he doesn't understand why I'm here or why I'm asking, then gently nods and casts his eyes back down.

Denny begins going into a speech, telling them everything was perfect until it wasn't. Each player hangs their head in shame as if what Brayden had done, they have all done. It's clear they're a team. They don't blame Brayden; they don't even seem angry with Brayden. They all take the blame for what happened, and it makes me realize why Den respects them so much.

"You can all go. Brayden, I want to talk in my office when you're changed." Den shouts while everyone gets up and walks past Brayden, slapping him on the shoulder. I hear whispering from Kal, who is kneeling between Brayden's legs, talking to him. Brayden doesn't look at Kal, but Kal keeps whispering to him. I catch on to a few of the words, and it's clear Kal thinks the world of Bray.

"Don't lose your cool. Listen to what Coach has to say," Kal whispers. "You killed it today. Don't let one small fuck up ruin the entire season." His hands land with a slap on Brayden's shoulder. "Come find me after, okay?" He finishes before standing up and walking toward the doors.

"Professor." Kal nods at me and drops his head quickly. It's as if he is shy or scared of me. I can't quite work out which one it is yet.

"What did I say about professor?" I mutter as he walks past.

"Sorry, Mr. Stiles," he says bluntly, with his back to me as he continues walking, which is weird, but whatever. Trayton stands there frowning at the back of Kal's head and then swings his attention at me before subtly nodding and walking off. I can see Trayton pick up the pace to catch up to Kal and whispers to him. I'm not taking it personally; they have been through a lot tonight. When I turn back, Brayden is nowhere to be seen. I assume he has gone into the office, which I won't interrupt. Sitting down where Kal was sitting, I wait. I hear a door open about ten minutes later and out walks Denny. The stress was clear in his face, the frown lines across his head, with a fixed scowl. The bloodshot, tired eyes, and the darkening circles that surround them.

"I'll meet you at the bar in a little while," I say as Denny approaches me. He frowns, his eyes flickering back to where he just came from, and then back to me. I smile and nod at him again, showing it's okay. "I'll be two minutes."

Denny finally nods and leaves without another word. Brayden turns the corner and stops in his tracks.

"I know I wasn't in class yesterday. I had something to deal with. I don't nee—"

"I'm not here for class. I'm not Mr. Stiles tonight, Brayden. I'm just Bohdi. Pretend you don't even know me right now." Where I'm going with this, I don't know, and why I'm even sitting here, I still don't fucking know. Something draws me to this boy. It's as if I can see him drowning and I need to save him.

He lets out a deep sigh and moves beside me, opening his locker and grabbing his clothes. "Look, I'm tired. I don't know what you want me to say. I got a temper on the ice, everyone knows. It got the best of me tonight, I guess."

"It wasn't anything else that made you switch in that moment? You were really fucking good out there, Brayden. What happened?"

"Why do you want to know?" he shoots back.

"Curious, I guess."

Brayden grabs more of his clothes in his hand, still in his hockey gear, and turns to walk away. He stops and turns around.

"Sir." His scratchy voice, as if he is beyond tired, breaks through the silence. "I don't know what you're trying to do, but whatever it is, it won't work with me. Just leave it and leave me, okay," he says, and not even in a rude way, but in a tired and fed-up manner, as though he's given up on everything, including hockey.

I don't push because what can I say? Why am I even here? Why do I even care? I don't know, that's the thing. The only thing I know is that seeing Brayden sad chips away at me.

I don't like it.

I really don't fucking like it.

13
Brayden 'Quake' Anders

Chapter Nine
Brayden

Why does it seem as if my head is being smashed with a bat, and why is it unbearably hot?

Reluctantly, I open my eyes, only to shut them immediately. The sun shining into my room has me squinting and trying to roll over, only to be greeted by more warmth. What in the actual hell? A hard body lies between me and my wall. With a groan and a struggle, I finally free myself from my cramped single bed. I can't recall anything, especially how I ended up completely naked. My eyesight follows my clothes and someone else's from the door to my bed. I spin on my heels and look at the body in my bed. Lance or Lanson lies on top of the covers, butt-naked also, catching flies. I glance over at the bed on the opposite wall and tucked up fast asleep is Cope. I really don't deserve him as a roomie. Not only is he one of my best teammates, but the unlucky fucker got saddled with me. The number of mornings he had to wake up to not only my bare ass, but someone else's, would put you off asses for life.

I wince, hoping we weren't loud last night, not that Cope ever mentions it, but still. After everything yesterday, I think I'm being quite a jerk right now. I face my bed and lean down, gently shaking Lanson or Lance.

"Mmmm," he mumbles, pushing his face further into the pillow.

"You gotta go," I hiss, trying to keep my voice down. I don't think I can face Cope this morning, not even for this, but for how I acted yesterday. I know the only place that will help is the gym, and having Lan here is delaying that. "I've gotta go out. Get up and go." I sigh before grabbing some gym clothes and walking into the bathroom.

I slouch myself against the door and let my head lull back. Closing my eyes, the disaster that happened yesterday replays over in my head. I was on top of the world on the ice. I was home. Then a few words and it was ruined. I always get told, not only by Coach, but by Kal, "Don't rise to it. Control your anger on the ice, Quake." That's all I ever hear, and I try, I really do. But when it comes to my brother, that's the one person I can't hear bad about. They don't know what it was like growing up for us; they don't know the sacrifices he made for me. He is the way he is because of me. Images of plumbing Mackey's face come into a clear vision in my head. I don't even know where Bexley went after the game.

Leaning down, I pull my phone out of my pants pocket and see I tried to call him last night. Thankfully, he didn't pick up. God knows what I would have said. I don't want him to know that the fight started over him. He pulls himself away from me too much as it is. If I tell him I potentially fucked up my future because someone bad mouthed him, he will pull even further away from me. Him being there yesterday was huge, and I don't think he realized what it meant to me.

I scrub my hand down my face, trying to get rid of the destructive energy that fills me, and walk over to the sink. I splash water on my face, trying to wake myself up and brush my teeth. I'm praying for everything; Lan is gone by the time I'm out of this bathroom. He knows this dance; he knows that he always has to go in the end. He's a bit of fun. Someone I need when I need to let steam off.

I take more time than needed to be in the bathroom and stroll out. Cope is still fast asleep, thank God, and my bed is neatly made, and there is no longer a body lying there.

I slip my trainers on and grab a bottle of water before leaving. It's 9 a.m. on a Sunday, I can't imagine the gym is full. I make my way across campus, barely seeing anyone, thankfully. I need to sweat this feeling out of me. The sense that I let everyone down yesterday, followed by getting wasted at a bar and not remembering anything, is quickly filling me with dread and anxiety.

No one likes not knowing what they did when they were drunk.

As I get closer to the doors, I break into a small sprint, eager to get inside the gym. As soon as those gym doors open and I see the empty space, I let out a sigh of relief that I felt I've been holding in since I left my dorm. This is what I needed, no one to disrupt me and to sweat all this alcohol out of my system. I jump straight on the treadmill to get myself warmed up.

Images of yesterday still filter through my brain even though I have music filling my ears, which normally always distracts me. Even with increased speed and pushing myself to the limit, nothing changes. As I step off the treadmill, anger consumes me, and I crave to unleash my fury on Mackey's face once more. I need to get this anger out of me.

With the sweat running down my back, I strip my top off. I know Coach will kill me if he finds out, as well as Kal, but I need to get this out of my system and the only way to do that is the boxing unit. This is connected to the gym, but Coach is skeptical about us using it. He says not only are our legs precious, but our hands need to hold those sticks so we can't fuck them up. Even though I played a game and scored with a fractured wrist, the coach is strict about things such as this. Fuck it.

As I open the door, I freeze in place. Right in front of me, there's a guy facing away, shirtless, and he's intensely going in on the bag. Like a continuous cycle, he holds on to anger and must release it with every connection to the bag. The exposed back is coated in sweat, creating a shimmering effect when the light hits it. Every punch causes his broad back to flex and his muscles to contract. My gaze follows the perfectly shaped ass embraced by tight shorts, revealing strong, muscular legs. My cock stirs in my shorts as my eyes meet the tattoos that run down both arms and across his upper back. His back is fucking beautiful. I can't imagine what his front loo—

There's no way.

Sweat drips down his face as his sapphire blue eyes, surrounded by darkness, fixate on mine.

"Brayden." Hearing my name spoken breathlessly by him catches me by surprise, causing another unexpected stir in my pants.

"Sir." I give him a tight-lipped smile and nod, turning on my heels and heading straight out of here. What the fuck was that reaction? How am I getting hard over my teacher? Fuck. I needed the outlet, but not with him around. I don't see why he can't back off, why he has to be one of those meddling teachers who think they can fix everything.

"Hey, wait up." I hear Mr. Stiles' voice reach my ears.

For fuck's sake.

I keep my head down and quicken my pace. The last thing I want to do is talk to anyone, but especially him, after yesterday and, uh, just now. It was only a reaction; I get them a lot. I don't need to freak out. I obviously didn't know it was him.

"Brayden." His urgent voice is now louder, right next to me. When his fingers brush my arm, the touch sends an electric jolt through my body.

I instinctively step away and turn to face him. A deep frown mars his face, concern etched in every line. He stands a few inches taller than my 6-foot frame, but in this moment, he seems to tower over me, his presence overwhelming. It's as if he surrounds me, his intensity wrapping around me like a cloak.

"You good?" His eyes search mine, the frown still prominent on his face. I didn't realize how blue his eyes we— Shit. Why am I thinking about his eyes?

"Yeah." My voice comes out cracked. "I'm on my way out." I follow up while moving away and continue to walk toward the door. Mr. Stiles doesn't leave it there, though, as his fingers tap my arm once more.

"I'm finishing up if you wanted to go in there." I stupidly allow my gaze to connect with his again and hate the way my eyes track every drip of sweat that runs down his head. Fuck. Clearly, Lan wasn't enough last night.

"Nah, you're good. I'm heading out."

Confusion still mars his face as he gently nods, but before I can say anything else, the sound of my phone ringing fills the awkward silence. I pull my phone out and see an unknown caller pop up. I frown as I answer the call and bring the phone to my ear.

"Hello?" I ask, more of a question than of a greeting.

"Uh, Brayden?" The person also sounds as if he's asking me a question.

"Yeah, who's this?" My eyes meet Mr. Stiles again, who stands there still staring at me. He's waiting for something. I nod at him as a gesture of goodbye because I cannot have his body this near me for a second longer. I begin to walk and then freeze.

"It's... Never mind. You need to get back to your trailer. It's your brother—" The noise of an ambulance or cop car, the latter probably, blares through the phone.

"Shit. I'm on my way." Before I can get a reply from whomever that was, my phone is already in my pocket and I'm pushing through the doors. My mom's trailer is at least twenty minutes in an Uber from here. I pull my phone back out, opening the Uber app, and notice the phone shaking in my hand. My heart thumps in my ears. What the fuck has happened? Every dreadful thought goes through my mind. Is he hurt? Has he hurt someone?

"Why won't this fucking app load?" I shout in a panic at no one but myself. When it eventually does, my stomach sinks. "What do you mean, there are none available?" I shake my phone, as if that will magically make one available.

"Brayden."

As if forgetting about Mr. Stiles, my eyes swing up and he stares at me, panic laced in his eyes as they flit between mine. I swing my head back and forth as panic begins to settle in.

I need to get to my brother now.

Chapter Ten

Bohdi

I witness Brayden's flushed complexion fade away, leaving a paler tone. Whatever the person said on the other end of the phone, he didn't even reply. He ends the call and bursts through the doors, walking away from me without a second glance.

Running to catch up with him, I avoid making contact. It's clear from the tension in his shoulders that he either dislikes me greatly or wants to avoid me entirely. Furiously tapping on his phone, he shoves his hand through his hair, aggressively tugging at the strands causing his back muscles to flex.

"Why won't this fucking app load?" He vigorously shakes the phone in front of him. A distressed and agitated tone emerges from him as he anxiously stares at the screen, questioning, "What do you mean, there are none available?"

"Brayden," I call out, trying to snap him out of his obvious panic. The touch of my fingers on his arm seems to free him from his trapped state of turmoil. Yet, his eyebrows furrow and his chest heaves.

"It- it's my brother. I need to get home. No Ubers," he says, his voice cracking with desperation, his eyes never leaving mine.

Realizing I've gotten too close, I quickly step back while nodding.

"Don't worry, my car is parked in the parking lot. I can give you a ride."

Rapidly nodding, he takes deep breaths as his eyes constantly shift between mine. Brayden keeps pace with me while I walk to my car, focused on his phone as he types frantically. We get to my car in record time.

"You're gonna have to direct me."

He silently nods, getting straight into the passenger side. His leg furiously bounces as we drive, showing anxiousness. What the fuck has happened to his brother? We've been driving for about ten minutes, and I've noticed his head constantly moving in different directions. We must be getting close. I don't know the area that well, but what I know is this isn't a pleasant side of town.

Not one bit.

With a signal, he points to a narrow pathway ahead as I drive carefully. He's already beginning to remove his belt. My eyes scan over the small trailers surrounding the car.

The place he refers to as home is a trailer park.

Without waiting for me to fully stop, he immediately opens the car door upon seeing a small group of people. Startled, I abruptly hit the brakes, unbuckle my seatbelt, and jump out of the car.

I call out, "Wait," and Brayden comes to a stop, spinning around.

"Thanks for the ride, but I got it from here. Please go." His eyebrows draw down, and a look of pure worry settles on his face. He really doesn't want me here or to see where he lives. He briefly glances behind him before returning his attention to me.

"Please." His pained eyes instantly have me retreating and slipping back into the car. Once my car door shuts, he swiftly turns and sprints toward the crowd and the cop car. I grip the steering wheel in a vice grip and grind my teeth together. The last thing I want to do is leave him here, but the way he asked me to go, how can I not? On the other hand, he is my student. I need to make sure he's not in harm's way, right?

Without thinking, I grip the door handle and pull it open. I see him in the distance, bending down to someone on the floor, with the back of his head in view. It must be his brother, but what the hell happened? Something stops me from leaving. I have this sense of need to stay here and make sure he's okay. Make sure he's safe. I head toward the group of people in the distance before overthinking it. Praying he doesn't notice me before I reach him. I've seen his temper and the last thing I need is him showing the cops. My eyes wander across the area until they fixate on familiar black boots and a slipknot sweater.

"Daxton." I raise my voice slightly so he can hear me. He quickly shifts his attention from Brayden and the others to focus on me. Assessing my approach, his eyes widen, and he lurches forward, only to glance over his shoulder quickly at the trailer door he was leaning on. He approaches me with quick steps as I get nearer.

"Mr. Stiles?" His face contorts in confusion and panic as his eyes dart between Brayden and his trailer, scanning the surroundings.

"What are you doing here, sir," he rushes out.

I gesture with my head toward Brayden. "While we were both at the gym on campus, he received a phone call, and since there were no Ubers around, I offered to bring him here." I maintain my gaze on Daxton, attempting to detect any reasons why I might not be welcome in this place.

"Sir, respectfully, I think it would be best if you leave. People won't appreciate—" He hesitates, clearly searching for appropriate words that won't offend me, all the while subtly assessing me.

"You can say it, Daxton." He runs his hand along the back of his neck and glances over his shoulder, presumably at his trailer door. With a deep inhale, he turns to me, appearing completely worn out. "Please, Mr. Stiles." His eyes plead with anxiety. I stare at him for a moment, tight-lipped, and after both he and Brayden appear anxious about me being here, I decide it is likely best I leave. Although, I will be talking to them both on Monday about this. Right as I'm about to leave, a deep and snappy voice catches my attention.

"Who the fuck is that?" Daxton's shoulders visibly tense as a slight cringe appears on his face, his eyes flitting between mine.

"Go," he hisses, but the bulky man wearing a stained tank top and oversized jeans is charging toward me with a threatening appearance, as if he intends to pummel me into next Sunday. He stops next to Daxton, and even though he is a good yard from me, I can smell the booze that wafts off him. His stained yellow teeth are exposed as he comes closer, sneering. Well, the ones he has left.

"Who the fuck are you?" He scans me from head to toe, noticing my tank top and basketball shorts that I'm still in after the gym.

My eyes move over to where Brayden was standing and he's now staring at me. I notice he's stepped aside, and I can see his brother crouched down on the floor with his knees up and cuffed hands leaning over his knees. He glances at me with his eyes lowered and his shoulders droopy as if he's carrying the weight of the world on them.

I notice one cop standing next to them, a clear bag in his hand, with something inside it, but I can't see what from here. Three other officers walk out of the trailer. Daxton and the brute stand still, resembling statues, as they observe the cops departing while I steal a sideways glance at them. Tension fills the air as we all watch to see what happens. An officer bends down and lifts Brayden's brother's handcuffed hands, pulling him upright.

At that moment, Daxton and the brute stand motionless, as if anticipating what is bound to happen. I take the opportunity to side-eye them once more, discreetly analyzing their tense posture and Daxton's rapid breathing, which reveals his unease. If he isn't friends with his brother, then he must be friends with Brayden. The brute's hands are clenched, his unwavering stare fixed on the unfolding scene, apparently unsettled by Brayden's brother's arrest. It appears they're a close-knit community in this area. The cuffs are removed from Brayden's brother's wrists as the cop distances himself. Brayden's brother places his hand in his pocket. He gives me a lingering gaze, then his eyes dart to the brute, and I'm convinced I saw fear briefly appear on his face. Brayden tightly embraces him before they enter a trailer. At the door, a petite woman with a cigarette in one hand and a beer in the other gazes down at the two boys. As the door begins to close, she quickly glances at the brute beside me, and once again, fear appears on her face before she softly shuts the door. The brute watches as the cops slowly drive past, their eyes lingering on us standing there. Once they're out of sight, the brute turns to me.

"Who the fuck are you?" he asks, his beer-laden breath hitting me hard. Daxton appears completely terrified as he nervously glances back and forth between me and the man.

"He's only my teacher, Dad. Let's go back inside."

The brute's swift swing catches me off guard, causing me to step back instinctively. He then directs his anger at Daxton, seething, "I wasn't talking to you. Shut the fuck up."

With hesitation, I step forward, extending my hand toward the brute's arm, not wanting to make contact, but Daxton's frightened response fills me with unease. A feeling I can't ignore. He spins at such a rapid pace that I can't react before he grabs my neck and begins squeezing.

"Listen up," he forcefully says, and the feeling of spit hitting my face makes me nauseous. "I don't give a fuck why your pompous self is here, but what I know is you have outstayed your welcome and you need to leave now." His eyes widen and his face gets closer. With a menacing tone, he cautions me. "People like you are not welcome here. Fuck off." As he releases his grip, leaving me struggling for air, I swiftly take hold of his dropped arm. I twist it around his back and forcefully strike the back of his knees, causing him to collapse onto the floor.

"Mr. Sti—"

"Give me a moment, Daxton." I take deep gulps of air, trying to steady myself while the sack of shit tries to get out of the tight grip I have on his back.

"Why don't you listen up?" I echo his words. "Lay a hand on me again and I'll ensure your arms are broken beyond repair, leaving you unable to use them ever again." I apply pressure where I know it will hurt.

"Ahhh!" he cries out, struggling to roll as I keep him restrained. I let go and stand up slowly, keeping my gaze fixed on him to ensure he doesn't make a sudden move toward me.

Daxton utters, "Shit!" Before following up, "Mr. Stiles, I'm so—"

The brute turns his head sharply to give Daxton a menacing glare. "If you say a single word to him, boy, you'll deeply regret it."

Without even thinking, I take a step closer and swing, my fist connecting hard with the brute's cheek as he drops to the floor. He sits up on his ass, holding his cheek and glaring up at me.

"I don't appreciate anyone speaking that way to my students. I suggest you fix how you treat your son, Mr. Rivers." I smile broadly at him and turn my gaze to Daxton. "You good?" When I raise my eyebrow in question, Daxton quickly nods, averting his gaze from me and focusing on his dad, who struggles to stand up.

Once he stands, he sneers at me before grabbing Daxton by the scruff of his collar and dragging him back to their trailer. They get to their door, and the brute walks in. Daxton glances over his shoulder at me, his eyes cast down as he mimes.

"Sorry."

I turn and notice Brayden staring at me from inside his trailer. Dropping his head, he shakes it from side to side before disappearing from my sight. Well, shit. The sunny Sunday afternoon turned out to be entirely unexpected.

What the fuck is going on in this place?

13
Brayden 'Quake' Anders

Chapter Eleven

Brayden

"What the fuck is going on with you?" I stare down at Bexley, who lies on the bed, staring blankly up at the ceiling. "Bexley," I snap.

His eyes meet mine.

"What?" he sighs, his feet crossing at his ankles. He likely doesn't have much reaction after the joint he smoked to calm his nerves after the cops being here. This is the second time this week shit has gone down with Bexley.

"I thought it was a fucking ambulance." I run my fingers through my hair for the fourth time in the past minute. As he lies motionless, I walk back and forth across the short width of our small room.

"You don't need to come here every time I fuck up, Bray. It's not your problem," he mutters, and then sighs, giving off exhaustion and disinterest toward everything and everyone.

"Yes, I do. You're my brother, Bex. Is there a part of you being my brother, my fucking twin, the person I'd risk everything for, that you fail to comprehend? Fuck!" I throw myself onto the end of the bed, slouching with my elbows on my knees and my knuckles pressed against my chin. "What happened?" I sigh, too tired to fight with Bexley.

He swerves my question with a question. Something Bexley is good at, no matter how high he is. "Why don't you tell me what happened at the game yesterday?"

"It doesn't matter," I mumble as I stare at a picture of Bex and me pinned to the wall. We stumbled upon ten dollars at the fun fair when we were ten. Instead of using it for rides or candy, we used it to get a cartoon sketch of ourselves in the picture booth. Both of us are captured on camera, Bexley laughing with closed eyes and me smiling. Right before the picture, I let out a fart and Bexley couldn't stop laughing. I miss those days. Even though we hated being in the trailer with Mom and we never knew if we would get fed or not, it didn't matter. We had each other. That was enough to keep a smile on our faces.

"Bray, you're lucky your teammates were there to pull you off. It could have ended a lot worse." I feel the bed shifting, and I glance over to find him sitting up. I lock eyes with him, his bloodshot, hazy blue swirls meet mine. "What did that guy on the ice say to make you react that way?"

I gesture by shaking my head, locking eyes with him briefly, and then redirect my attention to the picture.

"It doesn't matter," I whisper, wanting to forget about Mackey and every bad thing in our life. It seems Bexley gets the message that I'm not interested in discussing it. He gently nods his head.

"You were amazing out there, Bray." Bex moves next to me on the bed, his knee knocking mine. Both of our bodies taking up the small bed. "I missed watching you play." I shift my eyes to Bexley's face and find him fixated on the Pinboard picture. He doesn't look at me. Seeing him fixate on the picture of us, I instinctively turn my head and do the same. If we shut our eyes, even for a moment, we might be transported back there.

"The OG Quake." He inwardly laughs. "I don't think you realize the buzz it gives people watching you."

"Maybe if you keep watching me, that buzz will be enough, and you won't have to go searching for other things to give you a buzz. I would play for you every minute of the day if that were the case." I blurt it out without a second thought, instantly draining all the joy from Bexley. It feels as if a dark cloud has suddenly engulfed both of us. The black cloud constantly lurks in the shadows, prepared to show up.

"I wish it would be enough too," he sighs. He is aware of his addiction, but rarely acknowledges or discusses it. This is the closest I think I've ever come. We remain silent and content, our eyes fixed on the picture. I wish I knew what was going through his mind. Does he miss the old days? Does he wish to go back to those days? I want to ask him, but he hates me talking about our childhoods. They weren't great, but they weren't always bad. But I guess for him they were worse. He will get all twitchy and walk out of the trailer. He's right next to me, our knees touching. It's been a while since we've been this close. And if it means I can have him with me a little longer, even if we don't say a word, I'll cherish it.

"Who was the guy that brought you here today?"

"My teacher. While I was at the gym, I received a call and—"

"Call? Who called you?" Bexley interrupts me, before I can continue.

"Oh, I uh don't know. I was too worried about questioning it. It has to be someone in the park, right?" Bexley nods, his lips pressed together, as he turns to face the bed and stares at the floor.

"Is your teacher cool?" With a frown, Bexley studies the floor, likely pondering if Mr. Stiles will bring up today's events at my school. I mean probably, yeah. What teacher wouldn't? I've been too worried about Bex, that, per usual, I didn't think about how this will affect me.

I shrug. "I mean, Karl attempted to beat the shit out of him and failed." I smile a little. Seeing that guy have his ass handed to him has got to be number one on my wish list. That mental image of him lying on the floor will stay with me forever. "Maybe he might think it will affect his job, so he might say nothing. I will see what happens when I get to school tomorrow." I frown at the floor, taking another deep gulp of air. The familiar tightness in my chest emerges as I discreetly dig my nails into my wrists. The pain doesn't bother me; it distracts me from my racing heart and the sweat on my neck. The feeling of having a weight sitting on my chest slowly eases as I drop my head and close my eyes.

"Something tells me your teacher will be cool tomorrow," Bexley mumbles. He doesn't know him and neither do I, but it's not something I'm going to worry about now.

Our peaceful silence is abruptly interrupted by a phone ping, snapping us back to reality. Bexley shifts beside me, and I prepare myself with a deep inhale. I already know what's coming. Bexley rises beside me.

"Bye," I grunt, already knowing he's leaving, no doubt to get more drugs or sell them. Why can't he love me more than the drugs? Why can't he put me before the drugs? "You know what, no." I stand, coming face-to-face with my brother. His empty chilling eyes stare back at me, void of any emotion. "You're here with me. Why can't you chill with me for longer? Why do you have to run to that fucking prick Karl that has ruined our fucking life, Bexley?" My voice gets louder. "I'm fucking here. Stay here." I point to the floor and puff my chest out. Why? I don't know, but I'm mad. I'm so fucking mad right now. Every time that piece of shit rings or messages, Bexley goes running. When Bexley began selling drugs for that piece of shit, he essentially made a deal with the devil, and we all know the consequences of such a deal.

You never get yourself back.

Bexley pulls me closer, wrapping one arm around my shoulder and the other around my back. As he pulls me closer, I can't resist sinking into his arms. I nestle my face into his shoulder and squeeze him tightly. I can still smell my brother. He's still somewhere inside, deeply buried.

"Do me a favor. When people want to help you, don't shut them out or push them away." Bex's mellow voice makes me want to cry. I hate feeling weak, but the only person I would ever allow to see me crumble would be Bex.

"Letting people in hurts."

"Hey." Bex pulls back, his eyebrows draw down as a frown mars his face. "What makes you say that?" My eyes flicker between his, taking in this moment. Bex has always appeared to have a superhero complex in my eyes. He protected me and wanted nothing but good things for me. Until the drugs took over. I can't ever think of the good days without the bad days. He doesn't realize it, but he is the only person I've ever really let in. Kal is my best friend, and I love him for everything he has done and continues to do, but no one is Bex. No one shares the connection we have. It's not something that can be explained. I let Bex in the day I was born, but along the way, he left me. He left me on my own in a pitch-black room and I still haven't worked out how to get out. My silence must speak a thousand words as Bex palms my face, squishing my cheeks together while smiling.

"Are you heading to Brewtap later?" He releases my cheeks and puts his hands in his pockets. I frown but quickly mask it. I didn't even know Bex knew we went there. Brewtap is a bar near campus, but Tray, being the dodgy fucker he is, hooked us up with fake IDs. I'm pretty sure every single bar staff in there knows they're fake, but they say nothing. To be honest, half the fucking bar is filled with underage people.

"Yeah . . . " I drag it out. Wondering why he's asking. "I usually meet Tray and Kal there for a few." Bex nods, zipping up his sweater.

"Cool, I was thinking of stopping by tonight. I got an ID." He grins wide, and it seems as though the air has been knocked out of me. I can't tell you how long it's been since I've seen Bexley appear this happy. And he wants to go meet me for a drink and spend time with me, Tray, and Kal. The boys are going to be so happy. I nod eagerly, my grin matching his, no doubt bigger because of how happy I feel right now.

"Yeah, yeah. You can come whenever you want. We usually get there around 7, but if you want to arrive earlier, drop me a text me and I'll be there at any time," I rush out, and Bex smiles, but the smile doesn't quite reach his eyes as it did last time. His brow furrows briefly before he composes himself, but I caught it. The guilt at how excited I am right now. He doesn't realize how long I've waited for this moment.

"Sweet. I'll catch you later, Bro. I'll be there at seven." He nods, walking backward out of our room.

"Yeah, see you later." I shout through the trailer when I hear the door open and slam. I let myself sink onto the bed, lying back and grinning at the ceiling. Pulling my phone out of my pocket, I hastily open my group chat with Tray and Kal.

Me:

Bex is meeting us at the pub tonight :D.

Kal:

Sweet will be good to see him.

Monster dick:

Cool.

Me:

Tray, stop changing your name on my phone.

Kal:

What's it say this time? Nothing can be as bad as anal destroyer

Me:

Screenshot of chat

Kal:

Pft, he wishes.

I can see Tray has read the messages, but he doesn't reply. Tray wouldn't ever give up a conversation about his dick, but I know why it is. It's Bex. Something went wrong between Tray and Bex when we were younger. They got close as we grew, but then Bex changed, and Tray held on to Bex. We all did, but then Tray realized Bex wouldn't change for anyone, and I think Tray thought he might for him. It crushed him when he realized that wasn't the case. Trayton stopped coming to mine after long, I think seeing Bex the way he was hurt him too much. Tray never shared the details with me or Kal, and whenever I brought it up to Bex, he acted clueless. Bex overlooks the fact that he and I are essentially the same. Neither of us has ever been good at lying. Hopefully, they can handle whatever the problem is tonight.

With a burst of energy, I spring up and find myself walking with a bounce in my step. I have a lot of shit to deal with tomorrow, but that's tomorrow's problem.

Tonight may be the beginning of getting my brother back.

Chapter Twelve

Bohdi

Surprisingly, this bar is not as bad as I expected. I thought being nearer to campus; it was going to be a bit of a dive and full of seniors, but I've only seen a few around so far. There could be others here, but I haven't come across them on campus. There are a couple of bars around campus, but I've heard Pythons is quieter, and I need some downtime after the day I've had. I glance around the busy bar, which becomes more crowded with each passing minute. Suddenly, my attention is captivated by a gorgeous blonde who is staring directly at me from across the bar. She flashes me a larger-than-life smile, her pearly white teeth shining brightly. I tilt my head, racking my brain to recall where I've encountered her. Judging by her giggle and the way she heads toward me, it's from somewhere. I can't help but notice the way her curvy hips sway in that tight pencil dress and sky-high heels.

That dress would look fucking amazing on my bedroom floor.

"Mr. Stiles." Her mischievous voice causes my dick to stir in my pants. I can absolutely visualize her calling me Mr. Stiles while on her knees.

With a smirk, she wraps her lips around her straw, takes a sip of her drink, and asks, "Do you even know who I am?" It's hard for me to believe that I could ever forget a beautiful woman like her. It's annoying because I can't figure out where I know her from, even though I recognize her. Sipping her drink through a straw, she smirks at me and raises a quizzical eyebrow. I take a swig from my beer bottle, downing half of it in one gulp, attempting to buy myself some time, but my mind is completely empty. I flash a smirk while playing with the bottle top, spinning it between my fingertips, and then I place it on the table.

"I find it hard to believe I could forget a truly beautiful face such as yours." Flattery gets you most places. I've discovered that when it comes to women.

"To be honest, I think it's more I've seen you, not the other way round." She extends her hand. "Nice to meet you. I'm Amy, although my students tend to call me Ms. Banksy." Her smirk suggests that it's obvious from my expression that I've now twigged on who she is.

"Ahh, yes, Ms. Banksy, the one who teaches economics. I can't say I have seen you around Hawksview much. However, I do now remember briefly seeing you on my first day when I was having a tour of the College." I smile, grasping her hand and shaking it. Her addictive smile reappears as she casually flicks her hair over her shoulder.

"It is a pleasure to meet you officially, Mr. Stiles."

"Ah, please call me Bohdi." I rise to my feet, grabbing my nearly empty bottle. "Can I get you another?" I gesture toward her almost empty glass.

"Please. Vodka and sprite."

Once I bring our drinks back to the table, we get talking, and she tells me about her experience working at Hawksview. She describes the area and goes on expressing her passion for her job. Our drinks flow, and it becomes quite apparent after a few drinks she is flirting with me. The way her gaze flicks down to my lips when I bring the beer bottle to my mouth and take a sip. The way she throws her head back dramatically, laughing while laying her hand on top of my arm. I track her long slender neck as she throws her head back for probably the sixth time now, laughing at something that wasn't even that funny, but I don't care. I have no qualms about fucking a colleague. This is exactly what I need, to get lost in a tight wet pussy and try to forget about the shit show that was today. Despite that, I can't shake the slight sense of worry I have about leaving Brayden and Daxton there with that fucked-up guy.

"Did you want to get out of here?" Amy studies me with suggestive fuck-me eyes, hinting at her desire. As I'm about to reply, my attention is drawn to something at the bar entrance. When I glance at the door, I see Brayden, Kal, and Trayton.

Fuck.

Without noticing me, they walk through the pub and head straight for the bar. How the fuck are they buying drinks? They're nineteen. My old man thoughts make me inwardly groan. I was drinking at sixteen, for fuck's sake.

Amy breaks me out of the moment with her questioning voice, saying, "Bohdi."

"Yes, sorry. How about we finish these drinks and go back to my place?" I give her my signature smile that the woman can rarely say no to and let my gaze move slowly over her figure. When my gaze connects with hers, her cheeks are flushed, and her eyes are hooded. It's clear what she's thinking based on her squirming in her seat.

I can't wait to see her mile long legs hanging over my shoulders while I slide into her. My dick takes note while I pick up my bottle, downing the rest in one. She's already risen from her chair.

"I'll be back in a second." I quickly go to the bathroom, but on my return, I crash into a solid shoulder.

"Shit, sorry, man." As soon as I meet the eyes of the person, I internally groan once again. "Trayton." I greet him smugly. He peeks over his shoulder and then to the sides. His eyes widen in a frantic search for an escape route.

"Sir," he winces, awkwardly rubbing the back of his neck.

Raising an eyebrow, I ask, "Are we having a good night?" I want to see him squirm for a second, as if I'm about to call him out for being here, but I'm not. We've all been young.

"Yeah, chilling with my older brother, you know, catching up." His lie slips off his tongue effortlessly, leaving me slightly amazed.

"Uh-huh. Sure." I slap his shoulder playfully as I walk past, smirking.

"Stay safe and have a good night, Trayton." I gesture toward him, and he nods in bewilderment. Despite knowing he's lying, nothing can stop me from enjoying my night with what awaits me at the table.

As I approach the bar, I freeze when I see Kal talking to a girl, but that's not what's baffling me. Brayden is kissing another guy. I observe their open mouths connecting and Brayden's tall stature dominating the shorter, thinner person. His cap is on backward, tusks of dark brown hair peeking out of the sides.

I don't know why I'm stunned he's gay or bisexual. There was no reason for me to think otherwise. It just didn't come to mind. I detest that I'm unable to break my stare away from them. I track the way Brayden controls the whole kiss; the guy is like his opponent on the ice. A small puppet that he controls. Brayden repositions himself to have the guy's back facing me, firmly gripping his neck, and tilting his head to deepen the kiss.

Fucking move Bohdi. Walk away.

I experience a gulp in my throat as Brayden's hand slides down, clasping onto the guy's backside, and drawing him nearer. Understanding the exact reason. When you have that ache, you need to rub yourself just to get a slight release. Why am I thinking about Brayden being hard? How many drinks have I had?

As my eyes flicker up, the world ceases moving, and I am still in shock, sucking in a sharp breath as Brayden, with his crystal eyes, which sparkle under the bright lights, continues to consume the guy while intensely staring directly at me. Without looking away, he tightens his grip on the guy's throat. He's put me in a fucking trance. I can't move my eyes, my brain screams at me too, but I can't.

I'm just like one of his puppets, under his control.

No.

I'm his teacher.

His straight teacher.

I blink repeatedly as the music gradually returns to the room. I didn't notice I had completely tuned out until I heard the music and voices blending together. Refusing to look at Brayden again, I keep it moving toward the table. My heart beats erratically and I have to take deep breaths to calm my racing heart. There's a trickle of sweat forming at the back of my neck. Out of nowhere, my clothes seem too tight, and I urgently want to escape from this place. Now.

I don't make it to the table; I grab Amy's attention and gesture toward the door as she quickly nods and grabs her bag and coat off the table. I manage to get to the doors before she does and hold them open so she can duck under my arm. As I stare at her perfect ass swaying in the tight dress as she walks out, I tell myself to not turn around, but again, my body has a mind of its own.

Again, as if it's being controlled.

Holding the door open, I come to a stop and take a quick gulp of air before casting a glance back.

Fuck.

I quickly exhale before taking another breath. It's Brayden who I see, with a smirk on his face and a beer bottle gliding along his swollen, full lips as he stares back at me. He stands with his back against the bar, ankles crossed. He lifts his beer bottle toward me, then drinks from it, causing my eyes to fixate on the lump in his throat as it bobs with each swallow. My own mouth goes dry.

Swiftly, I avert my eyes and walk out of the bar, maintaining a fast pace with my head lowered.

"Hey, you okay?" Amy startles me as I reach the doorway.

I snap back at her, frowning, "Yeah, why wouldn't I be?" Why am I acting as if I've done something wrong? She rears her head back slightly and opens and closes her mouth.

"Fuck, sorry, Amy. I had a long day. Maybe we can rain check?" I cringe when I notice the disappointment in her eyes.

"Uh yeah, sure." As she glances around, intentionally avoiding meeting my eyes, I feel like a dick. I can't put into words what just happened and why I'm reluctant to invite Amy to my place now. Recalling the image of Brayden staring at me while he rubs against the guy, triggers a nauseating feeling in my stomach. Was he getting off on seeing me watch him?

Fuck.

It's not appropriate for me to be staring at him in that way. What caused my body to heat up when I saw his lips on that guy? What caused my stomach to flip when his stare burned through me intensely?

I quickly reach for my phone to order an Uber and one for Amy as my thoughts race at lightning speed.

Amy's Uber arrives first, and we exchange numbers before she gets in. I stare into thin air as I wait for my Uber, my stomach turning at what's just happened. Maybe there was something that could stop me from enjoying my night.

Brayden.

There are many levels on which this is wrong. He is my student, and I am his teacher.

Above all else, I'm straight.

Seeing Brayden leaning on the bar, smirking at me, instantly comes to mind and sends my heart into overdrive.

Well, at least I think I am.

13
Brayden 'Quake' Anders

Chapter Thirteen

Brayden

It's 7:30 and I still haven't heard from Bexley. He's obviously running late, which is fine, but I'm getting annoyed by my constant fixation on the bar door.

"He'll be here, man. He's likely got caught up." Kal studies me with a tight-lipped smile as he takes a sip of his beer.

I understand what "caught up" means. It's likely his phone is constantly buzzing and he can't find a moment to come here. I take my phone out of my pocket and select Bexley's number. Placing the phone against my ear, I hear the continuous ringing until it abruptly stops. With a loud exhale, I make it clear to the bartender that I need another drink by signaling with my glass.

"That's your third one in half an hour, champ. Slow down," Tray says, still on his first drink. With an eye roll, I grab my third drink from the bartender and take a long gulp. As the doors open again, I turn my head and realize it's not him. I take out my phone from my pocket and repeatedly check the screen for any missed texts, but there's none.

Nine o'clock comes around quicker than I had wanted. Still no sign of Bexley, but I'm past caring. He can fuck himself.

"Fuck him," I quietly mutter to myself as I take my second shot. I lost count of how many beers I had, but they weren't enough. I needed more to take the edge off, so I began on the shots, and I can already tell two will not be near enough.

"Quake, you need to slow the fuck down, man. Remember, it's a Sunday," Tray goes on again. I sarcastically roll my eyes and give him the finger before getting up and going to the bar. I push past people, prompting a few "Hey, watch it!" comments.

I could do with a fight right now. Hopefully, someone starts.

"Three shots." I signal to the bartender.

"Don't serve those," Kal's joyless voice interrupts, receiving a curt nod from the bartender before attending to another customer.

"Kal, what the hell?" I say, frowning and tightening my fists. Why can't my friends relax a little? Fuck!

Kal sets a beer bottle down in front of me.

"I'm not telling you to stop drinking, but ease up on the shots. Tray's right. Tomorrow is Monday and we have practice. You're already skating on thin ice with Coach."

"Sure thing, Cap." A sharp sting shoots through me as Kal slaps me on the back of my head. With a laugh, I grab my beer and join him at the table. I can't stand how frequently my eyes dart toward the door. I want to text him, call him out, but what's the point? The drugs will always come first. I pull my phone out and bring up a text thread.

"Who you texting?" Kal speaks from beside me, shifting himself so he can lean sideways to peer at my phone. "Who's L?"

"Lanson," I reply.

"Lance," Kal and Tray say in unison.

"Bro, get off my back. Lanson, Landon, Lance. What does it matter?" I huff. "Do you both want to suck his dick or something?" I sarcastically respond before shifting my focus back to my phone.

"That guy won't drop to his knees for anyone except you, even if I wished he would." Trayton laughs.

"Because he knows he won't get better elsewhere." I glance at Trayton with a smirk before going back to my phone, ignoring his trash talk.

Me:

Where you?

L:

Hi, I'm in my dorm. What are you up to?

Me:

Come out for a drink. Meet me at Pythons

L:

You know I can't. I'm not old enough.

I roll my eyes, laughing. He's too innocent for me. Why he keeps coming back, I'll never know.

"Tray, you can get *Lance* into Pythons, yeah?" I raise an eyebrow in question. He nods.

"Yeah, are we going there?"

"We are now. I want a few more drinks, and I need Lance awake and ready for me when I'm finished." With a smirk, I turn my attention back to our messages.

Me:

Don't worry about that. Tray will get you in. Meet me there in 20.

As I'm about to put my phone away, it pings, and it's L again.

L:

I can't do that. We have class tomorrow.

Me:

Do you not want to see me then? It's cool. I guess I'll see you around.

After taking a gulp of my beer, I can't help but smirk as I put my phone back in my pocket. Without a doubt, he'll make it to the bar in fifteen minutes, not twenty. This guy will do anything to see me.

Thirty minutes later, we're walking straight through Pythons and going to the bar. I didn't realize how much the beers I drank at Brewtap would affect me during the walk to this place. A part of me didn't want to leave Brews in hopes that Bex ends up turning up, but it's 10 now. It's not going to happen. He would have texted me. The thought alone makes me feel down and prompts me to order a beer as soon as I reach the bar. Engrossed in scanning the area, I take out my phone from my pocket and find three text messages. I open the text, expecting it to be Bexley with a valid reason for him not turning up, but it's not. It's L.

L:

I'm here. Are you inside?

Well, what do you know? He got here in fifteen.

L:

Brayden, are you here???

L:

You just walked right past me at the entrance. I can't get in.

Oops, my bad! I laugh and give Tray a friendly slap on the shoulder, then ask him to go get Lance. "He's outside."

Tray nods, walking back to the door. His older brother works security here. On weekends, we enjoy going to Brewtap because it has a better atmosphere, but we come to Pythons when we're with people who don't have ID, so Tray's brother can get them in. Lance approaches me, appearing terrified as his eyes nervously scan the busy crowd. I've never seen someone appear so out of their element. I'll loosen him up. As he approaches the bar, his timid brown eyes, framed by those black-rimmed glasses that are my ultimate weakness, meet mine. He opens his mouth, then closes it, finally giving me a shy smile.

"Hey." I lean down, kissing the shell of his ear. "You came," I utter quietly. As I lean back, our eyes briefly meet before he quickly averts his gaze, shyly peering down at the ground. I notice him wrapping his arms around himself, and a slight shiver running through his upper body.

"You cold?" I question. I can't imagine it; it's fucking hot in here.

Clearing his throat, he softly responds, "No."

Okay then.

"You want a drink?" I signal the bartender, and then glance back at Lance.

His gaze and mine collide once more.

He offers me a tight-lipped smile. "Water, please?"

"Oh, come on, have a beer with me." Flashing his straight white teeth, he smiles and nods at me. I haven't gone out with Lance in a social setting, but I know he's a responsible guy who goes to bed early on school nights and finishes his coursework well in advance. I barely pay him any attention in the few classes we have together, but I need him tonight. Burying myself in him is my temporary escape from this shithole life I'm currently dragging myself through. I gather the beers from the bar and hand him one. He accepts it and takes a drink. His attempt to mask his disgust is met with utter failure as he places the bottle on the bar with his face scrunched up.

Leaning one elbow on the bar, I shoot Lance a grin. I love watching him squirm and seeing him out of his comfort zone; it makes him all that more appealing.

All that more fragile.

"So, what made you change your mind, then?" I'm aware that questioning him makes him uncomfortable, but I still do it. He shifts his weight back and forth, adjusting his glasses on the bridge of his nose. With clenched teeth and a tight grip on the bottle, I envision him dropping to his knees, taking me in his mouth, and gazing up at me through his framed glasses. I gulp down some of the beer and turn, gesturing to the bartender again to order.

"Shot of sambuca, please." My focus shifts back to Lance. "Well?" I question, waiting for him to answer. His doe-like eyes dart back and forth as he sucks in his bottom lip.

"I wanted to see you."

I was already aware of this, but I simply wanted to hear him say it. I acknowledge him, tracing my tongue over my lower lip while his big, innocent brown orbs follow my every motion. He's gripping his arms tightly, with his chest rising and falling rapidly.

I take the sambuca shot and down it.

"Come here." I stare at Lance. His arms fall to his sides as he hesitates, but eventually he takes a step toward me and positions himself directly in front of me.

I lower my head, tracing my tongue along his lower lip. He inhales sharply, quickly licking his lips, as if trying to capture the taste of my tongue.

"You like the taste of that?" I ask, knowing he can no doubt taste the sambuca shot.

With eagerness, he nods while his eyes quickly dart from my lips to my eyes.

"Do you want some more?"

His eyes widen and fixate on my lips. I lean in, smirking, and kiss him. Instantly, he opens his mouth, practically pleading for my tongue. I hungrily dive my tongue into his mouth, taking everything I want. One thing about Lance is he can fucking kiss. He might come across as a shy boy but when this boy kisses, it says everything but. Our passionate kisses are like a battle for dominance, but Lance knows I will always come out on top. I tower over his slim, 5 foot 10 frame, claiming what I desire with each swipe of my tongue. Letting my tongue explore every part of his mouth, I lower one hand to his ass, firmly grasping and tugging him toward me while grinding against him. As he senses my semi-erect dick, he moans into my mouth. I steal a quick glance at his closed eyes, but my attention is momentarily diverted by something over his shoulder. Mr. Stiles focuses on my hand resting on Lance's ass. There's a slight hint of color on his cheeks beneath the stubble, and when our eyes lock, it's as if everyone else ceases to exist. Even Lance. The fact that I can't take my eyes off my teacher fills me with panic. My annoying, meddling teacher. With unblinking eyes, he stares at me, never once looking away. Even though I'm still consumed by Lance, thoughts of Mr. Stiles take over.

As he gazes into my eyes, he leans in and kisses me deeply, his stubble brushing against my soft skin.

Fuck.

I pull Lance into me more and would you guess? I'm rock fucking hard. I'm amazed that I'm not feeling faint, given that I'm almost certain every ounce of blood in my body has rushed to my dick.

Have I ever been this hard?

After a few blinks, Mr. Stiles averts his gaze and walks away. My lungs burn as I retreat from Lance, struggling to breathe as if I haven't inhaled for two whole minutes. What the hell was that?

I subtly re-arrange myself and survey the people gawking at me. Lance's face turns a deep shade of red as he lowers his head, resting his chin on his chest. I observe him slyly wiping the edges of his lips using his thumb.

"Couldn't have waited until you got back to your dorm? You practically put on a free kiss porno." Kal moans.

"I think I got hard from that," Tray follows up.

Lance's head jolts up, his eyes widening as he locks a horrified stare on Tray. Tray simply flashes his signature smile and winks at him. Lance's surprise is visible as his cheeks blush deeper and he directs his focus downward, avoiding eye contact.

"I need to go to the bathroom," Lance utters, and I point to where they are. I get myself another beer and casually lean against the bar. That's when I see him again. The sight of him walking out the door makes my entire body heat up. Wait a damn minute. Are Ms. Banksy and Mr. Stiles leaving together?

Well, well, well.

My eyes immediately drop to his ass in the tight jeans he has on, and then I snap them back to his head.

Don't look there. You have no business staring there; I tell myself.

Fuck me. Of course, I could get a hard-on for an annoying as fuck teacher.

Sexy as fuck. But also, annoying.

After this morning in the gym and now, I can say with certainty that my body is attracted to Mr. Stiles.

Of course it would be. The forbidden element is what makes it intriguing. The one person you can't have.

I wonder about that look he was giving me though, because that wasn't very 'Mr. Stiles, marketing teacher at Hawksview U' of him.

Mr. Stiles pauses, hand on the door, halfway out. Instead of releasing the door to close it, he simply halts.

Turn around.

Turn around.

He turns his head, and then, *boom*. When our eyes meet, it's like fireworks exploding in my stomach. His well-kept stubble and perfectly fitted T-shirt show the definition of the muscles I know are there with every slight movement. He always comes across as composed and professional. His chestnut hair is neatly styled, and his eyes, usually intensely focused and serious, hold a depth that's hard to ignore. I'm not sure why, but his intense stare is having an effect on me, so I use my beer to gesture toward him.

I know you're watching me, and you shouldn't be Mr. Stiles.

I slide the beer across my lower lip, then curl my tongue around it and gulp down a large mouthful. With a sudden movement, he whips his head back to face forward and then exits.

Well, fuck me.

Chapter Fourteen

Bohdi

Finishing my third glass of whiskey, I relish the fiery sensation and hope it can drown out my troubling thoughts. No matter how many I finish, I can't shake the memory of those eyes and the way they stared at me. But above all, I can't ignore the intense sensation that washed over me when he took a sip from the beer bottle. I sigh and pour myself a generous amount of whiskey, closing my eyes and tilting my head back as I drink it down. Fuck. Today was a complete cluster fuck. Maybe I wouldn't have stared at Brayden that way if I hadn't gone to the gym and ended up at the bar.

Could it be that my growing attachment to him is due to my subconscious inclination to support and ensure his safety? To make sure what happened to Jace doesn't happen to him? And it's not actually an attraction?

Fuck my life.

I drag my legs to the couch, flop down, and then realize I've brought the bottle of whiskey but forgot to grab a glass. I have class tomorrow, but I can't sleep tonight unless I drink enough to make me pass out.

I take a quick glance at the time and notice it's almost 11:30. Even though my alarm will ring in six hours, I'm not even slightly tired. I'm too wired to sleep.

Pulling out my phone, I light the screen up to do what? I'm unsure, but I see that I have a few emails. I reluctantly check my work account. This might be enough to make me fall asleep.

While quickly scanning my emails, I notice one from Denny, asking for me to provide an update on Brayden by the end of the week. It's a detailed report that showcases his work and attendance. I realize this isn't something the professors usually require. This is from Denny. He wants his players to excel not only in hockey but also in their work. He's always been strict about that and Brayden's grades slipping don't sit well with Denny.

My mind wanders back to the happenings earlier today at the trailer park. How do I keep this from Denny? I know he won't care that I punched the man; I mean, hell, if Denny was there, he would have done the same thing. Despite Denny knowing about Brayden's mom and brother, I'm not sure how he would handle the knowledge of Brayden's true home life and upbringing. He was already concerned about Brayden. That much is clear. I think this would send him over the edge.

So, my decision is to tell Denny or not?

I toss my phone onto the couch and reach for the bottle, taking a gulp. The burning sensation has disappeared while the buzz soothes my body.

I wonder if Denny knows about Brayden's sexuality. Who was the guy he was with tonight? I didn't know who he was, and he appeared way too small to play hockey. Despite my continued drinking, thoughts of Brayden plague my mind even more. *I was hoping drinking would stop me from thinking about him.* I use my fingers to find my phone, and then they take over control. Before I even realize, I'm already on Instagram, without pausing to think. I ended up downloading it because Rylee asked me to, even though I barely use it. When I search for Brayden's name, nothing shows up. Maybe he doesn't have it. I type in Devil Hawks. I'm sure they have a page, as I've seen Denny post some stuff on his personal page. It comes up straight away and I find myself going through the pictures. The team appears to have a strong bond, clear from the smiles in every picture and their serious game faces on game day. The way they celebrate each other on a win. There is no animosity among them. On the day I went there, I saw that after Brayden kicked off. I stumble upon a video of Brayden doing a trick, most likely during the warm-up. I observe his carefree smile and the impressive puck tricks he performs. How the hell do you essentially do kick ups but with a puck and a stick? That's the next level of talent. He pays no attention to the puck as it bounces on his stick. He's too busy skating toward the goal. There are a few tricks of him showing off. Even some teammates that get caught on the video are staring at him in awe as he flips the puck with his stick, while skating and shoots from some crazy angles.

He's addicting to watch. I could watch him play all day.

I read the caption, and it's only named 'earthquake' and then there's a tag.

@quakeontheice

I go against my gut feeling and click on it. I didn't think I would find much on here, but there are small snippets of his life. Not much, but still some bits. It appears as if most of the pictures are hockey-related, but as I scroll further, I discover a photo of him and Bexley when they were around eight years old. They are seen standing on what appears to be a table, pretending to play air guitar together, and both laughing. The caption *We will rock you* makes me smile as I gaze at the screen, but it also leaves a small ache in my gut. I feel a wave of sadness as I keep gazing at the picture. I'm not a twin, so I don't know how it feels, but I can imagine having one is like a right arm. Brayden likely feels a sense of loss when it comes to Bexley.

It's evident from this picture that they are filled with happiness and a sense of freedom. I bet Brayden would do anything to get that back. I scroll up to find more pictures, some of him with Kal, and some of him, Kal, and Trayton. Their tight-knit trio is apparent, but the friendship between Kal and Brayden stands out to me. When Kal watches Brayden, it appears as if he's ready to conquer anyone who dares to harm him.

I see a red circle around Brayden's profile picture, in which he is holding a trophy in his hockey gear. Clicking on it, there's a picture of him taking a shot at the bar tonight. I move on to the next one, and it's a video of him drinking more shots. I click once more, and now there's a table filled with empty shot glasses and beer glasses that says, *Fuck family*. That was posted five minutes ago. Glancing at the time, I notice that closing time is approaching. He's drank a lot. While I trust Kal and Trayton to keep him safe, I can't shake off the fear of something bad happening. What if he tries to go back to the trailer while drunk? What if he ends up coming across that waste of space from earlier?

I let my head roll back and stare up at the ceiling.

I need to know he's safe.

Before I can think twice, I'm opening the Uber app.

Less than twenty minutes later, the Uber I'm in pulls up near the bar and I see Brayden walking down the street with the person he was kissing earlier. It's obvious that the man is having trouble handling Brayden's height and solid structure as he leans on him. I watch the struggle for a minute, debating whether to get back in the car and head home. My legs have already made their mind up as I walk toward them. I try to convince myself that I'll only follow them back to campus to make sure they enter the building safely. But the longer I watch them from behind, the more my anger builds. But why? Why am I angry? Seeing them together is clearly bothering me, but why? As they walk, the smaller guy supports Brayden by rubbing his back and allowing him to lean on him slightly. It's clear to see Brayden is wasted. I can't handle this shit anymore. I increase my walking speed, and once I'm directly behind them, I clear my throat as a signal.

"Boys." I attempt to sound stern, but end up sounding even creepier, approaching two young boys past midnight on a silent street.

Huh, guess I kind of am.

The smaller guy's sudden jump startles Brayden, nearly causing him to drop to the floor. With a single arm, I secure Brayden by holding him up. As the smaller guy peeks at me with wide eyes, I hear Brayden muttering, "Jesus fucking Christ."

"Good night, I see?"

Brayden's drunken state prevents him from standing still, as his feet continuously jut out sideways. I release his arm and shift my focus to the other guy.

"What's your name?" I narrow my eyes at the boy, who appears genuinely terrified and on the verge of pissing himself. I guess I haven't made it clear I'm a teacher and not some random guy on the street. As I keep observing the guy and waiting for his reply, I can't help but think that Brayden and someone such as him don't appear compatible. I shouldn't stereotype, but he gives off the vibe of a classic geek. It's surprising that he's out at this hour, and even more so with Brayden.

"I—I'm."

"It's Lanson," Brayden sighs out. The man remains silent, staring at Brayden before glancing at me and promptly casting his eyes down to the floor.

"Lanson, I'm Mr. Stiles. I'm Brayden's marketing teacher."

As he shuts his eyes and lets out a deep sigh, a sense of relief washes over him, only to be replaced by fear as he struggles to speak.

"I...um...wasn't drinking. I swear it. You can smell my breath."

I raise my hand to silence him.

"I have no interest in what you are or aren't doing. My only concern is that you both return to campus safely," I reassure him, which has him nodding eagerly.

"Let's go then."

The rest of the way, Brayden stays quiet, doing his best to walk straight, but occasionally running into me and muttering, "Sorry." When we arrive at the campus, Lanson freezes and hovers near a few dorm buildings.

"Which dorm is yours, Lanson?" I inquire, and he gestures toward the one on the left. I glance at Brayden, who nods his head to the right.

Brayden winks at Lanson and says, "Lanson is staying at my dorm tonight, sir." I raise my eyebrow at Lanson, causing his doe-eyed gaze on Brayden to shift to me, and he immediately lowers his head.

"Goodnight, Lanson," I state.

"Wait, no," Brayden tries to argue, but I push him along to his dorm. Lanson continues to ignore Brayden and heads straight to his dorm.

"Respectfully, sir, but what the fuck? You know I'm nineteen, right?"

"Respectfully, Brayden, I don't give a fuck. Now keep it moving. You're too drunk to do anything right now and I'm pretty sure the school doesn't allow overnight stays in the dorms, right?" With a raised eyebrow, I observe the sulking face and his focus shifting toward Lanson's retreating.

"I can make my way to my own dorm," he mumbles as we walk through the main doors of the building.

"You're wasted. It wouldn't be right of me to leave you alone until I know you're safe." He hasn't even asked about how I found them or what I was doing walking the streets at the same time as him. And I hope he never does because I don't know what I would say.

Brayden stumbles a few times during our walk, but he quickly shakes off my attempts to steady him.

"What floor are you on?" I ask as we approach the stairs.

"Third," he says, taking the stairs. I'm trailing behind him, but he suddenly halts and wavers a little. I immediately jump into action, catching him as he crouches down on the step.

"Brayden, what are you doing?"

Without saying a word, he raises his hand and takes a few deep inhales. After a moment, he replies,

"Just give me a moment. I feel sick." He rests his elbows on his knees and lets his head hang between his legs. I stand there staring down at him, wondering how long he will sit like this for. After a few moments of silence, Brayden asks, "Why do all people suck?" I frown, wondering where the random question came from.

"What?"

"Why do all people suck?" he repeats. I hesitate to respond immediately because how do you even respond to that? Then I remember his Instagram story from earlier.

I position myself on the stairs next to him, bending down and placing my arms on my knees as I stare down the corridor ahead.

"I don't think all people suck," I reply. "I think it's the people you put your trust in and the people you love unconditionally, even though they don't deserve it and who let you down and disappoint you. Those are the people that suck." Brayden lifts his head and casts a sideways glance in my direction. Among the bloodshot that surrounds his sapphire eyes, his irises still shine brightly.

"Those are definitely the people that suck." Tilting his head upward, he studies the ceiling and lays back, resulting in the back of his head hitting the step. I want to tell him to get up and that his bed will be more comfortable than laying on stairs. But then I realize that if he goes to bed, I'll have to stop talking to him, and I'm not ready for that just yet. Selfish maybe, but it's what has me laying back beside him with my head on the step.

"I hate that I let him do this to me time and time again..." For a moment, I don't know who he's talking about. Is he talking about a boyfriend? Is he talking about Lanson, or is he talking about his brother?

"Who?"

"Bex," he sighs out. "I let him in every single time and each time he proves to me why I shouldn't." His voice cracks at the end.

I close my eyes, wishing I could ring Bexley's neck for making Brayden feel like this. I wish he could see what he does to his brother. Maybe he knows but doesn't care. It's understandable why Brayden is closed off and appears hostile toward others. Has anyone ever shown this kid that sometimes it's worth being vulnerable in order to let the right people into their life? That there's people out there worth being vulnerable for?

"Don't paint everyone with the same brush, Brayden. There are good people out there." Despite not knowing the reason, I have this urge to reassure him. "A day will come when you'll find someone who will patiently wait at the door until you're ready to open it. Even if it means waiting years. When the time comes, you'll understand why it's worth opening the door for the right person." There's a moment of silence before Brayden responds.

"Have you opened your door?"

"Not yet," I sigh. I'm still trying to gather my thoughts and emotions after what happened earlier today. Despite being with Brayden, I don't find it as strange as I thought I would. I'm not sure if being more content than I have been in a while is a good or bad sign.

"It's possible that Ms. Banksy might be the person you find at your doorstep," he remarks, his voice hinting at a playful tone.

I raise an eyebrow at him and smirk.

"I think it's time you got to bed," I say, leaning up and jumping to my feet, although I have to hold on to the railing. I forgot about the few whiskeys I had tonight. I motion my hand for him to hold on to. "Come on."

He shuts his eyes and grabs my arm to hoist himself up. My jaw clenches as warmth spreads up my arm. What the fuck is going on? For a moment, I don't let go and neither does he. There's something about his touch, his skin on mine, that feels almost perfect. Although, my mind is screaming for me to release him. I direct my gaze toward him, but he diverts his attention to his arm.

No, he's looking at my hand.

Nope, he's looking at my fingers that are brushing his arm.

When I snap my arm back fast, he sways slightly and then rights himself. I hurriedly pass by him, feeling the need for a moment alone, and climb the stairs. We are on the third floor in record time. Once he's inside the dorm, I must leave and go home. These feelings, or whatever they are, are a combination of drinks and sleep deprivation I've been dealing with lately. It has to be. This isn't me; it's as if my brain has malfunctioned.

As I walk past his dorm, his gruff voice calls out, "This is me."

I pivot on my heels, hands in pockets, and give him a firm nod. From his pocket, he retrieves his keys and unlocks the door.

Without a second glance, I casually say, "See you tomorrow, bright and early," as I continue walking.

"Mr. Stiles." His calm voice drifts through the air, leaving me motionless, my body refusing to turn and face him.

"Tha-Thank you for not only tonight, but today as well." I know what he means when he refers to today. He's talking about at the trailer park. I choose not to respond and continue walking, but when I reach the end of the hallway, I glance back and find Brayden staring right at me. He appears expressionless, as if he's lost in his own world. My feet suddenly become heavy, as if they are weights. Walking away from him feels like one of the hardest things to do.

What is this boy doing to me?

13
Brayden 'Quake' Anders

Chapter Fifteen

Brayden

Once more, I awaken to a pounding headache, but this time, I recall everything. I remember the anger that still simmers in my veins, waiting all night for my brother to turn up. I can still remember the doors opening and closing, and each time I held on to a glimmer of hope, thinking he might appear.

One night that is all I asked of him. One fucking night.

I told Kal and Tray too; they knew how excited I was for him to come out with us. He made me look like a dickhead in front of my friends.

Then the anger fades, and his images quickly come to mind.

Mr. Stiles.

What the hell was that last night? Was that all a figment of my imagination? The way he stared at me, the way he touched my arms and brushed his fingers along it. I hate the feeling it created in me. It was the drink it had to of been. When I see him later, it will feel as if nothing occurred, and the alcohol simply intensified the situation.

I think.

I grab my phone from my pants pocket and when it lights up; I see I have an unread message. It's from Bexley. I grip the phone tightly; the anger returning as I read the one simple sentence.

Bexley:

I'm sorry, bro.

That text was sent at 4 a.m. He was out all last night selling for that piece of shit instead of being at the bar with me. And not only my friends but people that want to be his friend as well. I know Tray would speak to him if he had only come.

Me:

Fuck you.

I'm not saying anything else. I'm too pissed right now. I know Bexley and he won't reply. He's a fucking coward sometimes.

I open Instagram, and then wonder if it was my story that prompted him to text me. I remember in my drunken, sulking state putting up an indirect story, clearly for him to see. Glancing quickly to check who watched the video, I don't spot Bexley's name. I have two hours until first class, so I scroll through out of curiosity.

Because my profile is public, I receive a lot of views on my stories from people who know me from hockey. I often get asked by puck bunnies if they can turn me bi for a night. My attention is drawn to a name, causing me to frown. Who the hell is @thestilestman? My mind is focused on 'stiles,' which is why I noticed it. But I'm also intrigued by the use of 'stilest.' Is it a different spelling for 'stylist'? Intrigued, I click on it too, which causes me to gasp.

It's Mr. Stiles. Why was he looking at my stories? And how the hell did he come across my profile?

There isn't a lot on here, only four pictures. There are three men: one who resembles him, possibly a brother, and another younger-looking man. All three of them are good-looking, clearly showing their familial connection. I proceed to the next one, and there he is, accompanied by a stunning girl. The camera captures their bright smiles. She appears slightly younger, but not by a significant amount. Maybe it's an old girlfriend. I notice a picture of him with a woman who appears to be roughly in her forties. I don't know why I'm so intrigued to find out who these people are. When I notice a comment on one of them by an account called @RyStiles, saying "two of my favorite people," I try to access her account, but it's private.

I return to Mr. Stiles' profile and check out his most recent photo. He captured a photo of the beach with an incoming storm indicated by the dark black clouds on the horizon. The caption of the picture reads, 'We hate storms, don't we, Jace?'

Who's Jace?

When I examine Mr. Stiles' pictures, I can't help but notice his lack of happiness in real life compared to these photos. I understand pictures don't reveal everything about a person, but something feels off. As I lock eyes with Mr. Stiles and smile, I can't help but wonder what caused him to lose his shine.

I arrive early to class and wait in my usual seat, but it appears Mr. Stiles is running late or not coming at all. I become restless in my seat, questioning if he changed his mind about revealing everything to the dean regarding yesterday's shit show.

"What's up?" I glance up at Kal, who is seated beside me, his brow furrowed as he gazes at me. His eyes scanning my face, likely attempting to figure out what is wrong.

"You know what I told you last night about Mr. Stiles coming to mine and the thing with Karl."

Kal nods.

"Well, last night—"

"Sorry I'm late, all." Mr. Stiles strolls into the classroom, his hair disheveled as if he's run his fingers through it multiple times and his eyes bloodshot as he scans the room. He looks like he didn't sleep a wink. My mind tracks back to the picture on his Instagram and how put together he appeared. How alive and energetic he looked. No sign of tired eyes, no signs of dark shadows under his eyes. I glance at him and notice how utterly drained he appears.

I give Kal a quick glance. "I'll tell you later."

"I may sound like any other nineteen-year-old student, but funny enough, my alarm didn't go off," Mr. Stiles says with a laugh, removing his blazer and hanging it on the chair. With a clap of his hands, he shifts his attention to the class. I fixate my focus on him the entire time, but he never once glances in my direction. I sneak a glance at Kal, who appears completely absorbed and oblivious. I don't know if it's only me, but it's becoming more and more obvious that he is avoiding me during class. I'm certain he hasn't glanced at this side of the classroom even once. He assigns us the task of researching our end-of-year presentation topic. Our task is to create a product and present it to the class. Additionally, he's developing an online poll that will be included in our college newsletter. This will allow everyone to view the presentations and vote for the best product.

I'm supposed to be researching, but my marketing teacher won't acknowledge me. I'm anxious that he might have told the dean, or that I said something wrong while drunk last night. Is he angry because he caught me drinking?

Tray kicks my leg. "Stop bouncing your knee, it's annoying."

"Sorry," I mutter, nervously chewing on the skin around my nails as a distraction.

I continue to stare at Mr. Stiles, hoping for that quick glance, but he doesn't give it. All it takes is one look to assure me that everything is fine. The more I worry, the angrier I become. How dare he have me here feeling like this? He's supposed to be my teacher. Are teachers meant to make you feel this way? Should teachers be giving you inappropriate glances? Should teachers be watching your Instagram stories? My mind abruptly stops at the thought.

What was the reason for him watching my stories?

As soon as the bell rings, people grab their belongings.

"I'll meet you at practice," I say to Kal and Tray as they eye me skeptically. "I need to speak to Mr. Stiles."

They both nod, walking past me as I pack away my stuff slowly. While making my way down the stairs, I catch sight of Daxton getting ready to leave. He pauses, peering up at me, and gives a nod. His left eye is marked by a dark black bruise, and a noticeable cut on his lip mirrors the injury. Even though I'm aware this is a consequence of yesterday, I can't muster up any concern. It may not be Daxton's fault directly, but it's his flesh and blood who is the reason Bexley is the way he is. His uncle and dad groomed Bexley. As I grew older, I began to realize that what they did was exactly like that. We needed money, we needed food. They were always at our trailer with my mom. They provided everything we needed, but it came with a price. My brother's fucking soul. I know Daxton deals, too. His dad isn't in charge, his uncle is. According to Bexley, that's how Daxton got into this school. He wanted an education, so he had to work for it. He may not take the shit they sell and may not be as weak as Bexley, but he's still one of their minions.

"Daxton, can you hold back a minute?" Mr. Stiles' voice causes me to snap out of my thoughts. I grit my teeth and focus on him. He still doesn't look at me. Taking a seat at the front, I slouch back and kick my leg out before dropping my bag on the floor.

I'm not going anywhere until he speaks to me.

"Brayden, you can leave." His voice, firm and commanding, ignites a violent desire in me to throw a desk against the wall.

While saying it, he doesn't bother looking up at me and instead busies himself with papers on his desk.

"I'll wait," I grit out.

"The matter I need to discuss with Daxton is confidential. Please, leave." His eyes finally meet mine, and I hate that it hurts to see exhaustion there. But I'm still mad and confused as to why he's being the way he is toward me today.

"What I have to tell you is confidential," I say, grinning. "Daxton, you can come back, right?" I arch an eyebrow at him, observing his gaze shifting between me and Mr. Stiles.

Mr. Stiles appears on the verge of scolding me, and Daxton mumbles a reluctant, "Okay," before promptly disappearing.

"I don't appreciate you dictating to my students when they can and can't be here. Don't forget that I am the teacher here, okay?" With anger oozing from him, Mr. Stiles walks around his desk and fixates his eyes on me. Strangely enough, I find solace in the fact that he's paying attention to me, even if it's with contempt.

"Why did you avoid me all class?"

For a moment, he stares at me in bewilderment, then chuckles and bursts into laughter, throwing his head back.

"This isn't the Brayden Anders show. I have other students." He shakes his head, walking around the desk and sits down in the chair beside his desk again. He continues, without making eye contact, "Brayden, I'm too busy for this immature nonsense. My afternoon is packed. Please, leave."

My veins throb with anger as he casually picks up his pen and begins to write, disregarding me like an annoying little kid.

"I'm immature, huh? If I'm that immature and annoying to you, what made your eyes stay on me at the bar? What made it impossible for them to stop staring at me when they shouldn't have? Could you please remind me, sir, how you found me last night? Oh yes, that's right"—I snap my fingers as If I remembered something—"because you watched my Instagram stories like a fucking stalker." My voice oozes sarcasm and disdain.

I lock eyes with him and only see pure fury.

Chapter Sixteen

Bohdi

How the fuck did he know I looked at his Instagram? Surely, it doesn't show you people that view your profile. Rylee neglected to include that important detail.

I tilt my neck from side to side, attempting to calm the simmering rage within me. Who does this kid think he is, acting all high and mighty? What he doesn't realize is, yes, he is right. I spent the entire class avoiding him due to my mind being overwhelmed by thoughts of his lips and the sensation of his skin. I've never experienced such a confusing mix of right and wrong in my life. Why am I feeling like this for a fucking student? I can't wrap my head around it. As I turned on my coffee machine this morning, all I could see were his lips. In the shower, all I could see was his hand on that guy's ass, which sent a jolt to my dick.

I fucking hate it. But how does it stop? How do all these consuming, overwhelming, and so-fucking-wrong feelings stop?

Right now, he's driving me crazy with his attitude, but I can't deny that I'm also captivated by the way he looks. Sitting there so nonchalantly in gray sweatpants, a tight white top, and a backward baseball cap. You hear girls talking about guys in gray sweats, and I've never in my life found this attractive, so why do I now?

I ended up searching for signs of a mid-life crisis at 3 a.m., all because of this boy. Apparently, finding your student attractive isn't a sign. It provided me with details of therapists in the area.

Maybe I should call one.

My eyes connect with his again. Brayden's gaze doesn't waver, and with everything he has going on, I admire the confidence he holds. It's clear the guy has some balls on him.

Oh fuck, don't think about the size of his balls.

What do I say to him? Do I admit I was staring at him inappropriately? Do I tell him, yes, I was stalking you on Instagram?

"Look," I sigh, raking my fingers through my hair, still contemplating how to handle this. I have to be truthful— Well, partially.

"I only wanted you safe." I keep it simple. I didn't acknowledge the way I stared at him because I don't think I can explain that to myself right now.

"That's why you searched me up on Instagram? To make sure I was safe?"

"Yes," I lie. What is the phrase for 'I had the urge to see your face again, so I searched you up?'

"You're really not going to inform the dean about what happened yesterday?" Without breaking eye contact, he asks me cautiously. It dawns on me that his reaction resulted from his worry about me telling the dean. And my disregard for him after yesterday's events made him anxious, thinking I had reported it to the dean.

Fuck.

"I have no idea what you're talking about," I state simply. His eyes meet mine, and I see the confusion slowly appear on his face as he furrows his brow and pauses, shifting his attention from me to the floor. His mouth opens briefly before shutting once more. "Nothing happened yesterday. There's nothing to tell the dean." I arch my eyebrow, hoping he catches on to what I'm implying.

He expresses his understanding with wide eyes and an O-shaped mouth, uttering, "Ohhh."

I'm too tired for this.

"Gotcha," he says, standing up and grabbing his bag. His back catches my attention as he leans down and effortlessly puts the rucksack on his shoulder. I gulp at the sight of his broad back flexing with a slight movement. Brayden stands awkwardly before me, peering at me intently. Our gazes lock, and for a moment, we share a silent connection, a mutual admiration that makes my heart race. I catch a glimpse of a blush spreading across Brayden's cheeks. It's a sight that I find irresistibly appealing. I had never noticed the delicate sprinkle of freckles that dust across his nose and cheeks, blending seamlessly with his soft, pale skin. This subtle feature stands in stark contrast to his dark brown hair, which, under certain lighting, appears almost black. His piercing blue eyes, partially shadowed by the baseball cap he never takes off, stare back at me with an intensity that makes the world seem to stand still. In that instant, everything else fades away, and it's only the two of us, lost in each other's presence.

Shit. No.

I audibly clear my throat and shift my attention to focus on the papers in front of me. I detest this newfound feeling that's causing my mind to race at 1000mph, and none of it makes sense.

"See you tomorrow, Brayden. Have a good day."

Despite my mind's warning, I can't resist glancing up after Brayden clears his throat and utters, "You too, sir." I'm watching him move toward the door, his back muscles flexing once more, making me feel nervous.

I'm not supposed to be attracted to those muscles. Despite Brayden making it to the door, I'm too preoccupied with admiring my student to realize he's turned back.

His chest rises and falls as he stares at me, mouth slightly open. I notice him visibly gulp as we become entranced in another stare, and I find my eyes drawn to his lips. Aching sensations arise from thoughts of his lips and tongue. I jerk my head back, staring at the jumble of words in front of me, expecting the sound of the classroom door closing. The moment the door shuts, a wave of relief washes over me.

Grading papers turned into a disaster because I couldn't stop thinking about someone, making it impossible to concentrate. I considered going to the gym to release my tension through boxing, but I still have to locate Daxton. I can't shake the feeling that his black eye and cut lips are my fault. If I hadn't intervened and done what I did, would he still have that black eye and cut lip? Probably not.

Despite searching the campus and asking multiple people, I still can't find him. As I make my way to my classroom, my phone rings, interrupting my racing thoughts. I remove it from my pocket and realize it's Rylee video calling me. How does she always know when I'm struggling? I hesitate to answer. She phoned me two times last week and every time I promised to return the call, but I didn't. I greet her with a smile on Facetime, but her initial happiness turns into a concerned frown.

"Boh, what's wrong?" I'll never understand how Rylee can detect something is amiss with a single look.

"I'm okay, Ry." I force a smile on my face, but she sees right through it. She hugs herself tightly, curls into a ball on the couch, and maintains a frowning expression as she stares at me through the camera.

"Please talk to me, Boh." Her face sags as she softly whispers. Ever since Jace passed away, my relationship with Rylee has become strained, even though she used to be the person I could confide in. Learning that your brother, who is the father of your nephew, is now dating your nephew's girlfriend less than a year after his passing has been difficult for me. To be honest, I'm still trying to process it. I forgave them. Their love for each other is clear, and I find comfort in knowing they have each other to share their grief. I acknowledge that the trauma they both experienced brought them together, but it's still tough. She and Jace and were together for six years, and each time I saw her, I saw my nephew. Every time I see her now, it's a painful reminder that he's no longer there. Whenever I catch a glimpse of her face, it seems as though a crushing weight settles on my chest, growing heavier with each breath. How do you express that to someone? You can't, so I do what I do best.

"I'm sorry, Ry, but I have a ton of papers to review and mark up. Can I call you on the weekend?"

I struggle to maintain composure as her teary eyes and trembling lip cause me to clench my jaw. Witnessing Rylee's sadness is excruciating, but the thought that I am the cause of it is physically agonizing. If I reveal the reason behind my avoidance, it will shatter her completely. She's already swimming in her own guilt as it is. I can't be the one to drown her.

"I promise I'll call you at the weekend," I say before cutting the phone off. The minute she is no longer on my screen, I let the first tear fall down my cheek, followed by another.

I snatch the cupboard key from my desk and swiftly unlock the bottom drawer. As I slide open the drawer, my eyes fixate on the one thing that momentarily numbs this pain. It makes breathing a little easier before the darkness swallows me.

Whiskey.

13
Brayden 'Quake' Anders

Chapter Seventeen

Brayden

There's nothing on this earth that calms me like sliding the puck back and forth with Kal. The smell of the ice, the slicing noises the blades make against the ice, the scratching of the puck as it glides and bounces off the stick. It's home. I always feel like I'm gasping for air, and my heart skips a beat, but when I'm here, I breathe more freely than ever.

Kal glides nearer to me, circling and fixating on the puck.

"Keep it on the down low, but I heard the scouts are coming back next weekend for our away game." I skillfully lift the puck onto my stick and flick it over to Kal, who smoothly catches it on his stick and sends it back.

"How about the person who lets it drop first, pays for all the drinks this Saturday night?" I say, passing it back. Kal wears a smile as we continue our back-and-forth with the puck.

I casually ask, "When did Coach tell you about this?" as we continue with our usual passes.

"Just before coming out here. He mentioned that he's letting you know to prevent a repeat of last time."

"There won't be."

"You promise?"

"No."

"You're known for your temper, but you're lucky you didn't get a match ban for what you had done to Mackey."

"I know, Cap. You don't need to keep going on about it." This causes Kal to fuck up, and he drops the puck. I lift my helmet, grinning. "Drinks on you, Cap." I wink.

"You fucker." He bodychecks me, slamming me into the side of the rink.

I shout, "Touché!" as he flips me off and continues skating toward Cope.

When practice is done, we all head to the showers. Trayton is talking nonstop about a guy he met at the bar and calling out Kal for not taking the girl back to the dorm.

Kal's sulking began after he returned from a trip he had to take with his dad last year and hasn't stopped since. There was a change and now he hardly pays attention to girls. I've asked him time and time again what's wrong, but he makes up some bullshit. I can tell it's not true because I know Kal. Kal has always been known as the "babe magnet," a nickname he dislikes, but stuck after Trayton used it. Kal used to lap up the attention and rarely had an empty bed. He was a man hoe, but a humble one. He may be my best friend, but that doesn't mean I can't acknowledge how incredibly attractive he is, both physically and in terms of his personality.

Kal is a fixer, someone who wants to help people who need fixing. It has always been part of his character since we first met. Hence, why we are best friends. Kal, being by my side is something I can't imagine being without. I furrow my brow in contemplation, observing him as he flips off Trayton when Tray reveals that Kal no longer likes girls and assumes he is now gay. Tray, of course, volunteers that Kal uses him as an experiment. I also noticed a slight increase in his drinking habits, not enough to cause worry, but noticeable, nonetheless. Especially when we are at parties. He will keep himself away from girls and only drink. It's not like him. Trayton noticed and attempted to talk to him, but he dismissed him the same as he did to me. I laugh as I see Tray twirling around a moody Kal, swinging his dick like a helicopter. Being friends with Tray means being okay with seeing his dick more frequently than you see your own. Trayton is as important to me as Kal. Kal is the one who can help me unwind, while Trayton is the one who supports me when I need to release my emotions. Honestly, I'm confident that if I told Tray I needed his help in robbing a bank, he wouldn't question it and would simply ask about my mask preference. Whenever I need to escape reality, they provide me with balance, and I will forever be grateful to them.

"Anders." Coach's deep voice booms in the locker room. I hastily put on my top and sweatpants, while the rest of the team watches me. Kal silently nods at me, indicating that this is exactly what we were discussing, before leaning in to whisper into Tray's ear, no doubt updating him. I put on my baseball cap and twist it backward. Strangely, my baseball cap provides me with a sense of security. I hate not wearing it.

Stepping into the coach's office, I offer a closed-mouth smile, noticing the overwhelming amount of papers on his desk. "Coach," I say, trying my best to sound cheery. The sight of me appears to offend him deeply, as indicated by his pinched eyebrows. I'm standing there, awkwardly rocking on my heels and clapping my hands in front of me.

"Anders, I'll get straight to the point. The scouts are returning next weekend. I need you to please get your shit together. Advise your brother to stay the fuck away from this game and find a method to release your anger beforehand. Nothing that will get you in trouble, of course." He points in my direction. "Your attitude is holding you back from reaching your full potential as my star player. Do you understand me?"

I nod. "Yes, Coach. Nothing will mess up next weekend. You have my word."

With a nod, he settles back into his chair, picking up his mug and sipping from it.

"Oh, and one more thing," he adds, fiddling with papers on his desk. "The dean and I have had a conversation, and your grades are declining noticeably." He stares directly at me, raising one eyebrow. "To help, you need to take an extra class." Before I can speak, he raises his hand. "It doesn't matter which class, but you must get extra credit. You have the freedom to choose, as long as it doesn't affect our practice schedule. I don't care what it is."

I bow my head and nod to show my understanding. Right now, I don't need an additional class, and this news has caught me off guard. I knew my grades were slipping slightly, and being on a scholarship, I know I need to be careful. But I thought I could pull it back, not have to take an extra class.

Leaving the coach's office, I trudge back to the boys. While most have left, Kal and Tray are still here, sitting and waiting for me.

"Gonna head to the gym," I grumble, trying not to sulk, but it's a bit hard right now. Kal's eyebrows knit together as he gets up and comes over to me, Tray trailing not too far behind.

"Was it not about the scouts?" Kal says.

I nod. "It was, but also about my grades slipping. The coach and the dean have decided that I should enroll in an extra class to raise my grades."

Tray drawls out the word, "Dayyyymnn," in a way that resembles Ice Cube and Chris Tucker's delivery in the Friday movies. Usually this brings a smile to my face, but currently I don't feel like smiling at all.

"Damn is correct." I sigh.

"What are you going to pick?" Tray asks.

"No idea," I say as I snatch my bag and leave the changing rooms, heading straight for the door. Behind me, Kal starts listing additional classes I can enroll in. I take a quick glance behind me and spot him on his phone, most likely browsing the college's website. I don't find any of them appealing.

"I didn't know Mr. Stiles teaches business management," Kal says, and this perks my ears up. I respond, attempting to hide my enthusiasm.

"Oh, is that an extra class?"

"Yeah, by the looks of it, not much information on here, though."

"Quake doesn't like him. Next one?" Tray says.

I stop and turn. "I didn't say that."

"You gave the impression you didn't like him," Tray mentions.

Kal agrees, "Yeah, let's forget about Mr. Stiles and try a different teacher."

"I think it's Kal who doesn't like him." Kal acts standoffish toward Mr. Stiles, and it has caught my attention once or twice, as it is unlike Kal. Kal simply shrugs and goes back to his phone. Opening the doors, I make a turn and abruptly stop when I come face-to-face with my twin brother. His foot against the wall and a cigarette in his mouth. This isn't what I need right now. I turn to Kal and Tray. "I'll meet you at the gym."

Kal nods in agreement, acknowledging Bexley, while Tray stands rigidly, fists clenched and jaw tight. I peer back at Bex, and he is staring at Tray. There's a softness in his eyes, as if he's on the verge of saying something but is unsure.

A moment later, he says, "Tray." I hear movement and glance back to see Tray turning around and leaving. What the fuck went on between them? As I turn around, Bex takes a long pull and flicks the cigarette.

A guilty smile forms on his lips as he says, "Bro."

"I've had a shit day and I'm tired, Bex. What's up? I don't need it to be any worse."

"I wanted to say sorry." His head dips, kicking at gravel on the floor.

"Sorry like the thousands of other times?" I respond, putting my hands in my pockets.

"Bray, I really am so—"

"No." I raise my hand. "I'm done with your sorrys, Bexley. All I wanted was one night, only one goddamn night, and you couldn't even give me that. One night with my brother."

I take my hands out of my pockets and run them through my hair, gripping the strands while Bexley's eyes grow heavy, observing my distressed state. "Seriously, Bex, we're nineteen. When have we ever gone to the bar together and just had a drink? When do we ever spend quality time as twins? It would have been nice if you had at least contacted me to say you couldn't make it, but you didn't answer my calls or texts. Fuck, even Kal and Tray thought you were coming." With a mixture of guilt and empathy in his eyes, he flickers his gaze between mine, his brow furrowing. "I put everything into you, Bex, every single part of me. I give, and I give time and time again, and I never expect anything in return, but for once, I just wanted this one thing. I reached out to you every day. Day after day, I waited with my door open, praying for you to come back to me." My hands fall and hit my thighs with a smack.

"I love you, Bex. I'll always fucking love you, but I'm done breaking myself for you. I'm completely drained from obsessing over where you are and what you're up to. You're fucking up my life and drowning me from the inside. I have nothing left to give Bex. I can't do it anymore. I need to close the door."

Bexley frowns and avoids eye contact, chewing on his bottom lip and tilting his head. He keeps flicking the lighter in his hand over and over.

"Bu—but what about BB for life? Brayden and Bexley?" His eyes are glassy as they stare back at me. It's hard for me to admit, but I need some time alone to clear my thoughts.

"BB hasn't existed for a long time, Bex. When you chose drugs over me, that's when it all ended. It stopped when we were twelve."

I turn and walk away, unable to face him again. Tightness in my chest comes back and my vision blurs. Following my therapist's advice, I close my eyes and take controlled deep breaths. The sensation of pins and needles moves up my legs while I'm still walking, making it more difficult for me to continue.

I switch from walking to jogging as I hurry to reach the gym, confident that once I arrive, I can release all my worries and clear my mind of Bexley.

Chapter Eighteen

Bohdi

Despite my temptation to drink the bottle at my desk earlier, I chose not to because of my afternoon classes. I hate relying on alcohol to take the edge off and I'm more than aware that it's wrong, but it's the only thing that helps. I can't win. When I consume an excessive amount of alcohol, I find myself consumed by darkness and haunted by thoughts of Jace, but when I withdraw completely, it becomes suffocating. I often believe my drinking isn't excessive enough to be considered a problem, but if I'm drinking to alleviate stress, isn't that problematic on its own?

I'm relieved that my day is done. I can go home and indulge in more glasses of my favorite evil juice. My eyes wander toward the chair Brayden usually occupies. There's a part of my mind that longs for his presence, staring at me with the same expression from earlier. Another part of me is screaming to let go and stop fixating on him altogether.

I can't though and as much as I need to, I don't want to.

Without even realizing it, my phone is in my hand again and the Instagram app is open. Instead of feeling anxious, Brayden's face unexpectedly brings a sense of calm over me.

Once again, I see the red-orange circle around his picture, but I pause before clicking on it.

He can see when I watch him.

Fuck it.

I've done it once. What's the harm in a second time?

I click it and it's someone with his phone recording him and Kal doing tricks on the ice. Kal and Brayden are impressively showcasing their skills by passing the puck to each other in midair. In another video, around six seconds in, Kal drops the puck and Brayden lifts his helmet up, winking at Kal with a smirk that makes my insides flip. The following image is a video of Brayden at the gym, lifting weights a few hours later. His toned arms in a tank top have captured my attention completely. A rush of excitement floods through me as I watch the muscles flex with each lift. With a focused expression and slightly flushed face, he lifts the weights in each arm, causing his biceps to grow with each curl. This was only posted fifteen minutes ago. I wonder if he's still there. I prefer not being in the gym when the whole team is present, but from the mirror's reflection, it appears only Trayton was there. A wave of exhilaration courses through me as I think about seeing him again, and I embrace the anticipation. I don't think about it, and I don't freak out about it. I let it go as I rise from my desk, knowing I have my gym gear in my locker. Grabbing my keys, I walk out of the classroom. I need to release some tension after today, anyway.

The gym is eerily quiet as I step inside. I scan the area, expecting to find people among the machines, but it's empty. Making my way toward the boxing gym doors, I open the door and am greeted by the sound of heavy breathing and the rhythmic thuds of fists meeting bags as I open them. Initially, I thought there were at least three people here based on the noises, but upon scanning the area, I only see one person in the corner.

One shirtless person.

Brayden.

I silently approach him, avoiding any sudden movements to observe him for a while longer. Brayden strikes the bag with remarkable speed, faster than most people I've seen. His swift and forceful strikes reverberate across the gym, giving the impression of multiple people pummeling bags, yet it's solely him.

And now me, secretly, the way I wanted it.

With each strike, Brayden's breathing grows harsher and sweat continues to stream down his chiseled body, effortlessly revealing the rippling muscles beneath his flawless exterior. His strength is palpable and his presence commanding attention from anyone that could catch a glimpse of his chiseled form.

I'm trying to convince myself to look elsewhere, but I'm unable to do so. I proceed to explore his body further, taking note of the loose gray sweatpants on his hips. My gaze wanders across his back and the air gets caught in my throat as a tingling sensation begins in my dick. All I can do is envision my hands gliding over his strong muscles, longing to feel their firmness. I move closer to him, as if being drawn by an invisible force, while Brayden moves in a circle now sideways on. Without warning, he comes to a halt and snatches the punching bag to halt its movement. Glancing sideways, his darkening swirls meet mine, and his shoulders rise rapidly as he takes deep breaths. It's as if the world moves beneath me as our stare connects. His usual backward baseball cap is missing. His disheveled dark hair looks like he has recently showered, but I know that's only from him sweating profusely. Dark shadows frame his blue eyes, while a few wet strands hang over his face. I can't resist the urge to let my gaze wander downward, taking in his clear and untouched skin. My gaze can't help but track the sweat droplets that shimmer on his glistening skin, emphasizing his well-defined form. Eyes widening, I admire his sculpted vee, a result of his hard work in both hockey and the gym. A solitary strand of hair stands alone in the center, beginning below his navel and vanishing under his sweatpants. I swiftly redirect my gaze to make eye contact with him before it can descend.

As the room remains dimly lit, his chest rises and falls quickly, his eyes never leaving mine, his breathing loud and heavy. Sweat drips down his forehead, shimmering in the low light. His eyes reveal his determination. His focus is intense. Despite appearing disheveled, he exudes a raw sense of power. He appears as if he's on the verge of releasing a flood of emotions with his clenched jaw and tense muscles.

The rawness in his expression creates a sense of vulnerability that pulls me in. His eyes, incredibly blue and full of emotion, reveal a hidden depth within him. It's as if he is baring his soul, exposing himself completely to me.

In that moment, I realize the strength in his vulnerability, the power in his imperfections. Despite his sweaty and disheveled appearance, he remains confident and determined. I'm captivated by the complexity of this kid, the way his eyes furrow as they watch me, yet the strength in his body when he clenches his fist.

I find myself wanting to get lost in him.

"Sir." His curious voice snaps me out of my observation.

"Brayden," I rasp, my voice baring all my emotions, yet I'm too consumed by him to mind. As we both take in a lung full of air, our eyes remain locked on each other. My eyes drop to his lips, his full fucking lips. The lips that devour without mercy. His tongue slips out, causing me to stumble over my words as I shift my gaze back to him, only to find that he's not looking at me anymore. Instead, his eyes are fixated on my slightly parted lips, as if inhaling through my nose has become too difficult. His piercing look lazily meets mine.

Our lustful trance is broken by a noise in the distance, causing us to snap back to reality.

"Yes, yes, Mr. Stiles." Trayton's voice resounds throughout the gym. "Have you come to get some tips off the youngsters?"

Brayden's scoff makes me grin as I raise an eyebrow at Trayton, who has joined me.

"Mr. Stiles would have you on your ass in three seconds flat," Brayden says, eyeing Trayton.

"What makes you so certain?" Trayton scans me from head to toe, as if trying to gauge me. Despite being only an inch shorter than me at 6 foot 3, Trayton is just as broad.

"I just know," Brayden says, as he turns toward the gym bag and keeps throwing punches. I don't think it would be as easy as Brayden makes out, but the compliment makes me puff my chest a little. I clear my throat,

"I will leave you boys to it." I offer Trayton a smile, keeping my lips sealed, then shift my gaze to Brayden, who is no longer interested in me. The only thing he's paying attention to is the bag that moves back and forth in front of him.

I retreat, moving toward a bag at the other side of the gym, and as I reach it, I can't resist checking over my shoulder.

Brayden stares straight at me, a slight smirk playing on his lips.

Why do I feel like this kid will be the death of me?

Trayton's voice echoes across the gym hall, pulling me away from my workout. "See you in class, Teach!" he shouts. I quickly glance at the wall clock. It feels like I've been in here for hours, even though it's only been fifty minutes.

With a wave to Trayton, I quickly wipe the sweat off my head. I take a quick glance at Brayden, who is using the jumping rope.

This kid has got some stamina.

I approach him, attempting to maintain eye contact, despite my mind's temptation to glance lower. "Don't you think you have done enough for today?" I say as I reach him, raising an eyebrow.

He throws the jumping rope aside and says, "Yeah," between gasps for air. "I have to go back to my dorm and take a shower." Taking a towel from his bag, he uses it to wipe his face. Evidence of his hard workout can be seen in the wet patches on the floor.

"Rough day?" I question him. His tense and fatigued demeanor hints at something weighing on his mind or an event that took place today. The sparkle in his eye from earlier is no longer vibrant.

As he sighs, he grabs his top and pulls it over his head, saying, "Long story."

"I'll walk you back to your dorm. You can tell me on the way." He suddenly stops and swiftly turns, tilting his head sideways.

"I was drunk last night. I'm good now. You don't have to walk me to my dorm."

I give a casual shrug, but on the inside, I'm anything but calm. I can't help but find reasons to be near him because he brings clarity to my mind, and I've missed that feeling of lightness.

"I want to know what's got my student hitting a boxing bag like he's trying to tear his way through it."

On a sigh, Brayden laughs. "Okay," he eventually responds, then hoists his bag onto his shoulder.

Once we're outside, we walk at a snail's pace to his dorm, which is only a 5-minute walk. I feel relieved he doesn't seem in a hurry to distance himself from me.

"So, talk to me."

"Take a guess." He sighs, his eyes fixed on the ground.

"Your brother," I state, eyeing him. He bites his lip, nodding.

"Yep."

"What did he do this time?"

"Apologized."

I frown, confused about why apologizing is a problem for him.

"Rightttt," I drag out. "What is the issue there?"

"I could have become rich if I had been given a dollar every time he's said sorry. I've had enough of him consistently screwing up and assuming an apology will make it right. I'm sick of fighting my way up and using all my energy to put him up high on a pedestal and him letting me down each time." I remember last night what he said on the stairs. "I put all my energy into him, and he gives me nothing back. I'm sick of it."

His eyes remain locked on the sidewalk.

"Did he call you?"

"No, he turned up at training. I said a few things which are now flooding me with guilt, but they had to be said."

"Does the gym help when you're feeling this way?" I want to keep him talking instead of focusing on Bexley. As he says, he uses enough energy on that boy when he doesn't even appreciate it.

"Yeah, a lot. It clears my mind." I understand that feeling and nod in agreement. The moment my fist meets the bag, a bubble is created, isolating me from everything else. Every negative thought in my mind travels through my bones, my hands, and into the bag. It's as if I can physically attack and eliminate all negative thoughts.

After continuously staring at the ground, he finally raises his eyes and peers up at me. "Is that why you go there?" he asks.

"Yep," I respond. I don't want him prying into my messed-up thoughts, so I divert my attention as we approach his building entrance. I open the door, letting him enter first before following him inside. He frowns at me. "I'll walk you up to your door," I say, stepping ahead slightly, hoping he doesn't ask why. I can't let him know how much I enjoy being around him. He will find that weird, surely.

"Sir, I wanted to ask you something." Jogging a few steps, he struggles to keep up with me as I bound up the stairs.

"Shoot," I reply. Brayden casually places his hands in his sweatpants pockets as we reach the top, but I catch the uneasiness in his quick sideways glance at me.

When we reach his dorm door, I face him. "Brayden?"

"Er, yeah . . ." He scratches the back of his head. "The coach might have informed you about my grades decreasing, and I'm sure you're aware that I can't afford to let them decline."

I make eye contact with him and give a nod.

"According to Coach, taking an additional class will be the only way to get them back up."

I nod again, unsure of where this is headed.

"I was looking at the college's website today and noticed that it mentioned you also teach business management classes?" Ah, yes, he's right. I am scheduled to start that in the upcoming semester.

"Not this semester, but I will eventually. I think they are starting next."

His shoulders slump in a disappointed manner as he nods.

"No worries," he says, placing his hand on his door. "I'll see you in class."

All I can focus on is the sickening feeling, observing his lack of happiness and hopefulness. He's unhappy now, and it's my fault, which is not acceptable.

My hand lays over his, that is on the door handle, and I blurt out, "I will run the class for you." Brayden stares down at my hand on top of his and I quickly snatch it away. I'm trying my best to ignore the tingling sensation that moves up my arm.

"Sorry."

He shakes his head, gazing down at his hand, rubbing it as if my touch physically burned him. "It's okay. What do you mean, you will run them for me?" With his head raised and a frown on his face, he directs his questioning gaze straight at me.

"It will mean after-school time." Clearing my throat, I continue, "Meeting me in the classroom at five on Mondays, Wednesdays, and Thursdays, and I'll teach the business management to you."

"Are you serious? You'd do that for me?" he asks, his eyebrows raised in shock.

"If my student needs help, then I will help them. It's as simple as that." I shrug. "See you in class tomorrow." I give Brayden a tight-lipped smile. Walking away, I close my eyes and inhale deeply.

I will help my students with whatever they need help with during school hours.

Brayden, however, is the only one I would help, whether it be ten at night or four in the morning and I have to make sure he never realizes that. My mind and body resist leaving Brayden, as I feel that same invisible tie once more, as I did last night and at the gym today. Pulling me, wanting me to look his way. When I reach the end of the hall and turn the corner, I quickly glance behind me. Brayden isn't looking at me. In front of his dorm room, he stands, fixated on his hand.

I wonder if he experienced the same sensation, signaling it's not only me.

13
Brayden 'Quake' Anders

Chapter Nineteen

Brayden

Waking up today feels harder than usual. Bexley plagued my dreams last night. My words to him replayed in my mind as a never-ending movie. He was drowning in water, but I didn't save him. I continued yelling at him, and suddenly, I found myself in front of a doorway. Water was consuming Bexley directly in front of me, almost as if this door were perched on the shoreline of a lake. He begged for my help; he begged for me to reach out to him, but I didn't.

I shut the door.

I let him drown.

Is that what it feels like to him? Like he's drowning? And I simply walked away from him when he needed me?

But I've been there when he needed me. I've been there my whole life. He could have asked me for help any of those times and he didn't.

I remember when it all began—the notes became fewer. He wouldn't get home until the early hours. It started young. I remember the first night we were twelve, and he told me at school that I needed to go straight home and that he would meet me there later. He claimed to have detention, but I sensed something was off. I spent the entire night waiting for him. Mom had no clue he wasn't there until he casually walked in at 3:30 in the morning, reeking of an unfamiliar and awful odor. His eyes were bloodshot, as if he had been crying for hours. I remember running over to him and grabbing him; I remember because my heart was beating so fast that I thought I was going to pass out. He watched me with glazed-over, bloodshot eyes as I fussed over him, but he simply yawned and fell asleep on his side of the bed. He skipped school the next morning.

That's when everything started to go wrong.

School stopped being a priority for Bex. He said I had to go.

He would say to me, "Bray, one of us has to be the brains, and I know it won't be me."

The truth is, he could have been the one, but he decided on a different lifestyle. He believed I desired the constant supply of new clothes he would bring home for me, the latest sneakers that would make all the neighbors envious. I no longer suffered from hunger during the night. I stopped going to school with shoes full of holes and clothes stained. He provided benefits to Mom without her ever questioning where he got all those things. Despite my repeated attempts, he would dismiss me or respond angrily, insisting I should be more thankful.

He assured me that he was working toward a brighter future for me.

And he wasn't lying. He was. But that's the thing. He was creating it for me and not us.

I began writing him notes to find when he arrived home late at night, and he consistently responded.

Until he didn't.

Until I would wake up and he wouldn't be there anymore.

It was when I was fifteen that I pulled the wool away from my eyes and looked at the big open world in front of me. And realized what Bexley had been doing since we were twelve years old.

Bexley was one of the biggest drug dealers in our area.

Despite his involvement in drugs, fighting, and insomnia, he gave up everything to improve my life. When I found out, I begged him to stop. I said he could go back to school, but it was too late. Dark shadows framed his sunken crystal eyes as they stared back at me. An altered version of myself that bore no resemblance to me. While his cheeks were hollow and sank inwards, I had full cheeks and a defined jawline.

Bexley's skeletal frame was concealed by loose, oversized clothes and his skin had a grayish, ashen hue.

How come it took me so much time to fully grasp the reality of what was happening to my brother, my best friend, right in front of me all along?

It all started with drug dealing at twelve.

At the age of fifteen, the drug dealing came to an end.

That's when the addiction took over.

After that, I paid more attention and noticed things. I found out about the Bexley situation and connected the dots. How did Bexley successfully skip going to school? The school wouldn't have allowed that. But they would allow it if the doctor approved.

Upon learning about Bexley's drug dealing, my mom not only found a source for herself but also someone who could supply her with an unlimited amount of drugs and alcohol. However, Bexley's operation was only of a small magnitude. My mom needed him to be bigger.

While my mom was unconscious on the living room floor after a wild night, I stumbled upon the doctor's note while rummaging through the drawers.

Anxiety.

Bexley was diagnosed with severe social anxiety by the doctor, who also suggested homeschooling as a solution. The doctor unknowingly did exactly what my mom wanted.

He's like this because of her.

A drug addict because of her, and I'll never forgive her.

Shortly after that moment of realization, I dedicated myself to my studies. I couldn't bear to look at her, let alone be near her. With no money for college, I realized a scholarship was my only option for escape. Yet, my scholarship was largely determined by my dedication to hockey.

I scrub my hands over my face, wishing I could scrub away this tiredness and guilt, but I know I won't be able to, no matter how much I try.

"You good?" Cope's voice causes me to twist my neck to catch a glimpse of him sitting on the edge of his bed, appearing as though he just woke up.

"Yeah." I stretch and turn in bed, grabbing my phone after unplugging it.

"You were saying some crazy things in your sleep last night." He laughs, getting up and heading to the bathroom.

"What was I saying?" I frown. Hoping it wasn't anything about Bex. All my teammates obviously know about him, but I don't want them knowing how he treats me. How much he lets me down.

Cope goes to piss with the door open, speaking to me through the open door.

"You weren't speaking in complete sentences. Just random words that made no sense."

"Fuck knows," I sigh, making out I have no idea what it was about. He doesn't know that Bexley's petrified face is a replay in my mind as the water swallowed him whole. I unlock my phone, open Instagram, and mindlessly flick through stories on various Instagram accounts. On most days, I mindlessly browse through their stories without paying attention, using it as a visual distraction.

When I check my notifications, I see numerous likes on my stories from yesterday and a couple of new followers. While scrolling, I notice that @thestilestman has viewed my story again. I click on the following videos and notice that he has viewed all of them. A strange mix of excitement and anticipation slithers through me, my lips tip up in a half smile. With a forced frown, I express my irritation at the screen as my mind unexpectedly reacts with happiness.

He's my teacher. That's it.

But do teachers gaze at you the way Mr. Stiles did yesterday?

I hate intrusive thoughts sometimes; he wasn't looking at me in any kind of way. I don't think, anyway.

Wait.

After watching my stories, he showed up at the gym. I frequently hit the gym after my classes and training sessions. I've never seen him there.

Is that why he came? To see me?

"What's got you happy?"

With a sudden jump, I send my phone tumbling down the edge of my bed. I scowl up at Cope, lips pressed firmly together. "I'm not happy," I snap. "Not unhappy, but I'm just me. You know. Straight faced." I stumble over my words as I speak.

Cope gives me a questioning look, a smirk forming on one side of his mouth.

"Am I mistaken, or did I not walk in here to find you grinning like the Cheshire Cat?"

"Nope, it's clear that you're still half asleep," I answer, fumbling around on the floor to locate my phone.

"Sure." He chuckles to himself, walking over to his wardrobe and grabbing some clothes.

After a short while, I'm still lying in bed, scrolling through TikTok, when Cope comes out of the bathroom already dressed. Since my classes start late in the morning, I decided to relax this morning. Cope picks up his bag and throws it over his shoulder.

"Catch you later, Quake." I leap out of bed, pat him on the back, and make my way to the bathroom.

"This is the reason why Quake was so happy this morning," I hear Cope say. I frown to myself.

"What?" I yell from behind the bathroom door, completely clueless about what his talking about. Muffled voices reach my ears before our dorm door is shut.

Weird.

After finishing up in the bathroom, I swing open the door and come to an abrupt halt when I find someone sitting on my bed.

"Laaann . . ." I say, drawing out the name as I struggle to remember it, but I'm pretty sure it starts with Lan, so I'm sticking with that.

"Lance," he huffs.

"Yeah, I know. I was shortening your name." Confidently, I flash him a grin and say, "I like it."

A subtle flush appears on his face as he absentmindedly fidgets with the strap of his backpack.

"How can I help you?" I'm standing with only my boxers on, and I notice his eyes repeatedly darting toward my abs.

"I...uh-" he stutters. "Your friend said something about you being happy this morning?" Adjusting his glasses, he peers at me with his innocent, pure eyes.

"He was half-asleep. Don't know what he was talking about." I brush him off and grab a pair of gray sweatpants out of my drawers, remembering the way Mr. Stiles stared at me in them. Pausing, I question my impulse to grab a pair, all because of Mr. Stiles.

That's not weird at all.

I drop my boxers, reaching in my drawer for a new pair and hear Lan clear his throat behind me. I sneak a quick glance back, catching him averting his gaze and pretending to be fascinated by my ceiling, as if he hadn't just been staring at my ass. However, his face turns bright red. His flushed face is always a dead giveaway.

He's kinda cute.

With a grin on my face, I hastily slip into my boxers and pull on the sweatpants.

I quickly put on a white T-shirt and then face Lan.

"Why are you here?"

He casually pushes his glasses up again, a clear indication of a nervous tick, and quickly stands, gripping his backpack strap tightly, his knuckles turning white.

"Well, we have our next class together. I wanted to know if you wanted to walk together."

I raise my eyebrows in surprise.

"Y-you don't have to. It was a silly idea. I'll see you in class," he rushes out, before pacing toward my dorm door.

"Wait." I tug on his backpack, causing him to pause. "It's cool. We can walk together." I laugh. "We have an hour until class starts. I want to grab a coffee first; you cool with that." He widens his eyes, smiling brightly and nodding with enthusiasm.

I hate the way he watches me sometimes. It's as if he sees all good and not bad. It's as though he stares at me with a sparkle in his eyes. I'll never be that person, but no matter what I say to him or do, I can't do any bad in his eyes and this has my mood souring.

I hate people seeing anything good in me because there isn't.

It's all bad.

His eyes shift back and forth, his brow furrowing as the light in his eyes fades gradually.

I snatch my bag and toss it onto my shoulder.

"Let's go," I sigh.

Lan's anxious eyes shift back and forth between mine as he urgently tells me, "We're running late."

I quickly check my watch. Technically, class started a couple minutes ago, so we're already late. Lan wanted to leave the coffee shop about half an hour ago, but I wanted to enjoy my coffee in the on-site café on campus. Throughout the last half hour, his leg bounced vigorously while his eyes constantly checked the wall clock and observed my remaining coffee.

"Chill. It's cool, Lan." I chuckle while smiling. There's no denying that Lan is both a massive geek and an even bigger time fanatic.

Once we're in the halls, Lan picks up the pace and moves into a jog. I struggle to hold my laugh in and stop, doubling over. The sight of me stopping fills Lan with complete horror as he turns around.

"Brayden, hurry," he whines.

His voice has me laughing even more as I wipe tears away from my eyes. Lan, in his current state, neglects to look ahead and unintentionally runs into someone. My laughter comes to an instant halt when the person turns around. As blue eyes meet mine, a rush of butterflies fills me.

For fuck's sake.

Mr. Stiles shifts his focus from me to Lan and then back to me, jaw clenched and eyebrow raised.

"Late to class, are we?" Mr. Stiles addresses Lan as I am transfixed by his face, unable to speak. A rush of warmth fills my cheeks and my heart quickens. My body is buzzing with a new energy.

My body needs to stop this shit and having these reactions toward this man.

Lan stumbles over his words, "We...uh...well, I'm—"

Mr. Stiles raises his hand.

"Yes, we're late, sir," I reply, walking to stand beside Lan.

"And why are you late?" As he crosses his arms, Mr. Stiles' eyes give me an icy stare. Curiously, I tilt my head to the side, trying to understand his attitude. When has he cared about the rules, let alone being five minutes late?

"We—"

I cut off Lan. "Time passed by, sir. We were too busy to be checking the time." With a smile, I attempt to appear completely innocent.

"Is that so?" Mr. Stiles' gaze bores into me, his sapphire blue eyes darkening with intensity. "It's clear to me why your academic performance has been declining so much. Class clearly isn't a priority."

This time, anger causes my heart to quicken as I observe his flexing jaw. I'm pissed that he would openly comment on my academic performance in front of others.

"It would be a good idea for you and Lanson to get a move on."

I casually drape my arm around Lan's shoulder and steer him forward, intentionally pushing Mr. Stiles aside. I pivot on my heels, bringing Lan along to face Mr. Stiles as we walk by.

"By the way, Mr. Stiles, his name is Lance." With a smug expression, I turn around and continue to walk down the hallway, pulling Lan tightly to my side.

Chapter Twenty

Bohdi

My leg bounces furiously under my desk as I keep peeking down at my desk drawer, wanting to open it and down the entire contents of the bottle that is inside. All day, I have thought about the encounter I had with Brayden and *Lance*. Instead of being in class, Brayden is fucking some guy. I can't believe I was willing to help him—in my spare time—when he doesn't give a fuck about his grades. I glance up, checking the time. He's due here any minute, and right now I'm so angry that I don't even know if I can teach this class to him. As I battle with my thoughts and debate getting up and leaving, the door opens, and in walks Brayden, head held high. He takes a seat at the desk directly opposite me, placing his bag on the floor. His eyes meet mine, emotionless.

My eyes roam his body, his hands, his legs, his neck, his lips.

Were they all over Lance earlier? Did Lance kiss those lips? Did those hands roam Lance's body?

My mind is fucked, but I can't help but accept it. Whatever these feelings are, I can't ignore them. I can't turn them off. This invisible string that connects me to him tugs at me day in and day out. He plagues my mind all day and my dreams are flooded with him all night. I can't escape him. I know he's my student and it can't go anywhere, but even seeing him, being near him, settles something in me, even when I'm angry. Well, was.

Now, my body instantly relaxes that he's here. In my proximity. Near me.

"What are you teaching me today?" He stares at me with a bored expression. I rise from my seat and take off my suit jacket, then roll up my shirt sleeves.

"What do you want to learn, Brayden?" Walking around my desk, I lean on the front, crossing my arms in front of me. His eyes scan both of my fully tattooed arms and then he shrugs his shoulders.

"I don't know. Maybe how to not be an asshole? Seems you could learn a thing of two in that department, too?"

The big guns are coming out today. Granted, the way I handled earlier wasn't mature of me. I hated seeing him with another guy, especially someone I know he's been with, well I assume he has been with by the way they kissed.

That still didn't warrant me speaking about his private work in front of other pupils, no matter who it was. I realize that . . . now.

I put my hands up in surrender.

"I was an asshole earlier, Brayden, and I'm sorry. I shouldn't have disclosed anything about your personal grades in front of your boyfriend." It slips before I can even think about it, and I instantly regret it. His eyebrows pinch together as he rears his head back. He tilts his head. Something I have noticed he does when he is confused about something, and I find it quite adorable. It reminds me of when dogs do head tilts. I bite my cheek to stop myself smirking.

"Boyfriend? Who said Lan was my boyfriend?"

"Your hookup or whatever you youngsters call it." I raise an eyebrow, a small smile tilting up on one side of my face. He gives me a closed-lip smile and shakes his head, glancing down.

"Lan is not my boyfriend. We have hooked up, yes, and I know I gave off the impression earlier that we were late because we were hooking up, but that wasn't the case. We were in the coffee shop for an hour. I don't enjoy drinking my coffee too hot. I prefer it warm, and it took a while to cool down before I could drink it." He exhales as if he's been holding that on his chest all day. "That's why we were late."

"Because your coffee was too hot." I hold my laugh in, but barely as I smile at him.

"Hey, I enjoy my coffee lukewarm; there is nothing wrong with that." He leans back in his chair, throwing one arm out to the side and leaning it on the chair beside him.

"Okay, now we have discovered that *Lance* and not Lanson"—I raise my eyebrow at him—"is your hookup and you enjoy lukewarm coffee, can we get on with the class?"

"Yeah, sorry. I always forget his name. That's why I stick with Lan now and he *was* my hookup." He mumbles the last few words as he leans down and grabs a pad and pen out of his pocket. My ears perk up at the *was*, but I try to mask it by nodding and returning to my seat.

"I had a thought, which I think will be brilliant for your grade, but it will take some work on your part."

"Shoot."

"I think we can link this with your marketing assignment. I want you to come up with a business idea. It can be anything you want. It doesn't even have to be a profitable business, it can be a nonprofit, whatever you wish. I don't know if you have thought much about your marketing assignment but—"

"I do have an idea, and I don't know if it's something I can class as a business," he says, tapping the pen on his desk.

"Let's hear it."

"On my marketing project, I wanted to market a charity and find ways of getting people to donate. By reaching out to multimillion dollar companies who could showcase their commitment to strategic business goals such as social responsibility and ESG objectives."

I stare at Brayden in amazement. I don't think he realizes how impressed I am. The thought he has put into this already and the fact he even thought out the larger companies and why they might donate . . .

"Wow." I'm speechless. My cheeks hurt from how big I smile at him. "It's perfect, Brayden." I can't help but stare at him in amazement.

"Thanks," he replies shyly, dipping his head, but not before I see the blush creep up his face.

"What's the charity?" I question.

"I don't know how it works, but it's more of a center, a charity to set up to fund the center." He pauses, fixating on his pen that he continues to tap away on the table. He doesn't peer up at me before he says.

"I want to create a rehab center. But not any old rehab center, and nothing like the state ones. I want to create a safe space, not only for people with addiction, but for the families who have had addiction affect them." He gulps. "Like me and Bex." As if he's trying to hold off bad memories, he winces. He opens his mouth to talk and closes it again, frowning down at the tapping pen.

"Talk to me," I whisper.

He swallows roughly. "Bex was a good kid." He smiles, as if the good memories flood his thoughts. "He was beyond selfless, always tried to hide me from the bad in the world. He protected me day in and day out. When Mom's drunk friend would turn up to the trailer, he would barricade the door with every bit of furniture we had so they couldn't get into our room. He would read to me out loud so I couldn't hear the fuckery that was happening outside the door. He was my twin brother and all he thought about was protecting me and nothing else. We had a shit childhood, but I can't say I would go back and change any of it, and that's because of Bex. He was my rock, my best friend. As long as I woke to him each day and got to spend my day with him, I was okay. I was happy."

A pain sears through my chest at hearing a tiny glimpse into Brayden's life. I can't imagine what it would be like digging deep. He must have many terrible memories, but I can't help but be thankful to Bexley at this moment.

"Bex had to see all the bad to know to hide me away from it. Of course, he couldn't hide me away from everything, but he did what he could." He stares past me at the wall, deep in thought. "No matter how hard it got, he was there, and he never closed the door on me." Frowning at the wall, he blinks multiple times.

"Sorry." He shakes his head. "So, how do you think I could link this to creating a business?"

"First, you never have to be sorry. I'm here if you ever need to talk. Second, that's easy, Brayden." I pause, smiling at him. "You create the charity."

His eyes widen, and then a smile I don't think I have ever seen on Brayden appears. In that moment, it dawns on me that I would do just about anything to see that smile again and again.

"It's perfect!" he excitedly exclaims.

I clap, standing up and walking over to him, taking the seat at the desk next to him, pulling the desk closer to his.

"Have you got your laptop?" I question.

"Yup," Brayden replies, bending down to grab his bag and pulling out his laptop.

"Okay, I think we need to start by writing everything you want the charity to be and everything you want to achieve from it. Is it open for all ages? Is it for a certain age range? Those sorts of things, then we can start working on a business plan and a name of the charity." I realize Brayden has frozen, and when my eyes meet his, the confusion mars his face, as his eyebrows drop.

"We?" he questions. I nod.

"We." I smile. "I want to help you, Brayden. And I know this is your assignment, and it's not technically real, but I think it's a great idea. Something tells me when you put your mind to something, you will achieve it. Just because it's not real right now doesn't mean it can't be in the future." Being this close to Brayden does things to me it shouldn't. Goosebumps rise on my arms, and the smell of his aftershave becomes one of the best things I have ever smelled. I notice things more, the way his eyes are blue, but they have small gray and white specs going through them, giving off a glowing effect.

"But why do you want to help me?"

I can't bring myself to say the many reasons, one because I enjoy being around him for my own selfish needs. He makes me calm; he makes me content. Weirdly, he makes me happy, and I haven't felt this calm and happy in a long time. But two, I'm not ready to go into detail about Jace, about how he died, why he died. The reasons if you dig deep into Jace's death all started with someone with a drug addiction. Someone who created a monster. How do I tell him I don't want him or his brother to be like my nephew's killer? It's not something I can even think about explaining right now, so with a smile and a small shrug, I lie.

"It's a great idea and something I'm interested in." He seems to accept it by nodding, but a small squint and the way his eyes roam my face, as if he senses the lie, makes me feel uneasy and has me glancing away. He doesn't push it; instead, he types away on his laptop, searching up ideas.

A while later, Brayden has already begun the start of his business plan. He hasn't come up with a name yet but looks happy with what he has come up with so far. I have been next to him on my laptop, researching larger organizations that he could contact that would help. In business management, colleges contact companies that the students select and notify them that the project is not real, but it is for the students' overall grade.

Some companies will express that they don't have time to take part in the pitches. However, larger corporate companies want to create added value to their business to show they work with schools and colleges. It helps their profile, and it helps bring in future clients.

I glance up at the time, noticing we have been here for nearly two hours already. These classes are only meant for an hour. He already has a lot of classes and training. On top of that, I can't overrun him.

"Let's pack away. We can carry on with this tomorrow. Go get some rest."

Brayden tidies up his papers while yawning.

"No gym tonight." I point to him with a smirk.

He smiles. "Absolutely not. I need to go back to the trailer and see if I can find Bex and then I'm crashing for the rest of the night."

Hearing that he's going back to the trailer floods me with unease.

"I can drop you there?" I say, not glancing at him while I tidy away my desk, trying to appear casual.

"Thanks, sir, but it's okay. I could do with a walk before seeing him, anyway."

I don't like it one bit, but I need to step back. He's a good kid; he knows what he's doing.

"If you're sure." I raise an eyebrow at him in question, and he nods, smiling again.

Moving over to my desk at the front, I begin packing papers and my laptop into my bag.

"Sir." I turn on my heels to find Brayden standing directly behind me. He stares at me, and I glance down to see his hand outstretched. He wants to shake my hand.

The minute my fingers brush his palm as I grasp his hand, my body slithers in goosebumps. My heart speeds up and I gulp, my mouth becoming as dry as a desert. My hand tingles as we both capture each other in a trance once again. Nothing has felt more *right* than his skin on mine. Nothing has made me feel so alive with just one touch. We continue shaking hands, and a weird buzz circles us as we both can't take our eyes off each other. Once again, my eyes move to his lips and I know right here, right now, I want to feel his lips on mine. I want to kiss him and revel in how alive he can make me feel.

As if thinking the same thing, Brayden's eyes flash to my lips and his hand tightens around mine as if he's trying to physically hold himself back.

I can't let this happen, not here, not now.

I pull my hand away, tucking my now clenched fists into my pockets.

"See you tomorrow." I offer a reassuring smile, and he finally drops his hand as if it takes him a moment longer to snap out of the trance.

"See you tomorrow, sir."

The invisible string is there immediately. Every time I walk away from Brayden, or he walks away from me, that string tugs as if I need to be with him. I allow myself to peer up at the door and a smile forms on my face when Brayden stares back at me, smiling as if he feels it too.

13
Brayden 'Quake' Anders

Chapter Twenty-One
Brayden

Mr. Stiles, no doubt, thinks I need to walk and clear my head before I speak to Bexley.

I don't.

I need to walk and clear my head because I've finally accepted something that has been brewing for the last week.

I'm hot for my fucking teacher and I'm pretty sure it's not one sided.

He makes me feel like I can do anything.

He has a way of taking me away from all the problems in the world when we're together. The ice is where I find that feeling, but outside of it, the only thing that provided that sensation was being lost in a tight hole. Mr. Stiles' presence does it alone.

The familiar dark cloud that hovers above the trailer park is noticeably powerful as I approach. The muddy, dead grass zaps all my energy as soon as my feet touch it. At the highest point in the park, my trailer sits, covered in rust and green moss. Similar to the rest of the trailers.

One part of me hates being here. I hate everything about it. I hate the views. I hate the smell. I hate the dead feeling it gives you inside, but then another part of me relates to being here with Bexley. It makes me think of the times I spent growing up with him, the overwhelming love he gave me, and his relentless commitment to providing me with a happy childhood.

I hope he's home. My conversation with Mr. Stiles made me realize I can't abandon him, regardless of what happened between us. I can't turn my back on him. He stood by me through thick and thin, never abandoning me even in difficult times; if anything, he risked his own safety to protect me.

How can I turn my back on him?

As I open the door, a cloud of smoke and the scent of old alcohol hits me. My mom's small, curled-up frame catches my eye as I glance to the left at the stained sofa with multiple holes. It's clear from her stained clothes she hasn't done laundry in weeks. My initial reaction is to always help her. The number of times I've had to shower, dress, and feed her has become impossible for me to keep track of. But now, I do nothing. It took me a long time to come to terms with the fact that she was no longer my mom.

Bexley can count on me to be there for him because we are brothers. A mother's primary responsibility is to shield you at all costs, but eventually, she changed. Instead of her two sons, she chose drugs and involved her own son to sustain her addiction. In the same way she betrayed us, I turn my back on her and move toward my old bedroom. Bexley's bedroom.

The moment I walk in, the smell overwhelms me, and my eyes water. Alcohol and God knows what else assaults me. Bexley is fully clothed and lying on the bed, holding an empty vodka bottle.

With a sigh, I shake my head and make my way to the bedroom window, opening it to allow some air inside. I quietly sit down at the end of the bed, being careful not to wake him as I fix my eyes on his vulnerable and messed-up state. I cannot walk away, but I refuse to stand idly by as my brother slowly destroys himself. I try to think of ways to help him while running my fingers through my hair and massaging my head, but I've encountered this before. I've been here time and time again. Without money, there is nothing I can do. I can't help him. It's up to him to help himself, even with venom coursing through his veins. He needs to try.

Gazing down, I see a white plastic bag that is filled with something. I bend over, snatch it, and open it, revealing a bag filled with candy.

Not any candy, but my favorites. All my favorites, but none of Bexley's.

I squeeze my eyes shut and inhale deeply, attempting to manage my emotions. Just like old times, he went out and brought back all the things I love. I put my hand in and pull out my number one candy. Nerds Ropes. My smile widens as I see he's brought me all the Nerds favorites—Nerds Ropes, Clusters, Rainbow Candy boxes in grape and strawberry flavors. No one knows me as well as he does. As I bite into the Nerds Rope, the rainbow flavor transports me back to our childhood. Despite never having money for candy when we were kids, Bexley claimed the cashier liked him and gave it to him for free. Every time, he made me wait outside while I gave him a long list of candy I wanted, and without fail, Bexley would bring out everything I asked for. It wasn't until a few years later, when Bexley was too sick to go to school, that I stopped being easily fooled. I wanted to make him happy, so I went into the shop and began filling my bag up. I wanted to make sure the man knew I was Bexley's brother, even though I'm sure he could tell simply by looking at me. The cashier was dumbfounded when I approached him, bag overflowing with candy, and explained that it was okay because I'm Bexley's sibling.

Bexley was not favored by the cashier at all. He had no idea who Bex was, or that Bexley was stealing the candy every single time. I suddenly realized that Bex only kept a few candies for himself, which was nothing compared to the pile he would give me. Despite sharing mine with him, he always ensured I had the most to eat.

That was the thing with having a mom like ours; she didn't care that at the age of ten; we were roaming the streets doing what we wanted after school. She barely paid attention. There was always some kind of food in the trailer. Whether it be moldy bread or chips, but Mom didn't always make us dinner. We would have to root around in the cupboards and try to find something for ourselves.

There were moments when choosing candy was the safer choice for us.

We were happy in those moments. Bexley's full face and chubby cheeks become visible in the images. He looked healthy and alive. I glance over my shoulder and see his face now, gaunt and pale, giving him an ill appearance. His cheeks, once full of life, are now sunken. Bexley no longer had any interest in hanging out with me after a certain point. He stopped going to the park. Despite everything, he never stopped bringing me candy. Tucked away in our shared room, we found solace while enjoying candy.

I drop the Nerds Rope, the taste becoming sour. It doesn't taste as it used to anymore.

My attention is drawn to an object on the nightstand—our book, accompanied by our UV pen. I get up, walk over, grab the book, and return to the end of the bed to sit down. It's an old one, one that we completed.

Has he been reading these? It's amusing to me when I flip through the pages and they appear untouched. No words written on them, but there are. There's an entire story written between these pages. Full of love, hurt, and pain. A whole insight into someone's life.

To many people, this is an unused diary.

To both me and Bexley, it's our entire world.

I shine the light on a couple of pages, the words bringing happiness to me in this moment.

I feel sick Bray I wish Mom wold give us somefin to make it better like she used to

Ew I don't It tasted like poo.

maybe I had to much candy.

I dont fink so candy is good for you they woldnt make you sick.

really

yeah nerd ropes have beries and grape and strawberys in dem.

my teeth hurt.

prob cos u havnt had enuf candy

I run my hand over my mouth, attempting to muffle my laughter and prevent Bex from waking up. I talked some shit when I was younger. Glancing at the end of the book, I see that the page is turned down like a dog's ear. When I shine the UV light, the text becomes difficult to read at first. The writing is scattered and chaotic. Writing blindly can be challenging, which is why this sometimes happens.

Writing fragments are cluttered across the entire page.

I'm going to get better, Bray. I promise.

Please don't let go.

Please don't close the door on me.

Please come back. I'm sorry.

I need you.

BB for life.

My best bro.

Fuck poison.

Fuck Bexley.

Tears well up in my eyes as I read further. Witnessing him write messages to himself filled with self-hatred and thoughts of death. Messages saying if he was dead, I would be able to get on with my life. A tear slips out when I abruptly close the book, startling Bexley. With a bang, the empty vodka bottle slips from his grasp and crashes to the floor, his bloodshot eyes fixated first on me and then on the book.

"Bray." His voice sounds gritty, causing yet another tear to escape. Bexley follows my tears and frowns. I rise from the bed and position myself next to him. Cupping his face with my hands, I bring our heads together.

"If you believe that your death would improve my life, you are mistaken," I grit out. "If you're gone, there's nothing left of me. Do you grasp what I'm saying? If you die, you may as well take me with you." As he nods, a tear rolls down his face.

"I'm sorry, Bray," he manages through choked words.

"I'm sorry too. I shouldn't have said what I did."

"You were right, though. I am fucking up your life."

"Without you, Bex, my life would be a complete mess." I close my eyes. The image of not having Bexley in my life feels void. My life wouldn't be worth living anymore. "You cared for me growing up. You were my mom and dad in one. You gave me food, you ensured my safety, you showed me unconditional love. I will never abandon you. We will beat this."

"Bray," he sobs, "I just want to live." I embrace him tightly as he sobs against my chest, his shoulders quivering. "I want to live for us. I don't want to feel like this anymore. I want to see life the way I used to. I want to see how beautiful life is. How do I make it stop?"

With tears leaving my eyes, my body trembles as his cries become louder. Tears stream down our faces as I cling on to Bexley, my hands trembling. I lie down, pressing Bexley close as he wraps his arm around my waist. Our large frames barely fit on the small bed, but I embrace him until his crying-induced exhaustion gradually sends him to sleep. I weep silently, tears soaking the pillow beneath me. Despite my muscles aching, I can't bring myself to let go of Bexley. I need to hold on to him a little longer.

The words *I just want to live* keep echoing in my head.

I can't lose him, and it's as if he's slowly slipping from my grasp. I need to do something now before it's too late and I lose him for good.

Because if I did, I don't think I would come out on the other end.

Chapter Twenty-Two

Bohdi

I glance down at my phone, frowning as I wait for Brayden to arrive, browsing his Instagram. It annoyed me he chose not to share a picture of himself on his story last night. I hate that because I couldn't see him; I drowned myself in whiskey instead.

I hate how weak I feel if I can't be around him.

The time on the wall ticks by. He's ten minutes late. I stand up pacing while I keep refreshing his page. Do I message him on here? I've never messaged him. I know he knows I found his page, but is it acceptable for me to reach out to him?

I struggle internally for a few minutes, but Brayden's arrival resolves it. His shoulders are slumped and dark shadows surround his eyes.

He looks drained. With effort, he moves toward a desk, throwing his bag down. Before dropping down in a chair, he mumbles. "Sorry I'm late, sir."

I don't say a word. I keep watching him as he places his forearms on the desk in front of him and stares down at it.

He remains motionless, continuing to gaze without responding. I move closer to him and delicately place my hand on his arm. Abruptly, he emerges from his thoughts and directs his attention to me. His tiredness becomes noticeable when I see him up close. His eyes are swollen and bloodshot, as if he has been crying. With a frown of concern, I hurriedly rush out, "What happened?"

He shakes his head. "It doesn't matter." With a sigh, he rubs his tired eyes, as if they long to shut and remain closed for the rest of the afternoon.

"In case you've had a tough day, would you prefer to reschedule?" I ask, not wanting to push him. If he's trying to catch up, all while training at the same time. I don't want him to burn out.

He sits up taller, his voice raised slightly as he firmly says, "No. Right now, this class is probably the most important one for me. I need this." His eyes, filled with pleading, dart back and forth between mine. It's as if I'm witnessing him struggle to stay afloat, desperately clinging to a ledge, not wanting to drown.

"We can do this class today. But first, fill me in on what's happening." I know this isn't fatigue from overdoing it. He hasn't slept. I know what that look is. I carried it with me for months, and I still do occasionally. He concentrates on me, as if he is deciding whether he can confide in me. "You know you can trust me?" I reassure him.

With a sigh, he admits, "I went to see Bex last night." His already deflated shoulders sink even lower. "I need to help him. I can't let this carry on, sir." Despite his focus on his hand on the desk, I notice his trembling lip. I lower myself into a crouching position to meet him face-to-face, extending my hand over his arm.

"Hey, I need you to talk to me." Unease settles within me. What has happened between them? Seeing him sad makes me feel physically ill.

"He's not good, sir." He takes a deep breath, and I can see him digging his nails into his hand. I frown and grab his hands, refusing to let go.

“Don’t do that.” With a grimace, I tightly clutch his hands. In an effort to contain his emotions, he inhales long and intense breaths.

“I need to help him. I can’t wait for a scout. I can’t sit back and wait any longer. I need to do something.”

“What do you mean, you can’t wait for a scout?”

“I love hockey.” He halts, studying my hands tightly, clasping his. Instead of letting go, I tighten my grip, encouraging him to continue. “My goal has always been to get scouted so I can support Bexley the way he’s supported me. I want to admit him to a rehab center.”

“You know you could probably get him into a state one?” I follow up.

“I know, but they’re not worth it. A few people in the park went into them and they came out and started using again. They release you too soon. It’s overrunning, so they want people in and out.”

I nod in understanding. Technically, they’re free, so it makes sense.

“What are you going to do?”

“I have no idea.” A sigh escapes from him. “By doing this charity project, I’m hoping I can find ways to help Bexley, even though I’m unsure what they may be.”

“Well, we better get cracking.” I let go of Brayden’s hands, which doesn’t feel good. I have an immediate desire to reach out and hold on to him once more. With a forced smile, Brayden opens his laptop and prepares for an hour of research.

Sleeping isn't coming easy as I toss and turn, remembering Brayden's face, witnessing how distraught he looked. It doesn't sit well with me. I need him to be happy; I need that smile on his face more than I need my next breath. I must be able to do something. The research today revealed companies we could present to, but they won't aid a drug addict in getting into a private facility. I wish I had the financial means to back it, because there's absolutely no doubt that I would go for it.

I turn on my laptop and launch the web browser, unsure of where to begin, but I start typing.

'What are some ways a family member can support a drug addict?'

Many things are displayed, but none of them appear useful, so I persist in searching and stumble upon a highly rated group. I visit their website and scroll through their page. It's a support group for family members with addicts as loved ones. They meet up regularly to offer each other guidance, but it appears they have plenty of suggestions for places to explore that could be useful. Something about this place reminds me of Brayden's plans, and I think it could be a promising start. They request a donation that supports the center's operations and provides refreshments for attendees, and I'm happy to contribute. I will just tell Brayden it's free.

I got additional information after speaking with the kind lady, and it could potentially be a promising beginning for Brayden. She clarified they hold them weekly, but it is not necessary for you to attend every week. You can go as many times as you want. To attend, you must make sure you register in advance as there's a limited capacity. I'm feeling hopeful and can't wait until tomorrow to tell Brayden. However, when I check Instagram, I'm disappointed to see that he hasn't posted anything. I enjoy watching his day-to-day life and what he gets up to. It calms me. I tap the message button.

@thestilestman: Hey

With impatience, I scowl at the screen until the word 'seen' appears below my name a few minutes later.

@quakeontheice: Hey

@thestilestman: I have found somewhere we can go for your brother. It's a support group for family members of addicts, but it's got good reviews and I think it will be a good start.

As soon as I send the message, I can see it's been seen straight away and eagerly await his response. What feels like an hour but is less than a minute. I get a reply.

@quakeontheice: this is amazing. Thank you so much, sir. I really appreciate this.

A sense of fulfillment rushes through me, realizing that I've made him happy based on that message.

@quakeontheice: But what do you mean by we? You don't need to come; you know that, right?

I frown at the message.

@thestilestman: You're not going on your own. I want to be there for you. I will go with you. End of discussion. We go this Saturday at 11. I'll pick you up outside Pythons at 10:15. Don't be late.

I shut down my app, convincing myself I don't have to see his response, but then my phone dings. Frustrated, I study the ceiling and clench my jaw, but I realize it's pointless. I grab my phone and glance at the screen.

@quakeontheice: Yes, sir.

Heat rushes through me. My body has a strange reaction when Brayden does as I ask and replies with *Yes, sir.* My pants tighten as vivid images race through my thoughts, ones that shouldn't be. Brayden's captivating smile as he kneels before me is burned into my mind. The smile I crave to see on him. Fuck. Rubbing the palm of my hand over my dick doesn't provide any relief. It's painfully fucking hard now.

This isn't good.

I type eagerly on the screen, consumed by my twisted infatuation for him.

@thestilestman: Tell me one thing. Are you smiling now?

@quakeontheice: I am, sir, and it's all thanks to you.

I let out a loud groan and forcefully cover my eyes with my hands, desperately wishing these images of Brayden smiling at me while undoing my pants would go away.

I'm so fucking gone.

My hand snakes down to my pants, unzipping and pulling my heavy, leaking dick out, and I pump myself until ropes of cum squirt out of me. And the sick thing is, the whole time, I imagine it's Brayden's hand and not mine.

13
Brayden 'Quake' Anders

Chapter Twenty-Three

Brayden

It's been a long time since I woke up feeling this happy. I went to bed with a smile on my face and had the best night's sleep in a while after receiving Mr. Stiles' message.

I know this group won't be the perfect solution, but it's a start and there will be people who can relate. They will understand the situation I'm in. They will give me advice and connections. I hope.

What brings me the most happiness is having Mr. Stiles there for me, meaning I don't have to go through this alone.

I have an extra pep in my step as I prepare for classes today, grateful that I don't have one this morning. I'm excited to see Bexley and share the news about this group. I want to be transparent with him. I want him to know that I'm finding a way out for him. I'm getting him help. It's about time I returned the favor and took care of my twin, exactly as he did for me when we were younger.

Last night, I couldn't stop grinning after rereading Mr. Stiles' messages.

Before putting on my sweatshirt, I think twice about it and bring my phone up to face the mirror in my bathroom. I rarely take selfies and post them, but I enjoy capturing moments when I'm feeling good. Just like now.

I flex my muscles, which are a lot more defined since I've been going to the gym more. With only my sweatpants on, I grin wide, letting my gray sweatpants hang low and snap a picture of my body and the top of my sweatpants. My smile is all you can see on my face, my nose and eyes, hidden under a low-hanging baseball cap. I post it on my story with a caption that reads:

It's going to be a good day

Because it is. I can feel it.

As I gaze at my reflection, a smug smile creeps onto my face because I posted that picture on my story for a specific reason. With the hope that one particular man sees it.

I think I spoke too soon about it being a good day. It was unrealistic to expect that, of course. I've been in a heated argument with Bexley for the past half hour, attempting to find the cause of his black eye and cut lip. I have a feeling I know who it is, but he's not willing to say.

"Just fucking tell me, Bexley." As he gets dressed, I maneuver around him.

"It was a stupid bar fight. Forget about it."

"You can't lie for shit. Now tell me."

He ignores me. Carrying on with getting ready.

"I came here with some good news to share with you. I was in a good mood before fucking coming here." I sigh, sitting on the end of the bed.

"Then go. I didn't ask you to come here, did I." I rear my head back, turning round, staring at him wide-eyed as he puts on his sweater. “Sorry,” he huffs. “I’m tired.” Next to me, he sits down and reaches down the side of the bed, pulling out a Nerds Rope for himself and offering one to me. We both open it and start eating them. I have my preferred rainbow flavor while he has his preferred berry flavor.

“I’m going to a support group on Saturday,” I rush out. I wanted to tell Bex and after the other night, I know he wants to help, but I don’t really know how to approach it. The best way to handle this is to rip off the band aid and say it. “For those with a family member struggling with addiction.” I take another bite of my Nerds Rope. He remains silent, and the awkwardness intensifies rapidly. I glance over and he stares straight ahead. “Bex?”

He continues to nod to himself, his gaze fixed on a specific spot on the floor. “I need out of here.” My heart breaks as I listen to his raw, vulnerable voice.

“I know. I’m trying, I really am. I think this group is going to be a good start.”

He agrees by nodding.

“Where did you find it?”

“Ahh, through a friend.” I don’t know how to tell him a teacher is involved in this. Despite witnessing Mr. Stiles knocking out Karl, I don’t believe he would be pleased.

I frown at Bexley, who continues to scratch at his arm. He seems considerably more agitated than his usual self.

“Hey.” I lay my hand on his arm. “Fuck, you’re ice cold.”

His hand trembles slightly as he pushes my arm aside.

With a downcast expression and drooping shoulders, he sighs. “I’m tired. That's all.”

“Bex, don’t lie to me. What happened?”

“I—I’ve.” He sighs. “I’m trying okay, Bray. I’m really trying.”

“Hey, hey, I know you are. Has something happened?” I scrutinize his appearance. He seems even more worn out than in his usual state. There's a noticeable shimmer of sweat clinging to his skin, and he appears paler than usual.

"I've been trying to stop." With a shy demeanor, he glances in my direction. "The d-drugs," he stutters. My heart swells. He's never made an effort before. Am I finally going to get my brother back?

"This is great, Bex. Trying is everything, and you're doing just that!" I exclaim, pulling him in for a hug. He embraces me gently, encircling me with his arms and resting his chin on my shoulders.

"I let Karl know I was stopping, and the situation became heated."

I'm quickly overwhelmed by searing anger.

I move away, observing his face. "I had a hunch that it was him who did this to you."

"I can't stop selling. I need the money, but Dax is holding on to the drugs for me, so I don't have it around me to be tempted." I embrace Bex tightly and plant a kiss on his head.

"You don't know how much this means to me, Bex."

"I can't promise, but I'm going to try." With a smile, he leans on my shoulder and whispers, "This is for us."

"BB for life," I mumble, my eyes fixed on the photo booth snapshot of us.

Good days are coming.

Not long after Bex fell asleep, I laid down next to him, not wanting to leave at that moment. However, I have a class coming up, so I get out of bed and lean down to give him a kiss on the forehead. He doesn't move. When I walk out into the hallway,

I find my mother sitting on the sofa, her eyes dull and her body swaying as a result of her intoxication. She can't even keep her head still. It's one in the afternoon.

"Pathetic." I exit the trailer with a sneer on my face. As I close the door, I notice Karl sitting on a chair outside his trailer, smoking a cigarette and smirking at me.

"Kid!" he shouts. "Tell your brother I need him over here pronto."

My resolve shatters at the same moment that he snaps his fingers. I storm over there and lean my hands down on the chair arms, caging Karl in.

"Listen the fuck here, you fat piece of shit. My brother is done with you. He won't come here anymore, and I'll make certain of that. Stay the fuck away from my brother." As I'm about to straighten up, a sharp, excruciating pain shoots through my head, blurring my vision and causing me to land heavily on the ground. My sweater is grabbed before Karl is in my face.

"I own your brother. You be good to remember that, boy. The next time you try to talk down to me, I won't beat you black and blue. I'll beat your brother black and blue." He releases his grip, causing my head to collide with the ground, intensifying my dizziness.

I raise myself on one elbow.

Fuck. My head.

"Shit, Brayden." Two arms embrace me and lift me off the ground. I grimace and hold my head, then shift my focus to Daxton on the left, who meets my stare. With his eyebrows furrowed, he forces a tight-lipped smile.

"I'm sorry." He sighs. Taking a quick glance at his trailer door, he redirects his attention toward me.

"Daxton, just make me one promise. Keep the drugs away from Bex. Please," I beg him.

"Daxton, get your fucking ass in here now and stop talking to that cunt!" Karl shouts from inside the trailer. Daxton winces and turns to walk toward the door.

Before he enters, he pauses and gazes at me. "I promise I won't, Bray." And I don't know why, but I believe him. Daxton has never really done anything; he was born into an unfortunate family. A bit like us.

Because of his father, he doesn't have a place where he fits in. No one at school likes him. He's a loner and his dad is notorious. How can I be friendly with him when his dad is part of the reason Bex is the way he is?

Chapter Twenty-Four

Bohdi

As I wait for Brayden outside Pythons, I can't help but study the photo I captured from his Instagram story. I couldn't resist, even though I knew I shouldn't. I needed this photo, and I hate how many times I've wrapped my hand around my dick while I stare at the photo, wishing I could dress him in my cum.

He's my nineteen-year-old student. What the fuck is wrong with me?

It might just be my imagination, but I had a dream last night that left me drenched in sweat and unable to fall back asleep. Jace's face was all I could see, a face I hadn't seen in my dreams for a while, expressing his disappointment in me. *He's your student, Boh. You're old enough to be his dad.*

I found myself in the shower at 4 a.m., pondering whether I was losing my mind or if this could be accepted as normal?

Of course it fucking can't.

Am I gay? No?

Am I bi? I guess?

Do I find other men attractive? No.

But do I find Brayden attractive? Hell yes.

Do I still have an attraction to women? I don't fucking know.

I made a decision this morning, but now I'm unsure if it's the right one. Before I contemplate it further, Brayden enters the vehicle through the passenger door. His aftershave clings to me, making me yearn to nuzzle my nose in his neck and inhale in his entire essence. Sporting gray sweatpants, a white tee, and a baseball cap pulled low, he always catches my attention. I know what his body looks like under that white T-shirt as I gaze at him. I can't help but feel a flood of heat wash through me.

"Hey, sir," he says, pulling his belt on and keeping his face turning toward the window and not at me.

That's weird.

"Brayden." I frown and start to pull away, sensing something is off. The tension feels wrong, like a taut string about to snap. I shift the gear stick with a deliberate motion and engage the parking brake, the click echoing in the silence. My eyes dart around, searching for any sign of what might be causing this unease.

"Are you ready for today?" It's possible that he's slightly anxious about the meeting.

Enthusiastically, he says, "Yep, all ready!" without looking at me. Maybe it's nerves. This could be his typical behavior since I haven't witnessed him being nervous.

We have approximately twenty minutes before the meeting starts, so we need to leave now or we'll be late.

Despite being five minutes into the journey, Brayden continues to ignore me and remains silent. No matter how many times I glance to the side, he keeps his head completely turned toward the window.

"Brayden, are you absolutely certain you're okay?" I question, frowning and stealing quick glances at him during the drive.

"I'm fine, sir."

"I'll believe it when you look at me and say that."

Despite his huffing, he refuses to make eye contact with me.

"Brayden," I snap.

He quickly turns his head and shouts. "I'm fine!" Just as I notice the darkness around one side of his face, he swiftly turns his head back to gaze out the window.

I abruptly hit the brakes, making Brayden instinctively grip the dashboard and lunge forward, saved by the seatbelt keeping him in place. The beeping of cars behind me gradually turns into a drumming sound in my ears. My heart is the only sound I hear as anger boils within me.

Someone fucking hurt him.

My sudden stop leaves Brayden staring at me in wide-eyed disbelief.

"Sir?" Brayden wrinkles his forehead at me, but his expression becomes more sympathetic as he observes my anger. "I'm fine," he says again in a softer tone.

I clutch his cheeks, grasping his face in my hand.

"Who the fuck did this to you?" I narrow my eyes, shifting my attention back and forth between his gaze. His eyes cast down.

"Please, drop it. We need to get going. I don't want anything ruining this meeting, Mr. Stiles. Please." The red mist lingers, despite his pleading blue orbs. I struggle to relax, squinting and clenching my teeth. The thought of anyone hurting him, even touching him, causes a strong response from me. Something that will obliterate anything that dares to even look at him the wrong way.

"I'll tell you after the meeting," he whispers.

I let go of his cheeks, noticing the red and white imprints my fingers made. I can't speak. I'm too afraid to speak because of what I might say.

I would kill anyone that even tries touching him again.

The thought scares me. I've never felt such an intense need to protect someone as I do for Brayden, and it terrifies me.

The rest of the journey is spent in silence until we reach our destination. Before I can step out of the car, Brayden grips my arm.

"Can we put it aside until later, please? I need your support in there." Upon hearing those words, I find myself sinking back into the seat, with one foot still outside the car. I slump my shoulders and sigh.

"Okay, but you promise to tell me after?"

With a forced smile, he assures me, and I nod in response.

The hall is huge. On the left, there's a lengthy table full of refreshments and a variety of sweet and savory snacks. In the center of the hall, there is a wide circle consisting of about twenty chairs. Brayden is already looking down at a table filled with leaflets to the right, picking up one of each. His eyes sweep the hall as he turns toward me, then he walks up beside me, waving the leaflets.

"I got these. Some late-night reading." He chuckles.

Smiling, I gesture for him to walk ahead. I'm here to support him today and encourage him to take the lead. He finds a seat and acknowledges the person next to him with a smile. As I sit beside him, I scan the room and acknowledge each person with a nod.

Directly across from Brayden and me, a small lady asks, "Is everyone prepared?" Several individuals grab doughnuts from the table, moving around and offering them to others. Brayden and I shake our heads, quietly declining, as they move on to the next person. Brayden's leg bounces nervously as we wait for the group to begin. I steal a glance at his face as he keeps his eyes fixed on the woman in front of him.

"Let me begin by saying how much of a pleasure it is to see each and every one of you here today. I can see we have a few new faces." I notice her smile at me and Brayden, but she doesn't request introductions. This brings me some relief, as I'd rather observe before speaking. "For those who are new, our group aims to promote mutual support, offer advice, and connect us with individuals who can provide assistance. When a family member is struggling with addiction, whether it's drugs, alcohol, or gambling, one thing takes precedence above all else." Pausing, she scans the group as they all murmur "support." Her eyes crease as she smiles broadly at everyone. "The support of family and friends is crucial for holding on. Without it, they'll feel like they have nothing at all."

I take another quick glance at Brayden. And he's laser-focused on the lady, hanging on her every word. "Nevertheless, it's important to keep yourself in mind, as supporting others can be draining and it's crucial to take care of yourself."

She smiles once more and then raises her hand in the direction to a man on her left. "Let's begin with you, Steven," she says, smiling at the man to her left who just finished his doughnut. "How has your week been so far? Have there been any challenges?"

Steven explains that his son, who initially got hooked on prescription drugs, had a tough week and realized $100 was missing from his wallet. According to his son, he had no knowledge of it. It's interesting to see everyone in the group nodding as if they've experienced this before, which makes me wonder if Brayden has ever gone through this with Bexley.

The lady smiles at Brayden. "Would you be happy to share why you're here?"

Brayden nods and smiles tightly, clearing his throat.

"Hey, I'm Brayden."

Everyone in the group says, "Hey, Brayden."

"My brother, my twin brother," he follows up. "He struggles with drug addiction. All kinds of drugs. He began at fifteen, but he started selling at twelve."

A sinking sensation drops in my stomach. I was unaware that Bexley began selling drugs at such a young age. Shit.

"He's my best friend and I want him back. His childhood was stolen from him, and now his teenage years have been taken away too. I want him to live, not just for me, but for himself. I want him to see the world, I want him to meet someone, have a family. Marry. I want him to witness what actual love is." His voice becomes hoarse, and I glimpse the woman across from me, her eyes glazing over. "He kept me safe during my childhood. We had, well, have a bad mom. She cared for us until she didn't. During my upbringing, he filled the roles of both my mom and dad. All he ever wanted was a better life for me, and I can't help but feel guilty about what happened to him. He started this because of me and then it took over him." His once upright stance crumbles as he fixes his gaze on the ground, his shoulders sagging. I don't want to cut him off by interrupting him and checking he's okay. I want him to fully communicate his thoughts. I think he needs this. He needs to speak to people who understand the struggle he is going through. "He wants to stop." He sighs and then continues. "He knows I'm here today. We cannot secure the necessary funds for his placement in a reputable rehab center, and the state options are not helpful. He's trying to stop for me, but I need him to do it for himself more than anything. As far as I'm aware, he has never tried to quit before. I see this as a promising start, but yeah." He shrugs his shoulders. "I'm at a loss and uncertain about my next move. Despite some recent regrets, I will always stand by him. He's my twin brother, the other part that completes me. I mean nothing without him. I'll stick by his side, no matter what. But I can't just watch him slowly kill himself because, to be honest . . . " With a pause, he makes eye contact with the woman, who brushes a tear off her face. "He's killing me along with him."

A man next to him places a hand on his shoulder, squeezing, and I have to clench my fists to refrain myself from leaning over and flicking his hand away.

I need to get a fucking grip.

As others murmur their admiration, Brayden inhales deeply and smiles at the man next to him, having impressed everyone with his sharing on the first day. Going into that level of detail immediately is not something many people can do, but he was able to. It further emphasizes how much he needed this outlet and to be around like-minded people.

"Can I ask a question?" the lady inquires.

He nods rapidly. "Go for it."

"Your face. " She points to his bruised face and cut lip by mimicking the motion on her own face. "Did he do that?"

Brayden vigorously shakes his head from side to side, saying, "No, no, no. He's never laid a hand on me."

She smiles softly. "Was the involvement of your brother and the drugs related to whoever did that?"

He sits in his chair, frowning and fidgeting, his shoulders drooping as the adrenaline fades. His body language reveals everything.

"Yes," he murmurs, his stare fixed on the floor. I guess he doesn't need to tell me who did that. A small part of me was praying it was hockey. Although I would have found out the player and probably hoped he broke his ankle on the ice, but I know now it's not hockey. It's that fucking Karl. I suddenly get up and head to the refreshments, pouring myself a glass of water, secretly craving something stronger. It's clear that my interaction with Karl has had no effect, and I'm clueless about how to go about this. I can't allow him to harm Brayden. Daxton is already bad enough, but Brayden is crossing the line. I drink two cups of water and then return to my chair, taking a seat. It's as if nobody said a word while I went to get water. I clear my throat.

"Sorry," I mutter.

"Michael can sympathize with you," the lady says to Brayden. She signals toward a man on the other side of the room. With a nod, the man reveals a glimpse of his bare stomach.

"I was stabbed three times by my son's dealers due to his outstanding debt," he grunts.

Jesus Christ.

Brayden's eyes widen as he stares at the three scars on his abdomen.

"The danger of addiction lies in its ability to cause harm not only to the addict themselves but also to those around them," she says with a sad smile.

"Is there anything you wanted to share?" The lady glances at me. Swallowing becomes difficult as a sharp pain stabs my chest. I have the option to inform them about Jace, but I don't feel comfortable discussing it, either with them or with Brayden. I'm not prepared to share that yet.

I understand all too well the destructive power of drugs and the havoc they can wreak on a family and individuals.

I put on a smile and shake my head.

"No, I'm only here to provide support." I motion toward Bray-den beside me.

"How did you find it?" I glance at Brayden, who looks a bit lighter. He smiles broadly at everyone and shakes their hands as we walk past. I'd say today was a win. "It was great." He smiles. "It felt good getting it off my chest, you know. It was good to hear other people's stories and know that I'm not on my own in this. Michael and Geoff shared their contact info with me and told me to reach out if I have any questions or need advice outside of the group."

"Why?" I snap. "Why can't you wait and see them in a group? Why do you need their number? What can they really do to help?" I fire at him. There's no need for him to have men's numbers. I'm here if he needs help. I can help him.

"Uh, I don't know. I suppose if I'm having a bad day with Bex." He shrugs.

"I'm here though, you know that. You can message or call me?"

He smiles. "I do." And then his eyes go wide as he looks over my shoulder. "Oh my god, it's been so long since I've had one of these. Do you mind if we stop to get one?" He gestures to the shop behind me, which is called Candy Shake. With a glowing face, Brayden gazes up at the sign. And there's no way I could say no at this moment.

"Sure." I nod as we walk in. Brayden orders some weird milkshakes. It seems that you can choose any candy you want for these milkshakes, and they blend everything together. I hadn't even heard of half the candy Brayden asked for. I opted to keep my teeth from rotting and didn't get one.

When he gets it, there's a generous amount of ice cream on top, with a multitude of rainbow sprinkles.

"That looks like a sugar rush in a cup." I laugh.

"It's so good!"

"What are those?" I point to the sweets on top.

"Nerds Clusters." He takes one with his teeth and crunches into it, saying. "My favorite."

"I'll take your word for it." I roll my eyes, smirking as we exit the shop. Once we reach the car and get in, he asks me to hold his shake while he fastens the seatbelt. I stare at the clusters on top while gripping the drink in my hand.

After fastening his belt, he smirks and teases, "I can tell you're curious to try it."

I'm not going to lie. I give in to temptation and lick the melting ice cream, gathering a few clusters. I notice Brayden's eyes following my tongue as he visibly swallows. The ice cream is enjoyable, but I have to close my eyes when I bite into the cluster.

"Fuck, they are sour." I blindly put the cup out in front of me for Brayden to take the cup and he howls out laughing. I open my eyes. "That's gross, Brayden. What the fuck."

My laughter can't mask the persistent sour taste in my mouth. Observing Brayden lick the same spot while never breaking eye contact ignites an instant, undeniable response as my dick begins to swell. I snap my eyes away and turn the engine on, making sure I don't let my gaze meet Brayden's again. I fear if I do, the next image I will get is him licking the ice cream off my dick.

As we approach campus, Brayden, who I need to remember to drop off at Pythons, breaks the silence.

"What are your plans for the rest of the weekend?" I can't shake off the thought of the decision I made earlier, and I'm unsure why I feel awkward telling him. It's true, I do like Brayden, but there are countless factors that continuously yank me out of the imaginary world I seem to inhabit whenever I'm in his presence. He's my student, he's nineteen, I would lose my job and Denny. Oh, and there's this other thing—I have no idea what's going on with me. Is this a moment that has just happened? Is this feeling going to last forever? Will I develop an attraction toward men now? Am I still attracted to women? That's what had me texting Ms. Banksy last night after I had wrapped my hand around my dick and came for probably the tenth time to a picture of Brayden, asking if she fancied dinner and drinks tonight.

"Uhh, I...um, have a date tonight." I quickly admit the remaining words and stay focused on the vehicle in front of me.

"With who?" Brayden's voice isn't angry, but it's not exactly cheerful either. I steal a quick glance at him as he maintains a blank expression while staring at the milkshake.

"Ms. Banksy," I mutter.

Without uttering a word, Brayden simply gazes out the window. In a matter of moments, we park outside Pythons.

"Thanks for today. It was appreciated." In a hurry, he gets out of the car, turns, and stoops down to say, "Enjoy your date."

There's clear anger in his eyes. I'm struggling to find the right words to tell him that I'm feeling scattered and need to sort things out. Brayden slams the door with excessive force, causing me to wince. I watch him walking toward a trash can, where he disposes of the nearly full milkshake before walking away with slumped shoulders and a lowered head.

My stomach sinks. A sudden wave of sickness washes over me as I come to terms with the fact that I'm responsible for his sadness. Why didn't I keep my mouth shut?

13
Brayden 'Quake' Anders

Chapter Twenty-Five
Brayden

Fuck him. *Punch.*

Fuck him and his sexy-as-fuck ass. *Smack.*

Fuck him and his beautiful as fuck smile. *Wack.*

Fuck him and his meaningless fucking words. *Thump.*

Over and over again, I unleash my frustrations on the bag in front of me. The rhythmic thud of my fists against the bag echoes my inner chaos. I'm confused about why he's going on a date with Ms. Banksy after the way he looked at me. What have these last couple of weeks been about?

I know he's my teacher.

I know lines have blurred.

And I know this is fucked up.

But I want him. I want him so fucking bad.

I side-eye the clock on the wall. It's 9 p.m., and he's probably out with her, having dinner as we speak. Despite not being allowed in here at night, Mr. Stiles understands my need for this place and provided me with the code to enter when it's locked.

Thank God he did. I wanted so badly to call Lan and get lost in him tonight. But I hate the fact that even the thought of touching another guy makes me feel sick. What the fuck has this man done to me? I've become an obsessed little boy who has a crush on his teacher.

Fuck, no. I beat the bag until my knuckles bleed.

I didn't wrap my hands.

I wanted to feel the pain.

I wanted to see the blood.

It's not enough.

I pause, reach into my bag, take out my phone, and send a text to Lan. Telling him to be at my dorm in fifteen. I need more, this isn't enough.

As I grab my bag and head for the doors, they suddenly open.

There he stands.

We both come to an abrupt stop. I observe his smart black dress shirt, buttoned up, and his matching black jeans. His disheveled hair, appearing as though someone had raked their fingers through it, causes my jaw to clench. Most likely Ms. Banksy. He looks wrecked, or is this his freshly fucked appearance?

His eyes wander over me, taking in my appearance before becoming fixated on my hands covered in blood. His eyes turn fierce, and he quickly approaches me.

Stepping closer, he grips my free hand, and exclaims, "What the hell did you do?"

I quickly withdraw my hand from his grasp. I don't want his hands on me, especially after touching someone else.

"Nothing." I pass by him and begin making my way toward the doors.

"Why are you here?" he questions.

I stop and turn on my heels abruptly. "Why am I here? Why are you here? Shouldn't you be on your date?" I raise an eyebrow at him.

He opens his mouth, but quickly shuts it, causing me to chuckle sarcastically before I turn around. I make it to the doors, but I don't make it through as the next words stop me.

"I didn't go." Exhaustion is clear in his barely audible voice. He didn't go. I feel a warmth spreading through me as my stomach churns. Three words are all it takes to wash away the anger and rage within me. *I didn't go.*

"Why?" I stay facing the doors, needing to know why he didn't go. If it's because she canceled, I'll leave and never think about that man again.

Lies, but okay.

"Why do you think, Brayden?" He chuckles, as if it's clearly obvious. "Look at me." I pause for a moment. His soft voice pleads, "Brayden, please," he begs, making my heart stutter. "Please look at me, Bray." The nickname *Bray* melts something within me. Slowly, I turn toward him, avoiding direct eye contact with him initially. Nervously, I avert my gaze downward.

His voice, shattered and weak, utters, "Bray."

I glance up. In that moment, our eyes lock, and it feels as if an invisible wall between us crumbles. Finally allowing us to be vulnerable and connected with nothing standing in our way.

"You," he says.

"Me?"

"Yes. You. You're the reason I didn't go on the date."

"Why." I need to hear him say it. I need to know it's not just in my fucked-up mind. I am certain of his feelings toward me, but I need to hear it from him directly. I stand frozen in place as he approaches me, watching his slow advance. Despite the dim lighting in the studio, I can see his face and the hunger in his eyes as he moves closer to me. My heart quickens, and I gulp, struggling to catch my breath through my nose.

"It's a scary moment when you realize that you have feelings for someone you're not supposed to, and those feelings are completely unfamiliar to you. Experiencing same-sex attraction after always being interested in a different sex can be both confusing and exhilarating." Mr. Stiles inches nearer, never breaking eye contact. "You have this sense of not really knowing yourself.

It's taken me forty years to find my true self." He pauses, reaching out and tracing a finger along my jawline and causing a gasp to leave my lips. "But do you know which feeling completely consumes you, Bray? The feeling that arises when you acknowledge these newfound emotions. You come to accept that this is who you are." He takes one more step, stopping dead in front of me, leaving only a few inches between us.

"And in that moment, you come to accept that no one else exists except that one person. Because if you go one more day without feeling that person's lips against yours, you will simply cease to exist." I gasp and take a moment to process his words, staring at him in complete disbelief.

"Brayden. Kiss me," he whispers, and I'm not sure why, but I become paralyzed. I am unable to move. I try to speak but end up closing my mouth. The air thickens between us, charged with unspoken desire. His gaze holds mine, a magnetic pull that defies reason. I feel the rapid flutter of my pulse, the heat rising in my cheeks. We're standing on the cliff of something forbidden, and it's intoxicating.

"I—uh."

His eyes darken. He knows what I want, what we both want. His fingers trace the curve of my jaw.

"Ahh, fuck it." Mr. Stiles twists my baseball cap around, and then he's kissing me—hard, urgent, as if time itself is collapsing around us. Our lips crash together, and it's a wildfire, consuming doubt and hesitation. In that stolen moment, I forget everything else—the rules, the consequences. There's only this ache, this hunger. And as our mouths move hungrily against each other, I realize that existence itself centers on this kiss. If I stop now, I'll cease to be. But if I surrender completely, I'll lose myself in him.

And maybe, just maybe, that's exactly what I want.

Tilting my head to the side, I open my mouth wider for Mr. Stiles' probing tongue. As soon as our tongues intertwine, a blazing fire ignites within me, spreading throughout my whole body. My fingers weave through his hair as our kiss becomes more desperate. My stomach flutters, my legs become jelly, and my dick fucking aches with how hard it is right now. Mr. Stiles moans into my mouth as our tongues urgently tangle with each other's. He backs me up until I hit what I think is the punching bag. I turn us around as I back him up into the wall.

Our lips remain connected, unbroken. He spins me again and my back hits the wall, hard. He pushes into me, and if it wasn't for his body flush with mine, I don't think I would be standing. The pressure of his hard dick against mine ignites my nerve endings, and I instinctively press back into him, grinding against each other. I have never experienced such an explosive kiss before, one that ignites a primal desire within me, tempting me to drop to my knees and beg for more.

In that moment, I am willing to do almost anything Mr. Stiles asks if it means having his lips on mine. Reluctantly, Mr. Stiles ends the kiss, leaving me wanting more as I lean forward to capture his lips again, not wanting this ride he has me on to end. This time, the kiss is more tender, as our tongues lazily graze each other, creating a rhythmic feeling that gives me spine-tingling shivers. Mr. Stiles grips my head tighter, then slowly withdraws, leaning his forehead against mine as we both struggle to regulate our erratic breathing. Filled with desire, his eyes lock with mine in a silent exchange as we regain our composure.

The room fades away—there's only us and our hunger for each other. Time cracks, and I surrender to the pull, knowing that in this stolen moment, we've crossed a threshold from which there's no return.

The room pulses with heat, our breaths ragged. He places a gentle kiss on my lips. His mouth travels from mine, mapping a trail of fire along my jawline. My skin burns where his lips touch, and I'm lost in him, totally and completely lost and honestly, I don't want to find my way back. I want to stay here with him.

The world outside ceases to exist. There's only us—two souls hovering on the edge of surrender.

"This changes everything," I murmur, my voice a fragile thread. His lips, warm and relentless, feathers across my ear, igniting flames within me. The world blurs, and I cling to him, craving more.

His raspy voice echoes, "Good." His harsh breaths fan my face. "It's never felt like that before," he whispers, and I don't even need to ask him what he means because I know. I've kissed dozens of guys, and none has even been on the same galaxy as that.

"I know," I reply as he places a gentle kiss on my lips, one time, two times.

"Your lips are so soft," he murmurs. I smile as he continues kissing my lips. My stomach flips again and again.

When will these butterflies calm the fuck down?

It's as if I've been on a ride that has pumped me with unlimited adrenaline. I feel like I could run to the moon and back.

I brush my hands against Mr. Stiles' stubbled beard. "I wish I could say the same."

"Shit, sorry." His eyes moving to my cheeks. "You have red marks around your lips." With closed lips, he smiles, as if he's attempting to contain his laughter.

"It feels good," I say, my eyes bouncing between his amused gaze.

"Yeah?" He raises his eyebrow before moving his face and rubbing his beard against the side of my lips and moving over to the other cheek.

"Stop." My voice pitches high as a laugh escapes me as I try to move away from Mr. Stiles, but he holds me in a tight cocoon, rubbing his rough beard against my face. Although it stings slightly, I welcome it. I want to feel him on me for days. I wish he could rub himself all over me.

"I meant—" I let out a squeal resembling a fucking girl. "My lips."

He stops immediately.

"Oh, yeah?" His gaze becomes intense as his eyes fixate on my lips. Once again, he tilts his head and gives me a tender kiss on the lips. I am overcome by the feeling of spinning, tingling, and an intense craving for him, as if I'm drunk on him.

"You're so fucking hot, Brayden. I could kiss you until the end of time and it still wouldn't be enough." His eyes focus intently on my lips, a smile spreading wider across his face.

As I observe him closely, I notice the charming way his eyes crinkle at the corners, the fine lines that frame them, subtly hinting at his age.

Despite these small signs, the rest of his appearance is flawless, exuding a timeless attraction. His hair, a rich shade of chestnut, is perfectly styled, complementing his strong jawline and high cheekbones. His skin is smooth and radiant, with a healthy glow that suggests he takes great care of himself. I never realized how fucking beautiful Mr. Stiles is.

"It was fucking breathtaking seeing you kiss, but to actually be receiving it, it's mind blowing," he exhales softly against my lips. With a forceful motion, he slams his lips onto mine and once again uses his tongue to explore my mouth. We can't get enough of each other, drinking each other up. While we devour each other, our tongues fiercely compete for control. Mr. Stiles snaps away so fast that I have to hold on to the wall behind me to stop myself from falling sideway. Our attention is immediately drawn to the door as we hear a loud bang in the distance. Mr. Stiles takes a few steps back and the door swings open. A dark shadow stands at the darkened door and then a body appears in the dim lights.

I narrow my eyes and make out the image before muttering, "Shit."

Lan's face becomes visible. With wide eyes, he glances at me and then shifts his attention to Mr. Stiles. With both of us breathing heavily, I can't begin to imagine what this situation looks like, especially when Mr. Stiles just stepped away from me.

"Lan, what are you doing here?" I rasp, trying to clear my throat.

"I...uh, thought you might be caught up here. I came to find you after waiting outside your dorm, just like you asked," he says, awkwardly hugging himself and shifting his weight between his feet.

"Oh, yeah. Uhm—"

Mr. Stiles stands there, his lips sealed, observing both Lan and me. He raises an eyebrow before uttering.

"I'm going to be heading off. Your form is better."

I frown, and then realize he is trying to make it come across that he was helping me with my boxing.

"Thanks." My stomach sinks. He knows I told Lan to come over. He knows I was going to fuck Lan. Shit. Usually, Lan avoids direct eye contact with Mr. Stiles, but I witness Lan's eyes lingering on Mr. Stiles' face as he walks past and says something under his breath. I draw nearer to Lan and notice his eyes wandering across my face as he frowns and furrows his brow.

Scratching the back of my neck, awkwardly, I say, "I'm tired now. Sorry. I pushed myself a little too much in here tonight." I gesture with my busted hand, and he nods rapidly, but never breaks his stare from my mouth.

"You have something on your face and around your lips?" He points to his cheek. "Looks like a rash, are you all right?" he asks, frowning.

Forcing a smile, I reply, "Yeah, just hot. Let's go." I walk alongside him as we exit the doors and pass through the gym.

Once we're outside, I turn to him. "I'll see you around, okay?"

Lan eyes me with a slight frown, appearing suspicious as he turns and peers over his shoulder at a retreating Mr. Stiles, who I hadn't realized I was watching. Lan catches my attention as he faces forward again.

"Okay." He nods slowly, and I turn around to head back to my dorm in the opposite direction. I hear my phone make a sound and I take it out to find an Instagram direct message. As I read the message, the butterflies that had settled down come back to life.

@thestilestman: If you touch a single inch of skin on that kid, I swear I will make you regret it. I don't share.

I try to suppress the grin that's eager to appear on my face by biting my lip. I type back.

@quakeontheice: The only skin my fingers will touch is yours.

Chapter Twenty-Six

Bohdi

I knew I couldn't go on the date on Saturday night. I was telling myself it's what I needed instead of accepting what my body and mind already knew.

It's him I want. Brayden Anders.

No matter how much I tried to deny it to myself.

He was my calm among my storm.

He was the person who had unknowingly picked me back up. Being around Brayden makes the grief a little easier to carry.

I don't dread my days when I wake up anymore. I look forward to them because I know I will see him. I finally found the person who, in those moments of them being around, the pain eases. It's barely noticeable when they are near or when you think of them. I finally found that person to make the pain go away.

After dropping Brayden off on Saturday, I went home, took the picture of Jace out of my nightstand, and placed it on top. I didn't stare at it and then put it away. Instead, I asked him what he would do, and I know what he would have done.

He would have told me to accept the feelings.

He wouldn't have been disappointed like my dreams.

He would have told me you can't help who you fall for, Boh. You can't help who you catch feelings for. You can't help what your heart wants.

He would have told me not to fight it.

I know he would have, because that was Jace. He was the purest soul out there. He accepted anyone and everyone, no matter who they were or who they liked.

They say grief reshapes us, often for the worse, but in losing Jace, I discovered my true self. This is who I am now, shaped by love and loss. I listened to my body and my heart when I left Brayden. I allowed myself to feel the ache in my chest from his presence not being there. The sickness deep in my stomach from wanting to see his smile and not his sadness. I imagined myself standing in front of him and telling him how I felt and his lips touching mine in a silent confession. I finally listened to my true self.

It wasn't Ms. Banksy I wanted. It wasn't any other women; it wasn't any other man; it was Brayden.

Only Brayden.

Is it complicated? Undoubtedly.

Difficult? Absolutely.

Could Brayden tire of the thrill of dating his teacher? Perhaps.

Yet, I couldn't continue day after day without confessing. The unknown—what it felt like to kiss him—haunted me. Nothing prepared me for that moment. It was unlike anything I've ever experienced. Standing before Brayden, my heart ached for his lips on mine. In that clash of need, barriers crumbled. He became the missing piece, filling the empty spaces in my life. One kiss, and I was whole.

"Good morning, sir." Matilda's voice jolts me from my Monday morning daydream. She glides into the classroom, settling at a front row desk, her fingers twirling strands of hair. "Did you have a pleasant weekend, sir?" Her grin is wide. Week after week, she emails me, seeking extra guidance on her project, struggling with tasks that should be straightforward. With one of the highest GPAs in the university, she puzzles me. And yet, my inbox overflows with messages from her and other female students. I chuckle inwardly—I'm their forty-year-old teacher. What delusion leads them to believe I'd risk everything for a fling with a student?

The irony of my thoughts is laughable.

If that person is worth it, then it's worth risking it all, and that's what I have learned. Brayden is worth losing it all. My feelings for him hit me out of nowhere. One minute, I was intrigued, and the next, I struggled to get through a day without seeing him. I don't know what happened and when, but all I know is I don't think I could let him walk away from me, even if he wanted to.

Once more, my mind drifts to Brayden, pulling me from the classroom's reality as students trickle in. "It was good," I reply to Matilda, my smile strained. "Thanks. I hope you had a good weekend, too." I aim to end the conversation, relieved when her friends arrive and engage her in chatter. But not before I catch a few glances from them as well.

Jesus Christ.

My heart races as a deep laugh echoes from behind the door. I recognize that laugh—it's the same one I heard only two nights ago when I held him close, our faces pressed together. It's a laugh etched into my memory, evoking the joy that grew within me. My focus remains fixed on the door as Kal enters, followed by Trayton and Bray. And there he is—my Bray. Our eyes lock, and the world fades away. The invisible thread that binds us pulls relentlessly, urging me to cross the room, to claim those soft lips that leave me tingling. Brayden's eyes hold life, happiness. Could it be because of me? I swallow, desperate to hold him, to touch him.

"Yes, yes, Mr. Stiles!" Trayton shouts, walking up the stairs, snapping Brayden's stare away from me as I glance up at Trayton, who takes his seat.

"Yo, you lot should see Mr. Stiles in the boxing gym!" Trayton shouts to the entire class. "Teach takes no prisoners."

Kal's shaking his head, drawing my attention to him as a few boys mutter, "I bet I could take him."

To save their ego, I don't say anything, but I know for a fact with one blink I would have them on the floor. My gaze moves to Brayden as he bites his lip to stifle a laugh as he walks past Trayton to sit between him and Kal. It always intrigues me. They sit at those particular desks and in a specific order, each time. Brayden is always in the middle.

"Let's proceed without bruising anyone's ego," I quip, rolling my eyes. Adjusting my laptop, I project the presentation on the screen as the class settles down, amused. "As you work on your projects," I continue, "remember my email is in the syllabus. Don't hesitate to reach out with questions—I'm here to assist." Guiding them through the slides, I emphasize the significance of marketing in business.

During the lecture, Brayden's gaze finds mine repeatedly. He doesn't glance at the presentation; instead, his eyes remain fixed on me. As I gesture toward the screen, stretching slightly, I notice Brayden's hungry examination. His emotions play across his face, visible to anyone observing. Tingles stir within me, a mix of anticipation and desire. When our eyes lock, a smug smirk curves his lips, teeth breaking through the tension.

This fucker.

I ask the class to get on with the project, needing to sit down behind my desk. As my dick hardens wondering what Brayden was thinking of in those moments, his eyes were wondering over me.

I have thought about the fact I haven't even touched another guy's dick other than my own and he's had plenty of experience. But it can't be much different from being with a girl, surely?

In this room filled with students, my thoughts veer to vivid images—Brayden addressing me as *sir* as I sink my dick into his tight hole. The heat of desire floods through me, prompting me to loosen a few buttons on my dress shirt. Why did he have to look at me the way he did? I wouldn't be sitting here in a full classroom with a dick hard as a rock and balls aching, begging for release. I hear movement, and I tell myself not to look up because I know that damn fucking force will have my eyes meeting his. No matter how many times I tell my brain not to try to find him, it's the first thing it does when he's in my proximity.

I glance up, and immediately I'm met with Brayden, jogging down the stairs and making his way toward my desk.

Fuck.

"Brayden," I mutter under my breath. My dick weeps just by his near presence and my heart flutters like a teenager sneaking a peek at something forbidden. How is it I'm forty years old and my dick is leaking over my nineteen-year-old student standing in front of me?

"Can I borrow a pen?" His voice, chirpy and upbeat, makes me grind my teeth because he has no idea what he is doing to me by being near me.

I extend my hand, holding my pen, while keeping my eyes firmly on my laptop screen and avoiding looking up at him again. I gasp as Brayden's fingers graze the back of my hand while he takes the pen. It feels like a lightning strike. He didn't need to do that.

He didn't need to touch me when he took the pen from my hand.

But he did. He knows what he's doing.

Our eyes lock, smoldering and heavy. A thousand words pass between us, unspoken yet screaming louder than anything else in this room.

Those fucking eyes.

"Stop watching me like that while I'm trying to teach, Brayden," I hiss, infusing my voice with a hint of danger. He leans down, ostensibly studying a paper on my desk, but those intoxicating eyes remain locked on mine, a smug smirk playing on his lips.

Close enough that I can feel the puffs of air that leave his mouth, he murmurs, "Stop acting as if you don't like it, sir." The fucker winks and turns his back to me, striding back to his desk. My eyes follow him and unfortunately drop to watch his ass in the slightly fitted sweatpants he wears.

My dick pulses with those leaving words. Because he is right as much as I voice he needs to stop. My body and mind crave his eyes on me.

13
Brayden 'Quake' Anders

Chapter Twenty-Seven
Brayden

This week has been harder than expected. I've barely been able to see Mr. Stiles. I could only do the two extra classes this week because I had extra training for the game today and in those classes, Mr. Stiles was annoyingly professional. I get it. He wants to help me, but it was painfully distracting when he was talking and his words blurred into nothing. Because all I wanted to do was leap on to him and crash my lips to his.

Lines blurred.

He was just any teacher.

Who I then found hot.

Who I then got feelings for.

I never truly understood what feelings felt like until I tasted Mr. Stiles.

It has to be feelings; I've never felt anything like this before. The butterflies that won't die the fuck down. They're constant from the minute I wake up to the minute I go to bed. And why is that? Because from the minute I wake up to the minute I go to bed, all I do is think of Mr. Stiles. His face, his lips, his body. It's a never-ending cycle of images in my mind.

But also, it hasn't escaped me, and everyone else around me, that for once I'm happy.

Cope keeps telling Kal and Tray that I'm whistling every morning and even hear me singing in the shower. Kal and Tray nearly dropped their drinks when they heard that. I eye rolled them and told them they were being dramatic. But they're not. When have I ever whistled or sung in the shower? Never.

Kal has been eyeing me suspiciously lately, and it's killing me not telling Kal and Tray about Mr. Stiles. It doesn't sit right with me. I never hide things from them, but I can't tell them this. They won't understand.

No one will. Tray is convinced it's because of Lan. Kal, being the weird detective he is, is adamant it's not Lan, and it's someone else, but he can't work out who.

I've told them I'm just happy that things are looking up with Bex, which I am.

Singing in the shower happily is a tad far-fetched though.

"I need you to make me proud today, boys. You have worked your fucking ass off this week. Now get out there and show these Chicago Cheetahs what the Devil Hawks are about!"

I go to put my headphones in, but the coach interrupts me. "Anders, get your ass over here." Here we go.

"Sure thing, Coach," I reply, trudging toward him, already laced up in my skates, eager to hit the ice.

"Your brother isn't here today, is he?" His gaze bores into mine.

"No, Coach." I chuckle.

"Good. I want nothing fucking today up, Anders. Fuck them up in play, shatter them with your mind, but no blood." He pauses. "On purpose."

"Nothing will go wrong today, Coach. We got this." I wink at him and turn around, going back to the locker to grab my phone.

"Shatter them, Quake," Coach mutters behind me.

"Always," I toss back, my gaze sweeping the room. Kal's lost in thought, plotting his next move like a seasoned detective. Tray, on the other hand, flips his lucky coin—a jewel no one dares touch. And then there's me, lost in a song that resurrects memories of better days.

Slipping on my headphones, I sink into weightlessness. Bexley's voice fills my mind, and I know those moments will return, the goofy friendship, the shared laughter. A smile tugs at my lips; today feels promising. I'm ready to shatter the cheetahs. If only Mr. Stiles could witness it. In a home game, he'd be there. But my phone buzzes, interrupting the song. I ignore it, appreciating the music. As the last note fades, I glance at my screen, grinning. Then, poof, my phone vanishes.

"Tray, I'm not fucking around. Give it back now." My heart races as Tray stands behind Kal as if he will do anything, but even Kal is raising an eyebrow at my reaction. My phone is locked, and Tray can't get on the text thread, but he can see what Mr. Stiles sent me and I have no idea what it even says. Hot flushes travel through me as I pin Tray with a serious expression putting my hand out for the phone. "I'm not fucking around." I should have known Tray wouldn't give a shit if he pissed me off. He peeks down at the phone and frowns, and then his eyes meet mine. They widen as a smile broadens into a full-blown grin.

"The fact I love you, I won't say anything out loud, but, Kal," he says, showing Kal the screen, who frowns down and then shifts his attention to me.

"Fuck's sake," I mutter.

Kal eyebrows meet his hairline as he says. "Not gonna lie, I'm shocked," he admits.

Tray, quieter now, approaches. His eyes bore into mine, curiosity laced with confusion.

"You? Brayden Anders. A sub?" he whispers. I open my mouth to protest, then it hits me. Snatching the phone from Tray, I glance down.

Sir:

S2R8S24

Mr. Stiles asked for my number and told me not to save him under something discreet. I didn't think about how it would look to someone else, though. Now they think I'm submissive, which is laughable.

"Is that some kink code or something?" Tray asks, walking behind me as I head back to my locker to put my phone away.

"No, Tray," I sigh out. Rubbing my temple, I try to work out what I can say, but there is nothing. I will have to let them think I'm a sub. This is a fucking joke. As I approach my locker, I glance down at the screen, frowning at Mr. Stiles' text. I have no idea what he's talking about.

Me:

??

What does that message even mean? I can't wait around for his reply. Everyone's streaming out of the locker room. I toss my phone into my locker and snatch my helmet.

"You're not getting off that easily," Tray whispers in my ear, leaning over my shoulder. "I want all the details."

"You're worse than a fucking girl," I snap back. Suddenly, a firm hand lands on my ass, and I whip around to find Tray grinning.

"My bad—you probably got turned on by that," he quips, erupting into laughter. Kal joins in. And I wonder why I'm friends with these idiots.

As we step out onto the ice, the stadium echoes with the collective roar of the crowd. The ice awaits, pristine and unforgiving. My eyes sweep across the sea of colors—the Devil Hawks' faithful in black and red, a stark contrast to the Chicago Cheetahs' white and orange jerseys. It's an away game, but our supporters are here in force.

Kal taps his stick against my knee pads, a familiar pregame ritual. His head collides with mine, helmet to helmet. "What's the plan today, Quake?" he shouts, adrenaline in his eyes.

"We're shattering," I reply, my grin matching his intensity.

"That we are, baby." Kal winks, then glides off to claim his position on the ice. The game awaits, and we're ready to leave them in pieces.

I come head-to-head with the Cheetahs' forward. He's built like a fucking brick house that isn't coming down from no earthquake. Of course, on the one day I need to show the scouts what I'm about, I'm up against the fucking hulk.

But they say the bigger they are, the harder they fall. People shatter upon impact. His eyes, filled with pure hatred, lock onto mine. He knows me, and he aims to break me.

Not a chance.

On the ice, noise fades; it's just me, my teammates, the puck, and the goal. The rest? Mere obstacles to skate around. The brute opposite me smirks.

"Quake, isn't it?" he asks.

"And you are?" I question. His eyes darken—I've hit a nerve. "Actually," I add, "you're the one with that . . . mom." His anger flares, and from the corner of my eye, I see the puck ascend. This is my moment.

"What mom?" he grits.

I wink. "The mom that sucks great dick."

It works every fucking time. The shock freezes them for that second just enough time to get the upper hand. I breeze past him, my speed too much for him to right himself. I instantly pass the puck to Kal as we push forward, but then, out of nowhere, the opposing brute blindsides Kal, stealing the puck. Kal collides with the boards, wincing. I'm already racing up the ice. Cope signals, and I know what's coming.

The brute may be a wall, but Cope's speed defies physics. He maneuvers around, leaving the brute bewildered. The puck connects with Cope's stick, slicing through the ice to meet Tray's blade. I surge forward, eyes on the opposing goal, seeking an opening. But a body check sends me sprawling. I'm up instantly, Tray passing the puck to Kal. He weaves through defenders, the puck dancing on his stick. And then, in a flash, the light ignites—the scoreboard confirms it. Kal scores.

We all skate over to him, and he hits my knee pads with his stick, smiling. The next faceoff—the puck escapes me, and the Cheetahs seize the upper hand, scoring within seconds. Annoyance simmers, but we stay in the game. They're a relentless team, one I underestimated during my hasty research. Body checks rain down—I taste blood, but it fuels me. The ache is my lifeline, the ice my sanctuary. Maxton, worn and bloodied, faces the brute. He won't let us down. Overtime looms—a single goal will rewrite our fate. The puck meets my stick; the goal consumes my vision. I unwind my brain—obstacles blur. You've conquered worse; this is no different, I tell myself. The opposing team come together, quick and merciless. I dip, weave, slide the puck to Tray. He passes it back—a dance of trust. I speed toward the net—the goal, my singular purpose. Their defense tackles me, stick against stick. The stadium vibrates—the fans' screams blend with the stick's echo. The net becomes my universe, the crowd a distant hum. I flick the puck, no longer bound by ice. It sails through the goalie's legs.

And then—the eruption.

We won.

Victory tastes like blood and echoes in my bones.

Chapter Twenty-Eight

Bohdi

This week has been a hurricane—a relentless storm of aching. I know the taste of Brayden's lips, the silk of his mouth against mine. It's etched into my senses, a craving that dares reason. The classroom becomes our battleground, and he tests me—those endless blue eyes like a vortex pulling me in. I want to touch him. Claim him. I stumble over words during my presentations. His gaze, intense, intoxicating, drives me to the edge. I ache to scream, to seize him, to make him mine in front of everyone. But we've only spoken through texts—a fragile thread connecting us. It's not enough. I hunger for more. His skin, his breath, the taste of him. He's an obsession, buried deep in the roots tangled with my sanity.

I need to see him, touch him, taste him again.

That's why I'm here.

Section 2, Row 8, Seat 24.

I couldn't go this weekend without seeing him. I knew when he arrived back from this game, he would be too tired to see me. As much as I know he would have, it wouldn't be fair. He needs to rest, especially with all the classes. That's why I've kept my hands to myself. My resolve teeters on the edge, because I know once I touch him, that will be it. My resolve will snap, and I won't be able to stop. I can't, not at work, not in the classroom—there, the air crackles with our unspoken tension. My desk, once a sanctuary, now holds memories of stolen glances, of lips that never met but hungered in those moments. His lingering scent alone is enough to drive me insane with need.

The rink echoes with ice scraping against skates. Bodies blur—a masterpiece of speed and desire. I pull my baseball cap lower, concealing my face. And hoping no one recognizes me. I can see the top of Denny's head, which keeps pacing, and I catch the odd glimpse of his hands wailing at his players.

I wonder if he knows he's going slightly bald on top of his head. I smile to myself because there is not a chance I will be the one to bring that to his attention.

My eyes lock onto number 13 as he glides across the ice, my heart pounding in sync with each swift motion of his skates. Brayden moves with the swagger of a man who owns not just the rink, but the very air around it. Even when the puck isn't tethered to his stick, he exudes confidence, weaving through opponents as if they're mere statues, leaving a trail of awe in his wake. Each time he's hit, my heart clenches. I grip the seat edges, torn between leaping to my feet and racing down to the ice. His passion, his unwavering commitment to the team—it's magnetic. Even when he falls, my stomach twists in knots. But Brayden defies gravity, rising in an instant. The collective tension in the stadium eases; the Quake still stands.

The opposing team hungers for his downfall, yet as I watch him, I realize how much he's overcome, the battles he's faced. Brayden shows resilience. He gets knocked down, he rises, unyielding. Overtime arrives, and the air thickens with anticipation. The puck finds Brayden's stick once more, and the crowd rises as one. On tiptoes, we witness the clash—the defenseman's stick, the flicker of the puck. Then, with precision, Brayden sends it soaring. Through the goalie's legs it slips, and the Devil Hawks' fans erupt.

And there, in that electrifying moment, my student becomes a legend. My heart swells with pride.

He's more than a player.

He's more than just my student.

He's mine.

The arena pulses with electric energy as the players exit the ice. The crowd envelops me, smiles and cheers washing over me like a tidal wave. A few people, drawn by my baseball cap, offer excited shoulder squeezes or friendly smacks on my back.

But my anticipation isn't for them—it's for Brayden.

I linger, careful not to overstay. The stadium empties, leaving me alone in the echoing aftermath. The distant echoes of the Zamboni scraping ice and the low hum of the overhead lights create an intimate feel. I don't know this place well, but I sent Brayden a text, telling him to wait in the locker rooms while everyone else leaves. I told him I wanted to call him without prying ears around. What excuse he'll make for his teammates and Denny, I can only wonder. Hopefully, his creativity works. Navigating unfamiliar corridors, I glance over my shoulder. The coast appears clear. I dash away from prying eyes. Near the tunnels, I discover what appears to be a cleaning closet. Testing the handle, I let out a sigh of relief when it opens. I slip inside, time stretching as I wait. The air smells faintly of cleaning supplies, a sharp contrast to the adrenaline-laden atmosphere outside.

It feels like I've been in here for an hour, but it's only been around half that time. Voices approach, a mix of murmurs and Trayton's unmistakable booming voice. That must be them leaving. Hopefully, Brayden stayed behind. I wait five more minutes and then crack the door, taking a peek out to make sure the coast is clear. Once I'm happy it is, I slip out, walking toward the lockers. As I get closer, I take slow quiet steps and open the door quietly. There's a small walkway to walk down and the locker room opens up before me—an expanse of anticipation. I scan the area for a moment, thinking Brayden must have left, and then, as if the universe conspired to test my resolve, I see him emerge from a door.

From the showers.

A pristine white towel clings to his waist, accentuating the contours of his body. His hands move with purpose, raking through wet hair as streams cascade down his skin, tracing the chiseled lines of his abs. My eyes follow each droplet, a silent ache building within me. The towel in his hand vanishes, revealing tousled dark hair that falls across his face. Leaning down, he retrieves his phone, an unmistakable frown etching his features. The air crackles with tension—he waits, and I know it's for my call.

He stands back up, and it's as if the temperature rises instantly. My balls ache, my dick fills.

Water droplets cascade from his hair as he casually brushes them away, a lone strand falling across his eyes. His abs ripple with each twisting motion, and I ache to trace my fingertips along the contours of his muscular arms. The mere thought electrifies my skin, urging me to abandon my restraint—I must feel his touch. Before stepping out from behind the wall, I stand behind. I loosen my belt and tuck my dick up. It's hard as a fucking rock and I know the minute I'm near him, it's going to be leaking.

Emerging from behind the alcove, I clear my throat, and Brayden's eyes snap to mine. His gaze sweeps over me, from head to toe, as if reading secrets written on my skin. The charged air between us hums with anticipation, and I wonder if he sees the desire etched in every curve of my body for him. As the tension between us thickens, I step closer, drawn by that invisible force which is stronger than ever. His eyes lock onto mine, and the world around me comes to a halt. Everything fades away, leaving only the two of us in this charged moment. Once I'm standing in front of him, my palms cup his face, my fingers melting into his smooth skin and my lips meet his. He instantly opens up for me, allowing me to take everything I have craved over the past week. Every swipe of my tongue sends jolts to my dick as it leaks for him.

They say addiction is bad for you, but is it always? Brayden is the sweetest poison coursing through my veins. There's nothing bad about him. He's pure, He's the healthiest addiction, and I ache to overdose on him, relapsing with every heartbeat.

We stumble backward, seeking refuge against the wall. His hands explore and ignite every nerve. The world tilts on its axis as his dick, only tented by the towel, stands up straight as he rubs himself against me, against my hardness only concealed in my jeans.

"Fuck," he gasps. My lips attack his as he tries to speak.

"You're," he breathes, I moan into his mouth, pushing harder into him. "Here," he says breathlessly, biting at my lip. I pull away and our eyes connect, keeping us still in our bubble.

"I couldn't resist seeing you." My gaze drops to the tented white towel.

Brayden's eyes lock with mine, a blush creeping up his face before a devilish smirk curves his lips.

"Are you gonna do something about that?"

Everything inside me screams yes as he confidently smirks at me. I've imagined this moment—the touch, the hesitation—but now, I'm anything but hesitant. I want to feel his bare skin in my grip, watch his face as I unravel him with my hands and more. The air thickens.

I step closer, my fingers trembling with need as they trace the edge of the towel. Brayden's smirk widens, and he leans in, capturing my lips with a hunger that ignites every nerve. The world continues to stand still, leaving only the heat of our bodies, the urgency of our desire. His hand slides down my spine, and I press against him, feeling the hardness beneath the fabric. We're suspended in our bubble, where time bends and rules blur.

My body pulses with heat, our breaths mingling as if they've become one. Brayden's hands find the curve of my waist, pulling me as close as he can until there's no space left between us. His lips trail down my neck, leaving a trail of fire in their wake. I tilt my head back, surrendering to the sensation, the hunger, the longing. The towel falls forgotten to the floor. I gulp as my hands move between us and I wrap my hand around the smooth skin of his dick.

"Fuck," he rasps, tracing lazy kisses over my neck.

My dick fucking weeps for him. I slowly pump my hand once and he groans as if it pains him.

"I'm not gonna last long." His voice is a tortured whisper, as though pain and longing have merged into one. The knowledge that I'm the one that's doing this to him ignites a burning flame within me.

"Sir," he groans loudly, desperate. The tingling sensation begins in my balls at that one word. There's no way I'm coming in my pants. No way. I squeeze Brayden's dick slightly, more so trying to hold off my own dick from exploding.

"Fuck," he moans again, and I lean my head back to gaze at him. His hooded eyes, full of desire, lock onto mine, threatening to unravel my composure.

"Your eyes don't leave mine, Brayden." My voice comes out raspy and he nods eagerly, his mouth open and more moans filter through. I speed up my hand, secretly loving the way his eyes close slightly and they roll back.

"Brayden," I growl, reminding him. His eyes snap back to mine, and then widen slightly and his mouth opens as a harsh puff of air fans my face.

"Sir, I'm going to come," he rushes out, right before ropes of cum squirt over me and my hand. I look down, watching his dick pulse and leak and it undoes me. The word "sir" and witnessing his release overwhelms me, and I shudder, my body betraying me as if I'm an inexperienced teenage boy as I feel ropes of my own cum leak from my dick. A guttural grunt escapes my lips, and I squeeze my eyes shut, grateful for my jeans concealing the dampness beneath.

We both regulate our breathing, leaning our head on each other's shoulders.

"Fuck, that was amazing." Brayden's croaky voice has me grinning when I lean back, his cheek flushed and hair disheveled. I've decided this is my new favorite look on Brayden.

His post-orgasm look.

His hands brush my abs as they move downward, and I react swiftly, capturing them. His frown deepens, but I shake my head.

"I'm fine," I assure him. "Besides, we're running late for dinner." I flash a grin and take a step back. If I don't put some distance between us, I won't be leaving anytime soon.

"Dinner?" He frowns, lifting the towel from the floor and draping it around himself. My eyes trace his well-defined abs, and I gulp as I stare at the dried-up cum.

"Yes, well, we're not dining out for obvious reasons. Instead, I have brought dinner and we're heading to a secluded spot I know." I smile, pleased that I've already organized our evening. His face brightens, but then his eyes widen.

"Wait, where are you staying tonight?"

"I'm driving back tonight," I reply. Brayden's face scrunches up.

"No way," he protests. "It's over a four-hour drive home. Surely you can stay somewhere and drive back tomorrow?"

"It's fine," I assure him. "I have a lot to get done tomorrow. It's best I get back tonight." Brayden nods slowly, avoiding my gaze.

He hesitates, our eyes locking, his cheeks flushed. "Did you come all this way just to watch me play?" His words hang in the air.

I lean in, my lips brushing against his. "And to kiss you," I admit, feeling my heart flutter as his cheeks turn crimson.

I love the way I can make him blush.

"You got a bit more than you hoped for, then?" He smirks, his confidence returning.

"That I did." I grin, longing to touch him more. But I need to leave; if I touch him again, we won't be leaving this locker room.

"Okay," I say, snapping out of my thoughts. I don't have time to think about that right now. "I parked the car about five blocks away. I'll go grab it, and I'll pick you up on the corner where Walmart is down the road, okay?"

He nods.

"Wait, your hat." Brayden's eyes lock onto mine as he lifts my hat from the bench. His smile, a sunbeam breaking through clouds, warms my heart.

"Did you have this made?" he asks, his voice soft, fingers tracing the embroidered *13*.

I nod, my pulse racing.

"You're number 13's biggest fan." He chuckles, stepping closer.

The hat settles on my head, his breath warm against my skin. I fight the urge to reach for him. "Wear it every day," he murmurs, eyes darkening. I pull it low, concealing my face, and promise that when it's just us, I will wear it every minute if he wants me to.

Brayden bites his lip, trying to conceal that beautiful fucking smile of his, and he turns around and walks back to the showers. I spin on my heels, pacing to the exit. An ache tugs in my chest, my heart begging me to turn around and walk back in there.

Fuck. My body needs to get a grip on itself. I'll be seeing him again in a little while.

13
Brayden 'Quake' Anders

Chapter Twenty-Nine
Brayden

The rush of victory and Mr. Stiles's unexpected presence linger as I step into the shower, water cascading over my skin. His soft, insistent lips haunt me, sparking a deep, burning desire. How can someone be so flawless? I used to believe winning was the peak of my happiness, but now I know better. It's him—the way he looks at me, the way he makes my heart race. I scrub myself clean, making sure I use plenty of soap and kicking myself for not bringing my aftershave with me. Once I'm out of the shower, I grab my phone and find a message from Kal and Tray in the group chat?

Kal:

Have you finished talking to Bex?

Tray:

I got beers, we're ordering pizza. Do you want your weird BBQ base, chicken and pineapple pizza?

It's not weird, but okay. I don't know what excuse I can say to them, so I do what I do best and ignore them. Getting changed quickly; I pull on my baseball cap, but not before brushing my hair back.

Kal and Tray took my hockey gear with them when they left, so I grab my phone, placing it in my pocket of my gray sweatpants, and leave the locker room. Anticipation seeps through my body with every step I take out of the stadium. Knowing I'm finally going to spend time with Mr. Stiles fills me with excitement. Maybe I can finally get to know him more. Ask him questions, dig deep into his life. I know nothing about him, only what I've seen on his Instagram.

Once I leave the stadium, I turn left and walk toward Walmart, pulling my cap down tight. My hotel is right next to this stadium, and I can't risk Kal and Tray seeing me. As I approach Walmart, I see a blacked out chevy truck parked up which sticks out like a sore thumb. Why do I have a feeling this is Mr. Stiles' truck? I pull my phone out and there is already a text from Mr. Stiles.

Sir:

I'm here. Black Chevy.

I smirk because I just knew it. I walk up to the Chevy, open the door, and I swear every time I see him; he takes my breath away. I get in the truck and those damn butterflies start up again when his scent wraps around me.

"Hey," he says, his eyes crinkling at the corners as he leans over, brushing his lips against mine, his voice low and intimate. His fingers trail along the edge of my jaw, leaving a trail of warmth in their wake.

"Hey," I reply, my cheeks flushing. Who the fuck is this person who keeps blushing? It's pissing me off. I've faced opponents on the ice, brought them down to their fucking knees, but this man has the power to turn me into a blushing mess.

"Two cars?" I question, arching an eyebrow. This isn't the one I've been in. He casts me a quick glance before turning back to the road ahead.

"This is my baby," he says, smirking and rubbing the dash.

As we drive, Mr. Stiles talks about my game today. His enthusiasm is contagious. He describes my plays, the precision of my passes, the agility in my footwork, as if he's analyzing a masterpiece. And I soak it all in, hungry for his praise. It's different from the locker room banter, the high-fives from teammates. This is validation from someone who matters, someone I want to impress. The cityscape blurs outside the window, and I realize we're leaving the familiar streets behind.

"Where are we going?"

Mr. Stiles' eyes dance with mischief. "Wait and see," he replies.

His hand rests on the gearshift, fingers tapping a rhythm only he knows. The tension in the car is palpable, a magnetic pull that draws me closer. He's shed his sweater, revealing a short-sleeved white tee that clings to his arms. One hand casually drapes over the top of the wheel, the other bent, elbow resting on the truck door. His profile is a study in contrasts—the strong jawline softened by the curve of his lips, the intensity in his eyes tempered by a hint of vulnerability. The urge to leap onto him and devour him while he drives—it's primal, raw. I fidget in my seat, the ache and want for him twisting inside me. This hunger, it's not normal. My body rebels when I can't touch him, making me feel needy—a sensation I've always despised. Needy isn't in my vocabulary; it never has been. But he changes everything. His presence ignites unfamiliar feelings, pushes me beyond my boundaries. I huff, gaze fixed on the passing landscape. His car veers onto a dirt track, and I raise an eyebrow, glancing sideways.

"Should I be worried?" I ask, half-teasing.

His smirk is wicked. "Scared that I'm taking you to have my way with you up in some mountains?"

"I could think of worse things," I reply, my pulse quickening. Glancing around, all I see are trees—no mountains. Not that you would see those in Chicago anyway. That's disappointing.

We climb, trees crowding the path until suddenly, it opens up. Mr. Stiles eases the car to a stop, reversing it to the edge of a cliff like top. I step out, and awe washes over me—it's breathtaking.

"What is this place?" I ask, staring across Chicago as the sun dips, casting a warm glow. The city lights twinkle, painting a canvas of the city's beauty.

"I call it the viewpoint," he says, his voice distant, lost in memory. "I'm not from Chicago. I'm from Baltimore, but my brother and I used to come here sometimes. He found it in his college days." I love that I'm already catching glimpses of him.

"Let's stay here for a couple of hours," he says, leading me toward the back of his car. With a precise motion, he unlatches the trunk, revealing blankets and a picnic basket.

"You didn't," I tease, biting my lip to suppress a laugh.

"Is it cheesy?" His wince is cute as he rubs the back of his neck.

"Kinda, but cute," I reply, walking closer to him. Standing face-to-face, I suddenly feel unsure—how do I act with him? Can I kiss him? His gaze locks onto my lips, and he leans in, brushing them with a tender kiss. I want to pout like a spoiled schoolgirl when he pulls away; I can't get enough of him.

"After you." He smirks, gesturing for me to climb onto the back of his truck. I laugh, throwing my head back, and jump up, settling down, overlooking the city. It's breathtaking up here. Mr. Stiles joins me, moving with a swift accuracy that somehow makes him even more attractive.

He opens the picnic basket, and my eyes zero in on the candy. "Candy?" I ask, my grin threatening to burst out.

His lips twitch. "Something tells me you have a sweet tooth. You didn't finish your shake the other day—that was my fault—so I thought I'd make it up to you." The memory of him mentioning a date, and my stomach sinking, floods back. And in Mr. Stiles's eyes, I see echoes of that moment, a shared vulnerability. "Plus," he says, as if unveiling a secret, "you have candy in almost every other Instagram photo."

"So, you do watch me?" I grin, our eyes locking in a silent conversation that goes beyond words.

"All the time," he confesses, his tone casual yet loaded with meaning. "I like watching you." My heart stumbles, caught off guard by the simplicity of his words. *He likes watching me.* The thought sends a rush of warmth through my veins. His gaze shifts, tracing the city lights ahead.

"You create a weird calm in my chaos," he continues, voice low. "To everyone else, you're a quake—a force to be reckoned with. But to me, you're my calm amid the storm."

The butterflies in my stomach take flight, their wings brushing against my ribs. No one has ever made me feel this way—valued, wanted. Happiness blooms inside me like a secret garden I never knew existed. "I don't like it when you don't post," he admits, shaking his head. "Everything gets too loud when I can't see if you're okay, what you're doing." His vulnerability hangs in the air.

"Sorry." He chuckles, self-deprecating. "I definitely sound like a weirdo who's lures you up into the mountains now."

But I'm already falling, tumbling headlong into something I can't name. "I like you watching me," I confess, heat rising in my cheeks. I've always been the one who leaves guys flustered, but when did the tables turn? "Some of my posts are for you," I reveal, digging through the picnic basket. Sandwiches nestle in a container at the bottom. This—this is an actual picnic, and I'm giggling and squealing like a girl inside. No one has ever done anything so thoughtful for me.

"Was that the mirror one the other day?"

Air gets lodged in my throat as I lift my gaze to meet his. His eyes, dark and intense, search mine.

"What mirror one?" I tease, my lips curving into a knowing smile. I remember the photo, the one meant only for him. He pulls out his phone, revealing the screen and there I am, captured in that stolen moment. "You took a screenshot of it?" My shock is genuine; I hadn't expected him to keep it. His gaze remains fixed on the image, hunger clear in his expression.

"How could I not?" His voice is low and gravelly. "Look at you." And suddenly, the picnic, the candy, the sandwiches, all fade away. There's only him and the magnetic pull between us. I lean in, my body moving on its own accord, and our lips collide.

He's so fucking addicting. All I want to do is kiss him all day. I lean up, and he stretches his neck to keep his lips locked with mine as I swing my leg over and firmly sit in his lap. I can't say I've ever sat on a man before, but it feels right. I ache to feel his skin against mine, to be so close that there's no space left for air. My fingers trace the curves of his face, threading through his hair, pulling him impossibly nearer. Our lips are hungry and desperate, as if we've been starved for each other. Our tongues dance, a wild rhythm of longing, and I lose myself in the taste of him—intoxicating, addictive. I grind myself down on Mr. Stiles's already hard dick, and he moans into my mouth. Mr. Stiles pulls back as he constantly fucking does.

"We have to stop," he grits out with his eyes closed, and his nostrils flared. He's teetering on an edge, and I'm ready to push him off.

"Why?" I moan, grinding myself into him harder as I kiss down his jaw. I want to fit his swollen dick in my hands, in my mouth, in my . . . Shit. I've never bottomed in my life, so why do I get a feeling as if I will die if I don't get fucked by Mr. Stiles?

"Bray." He grips my hips, making it harder to move, and I stop kissing down his neck and meet his eyes. His hooded and hazy eyes stare back at me, but he winces.

"I'm not doing anything with you here. And if you keep grinding yourself on me the way you are, my tiny bit of resolve hanging on by a thread will snap."

"I'll cut it for you, no problem," I rasp.

His laughter dances across my lips in a gentle kiss that leaves me breathless. His touch, a silent command, urges me to move. Awkwardly, I untangle myself and return to my seat. Shame swirls within me, threatening to consume me from the inside out. Mr. Stiles's fingers find my jaw, lifting my gaze to meet his intense eyes.

"Look at me," he demands, his tone sharp. I comply, but my eyes remain downcast, unable to meet his intensity. "Brayden," he snaps, and my heart races. "I ache for you, my hands on your skin, your touch on me. It's consumed my thoughts for weeks." His confession hangs in the air, raw and desperate. "More than you'll ever know." With a silent promise, his soft eyes hold mine.

"You mean more to me than fooling around in the back of my truck, exposed to the world. I already lost control in those locker rooms—it won't happen again." My pout betrays my frustration. "After group next Saturday, if you're still interested, I'd like you to come over. I'll cook us dinner."

"Me come to yours?" I ask, taken aback. Mr. Stiles reclines into his original position.

"Yeah. Why not?" His nonchalant shrug sends a shy thrill through me, and I nod, a smile lighting up my face. When I look at him, it's as if the world, previously dull, suddenly gains color. Mr. Stiles stands out, a vibrant color in this otherwise bleak existence. I can't make out what that means, but when he's near, the voices in my head hush, and the demons retreat.

A sudden flash startles me, and I blink rapidly, caught off guard.

"What the fuck was that?" I frown. Mr. Stiles turns his phone, revealing a picture of me, smiling, teeth on display, staring directly at him. In that frozen moment, I appear happy, content, someone in love.

Fuck.

Shit.

No.

No way.

My gaze shifts from the screen to Mr. Stiles, who studies the image as if it's the best piece of art he has seen. "This," he says, voice low, "is my favorite version of you. So fucking beautiful Brayden, and those eyes . . . "

He trails off, a soft laugh escaping. His finger traces his own lips. "The way you look at me with those endless blue swirls—it's become my addiction. I can't imagine a day without it." His head tilts, eyes locking onto mine, and then he studies the picture again. "Now I get to see it every day."

My heart races, and I'm suspended in a cloud of happiness, weightless and dizzy with possibility.

Shit.

I'm so fucked.

"Eat." He smirks, closing his phone. I unwrap the sandwiches and laugh.

"Peanut butter and jelly? Am I five?" I tease.

"I don't care how old you are. Peanut butter and jelly will never not be the best sandwich filling there is," he states confidently.

"You stand correct," I reply, taking a bite. The flavors explode in my mouth. "God, these are good. How have you kept them so fresh?"

"I had a cooler. Took them out when I picked up the truck," he explains, biting into his own sandwich.

"You really went all out just to see me, didn't you?" The city lights twinkle in his eyes as he focuses on me.

"You're worth it." His words hang in the air, and I try to swallow the goofy grin threatening to escape. To distract myself,

I take a massive bite of my sandwich and then rummage through the rest of the picnic to see what else I can distract my racing heart with.

"Tell me something about yourself," I say to Mr. Stiles.

We've devoured the picnic and now sit in the back of the truck, surrounded by darkness. The only light comes from the scattered city lights ahead. Mr. Stiles opens up a blanket, draping it over us. When he rests his arm on my shoulder, I feel myself melting into a puddle, my face nestled against his chest. It's the calmest I've felt since childhood—back when Bex would cuddle me in bed, shielding me from the world. In those moments, I was the safest person on the planet. Bex created tales of an invisible shield around us, protecting us from everything. I'm back to being protected by that invisible shield.

"There's nothing interesting about me," Mr. Stiles replies, his heartbeat a lullaby that makes me drowsy. "What do you want to know?"

"Everything," I whisper. Then a memory surfaces. "Who's Jace?"

His chest stills, freezing the surrounding air. I lean up, meeting Mr. Stiles's gaze. His eyes remain fixed on the city lights, their colors like shards of glass.

"My nephew," he finally says. "One of the best people ever to grace this planet." He smiles, taking a sip of water. "He was special."

Was?

"Mr. Stiles, I—"

"You can call me Boh, or Bohdi when it's only us," he interrupts gently. "You don't have to apologize for my loss or say the usual things people do. I can't talk about it right now, but he's gone, and no matter how much I wish otherwise, I can't bring him back. But one thing I believe." He pauses, running his fingers along my jaw.

"He brought me to you." He takes my hand, linking our fingers, and gazes down at our tangled hands. "I truly believe that."

13
Brayden 'Quake' Anders

Chapter Thirty
Brayden

Cloud fucking nine is the only way I can describe myself today.

Nothing is ruining this mood.

Nothing.

Everything has gone from zero to one hundred with Bohdi, but I can't bring myself to doubt it, like I would do everything else. For once I'm happy and I never knew being happy felt so good, how it changes so much around you, how it changes your view of life and people.

Since seeing Bohdi at and after my game yesterday, I have felt completely weightless. As if this boulder that was sitting firmly on my shoulders is no longer there.

And that's all because of him.

Last night, back in the hotel room, I realized I couldn't continue holding stuff back from Kal and Tray. I needed to reveal some truth. After they called me out and half the team searched for me out of concern, I confessed that I'd been with a man—not Lan, not a boy, but a man I genuinely like. They grilled me relentlessly until I drifted off to sleep. And this morning, at 6 a.m., I woke up to Tray staring at me. His expression studying me as he questioned whether we'd been in the same room as this person in the last month. Kal accepted my hesitation, but Tray's chaotic mind won't settle. We have not long got off the coach, and already, two more questions have come my way by text. Apparently, having secrets isn't acceptable to Tray. What I know, he has to know.

I roll my eyes, slipping my phone back into my pocket and exhaling as I approach the front of the trailer park. Each visit fills me with hesitation—it's a mood-ruiner, but I must check on Bex. I need to make sure he's still okay. Standing at the park's edge, I gaze up at the seemingly endless expanse of doom that lies ahead. Hopefully, Bex is having a good day today.

The warmth beams down on the day, and people lounge outside their trailers, lying in the sun. Strolling through the rows, some cast me looks of betrayal for leaving, while others offer smiles, relieved I escaped. Trailer parks can be like having a large family, and leaving is comparable to abandoning that family, making you a traitor. Yet some recognize the hellhole you emerged from and wish you freedom. The trailer park opens up, revealing a circular arrangement of trailers, with my mom's trailer standing directly in front. To my right, I spot people, and that's when my blood turns icy.

Bexley stands there, talking with Daxton's uncle—Marley Rivers. Karl's brother is the last person I want near Bexley right now.

Karl is bad enough. But Marley? He's the root of all this evil, the devil to whom Bexley sold his soul years ago.

While Karl controls Bexley, Marley feeds the addiction. It shows in Karl's appearance—he smokes, sniffs, and injects all his profit. Marley reaps the benefits from Karl and Bexley. He rarely comes here and as Bex is getting better, the last thing I need is him here now. Bexley steps aside, revealing Daxton, whose face is completely fucked up, swollen left eye, bust lip, cuts all over his face. It makes my stomach turn. It doesn't take a genius to figure out who done that. Karl fucks Daxton up, but Daxton can half hold himself with Karl due to him being high most of the time. This has Marley written all over it.

Bexley's eyes meet mine, and he sighs, his shoulder rising and dropping. He slaps his hand on the back of Marley's back and walks toward me. Seeing how familiar he is with Marley makes me feel sick.

"Bro," he murmurs, his hand on my shoulder as we head toward our trailer. I side-eye him, wondering why he's grinning the way he is. "Bex." He glances at me briefly, then averts his eyes.

His brightness, those wide eyes, it's unmistakable. He's relapsed. It's as clear as day. Inside the trailer, my mom's overly cheerful expression grates on my nerves.

"Brayden, my baby, why don't you visit me anymore?" she whines, pouting like a child. She approaches, reaching for my arm, but I recoil in disgust.

"Bray," Bex interjects, as if I need to ease up on her. I can't understand why he always defends her. After all, we're in this mess because of her. Brushing past Bex, I head toward our room.

"Why do you always defend her?" I furrow my brow.

"It's hard to explain, Bray. Addiction isn't a joke," he says, his smile strained as he takes a seat beside me.

"Why were you talking to Marley? Why is he here?" I question.

"It didn't take you long." He chuckles, nervously picking at the skin around his fingernails—a telltale sign he's avoiding the truth.

"Just checking in, I guess. Not sure." He shrugs, his thumb finding its way to his mouth as he nibbles on the skin.

"Fuck, Bex," I exhale, closing my eyes, already defeated. I don't need to ask; I know he hasn't stayed clean. I must've been living in delusional land, thinking it would be this easy. But it never is. That's why I've worked tirelessly for years to get him into a rehab center.

"Listen, there's something I need to tell you. Someone's been helping me explore options—for both of us." I pause, meeting Bexley's intense gaze. "He's incredible, Bex," I admit, my cheeks warming. "He's the one who found the support group. I'm going with him again this Saturday. The group isn't a charity, but they offer resources for addiction. And Bohdi has been so supportive. You'll like him when you meet him." Saying Bohdi's name sends flutters through me.

Bexley frowns, scanning our surroundings as if lost in thought. "Bohdi?" he questions. "I've never heard of him. Is he your new boyfriend?" His words twist something inside me.

"What? No, definitely not," I retort, my face scrunching up. "No," I add, my voice squeaking.

"Do you want to say 'no' anymore?" Bex's sarcasm stings.

"He's my teacher," I say, and Bexley's gaze locks onto mine.

"Which teacher?"

"You know, the one who beat the crap out of Karl?" I grin. Bexley's expression shifts, then softens.

"That's kind of him," he says, lips tight.

"Yeah..." I nod, unsure of his reaction, maybe because someone else is involved. "Anyway, we're getting you out of this mess, Bex. I promise. I talked to him last night, and—"

"You were in Chicago yesterday?" His frown deepens.

Shit.

"I...um. It was in text." Bexley raises his eyebrow.

"You have your teacher's number and are meeting him outside of school?"

His questioning gaze annoys me. Who is he to question what I do?

"Yeah, your point?"

Bex raises his hands in defense. "No point, just an observation." His face and tone drip with sarcasm.

A sharp knock reverberates through the trailer door, and Bex's eyes snap to mine before darting to the hallway. I spring to my feet as Bex tries to bolt out of the bedroom first, but my stronger build easily shoves past him. I fling the door open, unsurprised to find my mom gone. Instead, I come face-to-face with Marley, looking infuriatingly perfect in designer clothes, gleaming jewelry, and carefully styled hair. His cheeks are vibrant and full, and his eyes are free of bags, a testament to his worry-free, eight-hour sleeps.

Exactly how my brother should look—alive and thriving.

But he's not, and the person standing before me is one of the reasons why.

"Bex busy?" He smirks, fully aware that his mere presence grates on my nerves.

"Yeah, he is actually. He will be forever. Bye." I flash him a bright, mocking smile before slamming the door. Just as it's about to close, Bex grabs it, yanks it open, and shoves me aside.

"Sorry, Mar. I'll be over shortly." When Bexley slams the door shut, I stare at him, stunned and seething.

"Fucking Mar?" I stare at him in disbelief. "We're on nickname terms now?" I ask, my voice dripping with shock.

"Bray, don't." Bex raises his hand, a clear signal to stop, and walks back into the room. I follow, my anger simmering.

"What the hell was that, Bex? Why are you even talking to him? And 'I'll be over shortly?' Why are you going over there?"

"Because I still have to live, Bray. Damn it!" Bex snaps, running his hand through his hair, his frustration palpable as he paces the bedroom. "Every time you come here, you try to fix me, Bray. Don't you see how lost I am? I can't escape this life. I have nowhere to go, no money to live on if I don't stay here. You need to let go of this fantasy world you've planned for me. It's not me." His voice rises to a shout, each word laced with desperation and anger.

"This," he says, pounding his chest. "This is who I am." His eyes, filled with pain, bore into mine. "You need to start accepting that. You can't change me. Shit, Bray." He lets out a bitter laugh, gesturing wildly toward the door. "Even Bohdi saw me for who I am. I'll drag you into the darkness and strip away all the good in you. I hold you back, Bray. He was right. I didn't want to admit it, but I do. I always have." He sighs deeply, collapsing onto the bed. "The best thing you can do is leave and not come back, Bray." His chest heaves as he whispers, "I'm not well. And there's no way to save me." As he drops his head into his hands, a wave of confusion and hurt crashes over me.

"What are you talking about? Bohdi saw you for who you are? What do you mean he was right?" I demand, standing up and kneeling between his legs.

He leans back, appearing utterly exhausted. "Ignore that," he mumbles, trying to bury his head in his hands again.

"No," I snap, gripping his arms to stop him. "Answer me."

Bexley's eyes flicker between mine, guilt etched across his face. But I need to know what he meant. As far as I know, he and Bohdi haven't met.

"When I came to see you play." He peers down. "He caught me just after I came out of the bathroom, and I had, you know." Pausing, he takes a shaky breath. "He dragged me out back and had a few things to say to me." His eyes meet mine, filled with a mix of shame and resignation. "And honestly, he was right, Bray," he mumbles.

Anger blazes through me like wildfire. Everything from yesterday and last night evaporates in a haze of fury. How dare he think he can speak to my brother like that and spew such vile things?

"You listen here. I'm not going anywhere. I don't know how many times I have to tell you this. I am not going anywhere." I yank Bex into me, holding him tightly against my chest. Why does it hurt so much? Normally, I'd be consumed by rage, but now, the pain seeps in, raw and relentless. I can't let this slide. All the happiness he brings me has shattered in this moment, because no one on this earth comes between me and my brother.

And I will make damn sure Mr. Stiles knows that.

Chapter Thirty-One

Bohdi

As I finish grading the last of my papers, I begin tidying up my desk, preparing to leave. Suddenly, the room door slams open, and in strides Brayden, his face flushed with anger.

"What happened?" I ask immediately, concern etching my features. Why does he look so upset?

"How dare you?" Brayden's anger catches me off guard, especially since it's directed at me. Frowning, I rise from my chair and step around the desk to face him.

"Excuse me?" I question, bewildered by the sudden confrontation.

"I just visited Bex," he seethes. "He's a mess, telling me all this nonsense about how he can't escape this life. According to him, he drags me into the darkness, taking away any good in me. He's convinced he holds me back." A sinking feeling settles in my gut. "Who put those thoughts in his head?" Brayden's fury burns in his eyes; he clenches his jaw.

"Listen—" I begin, but he cuts me off.

"No." He points a finger at my face. "Bex is my brother. I can say whatever I damn well please to him. But you? You have no right. None." His voice echoes through the room, leaving me stunned.

The room feels charged, emotions sparking like live wires. Brayden's anger crackles in the air, and I tread carefully, my own pulse racing. "This was when I didn't know you or the situation," I reply, my voice steady, though my insides churn. His laughter is a bitter slap against reality.

"That's even worse," he retorts. "You didn't know him—you didn't know us." His face scrunches up, a mix of frustration and hurt. "Stay away from him," he commands, vulnerability flickering in his eyes. I want to reach out, to bridge the gap, but he steps back, shaking his head.

"Bray," I murmur, my voice soft, pleading. But he's solid.

"No," he says, finality in his tone. "Stay away from me too."

He retreats, walking toward the door. And all I can do is watch him leave. As the door slams shut behind him, my heart sinks. Chaos swirls in my mind, and I'm left wondering how everything crumbled so quickly.

I've messaged Brayden repeatedly, but he remains silent. The texts show as read, yet there's no response. It's driving me to the brink. I've apologized countless times, pouring my regrets into those messages. Despite that, nothing.

I realize now that what I said to Bexley was impulsive, a momentary lapse fueled by thoughts of Jace. It wasn't about Brayden or Bexley; it was James and Jace haunting me. Bexley bore the brunt of my anger and was unfairly compared to James. Now, cradling this whiskey bottle, I find comfort in its bitter taste. Glancing down at my phone which shows Brayden's profile, my gaze drawn to it repeatedly tonight, hoping for a sign that he's posted something—anything, but he remains silent. But when I glance at the screen again, the colored circle surrounds his picture, and my heart races as I open it—it's him. He's standing waist deep in a pool, droplets of water cling to him, clutching a bottle of what appears to be tequila. His bold middle finger is aimed at the screen. No need for a scientist to determine who this picture was meant for. I decide to respond to his story.

@thestilestman: If you're going to drink, at least do it with water.

My stress spikes as I notice the half-empty bottle in his hand and his bloodshot eyes. His immediate reply stings.

@**Quakeontheice** Fukc you.

Frustration clenches my jaw, and I slam the whiskey bottle onto the table. He's drunk in that damn pool. What if he's all alone?

@thestilestman: Where are you?

@quakeontheice: Yr brothas huse.

My brother's place, huh? I switch back to Brayden's story and observe the background. This little shit is in the school's gym, clearly using the code I gave to him when he needed to go in at night and let off some steam. To make matters worse, he's now drinking on school property. My frustration boils over. I jump off the couch, open the Uber app, and order a ride to the school.

Within fifteen minutes, I arrive at the school and head toward the gym building. From the outside, it's pitch-black, and there's no sign of anyone inside. Perhaps he keeps them off, so people don't know he's in here. As I enter the code and step inside, darkness envelops me. I navigate the gym floor and pass through the locker rooms, following the faint scent of chlorine. Finally, I reach the swimming pool area. The only illumination comes from the pool lights. In one corner, Brayden floats with his arms draped over the ledge, head tilted back, and body suspended in the water. He still clutches the tequila bottle. As I stand over him, our eyes lock, his lips curve into a smirk, but it's a fragile facade. His bloodshot eyes reveal a storm raging within.

"Get out, Bray," I plead, my voice raw. I lean down, desperate to break through the haze that surrounds him. The tequila bottle slips from his fingers, but he clings to it as if it holds his fractured soul.

"Go away," he rasps, then takes another swig. His eyes close, shutting out the world.

"I'll leave when you get out of the pool," I whisper, my breath catching. But he remains adrift, lost in the depth of his pain.

"Go home," he murmurs bitterly. Another swig, and the tequila burns its way down his throat as he winces. "You reek of whiskey," he adds, his gaze piercing mine.

I swallow my own ache. "And you stink of tequila," I retort, my voice breaking.

"Go bother someone who actually wants saving, Mr. Stiles," he says, and the absence of *Bohdi* cuts deeper than any blade. In this deserted pool, we're both drowning, clinging to our weaknesses.

"I'm sorry, Bray," I murmur. He remains motionless, suspended in the water. "I projected my own issues onto you and your brother," I continue, my gaze fixed on his face. "That wasn't fair, and I see that now. I'll personally apologize to Bexley." Still, Brayden doesn't react. "There are things I haven't shared with you," I confess, my voice faltering. "I'm not ready yet. It's not an excuse, but—"

"Can I ask you something?" Brayden's voice remains detached, as if my words barely registered.

"Yes," I reply, my heart racing.

His eyes open, locking onto mine. Coldness radiates from him, and I brace myself for what comes next.

"Tell me, Mr. Stiles, who do you think about when you wrap your hand around your dick at night?"

My jaw clenches, and I avert my gaze. I try to maintain composure, recognizing that he's drunk—this isn't the real Brayden.

"Because I think we both know it's not Ms. Banksy, is it?" Swimming toward the edge, he stops right in front of me. "It's me." An icy smile stretches across his face. It's as if I'm staring at an entirely different person. "Do you think about sinking your dick into my mouth?"

"Brayden," I stammer, my inner turmoil churning. Despite my hate at his words, my twisted mind has conjured these scenarios when I wrap my own hand around my dick in the darkness.

I despise my vulnerability, the way he sees right through me. And what I hate the most? How I'm hardening for him, despite it all.

He chuckles, the tequila bottle forgotten, sinking to the pool's bottom without care. His hands grip the ledge, pushing himself up. My eyes betray me, tracing the contours of his glistening body as water cascades down, leaving nothing to the imagination. He kneels before me, settling on the floor, his face inches from mine. The scent of tequila wafts from the puffs of air that leave his mouth. His lips brush my ear, sending an involuntary shiver through me—a connection he feels too, as his lips curve upward near my ear.

"Do you think about sinking yourself so far inside me until we both don't know what planet we're on?"

Yes, I've thought about it—more times than I care to admit. My body betrays me with a pathetic, guttural groan. His words hang in the air, a blade slicing through my defenses. It doesn't escape me that as he leans over me, his dick is hard against my leg, which causes me to gulp.

"I just want you to know that," he says, locking eyes with me, "those moments will forever be illusions of your mind. I'd sooner fuck a pig than let you touch me again." The venom in his voice stings, and I struggle to hold on to the truth: this isn't Bray. Not my Bray. Anger simmers, threatening to erupt.

He stands in front of me, his hard dick bobbing in my face. "Maybe Lan will handle this for me," he adds, and my resolve shatters. I rise, closing the distance from his retreating form, my hand wrapping around his neck. His eyes dance with mischief, a smirk playing on his lips.

"I meant what I said," I hiss. "Touch an inch of skin on that kid and you'll fucking regret it, Bray." He frowns, confused.

"Who said I'll be doing the touching?" His wink is a taunt. I tighten my grip. Fire blazes in his eyes.

"Let go," he grits out, my fingers constricting his windpipe. I release instantly, regret biting at me. My resolve crumbles.

"Bray," I plead, but he steps back, hands raised.

"Stay away." As he walks away from me for the second time today, shards of glass pierce my heart.

This time, it feels like heartbreak.

13
Brayden 'Quake' Anders

Chapter Thirty-Two
Brayden

Today's classes have been a slow, relentless grind. Last night's straight tequila was a desperate escape, a wasted attempt to drown my inner havoc. If it weren't for my slipping grades, I'd have skipped today altogether. But here I am, trudging through every class, including the extra one Mr. Stiles begrudgingly arranged for me. The timing couldn't be worse. This morning, regret weighed heavy and still does hours later.

I can't believe the venom I spewed last night, fueled by alcohol and my own sharp tongue. It's why I shouldn't drink when I'm angry. Nothing good ever comes from it. Bohdi shouldn't have shown up at the pool, but that's him—caring and concerned. And I repaid him with cruelty.

Anger still rumbles within me, yet, deep down, I know Bex's relapse isn't Bohdi's fault. An addict will always twist any excuse to justify his actions. I grasp this truth, yet it doesn't excuse what Bohdi said to Bex. I know Bex and that would have played in his head over and over. If Kal or Tray had uttered those same things, I'd react just as angrily. Perhaps I overreacted, but anger blurs the reason, but I hate how much my heart aches remembering what I had said to him. I wish I could walk into the next class and tell him how sorry I am for what I said last night, but my stubbornness won't allow it. Maybe heartbreak is the price of pride.

As I step into Bohdi's class, I keep my head down, avoiding his gaze. Will he be hurt? Angry? The weight of last night presses on me. I climb the steps to my usual seat, eyes fixed on the desk. Kal and Tray follow, flanking me on either side.

"You good?" Kal nudges me, concern etching his features.

"Just hanging," I reply, forcing a chuckle.

"Who were you with last night?" Kal glances at his laptop. "I saw your Instagram story. Who were you in the school pool with?"

"I bet it was 'sir.'" Tray nudges me, and my eyes involuntarily dart to Bohdi. He sits there, eyes cast downward, the pain clear as day to me, but to everyone else he appears as his usual self.

"Quake." Kal nudges me again, his focus shifting between Bohdi and me. "What's going on?"

"What do you mean?" I fake innocence.

"You were staring at him weirdly," Kal observes, his eyes moving over my face as if he's trying to read every emotion.

"I was just . . . being myself," I retort, my frustration bubbling.

"Well, I'd stare too," Tray whispers. "Did you see those muscles, the tattoos? And the way he swings that bag in the gym? Damn." His words hang in the air. "He's hot as fuck."

"Enough," I snap, my anger catching Kal and Tray off guard. Jealousy rears its ugly head before I can even think about it. Both Kal and Tray stare at me, wide-eyed.

My gaze remains fixed on him, the way he moves and commands attention. Not just from guys, but girls too, their eyes starry. Rage simmers within me; I clench my teeth, jaw ticking as I survey the room. All eyes are on Bohdi, and I despise it.

I really fucking hate it.

The class drags on, and he doesn't glance my way even once. Why do I feel so desperate, craving his attention like a needy fool? I'm supposed to hate him, right? I wanted him to stay far away from me. So why does the idea of our extra session, just the two of us, ignite a flutter in my chest? I leave my laptop untouched, Tray and Kal rising from their seats, their eyes fixed on me. Damn, I never told them about the extra classes.

"Uh, those extra classes? They're with Bo—Mr. Stiles," I stammer, scratching my neck under their scrutiny.

"How long have the classes been going on?" Kal's eyes bore into mine.

"Not long." I shrug.

Kal eyes me a little longer than I'd like, then nods slowly. "Okay. Cool. Call me later," he says, slapping my shoulder.

Kal's my brother, my personal diary. But right now, there are some things I can't share.

"Yo, who's going to Thompson's Thanksgiving party tomorrow night?" Tray's voice echoes through the classroom, drawing cheers from everyone as they pack up their laptops. "Remember, we're celebrating Halloween for Thanksgiving. No shit outfits."

Bohdi scans the room as students filter out. "Remember to stay safe this weekend. Don't do anything I wouldn't do." He smirks. His happiness grates on my nerves. Why isn't he as miserable as I am? Doesn't he realize how furious I am with him? Clenching my teeth, I leave my desk and stride to the front, chin held high.

"Daxton, can you wait behind, please?"

Daxton visibly sighs and stands by his desk, looking awkward as hell.

"I take it if I ask you to leave, you won't?" Bohdi raises an eyebrow at me.

"Nope." I smile, settling down at the desk.

Bohdi takes a deep inhale and moves his stare to Daxton. "I can't keep seeing you with your face like that. It's getting worse, Daxton. I'm going to need to tell the dean." Bohdi scrutinizes

Daxton's battered face, and even I must admit, this is the worst I've seen him. He can barely see out of one eye.

He exhales, fingertips grazing the raw edges of his face, wincing as they brush over the cuts and bruises. "Not my father," he mutters.

A bitter laugh escapes my lips. "Mr. Stiles hasn't met Marley yet," I interject, rolling my eyes, waiting for Daxton to reveal who Marley is. Bohdi's unwavering gaze remains fixed on Daxton.

"It wasn't Marley," he confesses, head bowed, avoiding eye contact.

"If not your uncle or father, then who?" I scoff, knowing he's evading the truth. "I tried, Bray," Daxton's eyes lock with mine, sadness and guilt etched in their depths. I furrow my brow, clueless about his hidden words.

"What do you mean, you tried?" I demand, the pieces finally clicking into place.

"Bex. I tried to keep him away from them," he admits, and realization dawns.

"No. I don't believe it," I seethe. "My brother wouldn't do that." I rise, and Daxton winces as I confront him.

"Hey, calm down. Bray. Daxton, take care of those bruises," Bohdi intervenes, tugging at my arm.

"I'm sorry, Bray," Daxton murmurs, head bowed, retreating from the room.

I spin on my heels to confront Bohdi.

"He's blatantly lying," I seethe. The little shit won't take responsibility for his dead-beat family and instead pins it on my brother. Bohdi's eyes soften, revealing a storm of emotions. He nods, as his gaze drops to his laptop, the silence between us heavy.

"Let me gather some notes I've taken," he finally murmurs, and my mind races.

Daxton's revelation is soon forgotten about because I can't stop wondering about why Bohdi isn't addressing last night. I feel the weight of my own words, the shame of my drunken outburst. Last night, I couldn't even call him Bohdi; his name on my tongue when I spit venom doesn't feel right. As if reading my inner thoughts, his eyes flicker to my neck, and he gestures to his own.

"I apologize for grabbing you," he says, his voice soft and weighed down with regret. "That wasn't like me." His gaze meets mine, sadness etched into every line of his face. The memory of my hurtful words echoes, I can't leave it like this. It's eating away at me.

"Look," I begin.

"Mr. Stiles, sorry to interrupt." The feminine voice slices through the classroom, chilling my blood. My attention snaps to the door. I recognize that annoying voice. Ms. Banksy strides toward Bohdi's desk, her eyes bypassing me entirely. She doesn't care about me, her focus fixed on the man before her.

"Sir," she purrs. The word grates against my clenched teeth, dripping with a provocative tone that sets my gears to grinding.

"Ms. Banksy, how can I assist you today?" Bohdi's smile radiates, teeth on full display. Her cheeks flush as she hovers near his desk.

Yes, bitch, his smile has that effect on me—*not you!*

"Did you see my message last night? I need to discuss something." Her widened eyes communicate an unspoken message, one inappropriate for a student's ears. The previous night, she'd been texting him. Was it before he got hard for me at the pool, or after? Did my words truly drive him to Ms. Banksy?

"Ahh, yes." He smirks at her, as if they share some secret joke. "I have a lesson, and then I'll come find you?" His wink adds to the tension.

He fucking winks. She places her hand on his arm—his biceps, I might add—and squeezes. That's when I spot his phone sitting on his desk directly in front of Ms. Banksy. Screw this. In a hastily pissed off decision, I pull my phone out, quickly bringing up mine and Bohdi's text and type out:

Me:

Hey, baby, thanks for last night. I can't wait to see you again tonight.

I click send and watch as the phone pings and the screen lights up. Of course, Ms. Banksy gets a front-row seat to the text message.

"Oh," she giggles, trying to mask her utter disappointment. Evidenced by her pinched eyebrows and the fact she can't take her eyes off the screen like she's reading it over and over, willing the words to disappear, she fails. Bohdi snaps the phone up, reading the message, his eyes snapping to me.

"Actually, I forgot I have training. Rain check?" I don't wait for Bohdi's protest; I grab my bag and bolt. The gym is my first stop, a place to eliminate this shitty feeling from my system. Although that right there may have helped a bit. I bite my lip, trying to hold back my smile dying to break free.

Suck on that, Ms. Banksy.

Chapter Thirty-Three

Bohdi

The music blares as I step into the house, surrounded by bodies swaying, drinks in hand, and who knows what else. But I'm not interested in the crowd. My focus is solely on one person: Brayden. The stifling heat inside my Halloween costume threatens to overwhelm me, but I had to choose something that would completely conceal my identity. Ghostface was my last-minute choice—a mask that clings tightly to my head, its black cape and gloves hiding my arms and tattoos.

Navigating through the crowd of people, I cringe internally as some of my female students fawn over Ghostface, their hands grazing my chest and shoulders. I tune out the inappropriate questions thrown my way as I continue pushing my way through the party.

When did Ghostface become a character for both girls and boys to romanticize? *What's wrong with these people?*

Ah, my age is definitely showing. I scan the sea of faces in the crowded mansion. The sheer number of people here is staggering. Finding Brayden will be a marathon. I weave through the crowd; the heat intensifying with each passing minute. Thankfully, I know what he's wearing from his Instagram story: Jason from Halloween. So far, I haven't seen a Jason, which is good, I suppose, because what if there were more than one?

I don't really know why I'm here, but all I know is I need to see him. I know his walls that he builds so God damn high were slowly crumbling for me earlier and then Ms. Banksy went and walked in. I get how it looked; it didn't look great, but she needed to ask me something about a presentation. I could see it in his face, in his eyes, his walls built back up quicker than I could blink. The anger, the false hatred, simmered in his eyes for me again. I need to see those walls crumble. I need him back.

He's never had to worry about Ms. Banksy, but he certainly doesn't anymore. She hightailed it out of my room as soon as Brayden left. I don't think she will be bothering me anymore. I gave Brayden a silent cheer for that text and also; I loved the jealousy that was clearly displayed on his face. He wouldn't have sent that text if he didn't care.

These last few days have been hell. I've come to realize that not only seeing Brayden is something I need, but seeing him happy is something I crave. Something I struggle to go a day without seeing. I have the picture—which I may as well frame and set next to my bed, with the number of times I stare at it. But knowing he's angry with me, it doesn't help. Scanning the crowd, I can feel myself getting impatient. He's definitely here . . . unless he's left already. I do another lap and as I walk into the kitchen, which heaves with people drinking from some type of punch. My eyes snag on someone dressed as a zombie-looking priest.

Trayton.

I hover, because I know if Trayton is here, then Brayden will be near. I haven't quite worked out how I'm going to get him on his own yet, but I'll think about that once I see him. I don't even know what the fuck I'm going to say to him. I grab a beer from the ice cooler, not planning on drinking it, even if I am gagging for it right now. But that would mean having to lift my mask and there isn't a chance I'm risking that. Trayton laughing draws my attention to him as Kal throws his head back laughing at something. When Trayton moves to the side, I see who he's laughing at.

Brayden sits on the couch with his arm around a flushed Lance, who, of course, is dressed as some kind of blooded-up zombie-looking nerd. Anger fuels me instantly, and before I know it, I'm barging through Trayton and Kal. I don't think about the consequences; I don't think about anything. The anger and jealousy consume me, and I grab hold of Brayden's arm, hauling him to his feet, dragging him along with me.

"Bro, get the fuck off me," Brayden hisses, his voice low and intense, as I pull him away.

"I'm not your fucking bro," I seethe close to his ear.

Trayton's sudden grip on my arm spins me around. "You better back the fuck off and let my boy go now before I fuck you up." My fingers dig into Brayden's arm, and he removes his mask, revealing dark brown hair matted with sweat. His eyes lock onto mine through the mask.

"Relax." He smirks at Tray. "I know him."

Tray's brow furrows as he studies Bray, then he performs an exaggerated triple blink. Brayden erupts in laughter and returns the peculiar triple blink. Tray's shoulders slump, and he scrutinizes me from head to toe before grimacing and walking away. Kal stands nearby, brooding, his demeanor suggesting he's prepared to tear me apart as he eyes my hand, squeezing Brayden's arm.

"It's cool," he says again, and without hesitation, I pull him toward the stairs. As I glance back, I catch Lance observing our every step. His gaze lowered. Normally, I'd pity someone like him, but not when he's laying claim to something that belongs to me.

Fuck that.

Ignoring the first bedroom at the top of the stairs. I pull Brayden toward the far end, pushing past some people who catcall and joke about Jason fucking with Ghostface. The last door leads to a dull cream-colored room with matching carpets, a king-size bed, and bland cream walls. Releasing Brayden, I pivot on my heels and slam the door shut.

"Scary," Brayden quips sarcastically. I turn to face him, yanking the mask off my face, my eyes drilling into his.

"What the fuck was that downstairs?" I grind out, my patience fraying. "Did you touch him? Kiss him?" My body trembles at the thought of his lips on someone else.

He scrutinizes me, his eyes revealing more than he lets on. He enjoys my jealousy, relishes the fact that I barged in and pulled him away.

"What's it to you?" he retorts, assessing me as if I'm insignificant. But I catch the glimmer in his eyes. He enjoys the possessiveness.

"What did I warn you?" My voice is edged with determination.

"And what did I say? Stay the fuck away from me. I hate you!" he spits. Closing the gap, I confront him face-to-face, our height difference barely noticeable as his rapid breaths brush my skin.

"There's something you should already understand, Brayden." I lower my voice, lips grazing his ear, and he inhales sharply. "I don't stay away from what's mine."

His audible gulp echoes in the charged silence; he neither protests nor retreats. I pull back, locking eyes with him, the turmoil evident as his gaze flickers between mine, and he clenches his jaw. I smirk.

"You hate me, huh?"

"I can't fucking stand you." He tilts his head up, jutting his chin out as he crosses his arms over his chest.

Tilting my head, I squint my eyes, ensuring my stare is locked with his. "Those hooded, ocean eyes that drink up every inch of me while I teach suggest otherwise." I wink, causing his resolve to slip as his breathing becomes harsher.

"I'm pissed with you," he mutters weakly, attempting to sound harsh. A smile tugs at my lips, but I suppress it. I know that would only further infuriate him. Truth is, he's pissed, but not as much as he'd like to be. And the truth is, he couldn't hate me, even if he tried.

"I know," I reply, my jaw clenching as I glance around the room. "I've apologized at least ten times now."

His jaw ticks, and he gazes down, then back up. "Why was she in the classroom earlier?" he huffs.

"To discuss a presentation," I answer matter-of-factly. His sarcastic eye roll and pursed lips follow. "Nice touch with the text, by the way. Luckily, I didn't have your name saved. Why do you even care, anyway?" I raise an eyebrow. "You'd rather fuck a pig than touch me again, wouldn't you?" I challenge. "Whether Ms. Banksy visited me—it's irrelevant, isn't it?"

Brayden inhales deeply, his gaze meeting mine, filled with regret. I understand he didn't mean what he said that night, but those words still haunt me, driving me to drink myself into a dark hole.

"I—" he huffs, shoulders sagging. "I'm sorry for what I said. I was drunk. I didn't mean it." His frown deepens as he stares back into my eyes.

"You're sorry?" he nods, our eyes locked, and I catch a fleeting glimpse of his gaze on my lips.

"Why don't you drop to your knees and show me just how sorry you are, Bray?"

His eyes widen, mouth opening and closing. I trace my thumb along his bottom lip.

"Put this mouth to good use instead of talking shit for once," I whisper, pressing a kiss against his lips and running my tongue along the edge.

He lazily closes his eyes and sinks to his knees, gazing up at me. As I lift the cape, his hands instantly find my belt, unclipping it and skillfully undoing the buttons. The slight tremor in his hands doesn't escape my notice, though. My dick is painfully hard as his fingers graze the fabric of my boxers. Pulling down the waistband, he pulls my dick out, and a groan slips from me.

"Fuck." I stare down at him. He licks his lips, his eyes fixed on my dick, and leans forward, licking some of the pre-cum on the tip.

My eyes roll into the back of my head, and I swear I see stars. Brayden on his knees is better than I ever imagined. Warm, wet lips circle over the head of my dick and suck. His tongue grazes the underneath, and I have to grab his hair and pull on it sharply to control myself from tipping over the edge too quickly. As Brayden sucks down my dick like a fucking pro, I can't take my eyes off him. His eyes closed, swallowing my dick. He flicks his tongue on the underneath again and I moan loudly. His eyes flick up, locking with mine as he smiles around my dick, flicking his tongue over my slit.

"Brayden," I say through gritted teeth, tightening my grip on his scalp, eliciting a wince. He withdraws from my dick with a soft pop, his gaze unwavering.

"Put the mask back on." He grins, flashing me my favorite smile.

"You're a freak," I retort, securing the mask once more. This time, I grasp Brayden's hair from behind.

"Open," I command, and he complies instantly, a smile playing on his lips. "You're so fucking sexy, you know that." Brayden's intense stare makes me feel alive, intoxicated by desire. I never want to come back to reality. I want to stay drunk on this feeling forever. His lips circle around me, and I lose myself as he takes me in completely. His tongue tracing every inch as he gags, causing the muscles in his throat to tighten, which makes my toes curl. He slurps on my dick like it's his favorite lollipop and continues taking me to the back of his throat as he swallows around my dick, making me see every fucking star in the galaxy. As Brayden's eyes connect with mine through the mask, they say a thousand words, and right there and then, he shows me just how sorry he is until I'm coming down his throat.

Chapter Thirty-Four

Bohdi

I had every intention of coming down Brayden's throat and then walking out and leaving him hanging at this party. Gagging for more. But I can't, not when he stares up at me on his knees, tears streaming down the sides of his eyes and drops of my cum dripping down his chin. I grab him by the scuff of his sweater, hauling him to his feet as I rip off the mask and smack my lips against his. He groans in my mouth, threading his fingers into my hair as I overpower him with my tongue, tasting the sweet tangy taste of myself on him, sending me into a wild frenzy.

Gripping his jaw in my hand, I push my tongue into his mouth deep enough he chokes on it. I want to consume his entire being. I want his world to start and end with me. I want him to wrap his hand around his dick every night and come to thoughts of me.

Having Brayden on his knees with my dick in his mouth and my cum dripping from his lips has awakened a beast. This need, want and obsession are not feelings I've ever experienced.

I wish I had a stamp so I could brand him.

He's mine.

He's fucking mine.

Reluctantly, I pull my mouth away from his. "I need you, Bray," I murmur, his intoxicated, hooded gaze shifting lazily between my eyes, as if he's just rousing from sleep and needs a moment to process my words.

"You have me," he breathes, his tongue tracing the edge of his lips, eliciting a groan from me as I nip at it, capturing it between my teeth. I sink my teeth in, causing a wince as he attempts to retreat. When he finally pulls away, blood oozes from his lips, and I eagerly follow, lapping up every drop.

"You've awakened a primal beast within me, Bray," I murmur, my tongue tracing the contours of his lips. His mews have my dick hardening again. "Make up something to Kal and Tray as to why you need to go home," I add, planting kisses along his jawline. "Tonight, you're coming home with me," I murmur as he retreats, his eyes wide.

"Your p-place?" he stammers, his shocked gaze darting between mine.

"My place," I reply with a smirk, savoring his bewilderment for a moment longer. He nods eagerly,

"O-Okay," he stutters again, and I find it endearing. I offer him a knowing smile.

"Meet me outside. The Chevy is parked down the street." As I approach the door and grasp the handle, I hesitate, pivoting to face a flustered Brayden. His gaze locks onto mine. "Stay away from Lance," I warn, narrowing my eyes. Brayden smiles and nods in agreement.

"I will," he quietly whispers. I shouldn't, but my eyes glance down to an extremely hard Brayden. He obviously sees where my eyes drop as he rearranges himself, but knowing I did that to him sets off another reel of possessive thoughts within me. I've felt like Brayden is slowly slipping through my fingers recently. I need him to know he's mine and nothing is going to change that. No, stupid words in the heat of the moment are going to change how much I want him and how I feel about him. I snap my attention away from him, putting on my mask and leaving the room quickly. If I don't, I fear I may claim him on that stranger's bed, and I don't want my first time with him to be at a frat party. No way.

I observe Brayden stride toward my truck with an uncaring swagger, exuding an air of cool composure. Yet, I'm aware of the demons that haunt him—the relentless search for perfection as a brother. As he opens the truck door, he hops in, grinning at me, and I find myself frozen. Leaning across the console, I grasp the back of his neck, our lips meeting in a leisurely dance. I crave more of him. When we break apart, I rest my forehead against his.

"You're dangerously addictive." I chuckle, drawing a bright smile from Brayden, the one I adore. "I've missed that smile," I confess.

"Did you delete the picture?" he asks, a frown creasing his brow.

I smirk. "No, but it's not the same when I know you're annoyed with me."

He nods, gaze downcast. "I'm not anymore," he whispers, sealing his words with a kiss.

Pulling away, I state, "All right, we'd better get going. If I linger any longer, we won't leave this spot for the rest of the night." Brayden smiles shyly, glancing out the window as I drive away.

As we drive, Brayden remains silent, gazing out the window. But I notice the nervous bounce of his leg, a telltale sign of his inner turmoil. I keep one hand on the wheel, my other hand gripping his thigh.

Abruptly, he snaps his head toward me, eyes locking onto my hand. "I can drop you off at your place," I offer, my voice low and steady. "You don't have to come back to mine." I'm happy taking him back to his dorm, but no way is he going to that party.

His brow furrows, and he shakes his head. "No, no," he insists. "I want to come back to your place." His vulnerability tugs at me. "It's just Kal." He sighs. "I tell him and Tray everything. Tray mostly stays quiet, except for a few snide remarks. But Kal worries, and I think he suspects something is wrong. I've been avoiding him whenever he brings up 'sir,' afraid he might start digging." He shrugs. "I guess I'm worried that whatever this is will end if someone finds out." His gulp is audible, and his head drops.

"If anyone discovers our secret," I say firmly, "we'll handle it." My grip tightens on his leg. A silent promise. I steal a quick glance at Brayden, and he smiles, nodding. His trust in me fuels my determination.

"Random question," I interject, my voice softer now. "What was with the blinking you and Tray were doing earlier?" The curiosity strikes me.

Brayden laughs, a raw sound that resonates with shared memories. I catch him in my peripheral vision, shaking his head. "Tray came up with this system when we were kids," he explains. "If we're ever in danger, we communicate through blinks—it stuck with us, I guess." He chuckles again, but there's an edge to it. "It's been a while since he used it."

"So, three very obvious blinks mean . . . ?" I prompt, waiting for his answer.

"Blink three times to let me know you're okay," he says, his voice steady. "Blink twice to signal that you're not, and I'll go all out on whoever's causing trouble. That's our motto—the unspoken pact between brothers. Bex was a part of it too." He grins once more, a mix of happiness and vulnerability.

"I like it," I murmur. It warms my heart to know that Brayden has good people around him—people who will protect him when needed, even if it means breaking the rules.

As we pull up to my house, the anticipation crackles in the air. It's nothing extravagant—a three-bedroom detached house in a humble neighborhood near the college. But Brayden's wide-eyed gaze tells me it means it's more than just a three-bedroom house.

"Wow," he gasps, staring up at the house.

"It's okay," I reply, stepping out of the car. Brayden follows suit, tucking his hands into his blood-stained hoody. We walk up the driveway together. Once inside, he takes in the open space, eyes darting around.

"Bohdi, this is amazing." His words hit me. To me, it's any old house, but I've glimpsed where he grew up—the struggle, the sacrifices. This must feel significant to him.

"Yeah, it's nice," I agree, not wanting him to feel overwhelmed. We step into the open-plan living room, the kitchen and dining area seamlessly connected.

"I'll give you a tour in a bit," I say, my voice low. "But first, can I go and shed this?" I gesture to my cape. "I feel weird."

Brayden laughs, nodding. "You look hot, not weird," he teases. Our eyes lock, and the intensity between us ignites.

"You think I look hot?" I challenge, tilting my head. I love when he blushes, but I also crave the fire in his eyes—the solid confidence that draws me in.

Husky and intimate, he murmurs, "You always look hot."

I step closer, my fingers tracing the contours of his neck, sensing the rapid pulse beneath my touch.

"Are you nervous?" I ask, my lips brushing against his skin.

"No," he denies, but his throat bobs with a gulp, and his pulse races, suggesting otherwise.

"I am," I confess. His eyes widen, and I lean in, our lips almost touching.

"Why?" His hoarse voice sends shivers down my spine. The answer hangs unspoken between us, a promise of want.

"Brayden," I whisper, my voice a raw confession. "The ache to possess you completely, it's unbearable. And when my lips find yours, I won't give in. Not tonight. Not ever."

His eyes widen, flickering between mine, and then his mouth claims mine. A storm of hunger and heat. I cling to him, fingers digging into his hips, pulling him impossibly closer. His touch trails up my spine, igniting sparks along nerve endings.

"Brayden," I rasp, surrendering to the intoxicating feel of his lips. "I need to know this is what you want."

He breaks away, confusion etching lines on his face. "I crave you," he rasps, lips mapping a path down my neck, leaving a trail of fire. "More than I've ever craved anything." His whispered words are the spark that sets my restraint ablaze—a fire consuming every last vestige of self-control. Without hesitation, I guide Brayden toward my room, the air thick with anticipation. Once inside, I press him backward until the edge of the bed catches him, and he sinks onto the mattress.

His eyes—those hungry, primal orbs feast upon me. I raise the cape, revealing my skin, and his gaze traces over my inked chest. His breath hitches as his eyes move lower, my dick poking out the top of my boxers.

I drag my boxers down, noticing my hands are trembling. My nerves pulse through me, electric and insistent. Brayden rises, stripping out of his clothes and before I know it, we're both standing in front of each, completely naked and rock hard, our breaths colliding in the charged space between us. I step closer, then our lips meet again. This time is slow and passionate. I put everything into this kiss. What's about to happen. Everything that's led up to this moment. It's what I want, and I know it's what Brayden wants. Brayden slowly pulls back and drops himself on to the bed, his dick standing up straight. I lean down, our lips meeting again, becoming more urgent. Our tongues tangle and the vibrations in my mouth from Brayden's throaty groan sends a shiver through me. I lower myself and when mine and Brayden's dick touches, I turn into a feral beast. I rub myself against him with urgency as he claws at my back, pulling me close as possible.

"Fuck, Brayden," I grunt.

"Bohdi, I haven't." His eyes stare wide up at me as I slow down, already feeling as if I'm about to come.

"You haven't what?" I frown, wondering what he's about to say.

"I haven't bottomed before." He exhales heavily, and I instinctively lean away, my expression registering surprise.

"Oh," escapes my lips, though I'm uncertain why, but I don't really know what I'm doing. I've been watching gay porn the last week just to get an idea of how it works, and I have to say I don't think I could take it in the ass. Not yet anyway.

"But I want to. With you." He chuckles as the words tumble out. "My first time, I mean."

My heart swells. He wants his first time to be with me and I've never felt this happy. A tidal wave of emotions rushes through me as my lips meet his one more time, lazily lapping him up, wishing this night would never end. I want to take my time with him. I lean up on my knees, my dick standing to a sharp point which Brayden's eyes immediately take notice of.

"I—uh, did some research," I mutter. Brayden bites his lip, trying to suppress a laugh. "Hey, don't mock me," I smirk.

"I think it's hot you done research." He frowns. "Well, as long as it was for me, you did the research for."

"Who else?" I raise an eyebrow, brushing my lips against his.

Leaning over to the nightstand, I open the second drawer, pulling out a small tube of lube.

Brayden's eyes follow my every move. I sit between his open leg, his dick fucking straining and I'm tempted to lean down and lick the head, but I know once I start, I won't stop. When he comes, I want to be inside him. I uncap the lube and squeeze a small amount on my finger.

My eyes flick up to meet Brayden. He pants, his mouth open as he lifts his legs up slightly for me, baring himself fully.

"I want to make sure you're ready for me first." My voice is raspy as I stare down at his untouched hole. "If it gets too much—"

"Bohdi, please shut up and touch me," Brayden begs, squirming. As soon as I touch his hole, my dick jumps for joy like it's congratulating me for touching him. My balls tingle just from touching him. How am I ever going to fuck him without coming instantly? Fuck. I push one finger slowly into him.

"Shit, fuck," Brayden mutters. I push it in until my finger is completely buried, knuckles deep, and pull it back out, repeating the same thing again. Brayden squirms.

"You okay?" I ask.

"Yeah, just keep going," he pants as if he's been out running. I add the second finger, and as soon as the tips are both in, I feel him tighten around my fingers and my dick leaks pre-cum. I stare down at my dick as a bead of cum drips down the side.

Jesus Christ.

"Ommmffuckkkkk." Brayden's incoherent words and moans are doing things to my dick, because it fucking bounces up and down like a fucking cheerleader, cheering for Brayden's moans. I push my fingers in deeper, curling them slightly, like I read about.

"Jesfuckchrist." Brayden's words and moans spear me on as I pull them out and push them back in, picking up the speed.

"Fuck, fuck," Brayden grits out.

"Does it feel okay?"

"It burns a bit, but when you—"

I curl my finger as Brayden's breath hitches.

"That, do that again," he begs, his eyes squeezed shut. I curl my fingers and keep rubbing on the spot.

"That . . . I need it . . . Fuck . . . Bodhi . . . please . . . more," Brayden whines, my dick weeps with every sound, and I don't know how I'm going to hold out.

"Come!"

Brayden gasps. I pull my fingers out as ropes of cum soak his abs.

"Ahhhhh, fuck!" Brayden rasps, as I push my fingers back in. His dick continues to pulse, cum soaking his abs. I pull my fingers out and stare down at the fucking masterpiece that lies before me. Before I can even think about it, I rub my finger through the ropes of cum and bring it up to my mouth, sucking on my finger. Brayden's drunk looking eyes ablaze as he stares at me.

"So fucking sweet," I rasp, leaning down and capturing his lips. "You come so good for me, Bray," I whisper into his lips as he moans into my mouth.

"Please, fuck me." His eyes—once a tranquil blue, are now transformed into a deep, thirsty black—lock onto mine with an intense lust. The air between us becomes charged, almost electric. I can hear the faint, ragged sound of his breathing and feel the warmth radiating from his skin. As his eyes slowly close, he breathes out, his voice a desperate whisper. "Please."

"I love when you beg."

Chapter Thirty-Five

Bohdi

I pull a condom out of the drawer. Brayden watches my every move as I put it on. We haven't spoken about condoms, but I assume it's the thing to do. Brayden doesn't stop me.

I squirt lube on the head of my dick, covering it in the latex, and squirt some more on my fingers as Brayden lies on his back, staring up at me, his chest rising at a rapid pace. My hands tremble with eagerness as I hold my dick in my hand and stare down at Brayden, who gazes at me like I'm the answer to life.

Right now, I feel like I am.

Bringing myself to his hole, I stare down as my swollen head probes his opening. Brayden instantly tenses. My gaze moves up to Brayden's eyes, and he nods, relaxing slightly for me. His ass sucks on my swollen head and I have to grit my teeth.

Think of work, think of all the presentations you have to go back to and watch and mark. Work. Work. Work, I tell myself, begging my dick to not release already.

"Fucomffahh," Brayden mews. He whimpers as I push in further and I have to stop.

"Baby, I need you to relax for me. You're too tight."

"Ahh fuck, call me baby again," he whines, begging me like a thirsty, slutty boy desperate for my dick.

"You like when I call you baby?" I kiss down his jaw, and his whimpers intensify as I push further into him. "Baby, if you keep squeezing my dick like that, I will come in two seconds," I grit out. Stars begin to field my vision. This is the tightest, warmest feeling I have ever felt, and I never want to leave.

"Relax, baby. Relax, baby," I repeat as he relaxes and I slide into the hilt, holding myself there as Brayden gasps and whines beneath me. Sweat drips from my head at how much I'm holding back. I could come right now, but I need to hold out for a little while. I need to experience what it's like to truly *own* Brayden.

"Fuck. I feel so full, Bohdi," he gasps.

"I'm going to move." I kiss his ear before sitting up and pulling out. Brayden winces, but when I push back in, his back rises off the bed.

"Holymotherfuck."

"You got that right." I try to hold myself back. His ass squeezes my dick incredibly tight.

"Bohdi." Brayden grabs my arms, and I stop, gazing down at him.

"I've been tested since I last had sex. I'm clean." He gulps, his cheeks flushed. "I want you to come inside me."

"Fuck." My voice comes out hoarse, squeezing his thighs as I hold myself still. I know if I move right now, I'm going to come. I wait a minute. After a few deep breaths and an image of my workload, I pull out slowly, pulling off the condom.

"I'm clean too."

Staring down at his hole, I add more lube before I push my swollen, leaking dick into him slowly and *Jesus fucking Christ.* This is what heaven must feel like. His warm, tight hole squeezes my dick like it never wants to let go, and I'm happy to oblige. If someone asked me where I wanted to die, this would be it: in Brayden's arms, buried deep inside him.

"There are no words to explain how fucking amazing you feel, baby."

Brayden whimpers and whines, pushing himself further onto my dick as he shuffles on the bed. Gasps fly from his mouth as I push further in.

"Fuck me, sir."

"Fuuuuuuuuuckkk!" I pull out and push myself in to him until I'm buried as deep as I can, and I pull back out again.

"It feels"—Brayden gasps as I push in a bit harder this time—"so good," he whines.

"My dick was made for your hole."

"Fuck me harder, sir, please." Brayden's words turn me into some crazed person as I pull back and push in hard, my balls slapping against his ass.

"Right there. Ommfffckkk."

"Right there, yeah." I continue with my pace. Brayden's eyes close as his head pushes into the pillow. A tingle begins at the bottom of my spine, and I know I can't hold out anymore. My balls tighten.

"Brayden, I'm coming in this tight fucking ass. I want you to take every drop," I grit out, squeezing his thighs.

"Yes, come in me, please," he begs. I wrap my hand around his rock-hard dick that has pre-cum leaking down it and begin pumping.

"I want you to come with me, and I want your eyes on me when you take my load into your tight ass. I want you to watch me when I claim and own every single fucking inch of you, baby."

"Myfuckingod!" Brayden screams as he pants, and his eyes flutter closed and then open up again, locking with mine. My balls tense up and then I let go, pushing my dick deeper into his hole as I empty myself into him.

"Fuckkkkkkkkk!" I roar, pumping myself so deep I feel like I start and end with Brayden. All I can think is he's mine now.

I've laid my claim. I've made my mark. Brayden Quake Anders is mine.

"I'm coming," Brayden groans, as his dick shoots out cum, and his ass tightens around my already sensitive dick which sends me into an overstimulated spiral as I twitch inside him watching him shatter in front of me.

I drop myself so my arms are either side of Brayden's head and place a gentle kiss against his lips between gasps of breaths from both of us.

"There's no word to describe that." I lean up and my dick slides easily out of Brayden's ass, causing a wince to leave his lips. I stare down as I watch a trail of my cum leak out of his ass. Gathering some up with one finger, I push it back inside him.

"Fuck, Boh." Brayden winces, tensing around my finger.

"Sorry," I whisper. "I want it to stay in you a little longer." I frown down at some of myself leaking out of him, not liking it. I want him to walk around with my cum inside him, feeling how wet and warm it feels. Remembering that I was there and no other man can put their dick inside him where my cum lays.

Shit. When did I become such an obsessed caveman?

I roll over and lie next to Brayden, bringing my arm up. He glances up at me as I pat my chest. With a smirk, he rests his head on my chest. We lay in silence for a few minutes, basking in the aftermath of what just happened. His breath, warm against my chest, creates a cocoon around us.

Time seems to stretch, each second etching the memory deeper. It's as if the universe holds its breath, allowing us to exist in that perfect suspended space. It doesn't surprise me that at this moment, my mind is clear. Clearer than it has ever been, and nothing seems more perfect than it does now. It's like everything around me has aligned, as if my whole life was leading up to this moment.

"You okay?" I break the silence. Brayden shifts up to lean on one arm.

"More than okay." His disheveled hair falls over his forehead, and his bright blue eyes bore into mine as my heart skips a beat.

"I needed to talk to you," I murmur, my fingers threading through his hair. His eyes flutter closed, a smile playing on his lips.

"Mmm," he responds, keeping his eyes shut as I lean in and kiss him. His teeth peek out in a wide grin, and I can't help but smile back.

"My favorite," I whisper, tracing my finger along his lips.

"I attended the meeting today." Brayden's smile falters.

"Without me?" He frowns.

"Well, yeah. I didn't think you'd want to come along," I admit.

He sighs, nodding. "Fair," he mumbles.

"During the meeting, they went over how family and friends can support someone struggling with addiction. One key point was keeping them away from drugs."

"Well, that won't be easy. It's practically next door to him," Brayden interjects.

"I know. I've considered that." On my drive back from the meeting, I realized waiting wouldn't help Bexley. We need a big change. "How would both Bexley and you feel about him moving in here?"

Brayden freezes.

"Wh—what?"

"I want to do everything I can, Brayden. If it's too much, I understand. But I want your brother to have a chance at life. I want him to see how amazing you are and how beautiful life can be. I want him to live, and I want to help him achieve that."

Brayden stares at me, wide-eyed and silent. "Bohdi . . . I—" He leans up, crashing his lips against mine. "I love you." The world seems to freeze, Brayden included. "Oh my god, I didn't mean that. It just slipped out in the heat of the moment. Please don't kick me out or think I'm weird. I swear—"

"Shh," I hush him, pressing my finger to his lips and kissing him to silence the babbling. He hesitantly kisses me back, and his eyes move away from me as I pull away.

"Hey, don't worry. I know you didn't mean it," I say, even though it stings to admit. I wish he had meant it. I wish he hadn't taken it back.

He nods, exhaling. "It truly was a mistake. I'm sorry," he repeats, another jab at my heart.

"I understand. It's okay." I force a smile, hoping he doesn't notice my hesitation. "So, are you on board with my suggestion?"

He nods, his smile growing. "Yes. You can't imagine what this means to both of us. I'll need to talk to Bex. I don't expect him to accept it immediately, though." He pauses, brow furrowing. "You do realize how challenging this will be, right?"

I nod, pulling his head back down to my chest as he snuggles in.

"I've considered it, and I'll need your help as much as possible without disrupting your college and training. Plus, we'll have to be discreet. No one can find out, especially given how close I live to the college."

Brayden sighs. "I feel like it's impossible."

"We can only try. I also want to start Bexley on some basic homeschooling, if he's up for it." Brayden raises an eyebrow at me.

"Were you made on planet perfect or something?" Bray teases, his eyes dancing.

"Far from it," I reply, pressing a kiss to his forehead.

13
Brayden 'Quake' Anders

Chapter Thirty-Six

Brayden

As I approach the trailer park, the cloud that hovers over the park is thicker than usual. Every time I come here, the cloud seems darker and heavier. I need to get Bexley away from here. It's as if all the good in you is drained away the moment you step on the grass, although today isn't like that for me.

Trudging through the muddy grass, I try to keep the smile off my face with memories of Bohdi. Everything seems perfect when he's around. I can't help it; every time I think about him, a rush of warmth and happiness washes over me, and I can't stop smiling. He brings me joy and makes me believe I can achieve anything I set my mind to.

I don't know where I'd be without Bohdi now. I know it's going to take a lot of persuasion to persuade Bexley to stay with Bohdi, but this is going to be the best thing for him. I just need to make him see that if I can get him away from this park, from my mom, from these awful people and from the drugs, I think he has a really good chance of overcoming this addiction. And I know Bohdi will be there for me every step of the way to help me as well as Bexley.

Last night's memory of saying I love you to Bohdi makes me cringe. I can't believe I blurted out those words. They've been replaying in my mind all night. Love, what a tangled, mysterious thing. I've never experienced it before. How would I even recognize it? According to Google, love hits you like a thousand emotions at once. A feeling you've never felt before. It's happiness, a lighter breath when your loved one is near, and an ache when they're not. Life suddenly loses its logic without them. And Bohdi? Well, he's turned my world upside down. Even those few days we didn't talk felt unbearable. But can love happen this quickly?

Earlier, I called and texted Bexley but received no response. Now, standing at the trailer door, I'm assaulted by the familiar smell of alcohol and unwashed laundry. It makes my stomach turn every time I walk in here.

My so-called mother is not here, likely indulging elsewhere with Karl. The cluttered kitchen, covered with used pans and dishes, prompts a mental note to tidy up—not for her, but for Bexley. As I step into the room, an unsettling feeling washes over me.

Something's not right.

Bexley lies half-covered, half-exposed, fast asleep at three in the afternoon. Perhaps his recent relapse has left him utterly drained? I approach, perching on the edge of the bed, and gently shake his leg. No response. His eyes remain tightly closed, no movement. The air thickens, and my heartbeat echoes in the silence.

"Bex," I murmur, shaking his leg again, desperation clawing at my chest. Still no movement. I shake him harder.

"Bexley!" I shout, but the room absorbs my voice. My heart thumps violently as I rise, crossing to the side of the bed. My trembling hand reaches for the cover, and that's when I spot the sickly stain on the pillow by his mouth. Panic surges through me as I yank the covers back, and something falls to the floor.

A needle.

My fingers dig into Bexley's skin, shaking him franticly. "Wake up. Please, wake up!" I plead, but silence taunts me. I cradle the back of his neck, lowering my ear to his chest.

Nothing.

No heartbeat.

No movement.

His lifeless form lies before me. "Bexley, stop messing around!" I cry, my voice breaking. "Please, stop this." Desperation fuels me as I begin chest compressions. "Help me! Fucking someone, anyone, please help!" I cry.

"Remember when I hid in the wardrobe all day, and you thought someone had taken me?" My voice trembles. "You were furious when I finally came out, vowing to get me back someday." Tears blur my vision. "Well, Bex, you've got me back now. Wake up. Please, wake up."

But the room holds its silence, and my world shatters around me.

"Shit," Daxton's voice pierces the room, his paleness mirroring my dread as he gazes at my hands pressed against Bexley's chest.

"Call a fucking ambulance," I plead, my voice cracking.

The world fractures around me. It's as if I'm an outsider, watching my own undoing. Bexley's life flashes before my eyes. The laughter, the shared secrets, the promises we made when we were young. We promised to explore the world together.

"London was your dream, Bex. Remember? You wanted to ride that giant Ferris wheel, see all of London from above. I said I would wait at the bottom because heights terrify me, but if you wake up, I swear, I'll ride it with you. Every stomach-churning moment. I swear." Tears blur my vision as I choke on a sob. I lean down, pinching his nose, covering his mouth with mine, desperate to breathe life into him.

"Stop playing games!" I scream. "Fucking Stop!"

My hands press against his chest, rhythmically, desperately. He's just messing around. He has to be.

"Okay, London isn't enough," I babble, my laughter mingling with tears. "How about Reese's Pieces every day for a whole year? You can't resist that, right?" But my words echo in the silence, and I cling to hope, repeating it like a mantra: *He'll open his eyes. He has to.*

"BB for fucking life, Bex. For life!" I scream, my voice cracking. "This isn't life, Bex. Wake the fuck up. You owe me at least another sixty years."

My resolve crumbles, muscles turning to lead as I continue pressing down on his chest. Each compression feels like a desperate plea to the universe, bargaining for more time. But Bexley remains immovable.

"Remember when Mom told us once that after we were born, they placed us down next to each other. The first thing I did was turn my head to look at you and smiled? Five minutes old and all it took was one glance at you and I was content already. That still hasn't changed Bex." Sobs rack my body.

"Blink three times, please. Blink three times and let me know you're okay," I weep.

A gentle tug on my arm interrupts my frantic rhythm. A lady, her face blurred by my tears, pulls me away. My hands lose contact with Bexley's chest, and I watch as others sweep in. They surround him, taking over from my trembling desperation. Time hangs suspended, and I'm caught between disbelief and anguish. Bexley—my brother, my partner in mischief, my fucking twin—lies there, lifeless. The room pulses with urgency, but my world narrows to that unmoving form.

I whisper it again, a fragile chant: "Wake up, Bex. Please, wake up." But the silence mocks me, echoing through the shattered pieces of my heart.

"Bray." I hear Kal and Tray's voices, their tear-streaked faces etching pain into my soul. They stand in the doorway of our bedroom, where Bexley lies on the bed, surrounded by paramedics. Daxton retreats, fading into shadows. My legs waver, threatening to collapse, but Kal and Tray rush to my side. Their arms envelop me, holding me upright as my world crumbles. I bury my face in their chests, sobs racking my body.

"Please, Bexley," I whisper, my voice raw. "Come back." Over their shoulders, I glimpse the paramedics—desperate, skilled, repeating the motions I'd attempted. But Bexley remains still. Time stretches, a cruel elastic, and I cling to hope, even as it slips through my trembling fingers. He's still not moving.

"We got you, Bray." Kal's voice brushes against my ear. I watch as the paramedics falter, their movements suspended in cruel stillness. My world grinds to a halt alongside them. The lady who pulled me away—her eyes, brimming with sympathy, lock onto mine. She doesn't need to say it. He's gone. I sensed it the moment I stepped into this room. His soul, once tied to my life, has slipped away.

"I'm sorry," she murmurs, her voice weighted with sorrow.

"We did everything we could. And so did you." Her eyes squint as if it physically pains her to say the next two words. "He's gone."

The world around me crumbles, surrounded by flames.

My brother, my twin, my best friend, is gone. In that burning moment, I realize life holds no purpose without him.

Chapter Thirty-Seven

Bohdi

I find myself frowning at my phone, baffled by Brayden's radio silence. He hasn't answered my calls or texts all day, and it's unnerving. He was supposed to meet with Bexley yesterday to discuss what I mentioned, but there's been no word. I've searched the campus, but neither Brayden, Kal, nor Tray are in sight. Perhaps they're caught up in extra training?

As the minutes tick by, anticipation builds. Class is about to start. Could Brayden have confided in Bexley, only for things to go wrong? My pen taps nervously against the desk, and I fixate on the door, waiting for answers. But as more students file in, Brayden remains noticeably absent.

A sinking feeling settles in my gut. Is he struggling with the weight of saying he loves me? Even though he made it pretty clear, he didn't mean it. My phone jolts to life, Denny's name flashing across the screen. But there's no time. I'll call him later. I silence the phone, tucking it into my desk drawer. A quick check after Denny's call ends reveals nothing from Brayden—no text, no missed call. Silence hangs heavy like a dark weight in the air.

Then Daxton enters, his posture defeated, head bowed lower than I've ever seen. He bypasses his own desk, heading straight for mine. When he looks up, his eyes are a raw, swollen mess, bloodshot and half-closed. I recognize that look—it's etched in my memory, the aftermath of nights spent crying yourself to sleep. Something has shattered.

"Daxton," I choke out, my voice strained. "What happened? Where's Brayden?" My heart races, and swallowing becomes a struggle. Daxton's trembling lip betrays him. His gaze flits between mine, and then the wall breaks. Sobs rack his body, shoulders convulsing.

"I'm sorry," he manages, voice cracking.

I grip his shoulder, desperation rising. "Where is Brayden?" The room tilts, and everything inside me plummets.

"You. You fucking piece of shit!" A primal roar pierces the air, and suddenly, Daxton is no longer in front of me but sprawled on the floor, a fist having collided with his face. The violence unfolds in a blur. I can't process it immediately.

Trayton jumps over Daxton, raining blows upon him, while Kal remains frozen, a marble statue caught in an out-of-body trance. For a heartbeat, I'm paralyzed too, shock gripping me. Then reality snaps back.

"Trayton!" My voice echoes through the silence as I stride around my desk, seizing him by the back of his sweater. "Explain what the hell is going on!"

The class holds its breath, and nausea churns within me. My mind races through countless scenarios. "Where is Brayden?" I grit out, not caring as Daxton lies on the floor beneath my feet, blood all over his face. But he just stares up at Trayton, who takes uncontrolled gasps, while gritting his teeth down at Daxton.

"Where's Brayden?" I shout again, my concern overwhelming me. Trayton's eyes remain fixed on Daxton.

"Ask him," Trayton spits, physically directing his disdain at Daxton. "He's the cause. Him and his junky family."

My resolve snaps. "Take yourself to the dean, right this instant!" I bellow in Trayton's face.

"You're as good as dead, Rivers." Trayton's parting glare at Daxton lingers in the room as he exits. I snatch tissues from my desk, offering them to Daxton. He stares blankly, shaking his head. My focus shifts to Kal, desperation etched across my face.

"Please, tell me what happened?" A solitary tear traces Kal's cheek, and the world tilts. "Is it Brayden?" His eyes assess me, up and down.

"You heard Trayton," Kal replies, voice frail. "Ask him." He retreats, another tear slipping free, and then he turns away. Head bowed, he walks out of the classroom, leaving me grappling with uncertainty.

"Daxton," I murmur, my voice a fragile thread. "I'll take you to the nurse, but please—I need to know—"

"It's Bexley," he whispers, and time fractures. I wait, suspended, as Daxton's trembling subsides. The entire class watches, a collective breath held. His tear-streaked face lifts, anguish etched in every line. "He's gone, sir. Fucking gone, and it's all my fault."

Sobs rack him, legs buckling, and I can't even steady him. My own legs waver, threatening to crumble beneath the weight of his confession. I cling to my desk, the room spinning, distant murmurs a haunting echo.

I don't look back at Daxton. I don't meet my students' eyes. Instead, I stagger toward the door, desperate for air. My lungs constrict, suffocating. Fingers fumble with my tie as I loosen the buttons and heat engulfs me. Outside the lecture hall, I clutch the wall, knuckles white, and stumble down the corridor. Concerned faces blur past, and when the cool air hits, I gasp—a panicked breath in a world that's shattered once again.

The trailer looms before me, its old, battered remains holding years of agony. But today, the pain is a relentless hurricane, tearing at my insides. I sense it even from this distance, an ache that defies walls and doors.

Inside my car, I remain motionless, fixated on that door. The silence envelops me, thick and suffocating. It's as though Brayden's sobs echo through the air, haunting me. The pain seeps out, oozing like a wound that refuses to heal. I scan the surroundings, a park, a community that now wears its own cloak of mourning. A loss it didn't care for, yet one that hangs heavy in the stillness.

Isn't that how it goes? When you're alive, people pass you by, indifferent. But when death claims you, suddenly they mourn as if a piece of themselves is forever fractured.

My car door creaks, and I step out into the hole of pain. Each heavy footstep stabs at my soul, drawing me inevitably closer. I can't be certain if he's here, but the invisible thread tugs at my core, pulling me toward him, toward his agony. My hand hovers, prepared to knock, but hesitation grips me. Instead, I push the door wide open.

Silence greets me, a suffocating veil. Then the smell—a haze of decay and misery—hits like a physical blow. My eyes scan the room, desperate for Brayden.

There, on the tattered sofa, lies the woman I glimpsed at from the door that day I was here, their mother. Her frail form crumples against the torn fabric, arms wrapped around herself. My heart bleeds for her, even as memories flood back of Brayden's whispered confessions, the fractured glimpses into their fractured lives. She's responsible for this wreckage. Had she raised those boys as they deserved, Brayden wouldn't be mourning his brother now.

I turn away from her, leaving her to wallow in her pain. A fraction of what she's earned.

A door to the right catches my attention, slightly ajar. Inside, a mattress rests on the floor, a grimy quilt atop it. A broken cupboard, walls veiled in mold. But it's the room at the end that seizes my breath. The loose doorknob rattles as I put my hand on it and push down. My heart ignites with agony.

There, curled into a ball on the bed, Brayden trembles. Guilt and pain are etched into every line of his body; face buried. The room showcases a life I haven't seen—old posters clinging to the walls, memories held together by frayed tape. Brayden and Bexley's childhood is captured in faded photographs, a photo booth moment frozen in time, their laughter denying their hidden struggles. Life, to them, was bearable as long as they clung to each other.

My throat constricts. A lump lodges there. Brayden clings to the sheets, knuckles white. His sniffles echo through the room.

"Brayden," I rasp, my voice cracking. His head tilts up, and his destroyed face shatters me.

"B—Boh." His voice, a raw whisper, pushes me toward him. He extends a trembling hand as I reach for the bed. "No," he pleads. "Please don't—touch."

I hover, lost, my heart echoing his pain. What can I offer? There's nothing, no remedy for this depth of loss, this heartbreak that splits existence in two.

"It still smells of him," he sobs, eyes swollen and desperate. "I can still smell him. It's as if he's still here."

I meet his gaze, helpless.

Every word he utters mirrors my own past, the ache, the void. I silently beg the universe for comfort, for something to ease his torment. His pain booms, and my heart fractures over and over. I walk to the end of the bed, hating that I can't touch him, that

I can't hold him and his pain. I sit on a stool at the end of the room, staring at him on the bed as he clutches to the quilt like it's his lifeline.

"Tell me about him," I whisper. "I want to know everything about him."

Brayden doesn't hesitate. "He is—was"—he chokes on a sob—"was my other half. Not just a brother, but a mirror reflecting my soul. We shared everything, the good, the bad, the unspoken. When we were kids, we'd lie in this very room, staring at the ceiling, inventing patterns."

His fingers stroke over the quilt he holds in a tight grip in his hands. "He loved storms," Brayden says, his voice a fragile thread. "When thunder rumbled, he'd drag me outside, rain soaking our clothes. 'Listen,' he'd say, 'that's the universe singing.' And we'd stand there, drenched, believing we could hear the heavens."

My lips trembling, I ask, "What did it sound like?"

"Freedom," Brayden whispered. "Like every secret we'd ever shared was twisted into those raindrops. But now . . . " His voice falters. "Now it's just rain."

I listen, my own heart aching. "What was he like?"

Brayden's chuckle is bittersweet. "Fearless. He'd climb trees, scrape his knees, and laugh like it was the only way to breathe. But he had this quiet side too, the one that loved poetry and sunsets. We'd sit by the window, watching the world turn gold, and he'd say, 'Life's a canvas, Bray. We paint it with our mome nts.'" He chuckles. "I thought he was just high, but then I began looking at life with him and it was beautiful with him by my side."

"And now?" I ask, my voice barely a whisper.

Brayden's gaze turned inward. "Now, it's like half my canvas is blank. Bexley was the color, the vibrant strokes that made life beautiful. What am I going to do, Boh? Please tell me what I'm meant to do."

His eyes beg me, but there is nothing I can say that will help because the truth is, nothing is going to take this pain away. It never leaves, it just gets easier to carry.

"I don't know, Bray. I don't know how to answer that, but know I'm here, and I'm not leaving you. I'm not going anywhere."

13
Brayden 'Quake' Anders

Chapter Thirty-Eight

Brayden

The hours and minutes blur together, a misty haze as I lie here, clutching the quilt that still carries Bexley's scent. Sometimes, I shift the fabric, and with each movement, his soul slips away. But I scrape at the edges, desperate to find my connection to him again. It won't last forever, I know that, but for now, I have his clothes too. They're my lifeline, a fragile thread that binds me to him. As long as I can smell him, he's still here.

Bohdi sits on the stool, silent and solid. A quiet assurance that I'm not alone. I don't want him to leave. Just having him here, someone who knows the jagged edges of my grief, makes breathing a fraction easier. The room holds its breath, and I stare at the floor, lost in my thoughts.

Then Kal and Tray walk in. I don't care about their judgment or their raised eyebrows. Right now, it's all noise. My focus remains fixed on the wall beside my bed, as if I can etch Bexley's memory into the paint. I cling to it, to him, as if my life depends on it. Because maybe, in some way, it does.

"Bray." A soft voice reaches me from behind, and I snap around. "Don't touch!" I shout, my desperation echoing. Tray stands frozen, bloodshot eyes wide, hands raised in surrender.

"Please," I beg, a tear escaping. "Don't touch the quilt."

Tray nods, understanding. "I know," he says. "Sir said." His gaze flickers toward the door, a fleeting glance.

"Where is Bohdi?" I ask, my voice trembling. Tray inhales deeply, nostrils flaring.

"Gone home. Kal's making sure of it. Forget about him. Focus on you, Bray. Me and Kal, we've got you, always."

"Why is Kal making sure Bohdi goes home?"

"Forget about him," Tray insists, his voice edged with something I can't quite place. I frown up at him, seeking answers.

"What happened?" I press, panic clawing at my throat.

"Kal put two and two together when we got here," Tray explains. "It clicked when I called Mr. Stiles 'sir.'" He winces, and I sit up in bed, scanning the room.

"What is Kal doing?" My heart races.

"You know he protects you, Bray," Tray says. "Give it a few days, and then you can talk to me and Kal about whatever." He gestures toward me and then the door. "Right now, you need to focus on you."

Exhaustion pulls me back down, and I bury my nose in the quilt, inhaling deeply. Bexley's scent fills my lungs, and I relax into it, forgetting about everything else around me, Boh, Tray and Kal. I breathe in my twin, allowing his smell to drift me off to sleep.

My eyes flutter open, heart racing, and for a fleeting moment, I cling to the hope that it was all a dream. But the weight of pain in my clenched fists shatters that fragile illusion. It wasn't a dream; it was painfully real. Waves of agony crash over me once more, threatening to drown me.

I sit up, gasping for air, and lean over the edge of the bed, retching until my stomach is empty. The room spins, and I glimpse Kal and Tray standing there, their eyes wide with concern, their faces outlined with exhaustion. Kal approaches, a glass of water in his trembling hands. My dry throat aches for it. I gulp it down in one desperate swallow, and he refills the glass from a bottle, passing it to me.

His gaze locks onto mine, and he whispers my name, so softly it's almost a prayer. "Bray," he says, and the wall inside me crumbles further. Tray steps forward, holding out a handful of Nerds Ropes—the sweet, sticky candies we used to share. My trembling fingers reach for them, and as I tear off the first piece, tears cascade down my cheeks. The taste floods my senses, memories crashing like waves, and I hurl the candies against the wall, each impact echoing the ache in my chest.

"They taste like shit!" I scream. "They taste bland. They're fucking shit. I hate them," I cry, curling myself back into the pain that drowns me.

Chapter Thirty-Nine

Bohdi

Kal and Tray know. I guess Brayden saving me under 'Sir' in his phone was a little too obvious. When Tray turned up to find his teacher sitting in his best friend's room, and then echoed the word "sir" in question, Kal immediately realized.

For the past two days, I've existed in my truck, cocooned in grief for Bray, but my own grief that's resurfaced, banging away in my aching chest. Nightmares of Jace have plagued my mind for the last two nights. Every time I drift off, I wake up in a sweat with tears streaming down my face.

Sleep, snacks and whiskey, all confined within these metal walls. People knock on my window, urging me to move, but I offer them halfhearted grunts, my gaze fixed on the trailer door.

I venture out only for necessities: food, whiskey, or a desperate piss behind someone else's trailer. My suit, worn for two days straight, clings to me like a second skin. Deodorant from the glove compartment is my feeble attempt at freshness.

Kal and Tray take turns leaving the trailer, not once leaving Brayden on his own. Kal's disdainful glances cut through me, while Tray's sympathetic eyes hold a world of unspoken understanding. Yesterday, Tray approached the truck, offering small updates about Brayden.

He's not well. Of course he isn't. Grief isn't fleeting; it's a relentless ache that claws at you day and night. Nothing aligns anymore. Life fractures into senseless fragments. People blur into shadows. Everything crumbles around you into nothings.

Tray explained briefly what happened to Bexley. An overdose.

Intentional? That's uncertain.

They took Bexley's body for an autopsy, but there are no results yet. Daxton discovered Brayden, desperately performing CPR, pleading for life. Trayton holds extreme resentment toward Daxton, but I know blame is a lifeline we grasp when emotions surge and grief weigh us down.

Kal said if I step one foot in the trailer, he will call the dean and tell him everything. I don't know what he knows, but he made it clear he would act on his threat. I know through staff room whispers that Kal Jacob can have someone's job taken away with a snap of finger.

But the thing is, I've sat here for the last twenty-four hours and asked myself: Do I really care about my job? And I don't know. I thought I found my love in teaching. I thought it was my escape from the black hole I fell into, but last night I realized something. It wasn't the teaching that pulled me out of that black hole. It wasn't the teaching I fell in love with.

It was Brayden all along who entered my darkness.

He became the love I never anticipated, the light that pierced my shadows. And now I sit here, still not moving, still not being in there to bear his pain because I know if Kal does ring the dean, it's not only me it affects. What could Brayden lose? Could he lose his hockey, his scholarship? Would Kal really do that?

Opening my phone, I see multiple missed calls from the school, from Denny, but I can't talk to them. I can't explain why I'm not at school. My finger scrolls down my contacts until I stop and hover over the one person that knows how to help me when everything comes crashing down. Who has always picked me up and put the pieces back together again. I click on the name and the call connects.

"Hello," I force myself to say, trying to sound more positive than I actually am.

"Boh," Cash drags out, his tone cautious. "What happened?" he asks immediately after. It's my fault that Cash and I have grown apart, but there's one thing about him. He is an exceptional older brother. He has a knack for sensing when something is wrong.

"Everything," I say with a sigh. I'm already feeling a sense of relief as the world becomes less heavy.

"Talk to me, Brother." There's a rustling noise, followed by the sound of a door shutting.

"Are you certain you can speak?" I question. The last thing I want is to be talking to him while he's with someone, especially Rylee. I adore Rylee, but she'd refuse to let this go and wouldn't settle for the limited details I'd provide. Until I admitted everything and proved what a hypocrite I was, she would continue to hound me.

"Sure, no problem," he says hastily. "I'm heading out for a walk. Rylee is working from home and I'm getting the impression this isn't something you want anyone knowing, even one of your most favorite people." He laughs.

"Thanks, Bro. you're right. I love Ry, but—"

"If she suspected something was happening with you, she would be relentless and might even fly to Michigan."

I can't help but laugh, as he obviously knows Rylee better than anyone else. Silence fills the call as I listen to Cash's footsteps and the gentle breeze that filters through the speaker. Cash doesn't pressure me to talk, he simply waits for me to take the lead. I sink further into my seat, raking my fingers through my hair. I can't find the right words, but this is why I called Cash.

I don't need to filter my thoughts around him. I can speak my mind, and he will always listen.

"Did you attempt to fight when you realized you had feelings for Rylee? Even though you knew it was wrong?" The sound of Cash taking a deep breath reaches my ears. I realize he likely doesn't want to address this, particularly given my actions involving him and Rylee, but even though it's not identical, it's comparable.

"Of course." He speaks in a whisper, burdened by the guilt that I know plagues him. "I've always considered Rylee to be amazing. I acted the way I did because I found her incredible, and it made me uncomfortable. Lines felt blurred on my part when I got to know her after Jace introduced her to me." He exhales a laugh with a huff. "Although it might sound messed up, pushing her away and treating her poorly felt like the right decision, and I still believe it was the right decision at that moment." It's clear that he is being cautious in selecting his words. "When we lost Jace." Cash falls silent.

The mere mention of losing Jace feels like knives tearing at my heart. It causes physical pain, and it's clear that Cash is feeling the same way based on his silence.

I manage to utter, "Cash." My voice is barely audible. "Forget about it, I—"

"No. Whatever this is about, I want to be there for you and help you talk it out," he rushes out before continuing, "Although people had their opinions and views, it wasn't as people thought. I wasn't waiting on the sidelines for her. Fuck. I thought Jace was going to marry her and that filled me with so much joy, Boh." He would have if he wasn't taken from us.

"I fought hard, Boh. Words can't describe it. I fought with every bit of strength I had. Guess I'm weak as fuck, because I have never fallen for someone so easily." His voice cracks toward the end. "I tried my best to avoid being near her, but the reality is, she needed me as much as I needed her. We mourned as one, blending our pain and supporting each other, Boh."

"Do you recall the moment you knew?"

"The moment I knew I couldn't live without her and would do anything to keep her by my side?"

Softly, I respond with a whisper, "Yeah."

"It's when Matthew Richardson had the nerve to make her laugh, a real laugh. The thought of someone else bringing her happiness instead of me made me feel like my heart was stabbed. In that moment, I understood she was mine, regardless of her acceptance." As Cash's words linger, we sit in peaceful silence, lost in thought. The very notion of Brayden confiding in anyone else about his grief makes me sick to my stomach.

I stare at the trailer door, and my stomach turns knowing it should be me in there, not Kal, not Tray. Me. The idea of someone else being the reason for his smile makes me want to rip this state apart.

I'm so fucked.

"Who is she? For the way you're acting, I'm assuming it's not good?"

"Cash, I'm in big trouble," I admit, a tear slipping from my eye as I comprehend the consequences. "The one person I'm not meant to love is the one thing I crave more than anything else in this world. I'm at a loss for what to do."

"Boh." Cash stops momentarily. "I need you to talk to me. What's going on?"

"I'm in love, Cash. I'm in love and they saved me without even realizing it, but I can't—" Silence fills the air, but Cash is too smart. He knows there's only one thing that could make me feel this way.

"I—it's not a student, is it?"

It is impossible for me to say no. I can't lie to him. I answer his question with silence.

"Fuck, Boh," he says, and we fall silent again. Staring at the trailer door, my mind races. Brayden's world has come crashing down and me being around him could make it worse. I contemplate how to handle this. Can I walk away? Just thinking about it makes me physically sick. There's a faint sound of waves that I can hear.

"Are you at the beach?"

"Mhmm," murmurs Cash. "I had a suspicion I'd need to have a conversation with my son after talking to you, and it appears I was correct." The silence returns, and all I can hear is the strong wind over the speaker. I have a clear mental image of Cash's position, so I close my eyes and picture myself next to him on the beach.

"Brother, I'm really missing you." I sigh.

"Miss you too, Boh." Cash's voice drifts with the wind. "Come home for a bit," Cash whispers. "Come. Be with your family."

I imagine leaving here, leaving Brayden, leaving him to fester in his pain, and I can't. I can't leave him. I had family around me, but I know what it was like to go home at night. You feel so lonely. There's no one there to hold you while you cry yourself to sleep. No one to share your pain and tell you everything will be okay when you both know it won't, but you cling to that false hope. I know how ruined it made me, how much I crawled into this dark hole and shut everyone out. How much I resented anyone that was happy.

I know it all too well.

"I can't. I need to be with him, Cash."

"Him?"

"Cash, I've got to go." I put the phone down, opening the car door. I don't care what anyone has to say. I'm there for him. I'm going to hold his pain and treat it as my own. I'm going to be the one he cries too. I'm going to stand by him each day and even if I have to watch him grieve and there's nothing I can do. I want him to know he doesn't have to use any strength because I'm going to carry him through it.

13
Brayden 'Quake' Anders

Chapter Forty
Brayden

A commotion of shouting stirs me from my hazy sleep. Initially, I assume it's my mother caught in an argument, but the voices are too deep, too masculine. I turn my aching head toward the door, and there they stand: Kal and Bohdi, locked in a tense standoff, chests colliding, fists clenched.

"What the hell is happening?" My voice, scratchy and raw, pierces the tension. Both Kal and Bohdi snap their attention toward me.

"I was just telling our teacher here that he needs to leave."

Bohdi's tormented expression bores into me, as if he senses the pain I'm struggling with, like he'd do anything to ease it.

"Bray, please." His eyes plead with me, and I realize how much I've missed him. I can't gauge how long it's been since he was last here, but the ache of his absence is physical.

"Kal, please."

"No." Kal's face contorts. "He's taking advantage, Bray. I won't stand for it."

"Kal, it's not what you think."

Kal whirls around on his heels.

"Then tell me. You've kept this from me. Explain what it's like. Help me understand." His voice cracks. "I can't bear to watch you suffer like this and do nothing."

"I need him, Kal." My trembling lip betrays me, and tears blur my stinging eyes.

"Kal." Bohdi's voice breaks through, and Kal's head snaps toward him. "I know you said you'd report this to the dean, and you know what? Go ahead. I don't care about my job. I don't care about teaching. The only person I care about is lying there, shattered, while we stand idly by." His finger points at me, and I gasp, the weight of his truth settling on my exposed vulnerabilities. "I'd sacrifice everything for that boy. Everything." His gaze locks onto Kal's, a tear escaping from the corner of his eye. "But remember, it won't be just me you're hurting. It'll be him, too."

Bohdi stands tall, his beard grown out, stubble longer than usual. His greasy hair and rumpled suit make him look like a man unraveling, crumbling alongside me. I ache to reach out and touch him.

My legs move before sleepless thought. I rise from the bed, knees threatening to give out as I take tentative steps toward Kal and Boh. My legs that I haven't used in days shake as I buckle with my next step, but Bohdi pushes Kal aside, catching me, his eyes boring into mine.

"I'm here," he whispers, pulling me close. And then it all spills out. I cry until I can't anymore. Bohdi cradles me in his lap, Kal's hand rubbing my back as I choke on my own sobs.

I must fall asleep in Bohdi's arms on the floor, because when I wake, Bohdi is leaned up against the wall while I'm tucked in tight to his chest. I grip his shirt, leaning my head up. My head throbs as Bohdi runs fingers through my hair. Tray sits on the stool eating a sandwich while Kal sits on the floor opposite, staring straight at me with an emotionless stare. No, actually he stares at Bohdi's hands running through my hair.

"Bray." Bohdi's whisper draws my eyes upward. His tired blue gaze studies me, and a frown creases his forehead. "Can you eat something for me, please?" His eyebrows knit together in a desperate plea, and I nod instinctively. I can't bear to see Bohdi sad.

The sandwich tastes like sawdust, but I have to admit, I feel less sick, less empty once I finish half. My body only allows me to eat half of it, but I'm full already. I put the plate down and Bohdi whispers thank you, while pulling me in tight to his chest again. I close my eyes, but then I realize something doesn't feel right.

"Bex." I sit up, urgency flooding me. "Bex."

Everyone freezes as I leap to my feet, the room spinning. I scramble onto the bed, cocooned in the quilt, seeking the scent of my brother. It's there, faint but familiar, and I cling to it as if it can mend the fractures within me.

My groggy eyes flutter open, and Bohdi stands by the bed, holding a cup of water and another sandwich. I sit up, accepting the water first, then the sandwich. Bohdi crouches down, observing as I take a few bites.

"I need you to come stay with me for a while," he says.

"No," Kal snaps, and I turn my head to look at him. "He can stay with me. How will it look if he stays with you?"

"No one has to know he's staying with me," Bohdi counters. "We can tell the school he's with you temporarily. Given the circumstances, they'll accept it."

"I can't," Kal grits out.

"Are you really that awkward?" Bohdi's frustration seeps through.

"My dad is on the school board," Kal explains. "He'll know that Brayden isn't staying with me."

Their back-and-forth exhausts me. Kal's next words cut deeper.

"Why does he need to stay with you, anyway? Bray has been my best friend since childhood. My parents and I can take care of him."

Bohdi rubs his temples. "I don't doubt that, but I want Bray with me." His vulnerability melts something inside me.

The room pulses with tension as Kal's protest hangs in the air. "Well, I want Bray with me," he insists, but I'm too drained to intervene.

"Kal, stop this," my voice trembles.

"I've been where Brayden is. I lost someone close last year. I want to be there for him. Please, let me." Boh's eyes plead with Kal, and I swallow down the emotions threatening to engulf me once more.

"I know," Kal replies, his voice softer. I frown. How would he know? But my exhaustion doesn't let me ponder it anymore.

"I'll stay with Bohdi and tell the school I'm here," I plead with Kal. "If your parents ask, can you say that you and Tray are keeping an eye on me? Please."

Kal nods, lips pressed tight. "Okay, but you need to know something." His words hang heavy. "Mom is coming tomorrow to discuss the funeral arrangements with you and your mom."

I gulp, closing my eyes, taking a deep breath. "We don't have the money for a funeral." My lip trembles, tears escaping. Bohdi's hand reaches out, gently wiping them away.

"Don't worry about the money," Bohdi interjects.

Kal follows up. "My dad is handling it. We'll need your input, though, if you're up for it."

I nod. "Not today?"

Kal's voice is softer now. "Not today," he confirms, offering me a tight-lipped smile. He leans over the bed, careful not to touch anything, and places a kiss on my forehead. My eyes well up again.

I glance at Kal, who blinks three times at me. It takes me back to when I was urging Bex to blink three times, even though deep down, I knew he was gone.

A sob racks my body as Bohdi pulls me close, and Kal stares at me, tears streaming down his face. This pain won't leave, and I'm lost. How am I supposed to carry on without my brother? He was my reason for everything, the driving force behind my hard work. Now, I'm left with nothing.

13
Brayden 'Quake' Anders

Chapter Forty-One
Brayden

Two weeks later

When you're trapped in a cycle of tears, time slips away like sand through your fingers. These past two weeks blurred together—I can't pinpoint where the days went or who crossed my path. All I know is that each night, I bury my face in Bohdi's chest, Bexley's quilt buried between us, until sleep claims me, and then I'm haunted by Bex's face. But in my dreams, he's different. Happy. It's where I seek comfort in losing him.

His sunken cheeks have filled out, his face radiant. He smiles freely, and when I look at him, it's like gazing into a mirror—except I know it's Bexley because of that unruly, overgrown hair he always tucked behind his ears.

He tells me it's better where he is now. That he misses me but will remain by my side every day. I've asked him countless times why he did it, but he never answers directly. Instead, he insists I find peace in his newfound home.

He's okay now.

Every morning, I wake with the mantra: He's better.

But the truth is, maybe he is, but I'm not. I'm shattered, piecing together fragments of our shared soul that he left behind.

And I keep telling him, if he'd stayed, I would've helped him. But he only replies, "It was too late."

Yet every night, my dream unfolds the same way. Bexley waits for me at the park gate—the same one we hung around in as kids. His smile is bright, and in his hands, he holds those nostalgic Nerds Ropes.

It's a bittersweet reunion every single time, because dreams don't last forever, and my body won't sleep forever.

Yesterday, I learned I could go visit Bexley and say my personal goodbyes before the funeral today, but I couldn't. I knew that the body that lays in that casket isn't my brother. It's not the Bex in my dreams and I want to hold on to that version.

As I sit staring at the solid casket in front of me, I still can't believe that Bexley is in there. Kal and Tray sit on either side of me, while Kal's mom and dad sit beside Kal, with my mom in between them. She's crying like her life has ended when, in fact, she is the root of all of this. She is the reason Bex is in that casket. I've told her Bex was the only thing that kept me coming back to that trailer. I promised her once I had removed everything to do with Bex from there, she will never see me again. Of course, she wept and begged me and said how sorry she was, but she wasn't. Bex was her pawn, her drug line, and now he's gone. What is she going to do?

Fucking die, I hope.

There's no seat in heaven for her. Hell can have their way with her.

Staring across the casket, all my teammates stand in their smart suits, paying their respect as everyone's eyes are on the casket as the pastor reads words about Bexley. Every morning this week, Bohdi would ask me one thing.

"Tell me one memory of Bexley."

And then he'd ask me the same thing before I went to bed. I would sometimes get lost in my stories, but I didn't realize he was writing a eulogy the whole time. A couple of nights ago, he read it to me. A lifetime condensed into one speech. It held everything: the laughter, the unfulfilled plans, like that trip to London, and the ache of loss. Bohdi became my rock—the one who held me when my legs faltered, who cradled me through tear-soaked nights.

Denny questioned Bohdi's whereabouts, but Boh slipped through the cracks, leaving only apologies. I spent a week cocooned in his house, but grief doesn't hold to calendars. School couldn't wait. I returned, seeking relief in familiar faces. Kal and Tray stood by me, their silent strength supporting my fragile resolve.

In class, I found moments of respite, the dull lectures, the scribbled notes. But I was always dying to get back to Bohdi's so I could go to sleep and be with my brother again. Cope believes I'm still at my mom's, unaware that my old bed remains untouched.

I feel a nudge as Tray looks at me, his bloodshot eyes slicing at my already damaged heart. I forget how close they were sometimes; I wonder how much this is killing him deep inside.

"They're ready for you." He nods to the pastor, who has obviously finished, but I didn't hear a thing. I said I wanted to do my own reading. I wanted to write my own for Bex. I tried to make it long. I wanted everyone to know how special he was, but then I realized I didn't need everyone to know how special he was. I only needed him to know that.

So as I step up and walk toward the front, I don't read from a script. I don't read from notes I had jotted down. I speak the truth to Bexley and only Bexley. Staring at the casket, tears run down my face.

"To my other half, my twin: Why did you slip away, leaving me here? You told me last night in my dreams that you're better now, but can't you see the wreckage you've left behind?" Clenching my jaw, I dig my nails into my palm, taking a deep breath.

"Your laughter lingers in the breeze, teasing me with memories. I glimpse your reflection in the mirror—the same eyes, the same curve of lips—and I ache. Bex, did you take a piece of me with you? Or did I lose a piece of myself when you left?" A tear slips free, trickling down my face. I dig my fingers into my palms harder.

"I would have held on, Bex. I would have fought against the darkness that consumed you. But you slipped through my grasp, and now I'm left with the jagged edges of our severed bond. We were more than siblings; we were halves of a whole, stitched together." The sounds of cries slowly blend into nothing. All I hear is the gentle wind, and if I close my eyes, I swear I can hear his voice.

"When your heart stilled, mine fractured. Our laughter, that once brought me peace, now echoes and haunts me each day. I search for you in every gust of wind, every raindrop that trickles down my skin. Perhaps you're there, whispering secrets in the rustling leaves, urging me to find comfort in memories. But how can I mend when my crumbled walls were because you knocked them down? I carry your absence like the heaviest weight, like an open wound, bleeding grief into the emptiness. And yet, I cling to the fragments—the shared laughter, the silent conversations, the unspoken promises—as if they can somehow weave me back together." My head drops as I stare at the blood trickling down my hands, but I don't stop. I dig more.

"Bex, my twin, my missing half. I cry for the life we should have lived, the adventures we should have shared. Our souls were tangled, and now mine flutters, untethered, searching for you in every shadow. Did you know, in that final moment, that our connection would shatter? That the universe would crack our shared core into a thousand tiny pieces? I'll hold your memory close, tending to the shards of our shattered soul. Perhaps, in their jagged edges, I'll find a way to piece myself back together."

Then it hits me with the raw, intense pain. "I love you, Bex. BB for life."

My voice breaks as I crumble to the floor. Everything I have held in over the past two weeks tumbled from my lips. Begging to know why he left me. Kal and Tray pick me up, and Denny walks behind, holding me up. When I'm brought back to my seat, my eyes meet Bohdi's, wishing it was him holding me up. His eyes swim with unshed tears as he clenches his jaw. His eyes bore into mine, a silent message: I've got you.

And I hold on to that until I can lie in his arms again tonight.

I don't travel with my mom, but there are some bits of Bex's I want to get. Bohdi said for the time being I can store stuff at his place until I go through it and decide what I want to keep. There isn't a lot, but I can't see myself throwing any of his stuff out. My phone pings, and I pull it out of my pocket.

Sir:

I'll park down the road from your mom's. Take your time.

Apparently, Denny already questioned why Bohdi was at the funeral. None of my other teachers were, so that's why Bohdi couldn't give me a ride home. Kal's dad stepped in. Now, I sit outside the trailer, my heart heavy from saying goodbye to Bex.

People claim goodbyes are the final chapter, but they're wrong. Bex's memory lingers, etched into every reflection I catch in the mirror. Inside the trailer, I bypass the familiar surroundings, heading straight for our shared bedroom. A cardboard box awaits me, and I begin taking down photographs. It's a bittersweet task, each image capturing Bex's infectious joy. These snapshots are my life, like the physical traces of our happiness.

Next, I open the nightstand drawer, revealing a stack of old diaries. Nine of them, each filled with our secrets, dreams, and whispered promises. I place them carefully in the box. Knowing that on the toughest days, I'll reach for them, tracing Bex's words with UV pens, as if he's still here, writing them just for me.

Next, I open the wardrobe. I had already taken a few sweatshirts out of here. Wearing Bex's clothes is something that makes me feel closer to him, but now I can have his whole wardrobe. Once I've taken everything off the hangers, I glance down at some screwed up clothes at the bottom. Picking those up, I notice a zipped duffle bag.

I place down the clothes I had in my hand and open the duffle bag. It's filled with clothes, shoes and two diaries. I pick the diaries up and open one up which has a UV pen buried into it. With trembling hands, I shine the pen on the first page, but there's nothing. My gaze shifts to the second diary, where faint indents reveal hidden writing. My heart races, and I sink onto the bed, the UV pen quivering in my grasp.

"Please don't let this be what I think it is." Shining the UV pen on the page, I read the writing.

Bray,
Do you remember when each day you didn't wake up with that tight feeling in your chest like a weight was bearing down on you?
Do you remember the days when breathing was easy?
Do you remember the days when you woke up with a smile and not a sinking feeling in your stomach that something wasn't right, but you couldn't pinpoint what it was?
Do you remember the days when I didn't have this

monster swimming in my veins and drowning me from the inside?
Do you remember the days when you woke up happy?
Do you remember when I was your best bro?
I miss those days.
I need you to think of those days for me and hold on to them.
I need you to do that for me, okay?
I promise, those days will come back. I need to go away for a little while and find myself again. I need to be on my own and clear my head. I can't be here, around these people, around that poison that I crave so badly.
I'll never get better and I want to.
For us.
I'm not saying goodbye. Because this isn't goodbye. Your twin, your other half, is coming back like he used to be, I promise, Bray.
I have taken one of our diaries we used to write in so I can read them back when I miss you so much it hurts.
You've been missing me for years now and I'm sorry.
You'll always find the old me in those pages, Bray. Just read back and I'll be there.
I'm going to write notes to you so you can read them when I'm back.
Don't stop writing to me, I'll be back to read them.
I know why it hurts you to let people in, Brayden. Because you let me in and it fucking hurt, didn't it? It cut like a knife to your veins, bleeding you out every single day. I'm so fucking sorry.
I never deserved you as a brother, but I thank the

lord every day I was blessed to enter this world with you by my side.
Keep shattering, Quake.
Love you infinite.
Bex.
Brayden & Bexley
Best Bros
BB for life.
P.S.: Can you do me a favor? Can you go to the store and buy some candy and save me some, bro?

"No, no, no!" My voice cracks, the words torn from my throat like shards of glass. The diary slips through my trembling fingers, crashing to the floor. I crumple, my chest collapsing as if someone's stomping on it. Breathing becomes a pointless struggle. It can't be true. It's like a cruel twist of fate.

"It was an accident." He didn't choose to leave me.

A primal scream echoes through me, reverberating off the walls. I rise to my knees, clutching the diary to my chest. Everything I've wrestled with over these past two weeks, the sleepless nights, the unanswered questions, the gaping void in my heart, it all unravels.

Today, at the funeral, I stood in front of his casket, silently pleading for an explanation. But he lied, he fucking lied in my dreams. He didn't mean to leave me. He fought for us.

The sobs come in waves, crashing over me. The room spins, blurring into a chaotic whirlwind of memories and pain. I can't stay here, can't bear the weight of this grief that blankets this room. I pull myself up, my legs wobbly, and grab the UV pen from the floor. It's my lifeline now, the secrets etched in invisible ink.

Stumbling toward the door, I gulp in ragged breaths. The world outside, a place where I can scream at the sky, where the grass cushions my fall. My knees buckle, and I collapse, unable to move. The pain wells up, threatening to drown me. I release the agony.

"Come back, Bex," I plead, my voice torn by desperation. I scream at the vast sky, as if my cries could summon him from wherever he's gone. But the heavens remain silent.

"Brayden." Daxton's worried voice comes from somewhere behind, but I stand up and I don't turn back. I stumble away as much as my legs will take me. Away from everyone. I can't see Bohdi. Not now. Not like this. The ache in my chest threatens to consume me as I stagger away from the trailer park and there's only one place I want to be right now.

Chapter Forty-Two

Bohdi

Today weighed on me in ways I can't fully express. The funeral, the raw grief etched across Brayden's face, shattered me. I gripped the chair, desperate to cross the distance and offer comfort. When he addressed Bexley, it felt like a thousand knives piercing my heart. His pain consumed us all, isolating them both in their shared loss. I felt every stab.

But it also resurrected memories of Jace, the ache, the unanswerable questions. Why did it happen to someone so pure, someone undeserving? Kal and Tray held Brayden, supporting him, and I wished it were me.

When Denny stepped forward, I was desperate to follow, but the questions buzzed around us like gnats. "Why's Mr. Stiles, the marketing teacher, here?" they whispered. I claimed my presence was for my student, but Denny's gaze sliced through my facade. He nodded, eyes squinting, and settled a few seats away. It felt as if his stare bore into me, yet every time I glanced his way, he wasn't watching. Glancing at the time in my truck, it's been over an hour since Bray was dropped off. I said to him he could take his time, but I'm worried he's not doing well and he's there on his own. I tap away on the steering wheel, debating what to do. I can't sit here wondering if he's okay. I need to hold him and tell him I've got him, no matter what. What was I thinking about leaving him on his own after everything that happened today?

Turning the engine on, I head toward the trailer park down the road. Pulling up, everything seems quiet, but once I pull up outside Brayden's mom's trailer, Daxton comes rushing out, fear drowning his face.

"Sir, sir!" His hands wave me down as his eyes go wide.

"Where is he?" I run toward the trailer door.

"He's not here." Daxton's gasps come out choppy. "He ran out of the park. He was in a bad way." Worry etches his face as his eyebrows pinch together. He gulps. "He was as bad as the day I found him. I tried speaking with him, but he stumbled away. He was a mess, sir. I didn't know what to do. I don't have anyone's number an—"

"What way did he go, Daxton? What fucking way." I shake him.

"That way." His lip trembles, but I can't think about that right now. I jump in the truck and drive.

I've been driving around for three hours, my mind racing. I reached out to Tray on Instagram, who informed Kal. We've searched tirelessly, but there's no sign of him. My fingers clutch my hair, desperate. Where the hell could he be? In his state, he could be anywhere. Kal and Tray searched all the bars around campus. But he's vanished. My phone rings and I pick it up instantly without even looking at who it is.

My voice trembles as I break through the chaos, shouting Brayden's name without even looking at the screen when answering.

Kal's urgent words pierce the air. "Bohdi, he's at Beaumont General. Me and Tray are on our way now." The phone clicks off before I can ask more questions. I slam my foot down, defying every speed limit, racing to the hospital. Fifteen minutes later, I stride through the main reception.

"Brayden Anders!" I practically yell at the receptionist. Jace's memories flood back—the hospital, the uncertainty. I clutch the counter's edge.

"Sir, are you okay?" A woman steadies me, concern etching her features. This won't be like last time. Brayden will be fine.

"Brayden." I gasp for air. "Anders."

"He's upstairs, sir. Follow me." I release the countertop, trailing behind her. The room spins, my heart galloping. Deep breaths.

"Sir, he'll be okay," the lady reassures me.

"He'll be okay," I repeat desperately.

She nods. "He has alcohol poisoning. He's had his stomach pumped. He's in recovery now." She points to a chair. "Wait here. Someone will be out to speak to you soon."

Kal and Tray appear, their eyes full of pain.

"I haven't heard much, but I've been assured he will be okay. He's had his stomach pumped." I grimace. "I knew I shouldn't have left him on his own."

"Do you know any more of what happened?"

I shake my head. "No." He was obviously broken after the funeral, but he was clear he wanted to go and have a moment on his own. "I don't know what happened in that hour. How did you know he was here?" I question Kal.

"He must have my dad listed as next of kin, since the hospital called him." I nod.

"Where's your dad now?"

"On his way." Kal rubs the back of his neck. Before I can say more, a man interrupts.

"Mr. Anders," the man calls, and we all turn to look at him. I spring into action.

They think I'm his dad. Great. "Yep, that's me." I raise my hand, walking over to him.

"I can let you in to see Brayden. Only one person at a time. He's exhausted and had a traumatic night," the doctor says, addressing Kal and Tray. I turn back to them.

"Please," I beg quietly, and Tray nods, as does Kal.

"Let him know we're here," Kal instructs, as I walk away. Following the doctor, he stops just before we enter the room.

"He's groggy but emotional. Kept screaming for his diary, which was recovered by whoever found him. It's in the bed with him, but he's fixated on a UV pen we can't locate. You might know what he means."

The diaries.

"Thanks, Doc." I step aside, entering the room. Brayden lies in the bed, wires connecting to his chest and wrist. "Fuck." I crumble, approaching him. His eyes lock onto mine, tears streaming.

"I'm sorry. So fucking sorry," he chokes, attempting to sit up.

"It's okay," I reassure him, my hands cupping his face as I press kisses to his forehead. Thanking whatever higher power exists that he's alive.

"It was an accident, Boh," he sobs, and I hold him close to my chest. "Bex didn't kill himself." I frown down at him. He must be confused.

"Bray, I think you're tired."

"No, it's in here." He leans to the side, picking up the diary. "He was going away to get better. It was an accident." His bottom lip trembles again as more tears leak down his face. "He didn't mean to leave me, and I don't know why, but that hurts more." I pull the chair closer to the bed, taking his hand in mine.

"How could he ever leave you, Bray? You were the best brother anyone could have asked for, there's no way Bex would have left you." I smile. "I know it hurts. Believe me, I know. But I can't have you doing this bray. I can't have you self-destructing. You mean too much to me."

"Bohdi." His head rises, his eyes rim with new shed tears.

"I think I'm too broken." He takes a deep breath. "Please, just let me go." A tear leaks from his eye as I reach out, brushing it away.

A bittersweet laugh escapes me. "I can't, Brayden. Even if I wanted to, I can't. I'm addicted to all of you. Even the broken pieces."

He shakes his head.

"You don't mean that."

I stand up, sitting beside him on the bed.

"I mean every fucking word. Don't ever question what I feel for you, because its' fucked up Brayden. My obsession and need to always have you with me scares the shit out of me. The way I'm a broken mess when you're not around and then when you are, it's as if all my pain floats away and I'm left with you. You're not my light in the darkness, Bray. You're my company in the darkness. You're my comfort. Nothing comforts me more than holding you among the chaos."

"We're a mixture of broken pieces, Boh, don't you see that?"

"We're picture perfect in a shattered frame, Bray. A beautiful broken fucking mess." I smile at him, leaning forward and capturing his lips in a gentle kiss.

"I love you too," I whisper. He gasps, sucking in a sharp breath as I capture his lips again and pull back. "So, fucking much."

"Boh." His pained eyes flicker between mine.

"I've been at your door for longer than you think, Bray. I'm knocking. I need you to let me in." He nods, a small smile appearing on his lips. "I promise you, Bray. Fall for me and you won't ever have to fall again." Tears leak from his eyes.

"How are you real?" he croaks, and I lean forward, kissing each tear that leaks.

"I'm real because of you."

"You love me?" His eyes flicker between mine, brighter than they were a minute ago.

"So much," I whisper, my lips touching his again.

This time, Brayden opens up for me, my tongue dancing with his, slowly, as I put everything into this kiss. The love I have for him, the shared pain we have. Everything that has led me to this point. To loving Brayden Quake Anders. Brayden moans as his head tilts to the side and in that moment, I get lost in him, my dick hardens with every swipe of his tongue. But then the machine starts beeping and as I jump back, just before the door opens, a nurse walks in frowning at Brayden's incredibly increased heart rate.

You're in a fucking hospital, Bohdi, where they think he is your son. What the fuck are you doing?

"Are you okay?" The nurse's voice cuts through the room, addressing Brayden's swollen lip and drowsy appearance.

"Uh-huh." He nods as she approaches the machine, monitoring his now slowing heart rate. I watch him, wide-eyed, as he smirks at me.

In that moment, I glimpse the playful side of Brayden. If it means just coaxing a small smile from him—even once a month—I'll gladly accept it and carry on risking everything. As long as each smile is because of me, I don't care how infrequent they are. I want him to grieve naturally. No fake happiness around me. Let him scream when anger consumes him over Bex's loss. Allow the tears to flow when the pain becomes unbearable. And yes, let him smile because of me.

Maybe someday, when he thinks of Bexley, it won't hurt as much and he'll smile for the life they shared, even if it was only a fleeting amount of time. Those precious memories deserve to live on. The nurse gives me a sidelong glance as she walks away from the machine. “You’ve got some impatient boys out there,” she informs me. “They practically demanded, in not-so-polite terms, to see their boy. The broody-looking one threw in a few choice swear words,” she says before leaving.

“Kal,” Brayden and I say simultaneously, sharing a chuckle. “I sort of forgot to mention they were here,” I admit. “Don’t tell Kal, he hates me already.”

“He doesn’t hate you—he’s just fiercely protective.”

“Sure.” I smirk, leaning over to kiss Brayden’s forehead.

“Yeah, stay away from my lips, please. I lose control around you,” he murmurs, adjusting himself discreetly under the covers, which is what I done while the nurse checked the machine.

“Got it.” I wink. “I’ll let Kal in before he stages a riot out there,” I say. “But I’ll be back as soon as they’ve had their one-minute visit.”

Brayden shakes his head, smirking. “Oh, Bohdi.”

I glance back, raising an eyebrow. “When you return,” he says softly, “can you tell me about Jace? I want to know everything—the good and the bad.” His smile warms my heart.

For the first time in a while, I’m ready to share memories of Jace, the ones that shaped us both. “I’d love to,” I reply, smiling back.

13
Brayden 'Quake' Anders

Chapter Forty-Three

Brayden

Kal stormed in, the broody asshole he is, and lunged at me, hugging me tightly as though I might vanish. Then, another pair of arms wrapped around me as Tray snuck in. They both hugged me for ten minutes while I sobbed into their arms. I've never been a crier, but lately, I'm leaking like a busted faucet. Everything hurts, talking, walking, even breathing. It's as if I'm navigating life with half my soul missing.

Kal and Tray allowed me to cry in their arms and even cried with me, begging me never to leave them. They told me I'm their brother, too. I didn't do this to die. I needed to get away from everyone. I needed to process everything I had read on my own. I still don't think I have processed it all.

I went to the park with my diary and UV pen and read. I read over and over what Bex had left me. With each word, my eyes moved over, I broke a little more. That's when I spotted a homeless man knocked out, clutching a bottle of vodka in his hand, barely even touched. I dragged my feet toward him, took the vodka, and curled myself up on the merry-go-round with my diary, my UV pen, and my vodka. And I drank. For every word that stabbed me, I took a swig and then the words didn't hurt so much. Then I wanted answers. I thought if I downed it as quickly as I could, maybe I'd fall asleep quicker and maybe I'd see Bex again to ask him why he lied to me.

Because it wasn't too late.

I realize now it was dumb.

The door squeaks, snapping my attention to Bohdi as he walks in. His smile blazes when he sees me.

"They said I can go home tomorrow," I tell him, my own smile matching his.

"I want you back at my place."

"I can't," I sigh. "People will start talking."

"Fuck what people say," he grunts.

I glance at him, a tight smile curling my lips. He nods. "I know. I wish I didn't have to hide you. Hide us."

His shoulders slouch as he walks around the bed, his eyes flicking up to the door and then me before he grabs my hand. Gently turning my hand over, his fingers trace the fresh, red cuts that mar my palm.

Touch tender, he whispers, "Please, don't do this anymore." Each word is accompanied by a soft kiss on the cuts, and I can feel my throat tighten, emotions welling up inside me. "Please, don't hurt yourself anymore," he pleads, his eyes filled with a deep, aching sorrow as he continues to kiss each wound.

"But it helps," I murmur, my voice barely audible.

"I want to help," he insists, his voice breaking with emotion. "When it gets too much, when the pain is unbearable, come to me. Let me be the one to take that pain away. Let me help you forget." His eyes search mine, desperate and sincere, as he holds my hand close to his heart. I nod, turning my hand back over and link my fingers through his.

"Tell me about him, Boh," I whisper and sink back into my pillows. Bohdi avoids my gaze, focusing on our linked hands. His fingers weave through mine, his thumb tracing patterns on the backs of my hand.

"Jace was the family's only child," he says, laughter tugging at his lips. "Spoiled beyond belief." His smile warms me. "Cash became a father at a young age. He was head over heels for Roxanne, and we all adored her. But then she discovered she was pregnant with Jace, and everything shifted. Her true colors appeared. None of us suspected she was involved in prostitution or drugs, not even Cash. She hid it so well. Given how young they were, Cash was still living with us in the family home. So, he didn't see her much at night. He thought she was home. It shattered him. She'd appeared pure and kind to us. I'd watch her and Cash, praying for a love like theirs when I grew older. But then she planned to terminate the pregnancy, claiming she couldn't afford to lose money. Cash panicked and spilled everything to my parents. Their fury echoed through the house. I can still hear the screams and tears, but they couldn't allow her to terminate the baby. Then, fast-forward to the day my nephew was born."

Bohdi stares down at our linked fingers, a soft smile playing on his lips like the memory is playing out in front of him.

"He was absolutely perfect, Bray. I held him, tears streaming down my face. From that moment, he became my everything. His tiny fingers, those chubby cheeks—he was such a plump little baby." Bohdi chuckles. "But it was his eyes. He had the Stiles eyes, big and blue. Our parents considered a DNA test, but there was no need. From the pictures, it was clear he was a spitting image of Cash and me as babies. And those eyes! They were huge. People on the streets would always fuss over him, mentioning his eyes and that infectious, toothless smile. No matter how tough your day was, his grin could turn it all around. You couldn't stay sad in his presence."

He pauses, taking a deep breath.

"When Jace was seven, my parents passed away within five days of each other—Mom from cancer, Dad from a heart attack. It was an unbearable time, but Jace became our lifeline. He held us together, the glue that prevented us from shattering completely. Each day, him being there helped mend our broken hearts." I squeeze Bohdi's hand, remaining silent, wanting him to continue, even if my heart is slowly breaking for him.

"Jace was my closest friend as he grew up, especially during school, when he got into mischief. That little shit changed Cash's number in his school records to my number, so if he got in trouble, they'd call me instead. I was wrapped around his finger, because I never told Cash with each phone call I got." Boh laughs, shaking his head. "Weekends, he'd stay with me. We'd watch football and boxing. To this day, Cash remains oblivious. But Jace's first beer? That happened at my place. Cash still thinks he was the one who introduced Jace to it. I could never tell him." Boh glances up at me, a smirk playing on his lips.

"As he grew older, we spent more time together. What an incredible man he became. He made our entire family proud. Then one day, he brought home a girl. Rylee Matthews. What a girl, Bray. You would love her."

I remember @rystiles on Instagram. Shit, they were married.

"I knew from the moment I saw Jace look at her, she was the one for him. I've never seen a guy look at a girl the way Jace did at Rylee and I got it. She's pretty amazing. She was perfect for Jace." Bohdi's hands slip from mine as he rubs his jaw, staring up at the ceiling. "He was happy, deeply in love. His entire life lay ahead of him." Boh's voice wavers.

"Then came the phone call from Cash. He had been involved in a car accident. Panic surged through me like a tidal wave." He gulps, his expression sinking. "I entered the hospital room, tubes everywhere, bandages hiding his face. Jace laid there, on life support, trapped in a coma." I suck in a sharp breath, leaning forward to grab Bohdi's hand again and squeezing. He offers me a pained smile.

"The days following were awful. None of us could sleep. Rylee and Cash slept at the hospital each night. I barely could bring myself to sleep. I sometimes would lie in my car outside the hospital all night, praying he would wake up. That didn't happen, though. We got taken into a room to say they had runs tests and confirmed Jace was brain dead." His voice hitches as tears fill up in his eyes. "I've never in my life felt pain like it."

I lean forward, my own tears slipping down my face. "Boh." My voice cracks. He squeezes my hand.

"They told us prior to this his body was filled with Xanax and Valium. That's what caused the crash. None of it made sense. Jace never took drugs; the odd painkiller to help with a headache, but that was it. No one could get their head around it. We had many unanswered questions that would never be answered." Bohdi stops and wipes away at the flowing tears that slip down his face.

"Everything is fucked, Bray. So much happened after his death." His voice breaks as his eyes meet mine. "None of it was an accident. We come to find out that someone he had called his best friend since school was hiding a lot." His teeth grind. "He drugged Jace's drink, knowing that his body wouldn't handle the amount he did, knowing it would probably end in a car accident and Jace dying."

"What?" My hand moves to my mouth, sickness threatening to come up. "Remember when I mentioned Roxanne, Jace's mom?"

I nod as the tears escape my eyes. Bohdi leans forward, brushing them away with his thumb.

"It turns out, she went on to have another child and created a fucking monster." Rage fills Bohdi as he lets go of my hand, running his fingers through his hair, tugging at the strands.

"His so-called best friend was not only his half brother, but was also stalking his girlfriend for the entire six years. He was obsessed with Rylee. He kidnapped her. Me and Cash found her, but it didn't stop there, the pain never did for our family. James got hold of Rylee again and this time, we nearly lost her and my brother. He shot Cash." He sucks in a sharp breath. "He's okay now, but he already took the glue to our family. Now he wanted more; he wanted to ruin everything, and it was all because of Roxy, bringing him up in her lifestyle. Jace's killer endured a lot growing up in the hands of Roxy and other people. Roxy died when James was young and he was taken into care, but he found out about Jace and resented the life he never got to live because of Roxy. So, he befriended him and then took his life."

Bohdi gasps for air as he finishes telling me, and I sit there in bewilderment. Everything he has gone through, and he sits here, holding me through my grief.

"Boh." My voice breaks. As I swallow the impending tears I feel like will rack my body. "You've been piecing me together," I whisper, my voice breaking. "But I didn't see how shattered you were. I'm so sorry."

He leans closer, his touch gentle yet desperate. "Look at me, Bray."

I tremble, staring down, hating how much he's been hurting all this time, and I never saw past my shit and own grief. "Please look at me."

His pained voice has me tilting my head up, and it's now I see it, I see the mirrored grief in his eyes. "Since Jace died, I've stumbled through life, hollow. I moved here to escape others' happiness. Twisted, I know. I resented their laughter, their love. Thought permanent sadness was my future, and I expected everyone else to feel like that, too. I thought being sad and wallowing each and every day was normal. I expected everyone else to do that." His thumb brushes my cheek, and I close my eyes, seeking warmth.

"And then you showed up." His voice cracks further, revealing vulnerability. "You stepped into my darkness, Bray. Taught me it's okay to smile, to feel something other than grief. A shared glance, a stolen laugh—they became lifelines." I trace the lines of his palm, heart pounding.

"But why?" I ask, barely audible. "Why fall for me?"

Bohdi's gaze never wavers. "From the moment our eyes met," he confesses, "I felt it, the pull. My heart recognized you before my brain caught up. Maybe I saw my mirrored pain in your eyes, or maybe it was your laughter echoing through my darkness. But I fell, Bray. Slowly, irrevocably."

I lean toward him, our foreheads touching. "Boh," I murmur, his eyes lock with mine and my heart pounds in my chest. "I will lie in grief, I will swim in grief, I will fucking drown in it, Boh, you know why? Because I found you in grief. I found a man who tests me, a man who ground every single one of my gears. A man who I dreamed of pummeling my fists into on more than one occasion. A man who saw every single crack and even watched me shatter before him, but still stayed. But most of all, I found a man that made me understand what love is. I found a man I fell in love with."

Boh's eyes shine with unshed tears. "You can't say you don't mean it." He smiles, a single tear escaping and trickling down his face.

"I fucking love you, Bohdi Stiles, and I mean every single word. I always did." We both laugh as his lips meet mine. "I'm staying with you in the darkness."

13
Brayden 'Quake' Anders

Chapter Forty-Four
Brayden

Three Days Later

For the past two days, I've been holed up in this dorm room, waking up to the sight of Cope, Tray, and Kal hovering around me like I'm some fragile baby. They won't leave me alone for a second. Yesterday, I dared to take a shower, and when I stepped out, guess what? The bathroom door was slightly open. Can't even shower in peace with the door shut.

They're convinced I intentionally wanted to join Bex on the other side, but truth be told, my head was a mess. I can't even say for sure what I wanted at that point. I know Bohdi has something to do with this as well. It's as if he's arranged for me to have a constant sitter.

I actually woke up this morning alone, which feels off. I check my phone, and no texts, and what's even weirder? I don't have a text from Bohdi. I normally wake up each morning to a text from him, telling me he misses me, and he can't wait to see me in class when I'm back.

The doctor told me I need to take it easy. I'm off for another week, and Kal's mom wants me to go see a therapist. I told her I'm okay but unlike my mom, Kal's mom actually cares and had basically insisted.

Sighing, I sit up in bed, bored out of my brain. I glance at the diaries beside me, running my hands over the smooth cover. Bohdi still texts me in the evening, asking me to tell him about Bexley. Anything, even down to his favorite color, and I can't help but fall in love with him a bit more. It keeps me thinking of the happy thoughts of Bexley.

When I was in the hospital, Bohdi went back to the trailer and gathered everything and took it all back to his place. I'll never have to go back to the trailer, and I'll never have to see my mom again. I have thought about her more than I should have over the last couple of weeks. People often fail to grasp the true nature of addiction. It devours those it traps, an insidious illness that embeds itself in their very bones and courses through their veins. It drowns them from the inside out. No matter how hard they struggle, they rarely break the surface, as it relentlessly pulls them back under. It holds them captive, slowly and painfully extinguishing their spirit. The only reprieve comes when the monster offers a fleeting lifeline, a brief moment of respite. But soon enough, it drags them back into the depths, suffocating them once more. My mom is an addict. But she is still a person, just like Bex was. She had choices and she never once chose us. Not ever. She turned her back on us entirely. We could have died in that very bed, and she wouldn't have known. I know my mom was in there somewhere, but she gave up. I begged her on more than one occasion, and I would watch as tears fell down her face. But she would shake her head in silence and storm out of the trailer. She could have fought for us, but she didn't. At least Bex tried. Not all the time, but he tried. He cared for me; he protected me. My mom would have used us for our last breath if she could.

She succeeded with that for one of us.

Do I tell her about the note I found? Do I tell her he didn't overdose on purpose like we were made to believe?

But you know what? She can live with that thought. She can live with the thought that Bexley was so fucked up, he no longer wanted to be on this earth, and I hope one day she wakes up and it hits her how it was all her fault. I hope one day it tears her apart even a fraction of what it's done to me.

Boh gave Kal two diaries, along with our UV pens, just in case I needed them. Thank God he did, because each night when I'm in bed on my own, Cope fast asleep, I open up those diaries and I read all our memories. It's bittersweet, but I'm so thankful I get to keep a part of this life with me.

There's a knock at the door and I push the diary under my pillow before standing up. Let's see who has been assigned to me today. Dragging my feet to the door, I swing it open, eyes rolling as I do so. The air gets lodged in my throat when I see Bohdi, dressed in a snug black suit, shirt unbuttoned at the top, sleeves rolled up, revealing tanned, powerful arms. His black blazer hangs casually over one shoulder, and my eyes widen in shock.

"Are you going to keep eye fucking me, or are you going to let me in?" One side of his lip tips up as he raises an eyebrow.

"Are you going to fuck me if I let you in?" I tease back.

Within seconds, I'm being pushed back into my room and my dorm door slams shut as Bohdi pushes his way in. His suit jacket is dropped to the floor and his hands cup my face, his lips finding mine instantly. A moan crawls up my throat as his tongue pushes through my lips, taking every single bit of me. My hands frantically glide over his arm, down his back. His lips, soft and wet, devour me like he can't get enough of me.

I have thought about Bohdi nonstop since we were in the hospital, the way he opened up to me, the things he said. The fact I could finally admit my true feelings for him. And then I had to come back to the dorm without seeing him. It's been hell.

"Fuck, I've missed you," I say between Bohdi attacking my mouth. Bohdi pulls back, his forehead meeting mine. "How did you get up here without being seen?"

"Had a little help from Tray. He said he would distract everyone."

I pull back, biting my cheek, trying to suppress a laugh. "You do realize he is no doubt currently running around this dorm building, buck naked? Any excuse to get his dick out and he will do it."

Bohdi raises one eyebrow at me, and then pinches his eyebrows together.

"Does he get his dick out in front of you a lot?"

I choke on a laugh. "I mean, I've probably seen it more times than my own, yeah, but that's what you have to accept when being Tray's best friend."

Bohdi's frown deepens. "I don't like that one bit. The only dick you should be seeing more than your own is mine." He frowns, with not one hint of amusement on his face.

"You're actually being serious." I try to not laugh, but my lips tip up as I bite my lip.

"Clearly, I didn't make it clear enough who you belong to, Brayden." Bohdi growls my name as his eyes darken and a shiver races down my spine.

"I think you need to remind me, sir." Bohdi's eyes glance at the bathroom door, and then he turns me so my back is facing it. His lips descend on mine as he pushes me back into the bathroom. Bohdi closes the door behind him, locking it.

"There's no such thing as privacy in this dorm. They can unlock the bathroom door from the outside," I pant as I make quick work of removing my clothes, my dick already painfully hard. Bohdi stops undressing.

"You mean to tell me not only do you see another guy's dick all the time, but they also see yours and just walk in here when they please?" he deadpans, his stare serious.

"Only since I've been back from the hospital." I won't tell him that Trayton sits on the toilet and has full-on conversations with me while I shower. That may push him over the edge. Although I'm kind of tempted. I love this side of Bohdi.

"If they walk in, I will pack your bags, and you will move in with me."

"Yes, sir," I tease as Bohdi stalks toward me, removing his shirt.

"Get in the shower, Bray." I walk into our walk-in shower. It's not the biggest, but it's enough for me and now Bohdi, I guess, as he stalks in after me. Turning the water on, I tilt my head back, allowing the water to run down my body as Boh's eyes move all over me. His eyes never leave my body.

"Turn around. Let me wash you," he says, grabbing some of the shower gel and squirting some onto a loofah.

When the loofah glides across my back, my body scatters in goosebumps. He rubs it across my back slowly. I lean one arm on the tiled wall and hang my head, allowing the water to hit the back of my neck. My dick stands up, the slit pointing up at me, oozing with pre-cum. All that it took was to have Bohdi stand behind me naked.

The loofah travels down my back and glides over my butt. My breath hitches as the loofah presses between my cheeks, playing particular attention to my hole. As Bohdi rubs the rough fabric over my hole, small gasps of air escape my lips as my eyes close and Bohdi's finger replaces it, rubbing over me over and over again. Boh gently pushes me under the water more, so it runs down my back. After a few seconds, he pulls me back and then I feel his dick nudging the entrance of my ass.

"Fuck, yes." I sigh. I needed this. I needed it so fucking bad.

Bohdi nudges me, the slight sting has me gripping the tiled wall, but Bohdi goes slowly. Treating me as if I might break, but I don't want that, not now. I want him to fuck me.

"Bohdi, fuck me," I grit out, pushing myself back into him, welcoming the burn. Bohdi hisses, holding my hips tight so I can't move anymore.

"I don't want to hurt you."

"So much for showing me who I belong to, you can't even fu—" I suck in a sharp breath as he slams into me with brutal force, it stings, it fucking burns but my god it's the best burn. Bohdi's hand wraps around my front, one hand snaking up to my neck as he wraps his fingers securely around my throat, holding me in place as he brutally fucks me. Taking everything he wants, and I love it. I love it so much.

"Fuck, fuck," I cry. Bohdi pushes my front up against the cold tiled wall and his lips find my ear.

"Who." Hips forcefully snap forward, hitting that magic spot. His fingers tightening with every snap.

"Do." Quick and hard, his hips snap forward again, knocking the air out of me as I claw at the tiled walls.

"You," he growls, fucking himself into me so deep.

"Belong." His voice breaks as if he's holding on and I know I won't be far behind him with each snap of his hips. The head of his dick brushes against that button inside. My balls tingle, ready for release.

"To?"

"You, you!" I scream, my voice becoming hoarse. "You, sir, I belong to you." His fingers loosen as they leave my neck and slide down my chest.

"Brayden, shit. Tell me you love me. I want to come in this tight ass while you tell me."

"I love you, Bohdi. I fucking love you."

"Again," he moans, his dick smacking into my ass in punishing snaps.

"I love you. I love you. I love you," I repeat and repeat until he stills and roars my name.

"Brayden, fuck, fuck." His hips slowly pump, and he slides his dick out of me, leaving me feeling empty, and I'm teetering on the edge of release. "Turn around."

His hoarse voice has me dizzy as his hands grip me and turn me around. Bohdi drops to his knees in front of me and my dick takes note as pre-cum leaks out of my tip and trails down my dick. Bohdi leans forward, licking up the pre-cum and then his lips cover the head as he sucks on it so hard it defies physics and logic. My eyes flutter, legs trembling and eyes rolling to the back of my head, seeing stars. Bohdi carries on paying attention to my head, and then his mouth slides down my dick, and he gags, his throat squeezing the hell out of my dick. Bohdi's finger slips into my hole, using his other finger to gather up his leaking cum as he pushes it back inside me. Over and over, he does this and I know I won't hold out much longer. I grip the strands of Bodhi's hair as a tingle begins at the bottom of my spine and my balls draw up.

"Bohdi, fuck. I'm going to come." Bohdi continues sucking the head like he's waiting for his favorite drink to pour out. While his fingers milk the fuck out of my prostate. And when that first rope of cum spills down Bohdi's throat, my brain short circuits as euphoria washes through me like a tidal wave.

"Shitmotherfuckingod!" I spew nonsense, not knowing what I'm saying as I spill ropes and ropes of cum down Bohdi's throat. Bohdi licks up every drop and as his tongue swipes over the head, my legs spasm, and I fall to the shower floor. Both me and Bohdi burst out laughing.

"Best blowjob ever," I pant, closing my eyes and leaning back against the tiled wall.

"Only blowjob ever," Bohdi growls. "In my mind, you've never had a blow job before. In fact, you've never been with anyone before. I'm your first and last." He grabs my cheeks, pressing a kiss to me. The slight taste of myself has me licking my lips and Bohdi's eyebrow raises as his eyes which darkens instantly follow the trail of my lip.

"I love your jealousy." I smirk.

Bohdi pulls up a loofah between us. "Your time to wash me."

My eyes widen. "Is that the one you used on me?" I stare at him, wide-eyed; his eyebrows draw together in confusion.

"Yeah, why?"

I burst out laughing. "That's Cope's."

Bohdi's mouth opens as he covers it with one hand. "Damn," he says before he burst out laughing along with me. "I'll buy him a new one."

Chapter Forty-Five

Bohdi

One week later

Brayden pummels the bag as if he holds a personal grudge against it. Each strike seems to channel the turmoil swirling in his mind, as if he can transfer the weight of his daily pain into the fabric. His bare hands are clenched, desperate to unload the burden they carried.

"It's been a rough day," Kal murmurs beside me. I shift my gaze to him, but he remains fixated on Brayden.

"What happened?" I question.

"Nothing," he whispers. "Absolutely nothing. Brayden's just having a tough time."

I nod, understanding. Those days ambush you when you least expect it. One moment, you're laughing; the next, tears or screams consume you. There's no specific trigger—it's as if pain strikes you out of nowhere.

"I don't need to remind you, but please watch over him."

"Always," Kal murmurs, striding toward Bray. The gym buzzes with activity today, and I blend in among the students, pounding the bag on the opposite wall, wanting to give Brayden some space. He needs this time with him and the bag. I should be at home grading papers, but a strange need keeps me close to him. I can't bear to be apart. It's as if a piece of me is missing whenever he's not near.

Time slips away. I lose myself in the rhythmic thud of the bag. Thoughts whirl in my mind about us, about Brayden, about everything. How do I navigate this? How do we move forward? As his teacher, an invisible barrier prevents me from being there for him the way I want to be.

My bed feels emptier each morning, devoid of his presence. The absence of his face, his scent—it's been a cruel few weeks without him by my side.

"Boh."

I snap out of my trance, realizing the gym is now empty. Kal stares at me. "I'm going."

My eyes scan the area where Brayden was last, but he's nowhere to be found.

"Where is he?" I question Kal.

"He's in the pool. Said he wants to swim some laps before heading back to the dorm. Told me to go."

I nod. "Okay. I'll see him before I leave."

Kal nods, lips pressed tight. He's a good kid; he looks up to Bray, which automatically earns my respect. I don't think he fully grasps the situation between me and Brayden yet, but he seems to be adjusting.

I unwrap my sore hands, always pushing a bit too hard. When it's just me and my mind battling the bag, stopping becomes nearly impossible. I roll my neck, heading toward the locker room. Once inside, I pass through the doors to the swimming pool.

But he's not here.

As I return to the locker room, I call out, "Brayden!" Silence.

I round the corner, spotting his belongings on the side. He's still around. Frowning, I double-check the gym—no sign of him. Back to the pool, still nothing.

My eyes catch the sauna. It's a recent addition, something Denny insisted helps the team's muscles. Brayden isn't typically one to use it all that much, but maybe he's inside.

I push open the sauna door, and the heat greets me like an urgent wake-up call. He's there, sitting on the lower bench, legs spread wide, arms draped over the top benches.

"I've been searching for you," I mutter, stepping inside and closing the door behind me.

"Here I am." He sighs. "Though you're a bit overdressed." His raised eyebrow follows as I peel off my top, leaving only gym shorts.

Sitting next to him, I allow the sauna to loosen my muscles; the heat sinking into my bones.

"Rough day?" I ask quietly.

"You could say that," he replies.

"Talk to me," I urge, recalling what I told him in the hospital.

He exhales heavily. "It's hard to explain. I feel like I'm about to burst, like there's a scream inside me—so loud, Boh. It shakes my insides, but no one else can hear it."

"That's grief, Bray," I say. "You can sense it and feel it, but it's uniquely yours."

"It's shit," he admits, running his hands over his face. "I've missed you," he adds, hair falling into his eyes as he rests his chin on his chest.

"I miss everything about you," I confess, laughing. "Not waking up to you—it's unbearable." I turn my head, meeting his gaze. Sweat trails down his body, and I can't help but follow every drop, every movement.

"Sir," he whispers.

"Brayden, don't," I grit out.

"Sir," he repeats. His voice signals to my dick as it takes note, and I should be put on a world record for how fast it hardens. My body rises in goosebumps as his fingers run along my arm.

"Please, sir," he taunts. He knows what that word does to me. He knows how much I love him calling me sir.

"Brayden, we are at school."

"That didn't stop you in the shower."

"Brayden," I growl, my composure tethering on the edge. He's next to me one minute, tracing his fingers along my arm. The next, he's in front of me.

On his knees.

"Tell me you don't want me. Tell me you don't want this, and I will stop," he utters. And he knows. He fucking *knows* he has me because there's nothing I want more.

"You're not playing fair," I say, gulping as his hands pull on my shorts.

My hips lift as if his touch is the magic passcode, and my body listens to him and him only. Pulling out my dick, he kisses the tip before wrapping his lips around the head and sucking. My toes curl into the wet, tiled floor as I grip the bench on either side of me. Brayden's eyes stare up into mine, his drool-slicked lips lapping at my dick, and I can't take my eyes off him. His eyes don't leave mine as his pupils dilate so much that his gaze almost appears black. His beautiful blue eyes no longer look up at me; it's just darkness. I need his blue back.

"My baby looks so fucking good, slurping on my dick."

His eyes lazily close as he groans around my dick, making my balls draw up. I pant, trying to hold back from coming. I want to come in his tight little ass as I watch my dick disappear into his bubble butt cheeks.

"How much does my baby want me to fuck him, mmm?"

I lean forward, causing Brayden to lean into me more to suck my dick down as I run my hands down his sweat-slicked back. Collecting as much sweat as possible before I run my hand down and move a digit around his hole. The moisture from his body and the air allows my finger to slip into his ass easily. He moans again around my dick as I add another finger, his ass swallowing my fingers as he tenses.

"Your ass is greedy for me, Bray. It wants to swallow my dick until I come deep inside."

Bray's lips pop off my dick. His head leans back under my arm, gazing up at me.

"Fuck me, please, Boh. Fuck me," he whimpers on his knees like the pretty good boy he is.

"If you want me to fuck you, you gotta come sit on it." I lean back, my arms mirroring the way Brayden's was, and I push my hips forward, my dick bouncing and slapping against my stomach.

"If you want it, fucking ride me," I taunt him.

Brayden instantly stands, his shorts drop, and his legs overlap against mine. He sits on my lap, rubbing his dick along mine as he leans in, grasping my face and attacking my lips with his own. Our tongues battle. He thinks he can be in charge because he's on top of me, but that's not how this goes. With his legs overlapping mine, I rise, a small yelp escaping his lips.

"What are you doing?" he pants into my mouth, between his lips on mine.

I turn us around and seat him on the bench. "I need you a little more wet, baby," I whisper into his lips, trailing kisses across his jaw. Lingering my lips over the shell of his ear, I remember the moans that left his mouth last time, and as if I were right, the same thing happens again.

"Sir." Puffs of air come out rapidly.

My lips and tongue explore every droplet of sweat, tracing a path down his chest. As I get lower, his dick nudges my bottom lip, and I suck on the head.

"Shit," Brayden gasps as his fingers dig into my arms on either side of the bench. I suck on the head of his dick a few more times. His mouth opens, his eyes closing as his head tips back. Gasps leave his mouth, but I let his dick slap against his stomach, trailing kisses down the rest of his dick, and then I kiss down his balls.

"Sir," Brayden pleads, his voice a desperate whisper. "Please."

"What are you begging for?" I ask, my breath catching.

"Everything," he exhales, his gaze intense. "Give me everything."

I use my hands to grip beneath his thighs as I push his back, his balls swollen and full hang there, begging to be sucked. I lean down, lapping at his balls, sucking, licking. Drool drips from my lips, some running down to his ass, as his legs twitch in my hands. Words leave Brayden's mouth, but none of them make sense.

His gasps are heavy, his knuckles turning white from their tight grip on the bench, and as I allow my lips to travel further down, I glance up at Brayden. Eyes wide but drowsy, he stares down at me.

"Please," he begs.

I lick his tight hole. Once, twice, and then Brayden's eyes instantly roll back. I lap at his hole as if it's the sweetest thing I've ever tasted, and right now, I think it is. Brayden ticks, pulses, and oozes pre-cum as I push my tongue inside him.

"Fuck, sir, fuck." Brayden's rushed words whoosh out of him as his body lurches forward.

"I'm going to come," he whines, and I quickly withdraw my tongue.

"Not yet." His devastated, stricken face looks at me. "I want to be inside you when you come, Brayden."

Holding his legs back, I line myself up and slowly press in, the head of my dick making it feel as if I'm pushing through a barrier. Rapid pants reach my ears, but I can't look at him; I stare down at Brayden's tight hole, squeezing the life out of my throbbing dick. I watch as his hole sucks me in inch by inch. Brayden tenses, and I gasp, halting my movement. I glance up at Brayden; his eyebrows pinch together as he stares down his body where we're connected.

"Have you ever seen something so fucking beautiful?" I rasp, my eyes moving back to his hole as I gather spit in my mouth and dribble it down on his puckered hole.

"Your tight little hole takes my dick so well. It's sucking me in like it can't get enough, baby," I drawl. "Do you think you can take me all, baby?"

"Yes, yes, please," Brayden pants. I pull myself out, and Brayden's gaze snaps to me. Before he can say anything, with my hands underneath his thighs, I lift his legs up, gripping his forearms while I stand. I bring him with me. His legs draped over my arms, I hold him tight against me, his balls grazing my abs as I turn around and sit down. Brayden leans up, his knees pressed into the bench.

"Ride me," I rasp. Brayden doesn't waste a single second. He leans up, his hands wrapping around my dick as he lines it up with his wet hole. He lowers himself slowly, sharp breaths whooshing from his mouth. His eyes widen, locked onto mine. Fluttering as he sinks further down, I grip one hip tightly and squeeze from how fucking good this feels right now.

"I feel so fucking full," he rasps as he takes me whole. I bring my other hand up, gripping his other hip, holding him still. I think I may spill inside him if he moves right now.

After a moment, we both catch our breaths, and the tingles settle. His hands hold each of my shoulders, and he slowly rises and then slowly drops himself down. I sit back, letting go of his hips and let him find his rhythm while I stare up at him as he watches me, his mouth open, eyes drowning in lust.

I bring my hands around the back of Brayden, gripping his ass cheeks as I open them and rut up into him.

"Jesus," he gasps as I speed up, fucking his hole fast and hard from beneath.

"I'm going to come so far inside this hole, and you're going to carry my cum inside you for weeks. When you walk, when you sit, you will feel me trickle out of you, and it's then you will remember each time who you fucking belong to, baby. You're mine, the meaning in every sense."

Being inside Brayden turns me insane, *primal.* I want to stay buried in him forever. Brayden moans and scratches at my shoulders as I get faster, my balls drawing up as I shiver. His eyes roll back as his body scatters in goosebumps.

"Paint me with your cum, Brayden. Fucking soak me!" I roar as my dick pulses with cum inside his body. Brayden's eyes flutter closed as he shudders out his release, each spurt of cum soaking my abs as moans filter out of him.

"Jesus fucking Christ, Bohdi." Brayden's head lands on my chest as he struggles to steady his breaths. Moments later, he starts to move, but I grip his hips, keeping him close. "I'm not ready for you to move yet. Can we stay like this?"

"With you still inside me?" he questions, a slight taunt to his voice. I drag a finger up his spine, loving the way his body shudders against mine.

"Yes. I want to make sure my cum stays inside you as long as possible," I rasp. With each rise of our chests, our bodies slide together, the sweat pouring from us. Somehow, I almost forgot we were in a sauna. I barely notice I'm on earth half the time when I'm with Brayden.

"You're a fucking caveman, you know that?" he teases.

"Your caveman," I whisper, placing a kiss on the side of his neck, and Brayden tenses, squeezing my sensitive dick inside him. A groan slips free, and he chuckles into my chest. I can already feel my dick hardening again, and I think Brayden can, too, because he sits up instantly, eyes wide.

"Do you think you could take me again?" I smirk, watching his pupils dilate as he rises and sinks back down on me.

I'll take that as a yes.

13
Brayden 'Quake' Anders

Chapter Forty-Six

Brayden

"Are you ready for this?" Bohdi's gaze locks onto mine as we stand outside the hall. The memories flood back, the time I stood inside, fighting for Bexley. But today, it's different. Today, I walk in to deliver the news that Bexley is no longer with us. I inhale deeply, my neck cracking as I nod. Bohdi has been my rock, and my anchor this past month. Every crash, every moment of doubt, I've leaned on him. He's carried me through it all.

Together, we visit the gravesite, and Bohdi speaks to Bexley. He apologizes for past words, regret etched in his eyes. He promises Bexley that Jace will help him. And then there are the little things—Nerds Ropes on my pillow, courtesy of Bohdi via Tray. His mission: to keep me smiling. And he succeeds every damn time. My smile barely leaves my face when he's around. Even on the bad days, as soon as I see his face, the day doesn't feel as bad anymore.

As I step into the hall, a few heads turn. Among them, I immediately recognize the lady who oversees everything. I offer a smile and walk over to her.

"Brayden." She squints, questioning, as if trying to recall my name.

"That's right, ma'am," I reply, smiling. "I apologize for taking so long to return."

She waves it off. "No need to worry, my boy. Help yourself to refreshments and find a seat. We'll be starting soon."

Her smile doesn't quite reach her eyes, and I wonder if my emotions are evident. I nod, still smiling. Boh and I turn toward the table, grabbing two bottles of water. Brayden leans in.

"I'm here with you every step. If it becomes too much, just let me know."

I smile back at him and glance around. Some faces are familiar from last time, while others seem new.

The lady addresses the group. "Everyone," she begins, "we have Brayden here, who some of you may remember from a couple of months ago."

Some people wave, while others nod and smile. "Hey!"

"How's your brother doing?" a guy asks, and I think I remember his name being Michael. I see Bohdi shift beside me, and I take a deep inhale, playing with the fabric on my sweater.

"He—" I pause, knowing I need to say it. "He's gone." Air whooshes out of me. I feel Bohdi's fingers link with mine and my eyes immediately snap to people in the room who pay no mind to Bohdi's hand. They just look at me, their eyes pained.

"I'm sorry," Michael mutters, his head dropping low. Everyone around the circle mutters their apologies.

"Thank you."

"If this is too much, please do say, but can you share what happened?" the lady gently asks.

"He overdosed," I confess, my voice a fragile thread. "By accident." The words tumble out, a desperate attempt to make sense of the senseless. Bohdi's hand tightens around mine, a silent promise that we're in this together. I glance up, meeting his eyes.

"He left me a note," I continue, my voice trembling. "He was trying to get better. Bags packed, ready to leave, to start over. He was coming back to me. But I still don't know why he took the drugs," I admit, my gaze dropping. "And I've learned not to think about it too much. It won't help."

"How have you been coping?" Someone in the group's question pierces through the fog. I force a small laugh, a brittle shield against the storm.

"I appreciate this isn't a therapy session," I say. "I don't want to waste your time with my feelings."

"No, my dear. We come here to help each other, even in loss. We're all here for you. There are people here that have lost people to overdoses too and still come here as a way of helping themselves heal." I don't know why, but it feels right being here. It's as if Bexley is in this room staring at me now, smiling, telling me to let it out, telling me to open up. My mind goes back to his letter.

I know why it hurts you to let people in, Brayden. Because you let me in and it fucking hurt, didn't it? It cut like a knife to your veins, bleeding you out every single day. I'm so fucking sorry.

"Some days, it doesn't feel real," I confess, my voice a fragile whisper. "People don't understand that losing someone so close isn't a single event, it's a series of small losses. Every time I pick up the phone and dial his number, I lose him all over again." The weight of that truth settles on my chest, suffocating me.

"I called him the other day, after training. That's when I would go and see him. But when I pressed call, reality slammed into me: he's not here anymore. Every morning, I wake up to a world where he no longer exists, and I have to accept that he'll only ever live in my dreams now. It's as if I was already grieving him while he was still breathing, while he was still here. I could touch him then, feel the warmth of his skin, inhale his scent, hear his laughter. Now, there's nothing. Just silence, an empty echo where he used to be. Honestly, I can't explain the pain.

It's so deep I don't think it will ever truly root itself out of me. I don't think I will ever truly grasp the meaning of gone forever." A tear slips down my cheek, and before I can wipe it away, Bohdi reaches out, gentle and steady.

He's always there, catching each tear that falls.

"I'm so sorry, Brayden. I really am." The woman wipes her tears away from her face. I offer her a soft smile. "Always remember, it's okay to be a little sad. Whether it's one year, or ten years from now, it reminds us they were real."

She walks over, opening her arms and her tiny frame holds me, and suddenly, everything tumbles out, the ache, the longing. Just having her hug me makes me wish my mom could have been there for us. Maybe then Bex would still be here. Maybe then he'd still be breathing.

"My sweet boy." Her voice trembles as she lays her hand across my heart. "He will walk beside you every day, and he will always exist in here." Her touch is both comforting and heartbreaking, and I feel the weight of loss settle deeper within me. I take a seat and Bohdi leans over, pressing a kiss to my head.

"I'm proud of you," he whispers.

The group session unfolds, a chorus of pain, strength, and shared struggles. People speak of loved ones lost to drugs, their voices cracking with grief. I listen, my heart aching in solidarity. In this room, we're bound by our brokenness, yet somehow, it feels like a delicate lifeline.

As the session nears its end, the lady questions if I will return. My answer spills, fueled by determination and a dream that burns brighter than ever.

"I'd really like to continue coming," I say, my voice steadier now. "And if it's okay with all of you, I want to volunteer. I'm working on a school project, a tiny seed of hope. But my ultimate dream is to open my own nonprofit rehab center. To help people like Bexley, who never received the lifeline they deserved."

Her response is warm, genuine. "We would be delighted to have you join our family."

We trudge back to the car, exhaustion settling deep within my bones. The group session, the shared pain, the whispered hopes, has left me drained.

"Can you stay with me tonight?"

"I'd love to," I reply, stifling a yawn. "Can we grab some take-out and eat in bed?" His smile lifts my weariness, and I nestle into the passenger seat.

"I couldn't think of anything more perfect," Boh murmurs, his eyes crinkling at the corners. As he drives, I steal glances at him, wondering how someone can be both my anchor and my escape.

We arrive at his place, and Boh scans the surroundings like a guard. Satisfied, he leans down, whispering, "Coast is clear."

I pull my hat low, hood up, and dash inside. The door shuts behind me, and before I can catch my breath, Boh's lips find mine, urgent, hungry, as if they've been waiting all day.

"I've been wanting to do that," he murmurs against my mouth. But a throat clears behind him, and Boh gasps, covering me with his body.

"Cash," Boh whooshes out. The man at the kitchen counter, older but unmistakably related to Boh, pours himself a beer. His gaze flickers from Bohdi to me, curiosity dancing in his eyes.

"Hi," I manage, offering a tight-lipped smile.

"Is that Boh?" A girl's voice echoes from one of the bedrooms as she strides down the hallway and into the open-plan kitchen. Her beauty is striking, long brown hair, big green eyes. It takes a moment, but then I recognize her. Rylee Stiles, Jace's wife.

Rylee's face lights up when her eyes land on Boh. Her expression softens, torn between aching and uncertainty. It's as if she's missed him desperately, but doesn't quite know how to bridge the gap. An awkward tension settles over us, and I wonder if Bohdi has kept secrets from me.

"Ry," Boh's voice cracks. Rylee shifts, her oversized sweatshirt revealing a bulging bump. A gasp escapes Boh, and I'm equally stunned. There's no mistaking it. Rylee is pregnant. She glances at Boh, sheepish yet hopeful.

"We're having a baby," Cash announces, and even I gasp. I clear my throat discreetly, not wanting to draw attention.

Boh remains frozen and silent. The revelation that Cash, his brother, is expecting a child with his dead son's girlfriend hangs heavy in the air. Did Boh even know about them?

"Boh." Rylee breaks the silence, and then it happens. Boh crumbles, tears streaming down his face. He rushes to Rylee, lifting her in his arms as she sobs.

"Congratulations," I manage, offering Cash a smile. He approaches me, introducing himself.

"I'm Cash, Boh's brother," he says, gesturing toward the emotional scene unfolding. "And that sobbing mess? That's Rylee, my fiancée."

Well shit.

Chapter Forty-Seven

Bohdi

"Boh..." Rylee's voice trembles, breaking through my shock as I stare down at her swollen belly. The reality hits me like a tidal wave—I'm going to be an uncle again. It all floods in at once: the guilt for not speaking to Cash and Rylee properly since everything happened. The realization that she's far along in her pregnancy, and the unspoken understanding that they kept this from me. But I don't blame them. Not one bit.

I have a second chance now—to protect this baby with every fiber of my being, to shield them from any harm. My gaze locks onto Rylee's, tears shimmering in her eyes. She bites her lip, perhaps wondering if I'll lose it, but it's not anger that consumes me. It's love, fierce and unwavering.

I rush toward her, pulling her into my arms. My whispered apology brushes against her ear. "I'll be the best damn uncle this baby could ever ask for," I promise. "And the best brother-in-law to you. I'll always protect you both. Always."

"I've missed you so much, Boh," she whispers, her voice raw with emotion. "I missed you so damn much." I pull her in tighter, not wanting to let her go. The weight of our separation settles on my shoulders—the days, weeks, and months when I walked away from her.

"I love you, Ry." Tears blur my vision as I bury my face in her hair. She needed me as much as I needed her, and I abandoned her and Cash. I walked away from the one man who'd pulled me through every kind of pain I'd ever faced.

When he lost his son, when grief threatened to consume him, I turned my back. I'll never forgive myself for that.

But maybe forgiveness isn't about erasing the past, it's about making amends. And right now, I realize something deep. You can't control who you fall for. Love defies logic, defies reason. It's a force that sweeps you off your feet, leaving you powerless. Your heart makes those decisions, and sometimes, you have to accept it.

Brayden entered my life at a time I didn't want anyone around me. He sat alongside me in the dark corners of my mind and made it less lonely.

I don't think people truly understand how beautiful the darkness can be if you have the right person there with you.

He made me find peace in my darkness.

He made me find peace in my pain.

Now, pulling away from Rylee, I glance down at her swollen belly. Her trembling lower lip mirrors the storm of emotions brewing inside me.

"We're having a boy," she whispers.

"A boy." My voice croaks as I struggle to hold back the tears and stare down at her bump, at my baby nephew.

"Thor Stiles."

"Thor," I whisper. "It's perfect." Tears continue to track down my face. Jace's addiction with Thor was next to none. The name couldn't be any more perfect if they tried.

"He will love it." Rylee doesn't need to ask who I mean when I say he'll love it. She knows. Her sad smile tugs at my heart as I pull her close, pressing a kiss on her forehead. But then I turn to Cash, standing next to Brayden. His clenched jaw and restless stubble reveal the emotions he's desperately containing. "I missed you, Brother," I say.

He steps toward me, our arms encircling each other. "I missed you more, Brother," Cash replies. We hold on, unwilling to let go.

"I'm sorry," I whisper.

Cash's response is immediate. "You have nothing to apologize for. I just want my brother back."

My eyes shift to Bray, who offers a soft smile. He's the reason for this reunion—the bridge that led me back to where I belong.

"I'm back."

Brayden's gaze locks onto mine, wide-eyed, as we stand in the kitchen. Cash, busy giving Rylee a tour of the house. "I know I failed to address that Jace's dad, my brother, is now getting married to Rylee. It's a story for another day, I think."

Brayden smirks, his lips curving. Just then, Rylee appears around the corner, her presence like a sunbeam breaking through the clouds. Pregnancy suits her; she practically glows. And Cash? Well, he's all over her. If he's not holding her hand, his fingers trace patterns over her bump, weave through her hair, or rub her back. It's only been twenty minutes, and I can already predict how hands on he'll be.

Rylee remains blissfully ignorant of what's coming. But I know. I know she'll eventually seek refuge with me, escaping Cash's overbearing ways. And honestly, I can't wait to steal my nephew. Watching them, I ache for Brayden, even though he stands right beside me.

I grab his arm, pulling him close, and press my lips to his. He pulls back, cheeks flushed, chewing on his bottom lip. My eyes shift to Rylee, who beams at us, caught in the moment between me and Bray. Cash smirks, raising an eyebrow my way. Pulling back, I sling my arm over Brayden's shoulder.

"I'd like to officially introduce you both to Brayden Quake Anders, my boyfriend."

Fuck, it feels good to say that.

Rylee's joy vibrates through the kitchen as she squeals and darts around the island, leaping into Brayden's arms. "It's so good to meet you, Brayden," she says, her voice warm. Her eyes lock onto his, and then she glances at me, her expression filled with approval. "Boy, did you do good."

Cash, being Cash, rises from his seat in an instant, pulling Rylee away from Brayden. His raised eyebrow speaks volumes. "Do you want to repeat that?" he challenges.

Rylee backpedals, her cheeks flushing. "Best not," she murmurs, casting a smirk Brayden's way.

Brayden, the silent observer, chuckles softly. His gaze flits to me, and I lean in, whispering, "Hey, are you okay?"

He nods, a bright smile curving his lips. "Yeah," he replies. "It's just nice seeing a happy family, that's all."

"Get used to it," I assure him. "You haven't met my sister yet."

Rylee interjects, her excitement contagious. "Oh, Bridget is going to love you," she exclaims. "She's currently in the Bahamas for work, but I promised her juicy details. Brayden, come sit, we're FaceTiming one of the best women you'll ever meet." With that, she drags a wide-eyed Brayden over to the couch, phone in hand, ready to connect him to Bridget.

Cash's gaze fixates on Rylee's hand as it clings to Brayden's arm.

"He's one hundred percent gay, Cash," I sigh.

"He fucking best be," Cash grunts, his jaw set. His eyes shift to mine, assessing. "So, a boy, huh?" His smirk dances at the corner of his lips.

"A man," I counter, my heart fluttering. Cash's grin widens as he glances back at Rylee. She hovers over Brayden, her joy palpable. And there, in the background, Bridget's smile beams through the phone screen. I can almost hear her laughter.

"You look happy, Boh. Really happy," Cash observes, his tone both teasing and genuine.

"Honestly," I confess, "I don't think I've ever felt this happy. I don't know how he does it."

Cash's next words cut through the joy. "I hate to be the one to drag you back to reality."

"But you're going to," I retort, rolling my eyes.

"What about teaching?" Cash's voice lowers. "What if you get fired? No other schools will touch you. You'll be blacklisted."

"I know, Cash. Trust me, I know." I lean against the countertop, my palms pressing into the cool surface. "Teaching wasn't a dream—it was an escape."

"Do you love him?" Cash's question hangs heavy in the air.

"More than anything," I reply, my voice unwavering. "I'll marry him, Cash. Mark my words, I'll have a ring on that finger within the next two years. Although I'm going to try for one sooner."

"Jesus Christ," Cash mutters, rubbing his hand down his face. "And Rylee thinks I'm bad?" He shakes his head, chuckling, then glances at Brayden and back at me. "Then you need to choose," Cash says, his tone serious. "It's Brayden, or the teaching."

I smile, the answer crystal clear. "That's not even a question."

It's simple.

"I choose Brayden, and I always will—over and over."

Chapter Forty-Eight

Bohdi

After my chat with Cash, I realized I need to make a move. Teaching while being in love with Bray isn't sustainable. He's not any student; he means everything to me. Until he graduates, I'll keep things low-key for his sake, but I can't keep up this act. Those classes I teach him? They're a struggle—I want to treat him differently, but I can't.

He's the love of my fucking life.

Plus, do you know how hard it is to teach him, knowing what it feels like to have his tight ass wrapped around my dick? It's increasingly distracting. I'm tired of constantly adjusting myself, wearing my blazer as armor during lectures.

Last night, Brayden stayed over at my place, along with Cash and Rylee. We gathered around the table, ordered takeout, and FaceTimed Bridget. Laughter filled the room as we reminisced about Jace and Bex. Rylee clung to Brayden, tears flowing freely. In those moments, it hit me—I want Brayden to be more than a secret. I want him to be part of my life, part of my family. Last night's glimpse of what could be confirmed my decision.

It's always going to be Brayden.

That's why I'm now standing outside his dorm room door, the number 13 biggest fan cap on my head pulled down low and a sweater on, with the hood pulled up. I need to tell him what I'm going to do.

I don't bother knocking. I know Cope has already left as I see him on my way up, to which he looked at me funny.

"Bra—" I halt my step as I open the door and see Brayden sitting on his bed, but that's not what's shocked me. It's Lance sitting next to him.

"What the fuck?" I growl.

Brayden's eyes widen as they move from me to Lance. Lance eyes squint up at me, taking me in, and then he looks at Brayden, wide-eyed.

"Get the fuck out!" I snap.

Lance looks at me like I've grown an extra head, but I don't care. I'm not thinking rationally right now. All I see is Brayden's ex fuck buddy sitting on his fucking bed.

"Get the fuck out, or I will drag you out myself."

Lance grabs his coat and bag and darts past me. Closing my eyes, I take a deep breath before Brayden is in my face.

"You fucked up. You really fucked up," he spits.

"I fucked up? What the fuck are you doing with your ex fuck buddy sitting on your bed with you?" I grit out, feeling my resolve about to snap like an overused elastic band.

"If you'd asked instead of going all caveman, I'd have explained. I invited Lan here to tell him I've met someone—someone I love. Lan has texted me a few times, and I never replied. I thought I owed it to him to clarify that I'm no longer available." Brayden runs his hands through his hair.

"He definitely knows who I've fallen for now." His gaze sweeps over me, head shaking. "This is totally fucked up. Shit, I need to go after him."

I grab Brayden's arm. "I'm resigning."

Brayden freezes, staring up at me, wide-eyed.

"You're what?"

"I'm resigning from this job."

"What why?"

"Because I chose you."

"No, no, you can't do this. This is your job, your livelihood."

"There are countless other jobs out there," I say, my voice trembling with emotion. "But what I want is a life with you, a real life. I want to wake up beside you every morning, share laughter, and proudly show the world that you're mine. No more hiding."

Brayden's expression shifts from shock to uncertainty. "I don't know what to say, Boh."

"Just tell me you support my decision," I plead. "Today, right now."

His eyes search mine, pleading. "If it means having you in every way possible, then yes," he says softly. "But promise me this is for you, not just for us."

"It is," I assure him, my heart pounding. "For my happiness, for our future." I lean in, pressing a gentle kiss to his lips. "I have one more class, and then I'm heading to the dean." Brayden nods, excitement lighting up his face. He leans in for another kiss, but I pull back.

"I want you out of this dorm. I'm sick of guys being around you. It pisses me off. You're moving in with me."

Brayden's mouth drops open.

"See you in class." I smirk, and with that I walk out of Brayden's dorm, ready to teach my final lesson.

Glancing around the class, I realize that this is a bittersweet moment. Although I haven't taught here for that long, it will be sad to not see the final presentations or see how well they do. Especially Brayden's. I know already I'm going to help him with every step toward his goals, whether that is the rehab center, or his hockey future. I'm going to be by his side, supporting him every step of the way.

My eyes immediately find Brayden as everyone settles down. His smile beams down at me, and I know with everything, the way he looks at me, the butterflies that take off with every smile he throws my way, this decision is by far the right one.

Kal sits beside him, typing away on his phone, but the seat to his right is empty. Tray's transfer to another class was necessary. His resentment toward Daxton weighed heavily on him. Every time they shared a classroom, Tray's actions spoke louder than words, whether it was a shove, a trip, or even hurling hate at Daxton. I couldn't bear to watch Daxton crumble a little more with each blow.

So, I took Tray aside and pulled him up on it. I explained that Daxton wasn't to blame, but Tray's hatred and grief had blinded him. Tray's removal from the class became the only option.

Daxton, surprisingly, never reported Tray's behavior. I offered my support if he wanted to, but he'd just nod and say he deserved it. Each time he uttered those words, it struck me. Now, Daxton sits at the front, lost in his own world, paying no attention to anything beyond that spot on the table.

"All right, everyone. Today, I'd love to hear about your projects. I would like a few of you to come up and share what you've chosen and why. Let's discuss our work—maybe we'll even spark ideas and support each other. So"—I clap my hands, scanning the students—"who wants to go first?"

Matilda's hand shoots up, and it doesn't surprise me.

"The stage is yours, Matilda," I say, stepping aside. She eagerly jumps up from her desk, bouncing on her tiptoes as she faces the front. Matilda proceeds to tell the class about her nonprofit veterinary and animal shelter for homeless animals. She envisions a team scouring the streets of Michigan, providing urgent care and rehabilitation for these vulnerable animals. Her passion shines through—words tumbling out, voice rising with excitement. It warms my heart because this is what it's all about.

Goosebumps prickle my arms, and my heart races. I can practically feel Brayden's eyes searing into my skin. When I steal a glance at him, he's already grinning. Kal, on the other hand, shoots me a look, then shifts his gaze to Brayden, rolling his eyes and shaking his head. Kal has warmed up to me, but he's still a broody ass boy.

My phone buzzes in my pocket, and I ignore it, trying to focus on Matilda's ongoing talk. But the damn thing vibrates again. Frowning, I pull it out, glancing at the screen, and nearly drop it. Clearing my throat, I place the phone on my lap. My eyes lock onto Brayden. He stares straight ahead, like a model A class student.

I gulp as my dick hardens. I glance back at the screen.

B:

I know how much you love having pictures of me, so I took this for you last night.

There, on the screen, is Brayden's dick, swollen with the tip shining with pre-cum and all I want to do is lick it. Brayden's large hand wrapped around the bottom, as the veins bulge like they're about to burst. My balls tingle as I stare at it and my mouth waters and then I nearly drop my phone when the class erupts into claps. I clear my throat, clapping and smiling at Matilda, telling her thank you. As the silence lingers, I understand why no one volunteers to share their presentation. It's nerve-racking to stand before your peers and present something entirely of your own making.

"All right," I say, trying to ease the tension. "If no one wants to share, that's perfectly fine." I know Brayden isn't ready, and I don't blame him. Heads remain down, avoiding eye contact with me.

"Okay, okay." I chuckle. "In that case, you can either stay here and do more research, or I'm happy to end class early."

The room erupts into motion. Chairs squeak against the floor. Hushed voices fill the air.

"Take care, everyone." I smile, realizing this is the end. No more teaching. Daxton grabs his bag and stands up. "Hey, Daxton." I pause, meeting his dark-rimmed eyes.

"Please take care of yourself," I tell him, my voice gentle. "And remember, none of this is your fault—none."

He nods, shoulders slumped.

"See ya," he mumbles, navigating through the classroom as people rush past him. He allows himself to collide with the wall, as if he doesn't even feel it.

I spot Brayden descending the stairs. "See you around, sir!" he calls out, saluting me with a wink.

"Actually," I say, "I need you to stay behind."

"Damn," Brayden sarcastically exclaims. Kal bursts into laughter as his fists bumps Brayden before raising his hand to me. As I push a chair against the door, I notice Brayden's hooded eyes follow my every move.

"You think that was funny what you just did?" I pace toward him, grabbing his hands, and rub it over my trousers, so he can feel how hard I am for him right now.

"It got the response I wanted."

"You were already skating on thin ice, but after earlier, having another boy in your dorm room when I'm not there. Tsk-tsk. Now Brayden, you are skating on shattered ice." I smile.

"You best get over on that desk. I want your pants down and your ass fucking up," I growl. Brayden's eyes dilate and he gulps, pacing over to the desk. He hesitantly drops his sweatpants and then his boxers. He leans over the table as a small moan breaks through, probably from his dick rubbing against the desk. I walk up behind him, undoing my belt and pulling my dick out.

"This is going to be rough and quick." I gather spit in my mouth and let it dribble on to his puckered hole while rubbing the head of my dick against it. His reaction causes his hole to pulsate, so I apply more spit to my dick and continue to rub it all around his opening.

"Bohdi."

"When we're in the classroom, it's 'sir,' Brayden."

"Fuck," Brayden moans. "Sir, spit isn't going to be enough."

I laugh. "It's gonna have to be."

Slowly, I push in and pull out, adding more spit. I do this two or three times, adding more each time until my mouth becomes dry. I bring my hand around to the front of a trembling Brayden.

"Spit." I cup my hand out in front of him as he spits in my hands. Slathering my dick with it, I slide myself in. Brayden's throaty moan sends shivers down my spine.

"Shit, sir," Brayden moans through gasps.

"I know you can take it, baby. Let me stretch this tight little hole."

Brayden's hands claw the desk as I push myself in, watching the saliva collect in my pubes.

Pulling my phone out of my pocket, I slowly rotate my hips inside him, which has him trembling and his legs kicking out as I swipe over his prostate.

"Ohmyfuckinggosh."

I get my camera open and move in and out of him slowly. The flash goes off multiple times as I take more pictures.

"What are you doing?" Brayden rasps.

"Now I have some pictures that I can send you when you think about talking to another guy when I'm not there. Call them little reminders of who owns every single inch of you."

Leaning over Brayden, I push myself in deeper as he chokes on the air, struggling to inhale. "Breathe, Brayden." I place a gentle kiss along the shell of his ear, just the way he likes it. His arms scatter in goosebumps and moans filter through his lips.

"See?" I bring my phone up in front of him. His hazy eyes meet the screen. Licking his earlobe and biting it between my teeth, he gasps, his eyes not moving from the screen as I slide along each picture, I took of me sliding in inch by inch.

"Be sure to remember how fucking perfect we look connected, Brayden." Slamming the phone down on the desk, I stand up, snapping my hips into his tight ass. His loud moans, which I love, echo through the hall as I get faster.

"Sir, fuck. Fuck. Yes, I want it. Give it to me, please." My spine tingles and my balls become heavy.

"Shit." I pull out.

"Turn around," I snap to Brayden, who stands on wobbly legs as he turns and I push him down on the desk. His legs coming up and wrapping around my waist as I pump my dick with my hand. I push his sweater up and paint his bare abs with my cum. Brayden lies there moaning with every squirt and my release must bring on his release as he tenses, his hands clawing my arms as his dick pulses with mine.

"The prettiest canvas I've ever seen," I pant as I stare down at mine and Brayden's cum mixed on his abs. I don't know what primal beast takes over me, but I lean down, trailing my tongue over his abs, collecting our mixed cum in my mouth as I lean over Brayden, kissing him and pushing my tongue into his mouth.

"Be sure to remember how fucking amazing we taste together, too." I smile.

"I won't be forgetting that any time soon," Bray pants as he licks his lips. Glancing down at his abs. I whip my shirt off, knowing I have a spare one in the drawer, and wipe away our cum.

"I won't lie. I was kinda tempted to make you walk around with us drying on you all day. But the thought of anyone smelling you makes me feel quite sick, so it's best we remove this."

Brayden shakes his head, laughter dancing in his eyes. "You've officially lost it," he teases, leaning up as I finish and pressing a gentle kiss to my lips. "But I wouldn't have you any other way." His smile warms me, and as he leans back, his gaze lands on my chest. His hand brushes up, tracing my most recent tattoo.

"I've never paid enough attention to your tattoos up close, but this one is beautiful," Brayden says. I glance down as his fingers brush over the large lion portrait inked on my chest. "The eyes are so blue." He looks back up at me. "Does it mean anything?"

I nod, smiling. "Yeah, it's for Jace."

Brayden smiles.

"Jace was a strong character. He held everyone's attention when he walked into a room, but not in a cocky way, just in a way that everyone loved him. He oozed power and loyalty. He reminds me he's always there, carrying me through everything. He's my courage to confront agony, pain, danger, anything that comes my way. He's my strength in pain and grief. Just like you are." I smile, pressing a kiss to Brayden's lips.

"That's beautiful."

I place a gentle kiss on his head and step back so he can clean the rest of him and sort himself out. Tucking my dick in, I put my blazer on and take a deep breath.

"Well, at least you're leaving with a bang." Brayden smirks, and I already know what's coming. "Quite literally."

I roll my eyes, shaking my head and laughing. "That was such a Tray line."

"Are you sure this is what you want?"

"Never been surer in my life." I press a kiss to Brayden's lips. "I'll see you at home."

Brayden frowns, and I wink as I walk out of the classroom heading straight for the dean's office.

I knock on his door, the echo of my knuckles reverberating through the room. His deep voice. usually steady and authoritative, booms, instructing me to come in. As I push the door open, dread floods through my veins. Before me stands a man on the brink of collapse, stress etching lines into his face. But it's not him who shatters my composure; it's Denny, standing at his side. Devastation mars his features.

"Please tell me it's not true." Denny's voice cracks, desperation clinging to each syllable. At that moment, I realize I've missed my chance. I should have spoken up earlier, but I wanted to be the one to explain everything—to soften the blow.

"Den, I—" I begin, but Richard, the dean, cuts me off sharply.

"Sit down, Bohdi," he commands, his tone leaving no room for argument. I comply, sinking into the chair as the door clicks shut behind me.

"Tell me," Richard demands, leaning forward, "why are you here?"

I meet Denny's gaze, his brow furrowing. His eyes silently plead with me to deny whatever rumors he's heard, to assure him it's all false.

"I think you know," I reply, my voice unwavering.

Richard slams his hand on the desk, frustration boiling over. "Ah, shit," he mutters.

Denny pulls at the strands of his hair. "I won't believe it. He's your student. My player. He's nineteen!" Panic twists his features.

"Den, please listen," I implore.

"I will," Denny says, desperation thickening the air. "If you tell me it's not true. Tell me, Bohdi, that you're not currently in a relationship with Brayden Anders."

My shoulders sag, and my head drops. There's no way I can lie. I'm not ashamed, but I need Denny to hear me out.

"Richard, Denny," I declare, my chin raised, "I'm in a relationship with Brayden Anders, and I love him." Both men gasp. "And I resign."

Denny's face reddens, his hands clenching. He strides around the desk, our faces inches apart. "You make me sick," he spits, storming out of the office. The door slams with such force that the room trembles.

My gaze shifts to Richard. “We need to talk.”

Three hours later, I trudge through my front door, tossing my keys onto the side table. Exhaustion clings to me like a heavy cloak as I survey the living room, now filled with Brayden’s belongings. He walks out of our bedroom, eyes wide with anxiousness.

“Boh,” he breathes.

“It’s done,” I reply, my voice weary.

“What happened?” Brayden paces toward me, pulling me into a tight hug.

“Can I just hold you on the couch for a while?” I ask.

Brayden glances back, concern etching his face. He nods, guiding me over to the couch.

We lie there in silence, the weight of the moment pressing down. Brayden rests his head on my chest, and I absentmindedly play with his hair, my gaze fixed on the blank white wall. The relief of completion mingles with regret over how it unfolded.

“Lance told the dean before I got there,” I murmur to Brayden, whose head snaps up.

“What?” he gasps.

I chuckle. “Yep, he mentioned a student stepping forward today. I assume it was Lance, given our earlier encounter.”

“That fucking prick. Wait until I see him.”

“Don’t.” I shake my head. “It’s done. I was going to tell the dean and then see Denny, but Denny was already there when I arrived.”

Brayden's eyes widen.

"You're good. I've squared it with the dean, but I doubt Denny will be speaking to me any time soon."

"So, what happened? What did they say?"

I sigh, pulling him close. "I really want to savor our first official night together. Can we discuss it tomorrow? Just know that nothing will affect you."

"Okay," Brayden whispers, but then he sits up, raising an eyebrow. "But you do know you're supposed to ask me to move in, not just arrange for removals. I thought I'd been robbed when I got back to my dorm."

"What are you talking about? I told you earlier."

"When?" His eyes scan the room, as if trying to recall when I mentioned it. I sit up, heading to the kitchen for a bottle of water. "I said you're moving in with me." I grab the bottle, smiling.

"Sweet Jesus." Brayden's head flops back against the couch. "I didn't think you meant today." He laughs, shaking his head. Then he leans to the side. Those ocean-blue eyes—capable of reducing me to a puddle—lock onto mine.

"You really do love me, don't you?" he asks.

Walking over, I plant a kiss on his forehead and crouch down to be eye level with him.

"Brayden Quake Anders, love doesn't even begin to describe what I feel for you. There isn't a word invented that captures it. I can't promise you it will be easy. No one else on this earth can test your patience and make you smile simultaneously like I can. But I promise you, for as long as I live, I'll bring a smile to your face on the worst days." I press a kiss to his forehead. "Some days, Bray, you'll be out there on the ice, sinking pucks and laughing with your team. Other days, it'll hurt just to open your eyes." I trace the line of his jaw with my finger. "But know this," I continue, my voice steady. "I've got you on both days."

13
Brayden 'Quake' Anders

Chapter Forty-Nine

Brayden

April

Training the last couple of months has been hard. After not being on the ice for two months, I lost a lot of strength in my arms and legs. But late sessions in the gym with Bohdi and him being relentless has built me up to this moment.

The last game of the season.

It's the one game we have been working toward all season.

The final of the frozen four.

Coach's decision to bench me during the semifinal hit like a slapshot to the gut. The team felt it, too—we were a tight-knit crew, and my absence echoed through the locker room. But fate had other plans. Our boys stepped up, playing like their lives depended on it. I watched from the sidelines, fists clenched, heart pounding.

And then Kal got body-checked, a brutal collision that sent him sprawling. I lost it. Kicked a bench so hard it splintered like my dreams of being out there on the ice. If Coach hadn't pinned me down, I swear I'd have leaped over the boards, skates on, and pummeled the guy who did it. My rage was a wild animal foaming at the mouth.

But the game ended, and the adrenaline didn't dissolve. No, it fueled me. I stalked that player, quiet and determined. When he least expected it, I booted him square in the back. His knees buckled, and a minor scuffle erupted. Fists flew, helmets rattled—it was hockey in its rawest form.

Kal has a new motto: "Sink pucks first, fists later." And damn, it's a great motto. Because sometimes, in the heat of the rink, you need both fire and ice to survive.

"Are you ready, Quake?" Tray slaps my back as I take my time lacing up my skates, making sure they're perfect. Never underestimate a good pair of laced up skates.

"Born ready."

"Did teach give you a good morning fuck to set you up for the ga—"

"King!" Coach bellows. "I will beat your ass if that mouth keeps moving."

"Yes, Coach," Tray mumbles, rolling his eyes. I know it's not the fact Tray was saying those words, it's who those words were about that has rubbed Coach up the wrong way. I glance up at Coach, whose eyes quickly move away from me.

It makes me sad Bohdi lost someone who has been by his side since they were young. The guilt has eaten at me more times than I can count. But Bohdi always pulls me back out of the guilt and reminds me that the people that truly care for him would be happy. He's not bothered, so why should I be? Coach acts weirdly with me now. He's pissed. I've tried explaining that it was as much me as it was Bohdi. But my age always comes into it, among other things that I can't even think about without feeling like I will lose it with everyone around me.

I get it sometimes. It's crazy for a now twenty-year-old being with a man twenty-one years his senior, but we have one life and one life only. We don't get replays of life; we get one shot at it and who am I to walk away from a love that I know I will never find again because of some stupid numbers?

Why would I not take the chance of being truly happy for once?

People stare. They can't help it. Sometimes it's a disgusted glance when Bohdi will grab me in the streets and smack his lips to mine, but sometimes it's in awe. Bohdi is a walking masterpiece. His stride and the way his eyes crinkle when he smiles, that alone draws attention.

It's fucking annoying. But I revel in it.

Jealous glances fuel my defiance. They don't know our story, the late-night talks, the shared dreams, the way his hand fits mine. This is the unexpected love story, the one I never imagined and never expected. Bohdi shattered my defenses, and he claims he knocked on my door and waited for me to let him in.

Little does he know, he kicked the door open long before that moment and forced his way into my heart.

No door was keeping Bohdi out.

When I was warming up, I glanced around the stadium looking for Bohdi, but I couldn't see him. He told me where he was sitting, in the first row, right next to the benches, which I'm pretty sure Denny was pissed about, but I still couldn't see him. Maybe he was getting a drink. Fucking best be. We came together, so he's got no excuse why he can't be here.

I pick up my phone, ready to put my headphones in, but Coach's voice echoes around the locker room.

"All right, listen up! Before we hit the ice, I need a quick chat with you all." I toss my phone aside and stand up, heading over to huddle with my teammates.

"This year? Damn, it's been epic. Feels as if I've watched you boys transform from wide-eyed kids to full-grown men in a matter of months. And let me tell you, you've made me damn proud, even if some of you raise my blood pressure like it's their part-time job." I shoot Tray a look.

"That was definitely aimed at you," I mutter to him.

"Eat ass," Tray fires back.

"Already did, twice." I wink. He bites his lip, trying not to crack up. Tray loves it when I mess with him. Meanwhile, Kal—our resident serious guy—stands across from us, brooding because we're not hanging on every word coach say.

And that's why he's our captain.

"Wayne Gretzky once dropped this wisdom: 'You miss 100 percent of the shots you don't take.' Well, tonight, we're taking every damn shot. I want your blades digging into the ice like talons, hearts pounding. This rink? It's our hunting ground. You hear me? You are the Devil Hawks!" The locker room erupts, helmets smacking together, cheers echoing.

"But listen up," Coach continues. "The best teams? They're not just a bunch of random folks. They're a brotherhood. And let me tell you, it makes me damn proud to be your coach. So leave no doubt out there. When that puck drops, we're not just playing a game; we're writing our legacy. Now go out there and make history!"

And with that, the locker room explodes, the smell of sweat, the clank of sticks, and the echo of pure determination.

"Let's do this, Devil Hawks!" Kal shouts, and then everyone's shouting, people bumping into each other. Everyone begins to filter out as I make my way back to my locker.

"Yo, Quake?" Tray's voice echoes across the locker room.

"Yeah, I'll catch up with you out there," I reply. The truth is, I wasn't expecting a pep talk, so I hadn't queued up my song. But that song, it's my ritual. Coach will probably chew me out when he realizes I'm not on the ice, but I don't care. I can't step onto that frozen surface without hearing it.

I glance around, searching for my phone. "I swear I left it here," I mutter, eyeing the bench where I was sitting. Panic flares up. "Where the hell is my damn phone?" I sing-song my frustration, scanning the floor. And then there it is—a glimmer of shattered glass.

"Shit." I reach down, picking up my mangled phone. It must've taken a hit during our pre-speech celebration. I press the power button, but the screen remains lifeless. Nothing. Nada.

I check everyone else's dressing area, no phones. Damn it. What am I going to do? I can't even text Bohdi. Panic claws its way up my throat. I have no choice. I'll play the frozen four final without my song. As I walk down the tunnel, the ice smell hits me, and my legs turn to lead.

I'll fucking mess up. I just know it.

As soon as my skates hit the ice, dread washes over me. I can't focus on anyone; I can't focus on anything. When I get a bad feeling about something, it's normally always spot on.

Kal skates over to me, his brow furrowed behind his helmet.

"Put your helmet on. What the fuck is that panic on your face? Quake don't panic," Kal says, skating in circles around me, tapping my pads. He smacks his helmet against mine. "We've got this," he says, his voice a steady anchor in the whirlwind of nerves. "Relax," he adds, his frown softening the edges of his determination.

"I'm going to fuck up, Kal." My voice trembles with panic. The weight of the game, the pressure to perform, it's all crashing down on me.

"What are you talking about?" Kal's eyes search mine, concern etching lines on his face.

"My phone just shattered," I admit, my fingers still trembling. "I haven't had a chance to listen to my song."

Kal's expression shifts from concern to understanding. He knows what it's like to play without our ritual, without that familiar melody coursing through our veins. In the last few games, when I wasn't there, he hesitated on certain shots. Doubt crept in, biting at his confidence.

I close my eyes, desperate to recreate the symphony in my head, the song that's become my lucky charm. But it slips away, vague as a dream when waking. Bexley's face flickers, a snapshot of joy, his air guitar, the way he laughed when we were just us. I cling to those memories, hoping they'll anchor me.

The opponent skates over, grinning. "Brayden Quake Anders," he mutters, taunting me. I remain silent, tongue heavy with lead. I've researched Montgomery Nathans, analyzed his moves, but fear grips me.

"The Quake has nothing to say? Well, shit."

"Shut the fuck up," I grit out, my eyes focused on the ice.

"I heard your teach was banging you up the ass in extra classes? I heard he's big. I might have a go on it and see what the fuss is about. I mean, by looking at him, you can tell he fucks like a pro. Does he make you call him Daddy?" he taunts, and I want to unleash my fury, pummel my fists into his face. But I'm frozen, trapped in my own doubt.

And then it happens—the stomping, the clapping. The beat.

I tilt my head up, scanning the stadium. Devil Hawks fans stomp their feet, clap their hands, and erupt into "We Will Rock You."

The collective voice reverberates, drowning out my fear. Bodhi stands by the players' benches, grinning wide, singing like his life depends on it. My team joins in, Kal, Tray, Cope, Jennings, Coach—all of us, united by rhythm and purpose.

Sticks raised high, we put our everything into the song. Memories of Bexley flood my mind, his bright face, his laughter, our shared happiness. It's like a rolling film tape, capturing our life together.

As the crowd reaches the final chorus, something shifts within me.

Quake steps onto the ice.

Nathans stares at me, fire burning in his eyes as I smirk at him. We both keep our heads down, facing the ice where the puck will drop, our sticks ready.

"He doesn't make me call him Daddy, actually. It's a bit tasteless," I quip. The puck rises and Nathan's shoulders go stiff.

"Although." I smirk. "Your dad loved when I screamed 'Fuck me daddy.'" I slide past, puck against my stick.

Rumors are great. Apparently, his mom caught his dad in bed with a man. I have to give myself an internal high five for that comment.

Flying up the rink, Kal streaks down the left, stick tapping for the pass. I pass it, threading the needle. As soon as it meets Kal's stick, he wounds up, unleashing a slapshot that screams toward the top corner. Steel, their goalie, lunges, glove snapping shut. But Kal grins, a near miss, but a warning shot.

The puck hits the ice, Tray intercepts, weaving through defenders. His stick handling was skillful, the puck glued to his blade. He swings, mesmerizing, and then the puck meets my stick. I spin, eyes on the net. Steel tracks my eyes and then the puck. Desperation is etched on his face.

I fake a left, then whip the puck right. The net calls to the puck like a siren's song. The crowd held its breath and then the buzzer goes off. My teammates swarm me with smiles and cheers.

The Frostbites keep pressing, and each time we sink the puck, they sink one after. It's back and forth all the time. Cope and Becketts, our D-man, battles in the trenches. Nathans, their power forward, crashes the crease. Cope slams him into the boards, ribs rattling. Nathans snarls, but Cope grins, he's our very own beast protecting his den. The puck echoes, chaos reigning. Cope clears it, eyes never leaving the play. Our team is moved around. Me, Kal, and Tray are all pulled off. Coach knows this is going to overtime. Our team fights with everything, Hawks score, Frostbite score, this goes on and before we know it, the whistle blows, overtime looms.

Devil Hawks: 6 Frostbite: 6

The rink throbs with desperation—an arena on the edge of eruption. Overtime—a sudden-death duel where heroes emerge, and hearts hang by a thread. The crowd's roar swirls like a blizzard, encircling us, amplifying the stakes. Coach reunites the nightmare line, our secret weapon, for this decisive moment.

Back to the faceoff, Nathans bares his teeth. No snide remarks, no playful banter—just raw intensity. This is the culmination of a year's need. Will the Devil Hawks win? The puck ascends, and time stretches thin. In that breathless instant, I send a silent plea to Bexley.

Wish us luck, bro. We're winning this for you.

The whistle pierces the tension, and the puck drops. Nathans's stick clashes with mine—a furious blur of motion. He's like a whippet, seizing the puck and streaking past me. My heart sinks, but there's no room for hesitation. Hockey demands constant awareness. Cope and Becketts zone in on Nathans as he winds up for a slapshot. Becketts blocks it, and the crowd erupts.

Tray, our speed demon, takes possession and rockets up the right side. His legs churn like turbines. Two D-men close in on Tray, but he threads a lightning-quick pass to me. I move with urgency, legs burning, lungs screaming. We need this victory; it's etched in our very bones.

I fake left, then right, before returning the puck to Tray. It's back to me in a heartbeat. Against my stick, the puck glides as I pass it to Kal. He blurs past the D-man, eyes locked on the goal. The arena collectively holds its breath. Kal shoots—but Steele, their tough goalie, saves it with a pad. Tray slaps his stick against the ice in frustration. I skate over to him.

"We've got this," I assure him, helmet to helmet. Determination fuels our veins as we reset.

The puck finds us again, and we know it's time to end this. We need this victory like oxygen. The crack of sticks fills my ears as the puck dances between our nightmare line. The crowd roars, drawing us closer. I glimpse an opening, but Kal taps his stick—a signal. I see it—the gap, the chance.

Kal slides the puck to me, right in front of the goal as if I'm about to take the shot. I fake a slapshot, and the last-minute slide left to Kal. The defense is too quick, though, and the D-men clash, sticks colliding, a riot of desperation with Kal. Kal flicks the puck up on his stick. We watch it spin and spin in the air as it comes back down, meeting Kal's stick before he slams it toward the goal, aiming for that sliver of opportunity. It slips through one D-man's legs, then another. The goalie's pads loom, but Kal's stick meets it again.

And then the buzzer blares.

We won.

The arena trembles beneath my skates. Scream, cheers and roars fill my ears. I blow a kiss to Bex, thanking him, and there's one person I zone in on.

Number 13's biggest fan.

Epilogue

Bohdi

Watching Brayden win is an experience that cannot be explained. It's the one time he sheds all worries, becoming unbelievably carefree on the ice. Seeing his happiness in those moments, it's what I live for.

Among the roaring crowd, a voice pierces through,

"Who's number 13? He's hot as fuck." My head whips around so fast I fear I might strain a muscle. The boy, wide-eyed, stares at me.

"He's mine," I growl, my tone low and possessive, and the boy's eyes widen even more as he nods frantically. As I turn around, I'm taken aback to see Bray, his eyes blazing with intensity as he stares at me, skating furiously toward the bench. He rips off his helmet, letting it skid across the ice. Crashing through the small gate, he shoves his teammates aside with raw determination. He bounds up the steps, vaulting over the small gate. My heart races as his hands seize my head, and he crushes his lips against mine with a fierce passion.

In front of everyone—the cameras, the gasping crowd, and the mingled cat calls and whistling. Our relationship wasn't hidden, but it wasn't flaunted either, thanks to the agreement I made with the college when I left. We'd keep it under wraps until Brayden graduated. They didn't want the news getting out and tarnishing their reputation.

Brayden thrives on breaking rules; it's in his DNA. And in this moment, to hell with the college, to hell with everyone.

Our tongues tangle, the noise around us fading into echoes. All that matters is him and me. With every kiss, he unravels me, leaving me breathless and wanting more.

"We fucking won, Boh," he whispers against my lips.

"You were fucking amazing out there, Brayden."

"Did you see that goal from Kal, Boh? Oh my god, it has to be the goal of the season." His eyes go wide with excitement as I smile, my insides doing flips at how excited he is right now.

"I'm sure it was," I mumble, my smile widening as I take in how happy Bray is at this moment.

His eyes go wide in disbelief. "Please tell me you saw his insanely good goal?"

"I didn't."

"What, Bohdi? How? Kal was battling it out with two D-man. How did you not see that stick flick with the puck and straight through the two"—he emphasizes two—"*two* D-man's legs and the goalies? What were you doing? Were you not watching the game?" his brow furrows.

"Bray, when you play, it may as well only be you on that ice. You're all I see out there."

His cheeks flame red as his eyes flick up to my hat. Number 13's biggest fan, and then his eyes move down to my jersey. I smirk and turn around.

"Number 13's biggest fan." He laughs, his smile brighter every time I see it.

"I love making you smile." I gently press a kiss to his lips and then "We Will Rock You" blares through the speakers on the stadium. With wide eyes, Brayden laughs as he gazes round at the crowd, who all point down at him, singing the lyrics.

"Did you start the song?" Brayden's eyes flutter as he looks up at me, his hair tussled as sweat runs down his face.

I smile, nodding. "Kal came skating over and told me what happened, so I started singing it at the top of my voice. Obviously, on my own, I wouldn't do much, but then Kal began singing it to the crowd, trying to rile them up, and one by one, everyone joined in. I even saw some of Frostbites fan singing it."

"Fuck, I love you." Brayden's lips smack against mine one more time. I pull back, excitement flooding through me as I tell him.

"Listen up." I smile, leaning in close. "Get showered and changed. I'm taking you somewhere."

He frowns, eyebrows knitting. "What about the team? The celebrations?"

I expected this. Would he rather party with his teammates? But once he knows the surprise, he'll thank me for dragging him away.

"Trust me," I assure him. "You'll have your late celebrations with them when we're back."

His frown deepens. "Back from where?"

"It's a surprise. Now hurry up." I grin, even though his questions linger. He backs away, teammates gathering around him, all smiles and laughter. Their joy is contagious.

Denny stands there, bright-eyed, smiling with his teammates. I approach the wall separating us from the benches. His eyes lock onto mine, and his smile vanishes.

"Bohdi." He nods, gaze shifting back to the players filtering down the tunnel.

"Den, can I talk to you?" I ask. Den huffs, walking over. Fans surround us, clapping Denny on the back. He smiles at them, but it's strained.

"Congratulations." I offer a tight-lipped smile.

"Thanks," he grumbles. "Look." Denny raises his hand. "Kal already told everyone about your plans for Brayden. I know he won't be celebrating. But I'm sure he'll love your surprise."

His words sound robotic, as if we haven't been friends since freaking school.

"Don't be like this," I say, wincing. His eyes bore into mine. He hasn't answered my calls. I've tried going round to him, but his wife tells me he isn't ready to talk to me. We're grown men, for Christ's sake.

"You were my best friend. I trusted you, Boh. Brayden isn't some damn project for you to fix."

I reel back. "What the hell do you mean, project?"

"You're a fixer, Boh. Always have been. Moving here? It was your escape from grief, from yourself. You found someone who needed fixing, channeled all your pain into him. It didn't matter who—it was your lifeline."

His words stab like glass, tearing through my heart. "You think Brayden's just someone I want to fix?" My voice cracks. "I fucking love that boy. I don't know how I survived without him."

"Well, he wasn't born when we were in college, Boh. Maybe that's how."

"Fuck you, Denny. Screw your stuck-up views. I don't care what anyone thinks. Brayden's mine, and I'll make him happier than any damn college kid could."

"Keep telling yourself that." Denny walks off, leaving me raw. His words echo, but all I can think is I wonder if that is what people think.

Well, there's nothing I love doing more than proving people wrong.

In the car, Brayden buzzes in his seat with excitement. "Please, can you tell me where we're going?" His eyes move to the backseat as he stares at our suitcases again. "I can't believe you packed for me," he mutters. "Did you include some hats? You know I can't go without my hats."

I chuckle. "And I love seeing you in those hats."

Brayden's eyes darken, no doubt remembering the other night when he was naked, and I went and put one of his beanies on his head as I fucked him over the arm of the couch. Something about Brayden in a beanie or a baseball cap does something to me and my dick.

In the moments after we pull up at the airport, Brayden's grin is intoxicating. I know he's never been on a plane before; every away game, they took the school coach, even if it meant hours of driving. But a few months back, I told him that Cash and Rylee wanted us to visit them once the season finished. He already asked me earlier if that's where we were going. I grinned, making him think it could be, but it's not.

"We need to hurry; we're a bit late," I say as we grab our suitcases from the luggage carousel. Inside the airport, the departure screen displays *Chicago*. His eyes light up.

"I've never been to Chicago." He grins, his smile bright. I think he's going to figure it out because yes, it says Chicago, but there's also another name underneath it.

"Chicago is just the layover." Smiling, I point back to the screen. His eyes dance over the display, then widen. Tears line his eyes, and I clench my jaw to stop myself from getting emotional.

"London?" he gasps. I nod, swiping under his eye before the tear falls.

"London." I smile.

"Boh." His voice cracks.

"Please don't cry, Bray. Two men can't stand in an airport crying." I chuckle.

"I can't believe it. You're taking me to London." His eyes move to the screen again, as if it's playing tricks on him.

"I want you to experience it all—for Bexley," I say, pulling a small bag from my carry-on. "I brought you this." I pass it to him, and he frowns down at it as he unwraps it. "It's a new diary. Write messages to Bex while we're on this trip, and when we're back, sit with him and tell him all about it."

Brayden chokes on a sob, trying to swallow it, but the tears fall free, dropping onto the diary in front of him.

"Boh, I really do love you. Thank you," he whispers quietly, leaning up to kiss me gently on the lips.

Kissing his forehead, I whisper, "Let's go make some memories."

Eighteen hours and two delays later, and we finally touch down in London. Once we ordered an Uber to the hotel, we basically crashed into the bed and fell asleep in our clothes, not waking until one in the afternoon, UK time.

It wasn't the best start, but thankfully I booked the main event for tomorrow. At least today we get to explore a bit. I booked a hotel in the city of London, so at least we are near to everything. I did a lot of research and Cash was able to tell me where to go and what's worth seeing as he's been here a handful of times.

"This is what you have been excited about since we woke up?" Brayden stares up at the blue sign in front of us.

"Hey, I have been told by more than one person that this place has some of the best food in London."

"Greggs? Who names a food shop fucking Greggs?" Brayden's clearly suffering from slight jet lag. He's grouchy when he's tired.

"Let's just go in." I sigh, dragging him in with me.

We sat in, and the fact Brayden went up to the counter six times, to order six sausage rolls. I think it's safe to say he likes it.

"Okay, I get it," he says, mouth full of pastry and sausage.

"Good, huh?" I smile, biting into a sausage and bean cheese melt. Honestly, it sounded horrible, but I promised Cash I would try it and boy was he right. It's fucking amazing.

"So, what's the plan?" Brayden eyes up the counter again.

"No more sausage rolls, that's what. Where the hell do you put it?" I eye him up.

"I can show you." His lazy gaze tracks me up and down slowly, pushing his leg out so it brushes against mine.

"Stop," I grit out, standing up as my dick starts to go semi-hard behind my tight jeans. Brayden stands up, following me out of the shop.

"Tonight, you best fuck me. I want to know what it's like being fucked in London while looking out my window and staring at Big Ben." He grins and starts to walk off. Now all I have in my head in Brayden bent over with me buried in his tight ass.

"We are making a pit stop at the hotel." I grab his arm, dragging him toward the hotel, my dick now painfully hard.

Okay, the vacation hasn't consisted of as much sightseeing as I thought, and we only have five more days here. We had a walk around London yesterday, after spending two hours in the hotel fucking the life out of Brayden. After that we were both exhausted and ended up having a daytime nap. We then woke up at ten at night. We haven't grasped the time difference yet.

But today is the main reason I booked this vacation. I had to set my alarm because at eleven, I booked tickets for Brayden to go to the London Eye. I know he needs to do this, and he mentioned it to me on the plane.

The London Eye looms before us, its massive wheel casting shadows against the bright sky. Brayden's eyes widen as we approach the queue.

"Oh my god," he murmurs, "it's so much bigger in person and high—really fucking high." Standing near the entrance, I retrieve the ticket from my pocket and hand it to him.

"I know you're afraid of heights," I say softly. "But you need this. Do it for Bexley."

His eyes meet mine, sunlight dancing on his face. "You brought us tickets?" he asks.

"I bought you a ticket," I clarify. "I won't be joining you. This is your journey, Bray. Take it all in, write it down, and read it back to Bexley someday." I cup his cheeks. "I'll be waiting right here when you finish. And I've arranged for you to have a pod all to yourself."

"It's really high," he stammers, doubt evident.

"You can do it," I whisper. "For Bex."

His voice trembles. "For Bex."

"Take this with you." I pass Bray a plastic bag. "Open it once you're up there."

And with that, he turns away, walking onto the platform, ready to enter the pod.

13
Brayden 'Quake' Anders

Epilogue

Brayden

The countless videos Bexley shared with me didn't do justice to the sheer scale of this structure. Seeing it in person—holy fucking shit. Honestly, I think Bexley would've chickened out. My legs tremble as I step into the pod, the doors sealing me in. Within minutes, the whole thing begins moving, and I don't even get a chance to glance at Bohdi before the massive support poles obstruct my view.

I hope those poles are damn sturdy.

In the center, there's a round, seat-like table, and I plop down immediately. Funny, I don't recall the videos showing this thing suspended over a large amount of water. Maybe that's a good thing. If it plummets, at least I'll land in water, right? Survival odds and all that.

The motion is subtle, barely noticeable, but as I peer downward, everyone on the ground becomes smaller. And that water? It appears rough. Maybe I wouldn't survive the fall.

Enough of this, Brayden. Stop spiraling.

"Right now, Bex, you'd be pissing yourself at how much sweat I'm drenched in. This thing—it's fucking massive and the height? Unbelievable. Why did you choose this over Buckingham Palace? I'd have endured boredom there for you, no problem. But this? It's pushing it, Bexley Anders." I glance out the window, then quickly shut my eyes. Damn, it's too damn high. Can I even stand? But I've got to do this for Bex. I stand, my legs heavy with each step I take. Keeping my eyes clenched shut, I walk as if on a tightrope, teetering toward my own death. I carefully open one eye, assessing my proximity to the railing. The glass surrounds me, but how tough is it? What if a bird smashes into it? Could it crack? I recall those airplane incidents, bird meets propeller, and suddenly, you're toast. Could that happen right now?

My fingertips brush cold metal, and I exhale in relief. Still, my eyes remain shut. Bexley's memory nudges me. His voice echoes: "Bray, it's beautiful. Open your eyes. Don't look down—always keep your head up and appreciate what's in front of you."

I can do this. I can.

I flutter my eyes open, chin lifted, gaze forward. And there it is—the view. "Bex," I gasp, "It's stunning. Really fucking beautiful. Why can't you be here to see this?" A tear slips down my cheek.

I chuckle, staring at the River Thames below. "Sorry, Bex, but it's uneventful. Looks dirty as fuck." Another laugh escapes.

"The buildings, though—they're something. You told me their names, but I only remember a few. They gleam, gold and strong. And the views? A lot like those videos you used to show me. You'd have loved it; the views are breathtaking."

Here I am, suspended in the sky, fulfilling the dream Bex held so tightly.

But he's not here. His laughter doesn't echo against the glass, and his eyes don't widen with wonder.

"Bex," I whisper, as if he's beside me, "I hope your soul lingers, laced into my veins. Can you see through my eyes?" The view unfolds even more. "I hope you're kicking your feet with excitement somewhere up there." I glance up at the open blue sky.

"Look, Bex. Look how beautiful life is underneath you." The bag rustles in my hand, reminding me what Bohdi gave me. I open it up, pulling out the smaller paper bag, and when I open it, tears fall from my eyes once again.

"Bodhi gave us some snacks for the ride, Bex." I laugh, pulling out a Nerds Rope and a Reese's Peanut Butter Cup. "Here you go, Bex." I place the Butter Cup on the seat behind me.

But it's bittersweet. "I want you here, sharing this moment."

His absence tugs at my chest. A phantom ache. "I'll be your eyes, your feet, your heartbeat. I'll carry you through the heights, and when the wind weaves through my hair, I'll pretend it's your touch." I try to swallow the sob that claws its way up my throat.

"Bex," I murmur, tears blurring the view, "I will come back here for you again. I will capture the memories for you. I will capture every single thing for you. I will research the buildings. I will tell you all about them. I will live for you, Bex. I will live every fucking day for you and appreciate everything you never got to experience. Life is beautiful. You always told me that. I never saw it, but now I do. I see what you saw. I see everything and I'm sorry it took me so long." I rub away my tears with my arm. Although it's chilly out, the sun beams down on the glass, warming my bones. The city below is alive, bustling with energy, but up here, it's just me and the memories of Bex. I close my eyes, imagining his smile, the way his eyes would light up at the sight of the skyline.

"Remember how we used to dream about this?" I whisper. "We'd sit for hours, planning our adventures, imagining the places we'd go. And now I'm here, living it for both of us. It's breathtaking, a moment of pure beauty that I wish you could see. I promise, Bex, I'll keep exploring, and keep discovering. For you."

Pulling out my phone, I snap a few pictures. "I'll make an album," I say, as if he's right beside me. "An album of all the places we wanted to see. I'll fill it with memories, with moments that should have been ours."

I turn my head, staring at the Reese's cup sitting on the chair "Here's to you, Bex," I say, raising the nerd rope like a toast. "To all the dreams we had, and all the ones I'll keep alive for you."

I take a bite, the sweetness mixing with the bittersweet ache in my heart. "I'll be back, I promise." Looking out at the city one last time. "I'll keep coming back, and I'll keep you with me, in every step, every breath. Life is beautiful, Bex, and now I see it." The wheel is nearly finished as people begin to come into sight.

"The journey isn't over, and neither is my promise to you. Every day, every moment, I'll carry you with me. Always. I love you always and forever. BB for life."

As soon as it ends, and the doors open, my feet can't move fast enough to find Bohdi. When I do, I jump into his arms, tears streaming down my face.

"When the moment comes, I know exactly what I want to name the charity, Boh," I say, my voice muffled as I bury my face in his neck.

I pull back slightly, my gaze locking onto his mesmerizing blue eyes, which seem to swirl with a depth of emotions. He smiles down at me, his soft eyes crinkling at the corners.

"Life is beautiful," I whisper, my voice filled with a mix of emotion and hope.

"It's perfect," he murmurs in response, his voice tender and reassuring. Leaning in, he places a gentle kiss on my lips, sealing the moment.

"You're perfect."

Our love, our defiance, it was our power play.

Bohdi took his slapshot and perfectly aimed it straight at my heart.

And he fucking scored.

"I don't know how I got so lucky to meet you, but to be loved by you is one of the most magical things to ever happen to me.

I love you, Bohdi Stiles. I love you so fucking much. You're my lifeline. Thank you for stitching me back together, one memory at a time."

The End.

Afterword

If you ever find yourself in a situation where you need help, please do not hesitate to reach out to your national help hotline. There is always someone there to help and listen.

Afterword 2

Thank you for reading *Shattered Ice*. I hope you enjoyed the sweet, heartbreaking, and emotional rollercoaster these characters took us on. If you want to talk about any of the characters or the storyline, my DMs are ALWAYS open!

For updates on the Hawksview boys, please follow my Instagram (PS. Black).

Stalk Me

Come join my reader group. That's where I do my most give-aways ;) and talk the most amount shiz. Also, my reader group get's all the teasers and info before everyone else :)

PS. Black's Brokenly Beautiful Romance

Instagram – PS. Black

TikTok – PS. Black

Trigger List

Large age gap (21 years)
Student x Teacher romance
Character Death
Mentions of Child Abuse
Mentions of Child Neglect
Depression
Drug Overdose
Drug Use/Addiction
Explicit Sex
Grief/Death of a Loved One
Murder
Violence

Printed in Dunstable, United Kingdom

70453008R00262